LIFE AFTER

THE ARISING

Life After: The Arising is a work of fiction. Names, organizations, places, characters, products, and incidents are either the invention of the author's imagination or are used entirely fictitiously. Any resemblance to actual events, locales, or persons, living or dead, is entirely coincidental.

ISBN: 0615851827
ISBN-13: 978-0615851822

Homepage of the Dead
For keeping my writing career alive when it tried to stay dead.

Mom and Dad
For letting me write instead of getting a real job.

Dani
For everything.

TO THE DUVIVIERS!

YOU CAN THANK YOUR MOM FOR STOPPING IN
TO VIVA VIDEO TONIGHT AND BRINGING HOME MY
BOOK! UNLESS YOU HATE IT... THEN YOU CAN
BRING IT BACK AND CHEW ME OUT!

~ Bryan Way

Character is determined more by the lack of certain experiences than by those one has had.

~ Friedrich Nietzsche

CONTENTS

10-11-04, MONDAY   1

10-09-04, SATURDAY   3

10-10-04, SUNDAY   49

10-11-04, MONDAY   95

10-12-04, TUESDAY   190

10-13-04, WEDNESDAY   225

10-14-04, THURSDAY   251

10-15-04, FRIDAY   279

10-16-04, SATURDAY   317

10-17-04, SUNDAY   337

10-18-04, MONDAY   359

10-19-04, TUESDAY   389

ACKNOWLEDGEMENTS   443

10-11-04, MONDAY

There is a newspaper clipping in my wallet that, for irony's sake, I will never remove.

"...The ground separated in front of the headstone, the newly poured dirt shifting with ease. The hands of the grave's occupant clenched at the air, the skin taut and brittle enough to split on the dorsal side. There came a low moan, muffled through the dust to which the corpses were supposed to return. Roger stepped away surprised to find himself unimpeded by fear, his thoughts instead turned to the notion that he had been correct that the returning dead have no use for the blood drained before their embalming. It's the blood that supplies muscles with their oxygen to allow them to convert potential energy into kinetic; you need it to move, you need it to live, yet here was Peter Thornton moving, living... when yesterday he was dead..."

This is an excerpt from Jeffrey Grey's award winning short story 'Their Insides Torn'. You'd never know it from looking at him, but behind his sincere blue eyes and easy smile lurks a morbid imagination nurtured by his carefree upbringing. "I had loving, supportive parents and a stable home. That just made the macabre more interesting." When asked if he thinks the dead could return to life, it's impossible to tell if he's kidding. "It would certainly represent a paradigm shift away from normalcy, wouldn't it? Then again, who knew about AIDS thirty years ago?" Is it paranoia, a dark fantasy, or does he know something we don't? According to him, paranoia and dark fantasy are the primary driving forces of his creativity.

His short story may seem pulpy at first glance, but he explains that the Zombies in his story are merely a vehicle "...to show what happens when the rules of society are removed." The absurdity of the subject matter dissolves in this melting pot, and whereas at first these Zombies seem like cannon fodder, we begin to see that they were human beings who lived full, normal lives. "It really shows what kind of person you are, dealing with Zombies. These are husbands, wives, and children... I think of the soul as the one thing about us that never changes; our bodies change from birth to death, as does what we learn and believe, but something is always inherently the same. Becoming undead, by definition, is the removal of that soul, and your survival largely depends on how you cope with that concept."

Every time he opens his mouth, he speaks in long passages with utter conviction, so much so that it's often easy to forget that he's talking about something so fantastic. It's the mark of a great storyteller, one who is almost certainly destined for a bright future. Whether he will become a filmmaker, *author, journalist, or philosopher, one thing is certain: his potential knows no bounds.*

So what was I doing the night of Saturday, October 9th 2004?

10-09-04, SATURDAY

The black patch of road stretching from the 476 off-ramp looks more like a noir cliché than a suburban interchange; it's empty, damp, and clean in a way that conjures the mysticism and freedom of the road as conveyed by country-inflected rock music, a type of freedom that I've always found illusory. As the song *Hands Away* by Interpol plays in the car, my mind wanders off the road to the soft grass and sparse, evenly spaced trees in the median, bouncing next to my formal reception via the *Welcome to Broomall* sign. I stop at a red light.

I glance at the digital clock on the dashboard: 7:31pm, or half an hour and one minute late to the event at my destination, which means I'm going to have a hell of a time parking. Fortunately the hosting band, that of Thomas Massey high school, colloquially referred to as 'the Mass', debuts last at this year's Bandrome competition, so I won't miss anything I had intended to see. I'm certain that I'll bump elbows with a few friends still tenuously clinging to their high school experience, and I'm fortunate enough to have an empty house in which to entertain with my parents gone by way of an extended vacation. I wonder if I'll be capable of funding a 30-year wedding anniversary in Bermuda, provided, of course, that I get married some day. The light turns green and I advance slowly.

I look to the left as I pass through the intersection, glancing at the small stretch of road that features one of the tiny commercial centers of Broomall; a hair salon, a mom and pop photocopy center, a leg brace store, a Chinese take-out restaurant, and not much else. The parking lot, which stretches behind the buildings, is surrounded by tall conifers and picturesque suburban homes. When I return my attention to the road, I make the conscious realization that I've stopped; it never ceases to amaze me that I can be lost in thought and still subconsciously follow traffic patterns. Despite seeing accidents often this close to the interchange, I'm stunned at my delayed reaction to possibly the worst series of car accidents I've seen in my life.

I rubberneck as I try to study the crash, but I quickly become dizzy from the wealth of visual information: Flares flickering against wet pavement. Black smoke pouring into the sky. Police standing around.

Reflections on bent steel. Shattered glass littering the ground. For a moment I consider rolling down my window, but my adherence to an unwritten social code of ethics stops me. Is it polite to roll down one's window to closer inspect an accident of this magnitude? I look at the cars around me to see that their occupants are all fixated on the series of smashed cars. Finally, my eyes settle on the median and begin slowly moving through the particulars of the crash.

One car is resting in the median on its side, propped up against a small tree that is destined to buckle within the hour. One car is facing into oncoming traffic, and the two central cars have pancaked against each other, their front ends smashed so that the only way to tell where one ends and the other begins is their color. Cars parked along the left side of the road have been trapped so that they now belong to the rest of the accident. It's too dark to make out every vehicle, but there are at least three in the middle of the road. One is upside down, fifty feet from the others in the intersection I passed. Smashed chunks of laminated glass glitter along the black pavement, catching the orange glint of the flickering flames rolling up from the hood of an overturned car and screaming toward the sky.

I continue peering down the line; a truck is on top of another car with a person nearly dead in the front seat of the former, a mutant gash across his forehead still dripping what's left of his blood that hasn't been spent on the windshield. I shiver as he defies my first prediction and opens his eyes to look in my direction. The cars in the lanes behind the crash have come to a halt without accumulating, which means this must have just happened. I count ten cars as I edge forward; the one in the intersection, two in the median, two pancaked together, three parked incidentally and the two horizontal ones.

I'm ashamed to find myself gracious of the fact that I'm not going back to Temple tonight. From the looks of things, police and EMTs are going to be there all night sorting this out, starting with blocking off the streets and intersections going back along Route 3, a task that is sure to occupy every cop in town. They'd better pray there isn't a bank robbery. As I stare at the two cars which have in essence become one, I can see something pinched between the bumpers; it's hard to make out with the flashing lights approaching from behind me, but it looks like the ripped top of a smashed canned ham. Is that someone's lower torso?

A car horn finally pulls me away enough to fill the space between my car and the one in front of me. I counted at least one certain casualty, but it was also certain that more were injured, maybe even dead, and I certainly can't discount the cylinder of meat in the middle of the accident. And just like that, I catch my focus drifting back to the road and to Bandrome as my capacity to move on from shocking events continues to astound me. A drive of less than two miles up the road brings me to the correct intersection, so I turn left through the median break and head for the school.

The car vibrates as it passes over a rough square of pavement, causing my hand to mechanically touch the small pocket that would normally align the right side of my pants. I instantly realize that I'm wearing corduroys as opposed to my usual carpenter's jeans, so I pat my upper pocket on the right side, then the left. "Dammit." I check my trench coat pockets while steering with one hand, and then check the cup holders to my right. I forgot my cell phone. No matter. Anyone I'd need to get in touch with is either at Bandrome or a few thousand miles away.

A flare illuminates the front of the school about half a mile ahead and I pray that it's not another accident. As it turns out, it's actually a police officer in the middle of the street directing traffic. Buses from the visiting bands line the right side of the street, parked next to the high school's front lawn. The adjacent grass is filled with arcs of tackily-clad students warming up under the illumination of grimy light produced by the half-dozen gas powered generators scattered on the grass. Beyond them, the school looks as ominous as ever with no lights in the windows and a heavy backlight from the football field that lies beyond.

I turn left on to a side street just past the end of school property to take advantage of an exiting vehicle at the end of the street. After parking, I get out of the car, pull up my decorative cane, pop on my bowler, and join a cluster of five people being waved across the street by the officer who is apparently too busy complaining about a motorist nearly striking some pedestrians to truly pay attention to our crossing. Great example of irony. I take a mint-flavored toothpick out of my fob and begin chewing at it as I stop and look up at my former high school.

Thomas Massey high school's Bandrome festival is one of the most celebrated marching band competitions in the area, having been around longer than any other such local competition and having the distinction of being the second or third oldest in the state of Pennsylvania. At this school, about three-quarters of the high school football season ticketholders are just going in to see the band. To be fair, most of that group is comprised of band parents.

Since the Mass' football teams have always been terrible, Bandrome is the gala event of the high school fiscal year, meaning that everyone from the mayor on down has to show up. It also attracts bands and their followers from as far as halfway across the state, but only if they know their band is good enough to compete. Understanding the intricacies of a band field show makes this no easy task, since even a minute mistake sticks out like a black eye in a Lamaze class. I walk past an arc of tuning band members clothed in tacky purple and gold uniforms. They sound awful. A few of them stare at me.

"Nice hat." One of them says. "Yours is better." I reply, not needing to look since all marching bands have goofy headwear. I walk along the sidewalk, staring at the thirty foot long, five foot high gardens that sit before rows of windows and sandwich a bank of silver doors. As I enter into the dim auditorium lobby, a pair of girls in purple holding flutes passes by me whispering, prompting me to consider myself; I'm carrying a black metal cane with a silver top, have a flavored toothpick hanging out of my mouth, and I'm wearing black corduroys, a corduroy dress shirt, a trench coat, and a black bowler. This self-inventory is mildly embarrassing.

I walk down the hall and turn the corner to find a Mass band member I've never seen perched next to a music stand in the middle of the hall upon which a sign stating *Band Members Only* is affixed. The hall forms a three-way intersection, but my path leads past a trophy case of band accolades to the practice room. As I walk toward the sign, the prick in uniform stops me. "Can't you read?" He says. "Totally illiterate." He's unable to construct a witty retort, so I keep walking.

I head down three steps and walk along the white cinder block hallway, pass through two sets of double doors, and stop outside of the band room as the memories flood back. The most potent one sees me enacting the type of full stop that would signify the end of a song in our field show, displaying my training to finish unless the band instructor himself, Mr. Weldon, came on the field and gave the signal to halt. Of course, most high school students rarely understand the mechanics of these orders; they train for specific commands and only function if everything goes right, failing to grasp something as fundamental as the drum major being present to keep the band in time.

I open the door to find the room buzzing with activity. Words in crepe paper adorn the white cinder block walls, streamers and beads line the doorways, balloons are sticking to the fluorescent lights and coating the floor in the school's shades of orange and black. Uniform bags are strewn all over the chairs. The drum major sticks out as the only one fully dressed in white as he talks to some freshmen in the corner as several half-uniformed instrumentalists walk past him wearing big black pants with built in suspenders and white thermal shirts beneath their black t-shirts.

It's both disappointing and gratifying to have my knowledge of names begin and end with juniors and seniors, and I don't even know most of them. A small wave of shock hits me simultaneously with a feeling of nervousness and isolation, since the only person I *really* know here is my girlfriend. Using sacred moves only entrusted to those with social cloaking devices, I slink to the instrumentation room.

Even though she's facing away, I spot her in an instant; a 5'5", short-haired, skinny, impressively curvy young woman in a band uniform bending over a French horn case next to rows of cheap plastic lockers. I sneak up behind her, slide my hands from just above her waist to the front of her stomach, and hold her against me. She inhales a deep, excited breath before squirming around, flashing her braces, and wrapping her arms around me. "Hello darling." I say with a smile. "Hello my love." She replies. I spit out my toothpick before I kiss her. She sits me down in a corner and starts giving me a back massage without another word; this is surprisingly standard, and though I love it, I could never fathom why she was always in the mood to massage me.

"How's the semester been treating you?" She starts.

"Damn good. My directing professor is a genius... makes getting up at eight tolerable."

"8:00am? How *awful*..."

"You're *incredible* at masking your sarcasm."

"...oh, I thought you were about to thank me for the massage..."

"Well, if I knew I had to *thank* you for it..."

"You're incorrigible."

"And you've been brushing up on synonyms!"

She playfully flicks the back of my neck before continuing.

"It's disgusting that eight is a standard of waking up to which I aspire."

"Well, high school's just one massive, annoying, embarrassing test to pass. Ask any graduate."

"So what's college?"

"The final exam. Then it's the workforce, where you trade up busywork for menial tasks and homework for taxes, loans, mortgages..."

"Trade childhood ambition for sustainability..."

"Then you trade down... work goes for retirement, and you trade life for death."

"Then what?"

I smile without her seeing it. "Always a step ahead." I reply, letting my last word trail off into a slightly exaggerated moan of pleasure. It takes a solid minute for me to realize neither of us has spoken, and when I do, I anticipate that she'll want to know what's on my mind. For some reason, as always, I jump to the conclusion that she might be able to read my thoughts and instinctively, though counter-pro-ductively, concentrate on all the worst things I've ever thought about her before my brain numbs itself and erases everything I was just thinking, making only one response appropriate.

"What's on your mind, love?"

"Nothing."

"Well, how's your band?"

"The Noctambulists? Didn't you hear? We're primarily responsible for Outkast's new album."

"I always knew you felt as though roses smelt like poo-poo-poo."

"Wow... you really *never* laugh at my jokes."

With that, she elicits a perfect airhead laugh.

"...that was terrifying."

"So, Noctambulists..."

"Right... well, we can't get much work done during the semester. Seen any Noctambulists tonight?"

"I saw Mursak earlier. Is Anderson coming?"

"Guard duty. One weekend a month and he doesn't get to pick it."

"There's no chance of him getting sent to Iraq, is there?"

"He won't say."

"You mean, he doesn't know, or..."

"He won't say. He doesn't sound optimistic, and the Guard comprises half the soldiers in Iraq. If there's such thing as karma, he won't have to go."

"Why do you say that?"

"You know... I mean his dad got him a suitcase for graduation... he was out of the house the day after commencement and homeless for about a week. So he went into the Guard... less chance of action and he'd get his college paid for."

"Not his first choice?"

"I think his options stopped at surviving. He's gotten pretty good at it. I've said this to you before, haven't I?"

"...yes."

"Wow, and for once I thought I wasn't repeating myself... how did you ever end up with someone who talks so much?"

Julia and I sit in total silence as she continues kneading my back. She stops massaging me for a moment, reaches her arms around and holds me up against her. I turn with a smile, gnash at her ear, and whisper my question.

"What's this about?"
"You're here."

She must be wearing a watch, because she suddenly gets up and informs me that her section has to warm up. A kiss, a hug, a smile, I'll see you later my love, you too darling, and she's off for practice. Since she's the only person here to hold my interest, I head out the back of the instrumentation room to the back parking lot. To my left is a chain link fence backed by a uniformly placed row of arborvitaes that block the view of an impressively dark cemetery which is also partially obscured by the towering trees planted throughout. To my right is the new wing of the school I've heard only too much about; with only four additional classrooms, it's really more of an extension than a wing.

When I come around the wing, I get my first glimpse of the new field. From this vantage, the artificial turf is obstructed by the bleachers, but the explosive new halogen stadium lights give the field the brilliant, ominous glow I noticed from the front of the building, and from here, the contrast against the dark pylons beneath the bleachers is stunning. I continue past the rows of cars in the enormous back parking lot, hook around the end of the row parallel to the field and continue past more cars. There's a ticket box next to the opening in the gate, but they're not going to charge entrance fees this late into the show. After this band there are only three more before adjudication including a final exhibition performance by the Massey Monarch band.

There used to be a flimsy wire mesh gate blocking the field, sealed at night by a weak link of chains and an uninventive padlock. Since I've graduated, they've decided that getting on the field has become a matter of life and death; the flimsy fence has been replaced by an eight foot high iron gate that seems to have been designed to stop a car travelling at forty miles an hour. The main gates appear to be locked solidly, having been constructed in a bulge facing away from the field. I walk around to the left to discover a small opening in the side, feeling as though there should be a turnstile as I walk through.

I pull the belt on my trench coat tighter as I walk down the path that opens up to the field, where I get my first real glimpse: the uneven, archaic grass has been replaced by beautiful artificial turf, the antiquated gravel of the running track traded for all-weather polyurethane, the rickety bleachers changed into gleaming aluminum with no spaces beneath the seats so as to prevent the passage of cold air, and the wooden light posts have been razed for uniform field lights that cut through the sky's darkness like kliegs. The band on the field is dwarfed by the massive crowd and geometric precision of every piece of equipment surrounding them; their subpar performance of Stravinsky's *Firebird* fails to provide the equally unimpressive visuals with the epic sweep the song so richly deserves. It doesn't help that this particular piece of music is so often played by marching bands it warrants inside jokes. I rest myself against the edge of the bleachers, but not for more than thirty seconds until I hear my name being called. "Grey! Jeff!"

All the way at the top of the bleachers a former classmate, Joe Harrington, lifts his arms with clenched fists and whips them around as if he's having a seizure in an effort to recreate one of our inside jokes, the origin of which I can never remember. Next to him are Paul, Mursak, Chris, Carlos, and Derrick, and aside from Carlos, the only black guy in band and one of few at our school, they are all unremarkable white folk from my class. Mursak is the most remarkable of the bunch; to friends, his name is a sound byte that conjures up imagery of a rubber face, an endless amount of impressions, and generally disturbing drawings. Over the past few years he had become one of my better friends and the singer for my band. As tempting as it is to sit with him and chat, I'm stuck below. Every square inch of space is taken up by local asses.

I wave to my erstwhile friends, shake my head, and finally shrug in defeat. I can probably find them after the show and tempt them to my house for movies and drinking, and Mursak may be desperate for an opportunity to hang out if he actually made the trip down from his college in Rochester. Naturally I'd love to spend the rest of the evening with Julia, but her parents are overprotective; for the years we've been going out, we've had to survive by seeing each other at gatherings such as these and timid parties at her friends' houses.

So I stand here like a knob, politely and lethargically clapping for each band as I wait for Mass. Once the unfortunate Firebirds are off, the next band gets on the field. At 9:40, Pennawanee goes up. The Mass band members don't like them because they have the same colors as our school and practically the same uniforms, except they substitute our black tops for orange ones. They also win more awards than we do, only because they put on a show with sickeningly easy marching configurations and stop frequently between pictures for increasingly tedious emphasis. A middle school band could pull this show off, but as usual, Pennawanee will take home a superior. The adjudication is graded as follows:

1. Superior
2. Outstanding
3. Excellent
4. Very Good (AKA get off the field before we have security escort you out)

In a given night, every band can get a Superior, but it never works out that way. Bands are rated on scale from 0-140 points, and because of the margin, there are never any ties and Pennawanee's usually on top. They put on their simple damn show to a roaring applause from their fan section in the bleachers, and then a silence settles over the field, followed by suspended snare taps in the background. The husky crack, carried by the cold air, takes me back to high school. *Bap, bap, bap.* "Two, three, four." *Bap, bap, bap.* "Two, three, four." *Bap, bap, bap-bap-bap-bap...* and with that the percussion explodes into the only marching cadence I've ever enjoyed.

The crowd starts roaring as percussive instruments being toted by people in black uniforms glide through the gate on the far left from my position, making a beautiful contrast against the rows of yellow school buses behind them. A hush falls over the crowd just for a moment before the announcer chimes in. "Ahh, Ladies and Gentlemen…" The crowed howls again, and I join. As I lean over the four-foot high chain link fence separating the masses from the field, I can't help but feel like I'm at a racetrack in the 1940's, or at least how film portrays racetracks in the 1940's: hundreds of people in warm coats packed against each other like so many sardines, all shouting and waving as their champion races toward them. I expect confetti to spray out of the press box.

Marching along the inside track, the front of the band hits the 20-yard line and the first row of band members behind the percussion snaps off to the right and marches onto the field. The last person on the field-bound line is then narrowly missed by the row of band members marching perpendicular to the field in an astounding first display of skill. At the 25 yard line, another line snaps off, and this continues until the only band members remaining on the track are the percussion.

Each line, a set of five, has formed little pentagons on the field. The band plays a warm-up song, the name of which I don't know. While they do that, the percussion continues around the track. By the time they reach the opposite side of the track and march onto the field while centering the 50 yard line, the band's warm-up is over, and everyone stops and drops to the ready position; feet spread, heads bowed, instruments down.

I didn't take notice, but the announcer was talking the whole time, introducing the positions and the field show music. "Drum Major Dan Kerry, is the band ready for exhibition?" Dan turns, salutes, turns back, and counts off, "One, two, one-two-three-four!" The percussion lets out an explosion before silencing and building back to a crescendo. On every count of three, another member in each pentagon comes up to attention. When they're all up, the instruments come up and they go.

It's a Spanish theme show, which is no real surprise since there's a Spanish theme every other year. The pentagons rotate, and then smash together in the center, slowly spiraling out, creating a pentagram. The pentagram stops and the lines break at the center and form a pentagon out of the band with the percussion in the center. The pentagon rotates around, and then the lines split in half and bend toward the center of the field, creating a diamond toward the far side that looks like a head. The lower sets of lines bend to create what looks like thin arms and legs with the percussion in the torso. The percussion continues wildly while the rest of the band gets quiet again; it looks like the percussion is supposed to represent a beating heart.

The band front has formed a circle around the top of the head extending between the hands; they continue flashing their flags one at a time so it looks like fire is being thrown over the figure's head from one hand to another. Then, where the mouth would be, the tubas rise up in a line and blast what sounds like a something taken out of Holst's *Mars*. I can honestly say I'm shocked by the ambitiousness of the field show, and even more shocked that such an intricate design can be so well translated at the ground level.

I spit my toothpick out as I start walking and fetch another one from the fob in my pocket. Once I'm finished struggling through 100 yards worth of people, I stand at the edge of the track. With a huge, irrepressible smile I turn back and look at the crowd; every eye is fixed on the show, and nearly every other mouth is hanging open. Having had my eyes trained by years of seeing competitions, I can still see the odd mistake, but none of them are serious enough to warrant anything more than a bit more practice, of which they'll get plenty. If they could clean it up by championships, the one place where marching bands are ranked, they could take home the gold.

The field show is an attack on the senses, vibrant colors from the instruments and movements on the field, so many sounds from so many loud instruments that it's hard to focus on anything else. Well, there's also the band front, all of whom I despise from years of dealings without disrespecting their function. The fire thing was pretty amazing, but I know I mostly have the band director to thank for that. I turn away for a moment when I think that no one's paying attention and I see something from which I can't pry my eyes.

Past the chain link fences that surround the field, through the gate to get to the track, beyond the blacktop and parked school buses is a blanket of dense tree cover that hides everything below, except for the enormous yellow school buses. In the darkness, it would appear as though the grass next to the blacktop on the far side is moving. Normally this would be worthy of dismissal with the show continuing to my right, but there is nothing in the cemetery that should move like that, particularly given its notoriety as a place of rest. Nevertheless, something besides the foliage is moving, poking forth between the buses and stirring in little waves.

As my eyes continue to adjust, I see hands, arms, and whole bodies trying to push through. For a moment, I try to assign the field show as background music, but I find myself unable to concentrate on anything other than what is seen; this image, like an impressionistic painting, is vivid without total clarity and stands out as starkly as a freshly shaved poodle, a seriously handicapped person, or a car accident. Maybe it's a bunch of kids squeezing to get through to the show? I'm immediately disabused of this conclusion as I see gray flesh hanging from someone's dried out, exposed, bony sternum.

I've always wondered when writing how I could possibly react to Zombies in person. I've written a great deal on the living dead and one of my fascinations has always been finding interesting ways to present them to the audience for the first time. In writing, I could always react through a character. If I can understand who they voted for and why, what kinds of food they ate, what they did with their spare time, why they cheated on their wife or resent their children, I can map a pattern that will see their reaction to encountering a member of a group best described as undead.

Gray flesh hanging from a sternum. Part of me wonders if it's a prank, but I can't imagine how any kids, no matter how resourceful, could come up with an effect like that. If they had, I'll have to get them involved in my line of work. As this would-be fatally injured person shuffles forward, I watch the flesh shake on the end of what looks like a husky rubber band, which is most likely a tendon.

Another person covered in dirt pulls his way from underneath the bus and keeps crawling. I get a good look at this one's face and confirm that there is no way this can be a prank; having listened to a lecture from someone who does make-up effects professionally, I know that one can't take down a person's face like that. One must build up before one can do something like pretend to expose part of a person's skull.

This fellow's head is more or less a skull with gray flesh about as thick as a piece of paper wrapped over it, and he's moving like a human being would.

I stop and reverse my thought train. I'm not reacting, at least not properly. Part of my research on the subject has yielded that humans behave very much the same way as animals in these situations. If an animal has never seen something before, the first reaction is one of curiosity before other emotions come into play. I'm not afraid, but I'm not curious either. I know exactly what I'm looking at, I'm just not reacting. In fact, I'm watching them as an Alzheimer's patient would stare at one of their close relatives, even though I know what will most likely happen next.

They're moving slow, ambling, just like in the Romero movies, and wearing tuxedos and dresses. They're covered in dirt; did they actually come up from the ground? I tap the person next to me; she turns, and I'm surprised that it's a former crush of mine, Kelly Immelmann. "Hey Jeff..." She says; normally I'd get a heart flutter from talking to her, but my heart is already beating fast. In spite of my anticipation of the next series of events and a nearly subconscious effort to map contingencies, I just stand there with Kelly. "Pretty good, right?" She asks in reference to the field show, obviously not looking at the same thing I am. They continue moving forward, ambling toward the spectators with their arms stretched out. More come crawling out from under the buses as I stand there staring in disbelief, doing what a bystander does best: watch.

They pass through the gate and out of the shadows as they are struck by the lights of the field, still about twenty yards away. Two people are standing by a steel shed next to the gate, one a tubby man in a blue windbreaker and the other a tubby woman in a white sweater. They haven't noticed, as evidenced by their continued discussion. I hear nothing as they are engulfed by a sea of rotting arms in unspectacular fashion, but I see the bright contrast of that white sweater against the forest of putrid earth tones moments before the splashes of bright red permanently soak in. That was probably someone's mom.

As the second row of undead push past, the blood begins trickling out beneath their feet. The skin on the head of the first one is putrid and grayish, pulled back around his mouth as if he's had plastic surgery to expose his perfect teeth. His eyes aren't open, but he is somehow targeting the group of people of which I am currently a part. I turn around to find that the crowd has no idea what's going on, and Kelly has returned her attention to the field, but I do spot a police officer standing at the edge of the bleachers. They are now forty or so feet away; at this point, the first spot of true terror tightens its grip around my spine as I see the unending flood of bodies spread out behind them.

"Officer! Officer!" I shout, trying to be heard over the band. Suddenly, the fact that I can move and speak reminds me that I am not dreaming. As he turns to look at me, I scowl and point to the corpses stumbling over to us. The officer squints and starts walking over; what is he doing!? When he gets within speaking range, he stops. I can barely hear him say "Can I help you?" Insane, utterly insane; how is it possible he can so nonchalantly ask a walking corpse if it needs help? The one in front opens his sagging eyelids to show that there is nothing left inside the sockets. His mouth drops open, sending drool spindling out as an answer to the officer's question.

"Holy shit! Stay back!" Everyone is still watching the field show, like this moment is following some sort of nightmare logic in which everyone is oblivious but me. The officer jumps back, and then starts walking backward with his hand on his gun. "Stop there! Don't come any closer! Put your hands behind your head and drop NOW!" He pulls out his gun and points it at their leader. "This is your last warning, drop to the ground now or I will fire on you!" They aren't listening.

The pistol going off should be loud enough to break everyone's concentration, but I rotate my head to see that it arrested the attention of only a few people in the bleachers. Despite the fact that I couldn't hear the shot particularly well over the band, the knowledge that a gun was just discharged a few feet away from me while being aimed at a walking corpse simultaneously makes me dizzy and wakes me up.

The drum major is watching the field and he can't hear because the percussion is in front of him. Band regulations state that the rim of your hat must be one inch from your nose so you cannot be distracted by the crowd and all you can see is the ground and the drum major, so the band plays on like nothing is happening. A second shot is fired, this time it's in the arm of the leader of the undead. A shot in the leg makes the creature stumble, but he still advances forward. "Shoot him in the head!" I shout.

"Shut up kid! Back off!" With the police officer only twenty feet away, I'm reminded of watching the events of September 11th on television. That didn't seem real either, because something like that just doesn't happen; it can't happen because it isn't possible. A shot in the stomach, the leader is unfazed. The others are now grabbing and clawing their way through the gate, but there isn't enough space to accommodate any more than a dozen at a time. I look to the right to see more of them, barely visible in the low light aligning the twenty foot fence behind the goal posts as they scrape at it with their bony fingers. There has to be at least a hundred of them.

The police officer trips over his own foot and falls back, pulling the trigger and sending a round through the leader's nose an instant before a dusty spray of brain matter vents from the back of his skull. He crumples on the officer, who must now finally realize that his situation is dire; with this lifeless body pinning him to the freezing concrete, he lifts his gun and starts firing into the heads of his assailants. Twelve shots, four kills, and he's out of ammo. He reaches down for another magazine, but the undead are three feet away, and the new leader falls on top of him, sinking his teeth into the officer's lips as he puffs his cheeks in a terrified, muffled screech that, if I could hear it, would surely give me nightmares for the rest of my life. More fall on him and start pulling strips of flesh off, but the officer disappears as the next wave passes.

They've come through the gate and they're spreading in all directions as a seemingly endless torrent continues staggering through the gate. With their hands close enough for me to register them as real, my feet start mechanically stepping backward to the running track as if I were a windup toy given a full charge. There are about six clueless people exposed to the outstretched arms of the undead, and though I open my mouth, no sound comes out. When Kelly is driven into the ground by another falling corpse, she does the screaming for me. The syllables suggest cries for help, but it's too late.

Surges of thoughts flood my brain, but the most important one surfaces immediately: *Julia.* I can feel the toothpick fall limply out of my mouth as I turn and run. As my legs take me onto the field, I can feel dizzying gesticulations at the sides of my brain, warning me that I'm already a few steps into shattering one of society's intellectual-territorial barriers, and that it's not too late to turn back and redeem myself. This notion disappears as I shove my shoulder into one of the clarinets, spinning him like a top as I search for the mellophone attached to that beautiful face.

"What are you doing!?"
"You're ruining the show you asshole!"
"Get off the *field*!"

Julia sees me coming like a freight train and ignores me like she's supposed to, so I pick her up at the waist and start running with her slung over my shoulder. One by one I see the instruments come down as the teenagers operating them turn to look behind me and start walking cluelessly toward the horde. The music seems to cut out a moment later, the echoes of dissonant chords ricocheting off anything that can reverberate before the deafening silence is replaced by clanging metal, pounding feet, and a rising chorus of bloodcurdling screams.

I notice Julia kicking at my thigh as I turn toward the front entrance, and as I stop to watch a stampeding crowd attempt to savage their way through, she unloads herself from my shoulder, tossing her hat and mellophone to the field. The crowd of screaming people attempting to escape through the gate is now twenty bodies wide and a hundred people long as the cluster builds in density with almost no one getting through. They must not have opened the gate.

Under the blinding kliegs, it's hard to make out much aside from the audience in the bleachers, though it would be impossible to miss the sudden velocity change of a person jumping off the side. I look back toward the rear gate to see the pile of shuffling corpses overtaking the field up to the ten-yard line. I know in that moment that there must be some way out of here that isn't part of the charge of the living exiting or the dead entering. I squint to look across the bleachers, the bathroom hut, the snack bar, the faint outline of the fence surrounding the tennis courts...

"Let's *go!*" The words burp out of me involuntarily as I grab Julia's hand and jerk her behind me. The fences surrounding the outside of the field are at least fifteen feet high, making this a giant feeding pen aside from the two crowded exits and the one small door that leads from the football field to the tennis court. The gate is locked by a rusty chain, and I forget myself for only a moment before realizing that I'm still clutching my cane, and after seven sharp whacks, the brittle lock crumbles and we advance to the courts.

I stare into the pitch black fence surrounding us as my asthma ravaged lungs beg me for a moment to recover; there are thin, bony fingers protruding through the chain-link gaps, nearly blending in with the densely packed branches that scrape across the metal with the wind. There are houses behind these courts, and it becomes immediately clear to me that they have the field surrounded. I look back at Julia to see others breaking away from the amorphous swarm of people and running toward the door I opened. Gasping for air, I drag myself along the fence, running from one court to the next shrouded in darkness, glancing out at the field to see people trying to climb the fences before being pulled into the crowd.

We finally exit the tennis courts to enter the poorly-lit parking lot maze where nearly every space is occupied; though I want to stop to extinguish the fires blazing in my lungs, I know I can't. I look back at the gate while staggering between two cars to see people punching, clawing, screaming, and trampling to get through. Every few seconds another body breaks free and darts toward one of the cars in the massive, dark parking lot, but the rest are left trying to squeeze through the entrance all at once while people crawl through their feet and climb over their heads. "Where are we going?" Julia asks. "My car!" I wheeze. I run as fast as I can down the rows of cars, never letting go of Julia's hand. When I get to the end of the row, I stop, turn right, and run along the back lot parallel to the field.

The exit that leads to the band room is blocked by a police car that was intended to stop motorists from running over the entering and exiting bands; whoever tries to leave that way is in for a surprise. A body spills over the hood of the car, rolls on the ground, and rights itself before advancing toward us. It's followed by another, then another, so I can't help but stop. "They're blocking the exits, how are they blocking the exits?" I grab my chest as I pull in as much of the cold air as I can. I look over to the main school building, which is straight ahead, and then move toward the series of giant glass windows that adorn the pool building to my left side.

"What are they?" Someone asks behind me. I turn back as more pour over the hood of the police car. For the moment, I can't string my thoughts together. I'm staring, lost in my own mind with waves of exhilaration reminding me that what's happening makes sense. *The dead are returning to life and eating the living.* "How do we get out?" *The dead are returning to life and eating the living.* "Jeff, how do we get out!?" *The dead are returning to life and eating the living.* "JEFF!" I turn my head back to Julia.

"This way." I say, looking past her toward the driveway entering the back parking lot from the street out front. The blacktop is darkened by shadow ten feet from the opening and the road is obscured by the structure, but soft light is emanating from the unseen road around the corner. When I look back, I notice about eight people behind me waiting for my decision, one of whom is on their cell phone. I keep staring at the exit while again noticing the distant screams from the football field echoing off the façade of the school. "*This* way!" There is a gap between the pool building and the cafeteria, and at the end of this gap, there is a basement access door.

People in the parking lot are getting in their cars and driving, but there's nowhere to go. They still have enough humanity in them to avoid the people running for their lives, but some of these people are actually the undead. A few cars try to go out the entrance, but there are reverse treadles that will destroy their tires, leaving them exposed to attack. "Look out!" Someone shouts; a beige sedan speeds toward us, showering two other cars with sparks as it blasts between them. I instantly wrap my arms around Julia and leap left just as the car swings right and coldly whacks into the side of the building with an impact that shakes the asphalt. For a moment, I hear nothing but the hot echo of crushed brick and steel.

When I look back up, all that remains of the horrible crashing sound is the ticking engine, squealing tires, and soft moans. One of the people in our group must have jumped the wrong way, because his body is pinned between the eviscerated hood of the car and the shattered brick of the building with absolutely no space between. The car interior is obscured by smoke from the deployed airbags, and the car itself is shaking as though two people are fighting inside. The wheels continue to spin, peeling the grass off the lawn and spraying dirt into the car's undercarriage.

The pinned person is a teenager wearing a band uniform and he's still conscious, evident by his vibrating hands absently clawing at the hood of the car. Before Julia can look, I pull her head to my chest. "It's... numb... m-my legs are numb..." he mumbles, blood dribbling down his chin. The hood descends as the wheels continue to dig ditches in the lawn. "It doesn't hurt..." His voice trails off in an anesthetized drone as his eyes drift shut. As the hood continues to a dip, a soft crack emerges from his lower back and his severed torso falls limp on the hood, firing thick jets of blood against the wall.

When I become aware of the screams again I look back at the glowing, ominous haze of the football field and watch the waves of people shuddering with fear as they run toward the lot. I absently touch my face and realize that my bowler has fallen off. I find it on the ground, grab it, and put it back on as I start running with Julia's hand. "Let's go, let's go!" I shout. We run along the strip of blacktop, past the cafeteria doors on the right, past the gymnasium doors on the left, through a small fence door, and finally down a set of metal steps that see us boxed into a square shaft of brick and mortar at the building's underbelly.

At the bottom of the staircase is a set of metal doors with light leaking out between the diagonal slots. There is no handle, only a padlock keeping it shut. I slide my cane between the latch and the door when a light hits us from behind. I turn to be blinded by the dim bulb of a flashlight with the shape of a man behind it. "What are you doing? What the *hell's* going on!?" He says, stumbling to his feet. It's a bum, and he must have been sleeping behind the stairs.

"Come on!" I say, motioning to him. "Jesus Christ, listen, come *on!*" He turns off the flashlight and joins the cluster as I snap the latch off, wait for everyone to file in, and shut the door, trapping us in a buzzing mechanical generator room lined with pipes. "Block the door!" I shout over the generators. We use a metal desk next to the doors to block them shut. I spot a metal tool cabinet, roll it over, and knock it down behind the desk, but I unexpectedly tumble over it. "The greenhouse, let's go!" I point to a door next to a bundle of piping. Julia helps me to my feet as I wheeze.

"You alright?" She asks softly. I don't want her to suspect that I'm seriously struggling, so I shake my head while swallowing hard and push her toward the door, which opens out to a hallway reminiscent of the subterranean missile complex in *Day of the Dead*. I turn right and they follow me; we go up a set of steps, make a right U-turn, run up more steps, and I stop to look out. We're at the stairway across from the front door, and luckily, the halls appear to be empty. We head up another ten steps or so and we're at the door of the breezeway that connects the middle of a horseshoe-shaped building segment. The giant windows overlook the courtyard where the band practices, but it is fortunately elevated to the second floor.

We start to run across when one of the group members stops. "Look!" They shout, causing the rest of us to turn around. He's pointing down into the courtyard between the building halves, toward the band room as two slowly ambling people turn the corner into the courtyard. "MOVE!" I yell. We trot through a set of double doors, up more steps, and into a hallway lined with lockers. We turn the corner to the right and keep moving.

After another hundred feet, we turn right again, this time into the science hallway, and finally stop at a wooden door upon which the word *GREENHOUSE* is stenciled; it's unlocked. Once everybody's in I lock it from the inside and we run up another twenty or thirty concrete steps, open the door at the top and finally stop in a small room with a few desks and random school supplies scattered around. From where we stand, there is a door to the left in the far corner on which *OBSERVATORY* is stenciled. Turning right leads to a twenty-foot greenhouse lined with windows and a glass door that face east; the glass is visibly shaking with a series of crashes and car horns.

I collapse on the floor, gasping as hard and deep as I can before shuffling the sullied air out for more oxygen. As I chase my breath, I become aware of someone weeping over the labored breathing of everyone else in the room, but I still can't focus enough to discover the party responsible. I look at the group of seven, immediately recognizing some of them as band members. Ava Vaziri, perhaps Julia's best friend, is in the far corner. John Johnston, a saxophonist we call John Squared, is across from her on a desk. Don Mason is sitting against the floor with his knees tucked against his body. There's a girl who looks as though she spent the evening primping, then there's the bum and two young kids I've never seen before, one wearing a band uniform and the other in plain street clothes.

As my breath finally starts to settle, I unscrew the top of my toothpick fob, take one out with my mouth, and screw it back on as I stand. "Everyone..." All eyes are instantly on me. "Uh... I'm going outside... *stay* here, and uh... once you catch your breath, try to breathe slowly. John Squared?" John stands immediately and walks over. "We'll be back in a minute. Just..." I open the door to be greeted by a frozen blast of air mixed with a variety of scents, most of which produced by cars. Once John Squared is out behind me, I yank the door shut and jump over the railing that separates the greenhouse from the rest of the roof. Still catching our breath, we walk straight out to the edge, roughly seventy feet from the back of the door, and look out over the parking lot.

Our enviable vantage gives us an uninterrupted view of the undiminished chaos on the field, the full breadth of which did not have a chance to fully sink in until now; to a blind eye, the gaming surface would simply be a mixture of brown and red with the occasional green and white intrusion, each color contributing to the undulating tapestry of desperation. The rear exit to our left looks to be packed with cars filling the width of space between the school building and the cemetery fence. It would appear, however, that many of the buses from beneath which the dead first made themselves known have already made their exit. To the right, the rear entrance appears to have suffered a similarly clogged fate.

A second glance at the field reveals that everyone who remained unmolested has made it out, but they have left at least three hundred people dead or dying on the synthetic grass. I reach inside my trench coat pocket and pull out my glasses. There are more people randomly positioned across the parking lot, and the undead are spreading through the cars, overtaking them, and overturning them. The humans desperate to escape the parking lot have blocked themselves into a feeding pen. There are screams every few seconds, cars driving in circles and crashing into each other, and people trying to run over the dead, but the cars are in such tight quarters that any maneuver is futile.

At either exit, from what I can see, the cars are pressed together so tight no one can get through, leaving much of the parking lot open save for the few cars trying to drive through the gates and hit the undead. There are about thirty people running through the parking lot, screaming for help, some of them in band uniforms. Looking below is surreal, as if I'm watching a rehearsed performance of the apocalypse at Universal Studios. The undead look so much like people in makeup I'm willing to bet that people tried to reason with them. Mothers. Fathers. With children.

I look over to see John surveying the atrocities below with just as much interest as me. If Mark Hamill were sixteen, gaunt, and had a bit of an acne problem, that would be John Johnston. He possessed a strange sort of silent, sarcastic humor that was executed mostly in response to other people, mostly just using his eyes. Every time he saw me again after I graduated he would meet me with an ever-present sort of half-smile which seemed to indicate that we were both in on some kind of joke. I don't particularly remember if we were.

"Anyone else try to follow us?"
"Yeah... they went for the front..."
"I mean... did we trap anyone behind us when we got in?"
"Definitely not."

I sigh.

"The kid... and the car... did you..."
"...Chris. His name was Chris."
"I'm sorry..."
"I... I can't believe that just happened. I mean that. I *can't*."

We sit in silence until I realize I haven't a clue what I could possibly say. He breaks the silence for me. "What are we gonna do?" I immediately regret the broken silence, since I honestly can't be sure if I want to be the one that has to answer that question.

"Think anyone called 911?"
"Well, yeah... but, *someone* in there's gotta have a cell phone..."
"Good point..."

The greenhouse is silent as we reenter with a cold wind at our backs. "You." I point to the relatively attractive, made up girl whose name I don't know. "Got a cell phone?" She stares for a second. "Yeah, yeah... here." She reaches into a pocketbook, pulls out the phone and points it at me. Expecting her to throw it, I stand still, but she continues looking at me with the phone in her hand. Finally, I acquiesce and take it. "Thanks." I say, dialing 911. "Busy. That's encouraging."

I toss the phone back to her, but it sails into the wall as she stares off into space. She reaches back to retrieve it, checking to make sure it's in one piece as her face retains the qualities of a confused child. One at a time, everyone in the group looks around at everyone else. As I lean back on one of the greenhouse rows, I can feel their eyes following me. "What next?" Don asks. I look back at him blankly. I don't know what to do. Should I tell them that, or am I better off saying nothing?

"They're... they're still out there... god... isn't there... something we can do?" The boy I don't recognize asks.
"What are *we* gonna do?" Ava asks.

"Kate's out there. Julia... I... Kate's *out* there. I couldn't find her...
I..."

"You wanna go out and *look* for her!?"

"I don't know, yeah! She's alone..."

"There are hundreds of people..." Don adds.

"...John, Lisa's out there..."

"Duh, *hundreds* of people are out there... what are we gonna *do*!?"

"I don't *know*! Everyone just started freaking *running*..."

"Jesus, calm down!" Ava butts in.

"Calm *down*!? Honestly, what the... I can't! I *can't*!"

"Well what do you wanna do about it!?"

"Bullshit, bullshit, there's plenty we can do..."

"I'm not going out there..." Don says. "...and I'm sure as hell not
staying *here*..."

"Oh, sure, you're just gonna walk out the god damn door..."
Squared interjects.

I look over at the girl I don't recognize, whose breath is slowly
beginning to shallow. "Guys." I say quietly. They continue talking over
each other in increasing volume. I turn my cane around and rap the
metal bulb at the top into the ground repeatedly until they all shut up.

"Relax..."

"F... I can't relax..." One of the young ones blurts.

"Can you listen?"

He quiets down. "Okay. I know this sounds stupid ... take a deep
breath, hold it, and exhale... please." Surprisingly, they all obey. The
silence that follows is utterly satisfying. "Okay, keep breathing slow...
we have three options... go back out, run, or stay put..." Everyone
nods or murmurs in agreement.

"So what do we do?" Don asks.

"...why are you asking me?"

"Come on, I'm asking, just, like, what do *you* think!?"

"I can't tell you what to do. *I* don't know what to do."

"You brought us up here!" Don shouts.

"Keep your fucking voice down! *You* followed *me...*"

"But why did you pick *here*!?" Ava asks.

"It's the highest point in the building, it has two entrances, and if worse comes to worst, we can always run out across the roof."

"Okay, so, I get *that...* so what do we *do*?" Don asks.

"I can't *tell* you what to do..."

"Can't you just tell us what *you* think!?" Ava shouts.

"No!"

That shuts everyone up.

"Look... what I'm trying to say is... let's think about this."

"You still didn't answer him."

"...I think we should stay put."

Don and the boy I don't know immediately bark retorts and Ava joins in after a moment. I hold my hands up to silence them, and then bang my cane into the ground again; it's surprising how effective it is. "*Shut up*! Before we do *anything* else, we're gonna have to start *listening* to each other... for all we know, both those doors come crashing down in the next thirty seconds..." The reaction to this is, to say the least, both extremely negative and extremely loud. More banging silences them again.

"Shut. Up. I made my choice... I'm up here... the rest of you... I don't know..."

"I got a question..." It's the girl I don't know. "What the *FUCK* is going on!?"

"Will you be quiet!?"

"I don't care, I don't care! Just tell me what the *fuck* is going *on*!"

"Jesus, will you *listen*!? Calm *down*!"

"How do you expect me to do that!?"

"I don't know, figure it out! If we sit up here shouting at each other, they're gonna hear us, got it!?"

Once again, everyone shuts up.

"*Fine,*" She starts. "*...you* brought us in here..."
"For the fifth time, you *followed* me, see?"
"Duh..."
"So you agree?"
"What?"
"...I came up here on an impulse. Can we just put that to rest?"
"Duh, but..."
"Would you *stop* saying that?"

She takes another long, deep breath.

"Okay... but why *here?*"
"I told you..."
"...you *knew* what you were doing... so you have, like, *some* idea what's going on..."
"Okay, yeah."
"Well?"
"Do you really want my theory?"
"Am I speaking German? Yes, I want your fuckin' 'theory'!"
"Okay..."

I start walking around the room, taking off my bowler and setting my cane down on the flowerbed. The girl takes off her coat, balls it up, and throws it in the corner. "I'm certainly no expert, but it is my *opinion...*" I start, taking off my black leather gloves. "That the dead have come back to life..." I throw off my trench coat and rest my arms back against the flowerbed, facing the group. "...and are after the living."

"Zombies." Julia says.
"What does that mean?" The girl I don't know asks.
"Seriously?" Squared asks. "Is there any person alive who *doesn't* know what Zombies are?"
"Could you just... explain?" She asks insistently.

"Well, they bite the living... and we turn into them." I offer.

"...how?"

"Does it matter?"

"You think the police are coming?" Don interrupts.

"Dunno."

"Can they stop 'em?"

"If they shoot them in the head... that's the only way to kill them."

"Do you *know* that?"

"I... watched a cop shoot one in the head."

"I get it..." One of the boys I don't know says. "...but what do we *do*? I mean... our parents, our friends...?"

The group murmurs in agreement, so I wait until the chatter dies down to continue.

"Look... I'm sorry, your name is?"

"Matt Hughes."

"Matt. I can't keep you here." I get up and walk to look out the series of dirty greenhouse windows. "But what's gonna happen if you leave?" I look back at the group. "Imagine going out there... even if you *could* make it to the field... could you make it back?"

"But they're slow... I mean, they're *walking*." Ava cuts me off.

"Did you *see* what they did!?"

Silence. I sigh and calm down, spitting out my toothpick.

"They surrounded the field... on *all* sides..." I trail off, pinching the top of my septum. "The noise... I *think*... they were attracted to the noise. If we stay quiet..."

"Be careful," The bum says. "You can't assume that."

"I know, I know... but... I'm sorry, you are?"

"Richard McKnight."

"Jeff Grey. What I'm saying... it's *really* important we figure out what we're gonna do..."

"What happens next?" Ava asks.

"Okay..."

I push my hands back through my hair and let out a deep breath.

"The people on the field haven't turned yet, so assume it takes a few hours..."

"And if they're not Zombies?" The other young man says.

"...and you are?"

"Jake."

"Jake... I just watched a hundred embalmed corpses covered in mud wearing formalwear attack and kill a cop... I think it's safe to assume they're not psychos."

"How long until we see the military?" Richard asks. His sentence carries with it the scent of decaying teeth and cheap alcohol.

"You're asking the wrong guy... more importantly, what are you planning to do? All of you."

"You were saying we should stay put." Matt says.

"Yeah... I think so."

"What's the point?"

"...what's the point of leaving?"

"It's death trap in here, no matter how you slice it."

"Well... what isn't?"

"Huh?"

"Where can you go that *isn't* a death trap?"

"I could just go... I mean... I could go to the police..."

"How're you gonna get there?"

"I... do you have a car?"

"Pretend I'm not here, what are you gonna do?"

Matt stays silent.

"Because you aren't *walking* with the town in this state..."

"Come on, it's not *that* bad." He retorts.

"Can we at least agree that, for the moment, you feel a *little* safe?"

"Not really..."

"...as compared to ten minutes ago."

"...okay..."

"Outside, you're exposed. No weapons, alone, at night, and out-numbered a hundred to one. If you call for help, what do you think the chances are someone answers?"

"Well..."

"You're talking about your life. I don't know if you're entertaining the notion of arming up with a shotgun and a chainsaw and going hog wild... it's not a video game. You run into the wrong house, you run out of breath... and that's it."

"...so what do we *do*?" Don asks again.

"What's the worst case scenario?" Ava asks. I really have to take a moment to think about my answer.

"Well... if this *isn't* a virus... then the hospitals won't catch it and send their patients home... and... these bands come from halfway across the state... if they go back, the infection's already in what, nine? Ten towns?"

"Ten, including this one." Don says.

"Right. Ten towns, some of which are halfway across the state." I sigh and sit back. "Actually, the more I think about it, the more likely it is."

"Oh god..." Julia says.

"That's... pretty bad." Ava says.

"So if you want my opinion, we stay on the roof."

"Shouldn't we be on the ground?"

"Not unless you want them scratching at the glass all night..." Don blurts.

"Don, not necessary..." I say, cutting him off. "If they can see us, smell us, hear us, whatever... we have less of a chance of any of those happening if we're above ground."

"And why are we staying put?"

"Look, I'm sure there's a dozen places you can think of to go that will be safer than this, but getting there involves going outside..."

"Duh." Ava offers.

"Look, I've *had* it with that, okay!? You want to keep interrupting me, then stop asking fucking questions!"

"Did you drive here?"

"Yes, but we're *not* packing eight people in a two-door sedan and I'm *not* making two trips. We don't *have* to make any decisions right now..."

"That's such a shit idea..."

I stifle my urge to strangle Matt when he finishes, pressing my hands on my cheeks and shoving them toward the back of my neck.

"Okay... think about it this way..." I start. "Outside, you have no control other than where you *plan* on going and how you *plan* to get there. There's no safe, just *safer*. We're all tired and shaken up... if you're scared, stay put, stay quiet, and wait for morning. I can't make it any clearer than that. If you want to argue, please do so to your heart's content. If you want to leave, there's the door... I can't tell you what to do. So... hands, who's staying here?"

Everyone raises his or her hand without hesitation.

"Okay. We have to block the entrances."

"So by tomorrow, what?" Ava asks.

"I don't know. If it gets taken care of, we'll *hear* about it. If it doesn't..."

"What about our parents?" John asks.

"What about them?"

I get several insistent stares.

"What?"

"We can't...?" The girl starts.

"B-... I'm sorry, what's your name?"

"Melody."

"Okay, Melody... it's not *safe*..."

"No, idiot, I'm talking about why you don't want to find our parents..."

"Melody, was it? Mind your *fucking* manners. *I* am not going out there, and I'm not explaining why again."

"What the hell does that mean?" Jake asks.

"Can't we go out see if they're okay?" Melody asks, breathing harder as tears well up in her eyes.

"Melody... I'm. Not. Leaving. You're gonna do what you're gonna do. If that means going outside, then do it. But don't even think about coming back... if even one of them sees you, we're all in a world of shit. Now... we *need* to block the exits."

"How?" Jake asks.

I get up and walk to the far side of the room, past the observatory. I open the door to the main stairwell to find a pile of loose ceiling panels that rest against the wall to my left. I sigh, bite my lip, and take a step back only to run into Melody. "Didn't I see some desks back there?" I ask. As she nods, I lift my arms and cross my hand over my mouth. "I figure we lay the panels across the staircase and reinforce the desks between them and the wall... it'll buy us some time if they get up the steps. Do we have any extra light bulbs in there?" Melody looks at me. "Light bulbs? What the...?" I motion toward the platform at the bottom of this set of stairs. "Shatter them... if anyone comes up the steps, we'll hear the glass break."

In ten minutes, the desk boundary is set up: six desks in a cube behind two panels and eight broken fluorescent bulbs. I next turn my attention to the other stairwell, which is just a thin concrete tube down to the science hallway. "Okay." I let out a deep sigh and push my hair back. "We put a note on that door saying that we're up here, and then we push the last three desks down the stairs." I flip my toothpick using my tongue.

"Push the desks down?" Don asks. "So if someone gets the door open, we'll know." Everyone nods in agreement. I get down on the floor and scratch out a message: *October 9th, 2004. Eight Survivors Upstairs. None of us has been bitten. Welcome up. ~Jeff Grey.* I stand up and pick up the stapler. "Okay, we make a new one every day, that way if someone comes through, they'll know we're up here. Who's coming down with me?" I ask. Julia immediately waves and smiles. I throw on my trench coat, grab my cane, and start down. "So... can I assume that you're all still here because what I've said makes sense?" I say, looking toward the top of the steps. Matt appears at the door, looking back at the rest of the room before he nods.

"Alright… no one ever goes anywhere alone, no excuses. There's a lot of us up here, so if you have to go anywhere… groups of three." I continue down the steps, Julia follows. At the bottom, I put my ear to the door, and then open it. Once I see that the halls are empty, I turn and staple the message on the outside of the door, then look around again. I catch a glance of Julia as she stands flat and expressionless, but when she notices me looking her face transforms into a coy smile. "Are you okay?" I ask, finally. "I'm fine."

"You know, you still look hot in that band uniform." I say, putting my hands around her. She reaches up to kiss me, but I hold her back and look off down the hall. "Shh…" A dull, rapid clapping sound echoes down the hallway as fear tightens its grip around my spine again. "Get inside, *now*!" I snarl, pushing her in. My legs spread apart and I look up, one hand on the door and the other on my cane. If they're running, I might as well kill myself now; I can outrun them if they walk, but when the asthma kicks in, I'm a sitting duck. A guy wearing a green band uniform comes around the corner running like hell, stumbling when he sees me. "Oh *god*!" He spurts, bumbling to a stop. "Get over here!" I yell. "Oh thank god!" He says, running for me. As he approaches, I notice blood on his arm.

"Were you bitten?"

"What?"

"Were you bitten, scratched, anything?"

"Oh god, yeah… someone grabbed my arm… his fingertips just rubbed off like… dried apple sauce or something…"

His sleeve confirms the story; there are a series of bloody rips in the uniform at his forearm surrounded by dark, gelatinous smudges. The smell induces my gag reflex. "…dug in pretty deep…" I consider that while he catches his breath.

"We… can't let you up here."

"What!?"

"I... I'm sorry, you... we can't risk it."

"Risk... what...?"

"...it didn't occur to you that they're Zombies?"

"Please! The bus left without me, I got nowhere to go!"

"I... alright, *one* condition..."

"Anything, name it!"

"...we're gonna tie you up."

"What? Tie me *up*!?"

"There are seven people up there, and I'm making their safety *my* responsibility. If you're not infected, we'll know by tomorrow morning and we'll untie you."

"I don't know..."

"I can't put them at risk."

"I won't touch anyone, I'll sit in a corner or something... wait... wait... you're saying I could turn into one of those things!?"

"I- uh..."

"Oh god... that's not true, right? I'm gonna be okay, right?"

As I look in his watery eyes, the urge to lie is nearly too easy to pass up. "...I honestly don't know. B-but... we can't take the risk. Do you understand that? Let's start there; do you understand why I need to do this?" He looks up at the ceiling, his mouth contorting as he holds back a sob.

"Okay, I guess it's okay."

"I... have you had anything to eat? If we tie you up, we don't want you to be hungry."

"I don't think I could eat now anyway."

"Come to think of it, I don't know if we have any food..."

I open the door sheepishly to reveal Julia standing there. Steve leaps back with a shout.

"Relax! This is my girlfriend Julia... Jules, this is..."

"Steve... Parmacek."

"Jeff."

He extends his hand to Julia. "*Don't* touch him!" Steve and Julia jump and I cover my mouth. "I'm sorry..." Julia nods and runs up the steps. I hold the door open for Steve, and he hesitates before going up first. As he lumbers up the steps, I try to be ready for him to turn and kick me down. He doesn't, but to be safe, I spit out my toothpick so I don't end up swallowing it. When Steve comes out at the top, he waves to everybody. "Everyone, this is Steve... he, uh... he's..." I watch Melody's eyes connect with the patch of blood on his left arm and it looks like she can't restrain herself from pointing at it as she gasps. The rest of the group follows suit and backs up to the wall.

"Alright! Relax... we're gonna tie him up."
"Are you *kidding* me!?" Melody sobs.
"We *have* to..."
"No, why would you even let him *up* here!?"
"...because I'm still human?"
"What..."

The door shuts and we all turn to see Richard reaching into the top drawer on the desk, producing a roll of gray tape which he then throws to me before pushing the desk back in front of the door. I feel Steve's nervous eyes on me as I find the end of the roll and pull out a swatch. "I'm sorry Steve." I start at his feet and wind up his legs, around his crotch, up his torso, and finally around his shoulder blades before winding down around his arms.

"Can you breathe okay?"
"Yeah, fine."
"Do you need to go to the bathroom?"
"No, I'm okay."

With that, I re-wrap his arms separately, and then re-wrap his legs again. There's still plenty left on the roll. "Uh, Richard... you want to help me get him up on the garden row so we can tape him down?" Richard nods and helps me lift him. As I continue to tape him up, his eyes stay fixed on the ceiling. Richard pops up with a half-full bag of dirt and slides it under his head as a pillow. "Warm enough?" I ask, taping down his feet. "Yes." His reply is dripping with irritation.

"Do you need any help?" John Squared asks.

"No, I've got it..."

"I was just thinking, maybe we should find a first aid kit for that bite."

"It's not a bite." Steve spits.

"He wasn't bitten?"

"No, one of them dug their fingers into his arm..." I say.

"So he could be okay?"

"Yeah, we just don't know... but it's a *long* way to the nurse's office."

"Right... tomorrow, though?"

"Definitely."

"If I'm still alive tomorrow." Steve bitterly interjects.

"Relax, Steve, try not to think about it..."

"Are you telling me *you'd* be able to not think about it?"

"...now that you mention it..."

"That's what I thought, so fuck off."

"I'm sorry..."

"You're *not* sorry, you're tying me up!"

"Steve, I know how upset you must be..."

"No you *don't*! You can't even... you know what, I changed my mind, take the fuckin' tape off..."

"You agreed to it... you *begged* me to let you up here..."

"And now I changed my mind, so let me the *FUCK* out!"

"Steve, I sympathize, really, but you're gonna have to keep your voice down..."

His spit sails past my head and smacks into the wall behind me. I look back at foamy, white streak on the wall and tear off another swatch of gray tape.

"I'm sorry, Steve... I'll let you go tomorrow."

"When you let me go I will FUCKING KILL YOU!"

"No biting…"

He tries to thrash against me, but he's been bound too tightly. I line up the tape over his mouth and push it down hard, taping it off under the row before tearing off two smaller strips to put under his nose and on his chin so he can't stretch his face to pull it off. I do feel sorry for him, especially since the windows provide such poor insulation. The greenhouse is certainly the coldest part of the roof interior, but not by much.

I turn around to look at the rest of the group, and, as if to make my point about the cold, my eyes fall on Melody's nipples poking through her shirt like she's smuggling pills in her bra. I shake this off and return my attention to the door to the science hallway. "All right, let's push the desks down the stairs." Richard opens the door for Don, but stops him just before he pushes the first one down. "Instead of pushing them down," Richard starts. "Maybe we should… it's gonna make an awful lot of noise."

Another rancid burst of air pushes out of Richard's throat, carrying the heavy, acrid smell of alcohol fused with stomach acid. I nod, so he and Don take the desks down. I pace in front of the doorway until we can finally lock the door and push the desk up against it. I have a seat on the desk and let out a long sigh as I try to imagine if there's anything I can do to make the roof safer. "Where do you come up with this shit?" I open my eyes to see Melody asking me the question. "Years of writing and loneliness." I rub my face and yawn. "Oh."

"Who's got a watch?" I ask. Melody rifles through her pocketbook and pulls out her cell phone. "Uh, it's uh… 12:03." I roll off the desk and get up, yawning. "Okay, Squared-ston, Richard, come with me." I grab my cane and walk for the greenhouse door. "Where are we going?" Richard asks. "Take a look at the front and back parking lots to see how things are." As I put my hand on the door, Melody stands up.

"No! I don't want to stay in here with… people I don't know."

"Well, you don't know *me*, so… what difference does it make?" I respond.

"We had art class together two years ago."

"Uh…" I start, staring blankly at her.

"Look, I don't want to stay here with Steve. Can I please go?"

Steve thrashes and moans at that, trying to talk. I sigh and look at Julia as she shrugs. I take out another toothpick. "Fine. Richard, stay here and keep an eye on things." As she pushes herself off the floor, I notice that her hair used to be bleached. I reach back and grab my cane, then pass Steve, who stares irately as I hold the door open for Melody and John. When we go outside, Melody's hands cross over under her breasts and she starts shaking. "It is soooo cold!" She says. I roll my eyes, strip off my trench coat and hand it to her. I look to see if John's okay, and though he's not wearing his band jacket, he was smart enough to wear a thermal shirt beneath his suspenders.

I try to hop over the railing but end up carefully willing myself over due to a weathered sting in my leg joints. As I walk out to the edge again, I become fully aware of just how tired my muscles are. The massive lights of the back lot are still cutting the darkness of the field to illuminate the flat, dark, lifeless bodies, while the ominously dim parking lot is littered with a sea of laminated glass crystals from several dozen windshields. The only cars remaining have been reduced to hissing heaps of metal; some haven't been started, a few have illuminated headlights, but none of them have drivers.

My eye catches a piece of white cloth dancing across the ground with a brisk wind, and the motion instantly makes me aware that there is not single body moving in the expanse before us. "Well, this side is fucked." I say as I turn off and head toward the other side of the building. "How do you know that?" Melody asks.

"I don't."

"Are you gonna leave them out there?"

"Haven't I answered enough questions?" I mutter.

"What?"

"Yes." I growl.

"…*what?*"

I continue walking, only glancing back to see the droll expression on John's face. I wonder for a moment what it is about her that aggravates me, but I then vaguely remember that art class where she distinguished herself as an arrogant bitch.

"There's nothing we can do. If they're infected, then they're already dead."

"But you already said you don't know that, right?"

"I don't."

"So what if they turn out to be alive tomorrow?"

I finally stop and turn back.

"What exactly would your plan be if you were in my shoes?"

"I don't know. I'm not you."

"What would you do about those people?"

"I don't know."

"Try to help them, maybe? What if one of them bit you? What if you were followed back inside? Do you actually *want* to go down there and look at a bunch of corpses?"

"Not really."

"Then why are you asking these questions?"

"Am I not allowed to?"

"Of course you are, but *why* are you asking them?"

"Look, you're like, leading the group, right?"

"...no, I'm not."

"Well, if I don't understand something, I'm gonna ask *you*."

"...alright. But can you keep it to a minimum when we're outside?"

We all resume walking. It's not exactly a quick trip to the other side as there are a lot of contours in the top of the building. We also have to walk along the top of the breezeway. Getting down to it and up the other side requires mounting a ten foot drop from the higher roof contour. There are surprisingly few undead in the courtyard that it overlooks, but I can already hear a chorus of terrible sounds coming from the front, and the giant gas-powered generators are the only instruments I can make out from here. All of the buses that were out front are gone, and there are more corpses on the lawn, but there are also several people running out from either side of the school. Melody's lungs fill with air, but I grab her before she can let any of it out.

"What do you think you're doing?"

"All those *people...* we've gotta tell them to come in! Get your hands off me!"

"Alright, relax... what can we do? It's quiet and safe up here, and if we bring in twenty or thirty screaming people, it's not gonna be anymore..."

"But..."

"Look... *I* want to stay alive... do you?"

"Duh!"

"Right... those people are the only thing keeping us alive. They're the one's getting chased, right? Not us. Like I said... there's *nothing* we can do to help them... we stay in here and try to make it through the night and let the police do their job, okay?"

She seems satisfied, so I return my eyes to the street. When I kneel down to approach the edge, John and Melody join me. The cars on both sides, from what I can see, are packed into each other to the point of being immobile after one last sedan slams into the cars behind it and speeds off down the street, but not before running over at least two people in the parking lot. People on both sides are bounding over the cars and funneling out, running to the street, and heading off in opposite directions. The middle ground, which is right in front of us, is largely unoccupied, save for the dying embers of a few flares. Screaming, footsteps, car alarms, and metal grinding are all still audible above the generators.

After sweeping back and forth a few times, I don't see or hear a single cop car. I look up over the houses, over the field of trees packed between them, and I can only see the clear, empty sky; no flashing lights, no fires burning in the distance. If the scene below me were removed, it would be an average, peaceful night. I sigh, pounding my hand on the roof before I turn to walk back. "So what does this mean?" Melody asks. "It's a puzzle… think you can figure it out?" John says. I force a soft laugh.

"What's *your* problem?" She asks.
"Haven't got one."
"Well, *something's* making you act like an asshole."
"Whoa, it's not possible that I'm countering a dumb question with a snarky answer…"
"You could just answer the fucking question."
"I was hoping you'd figure it out."
"You don't have to be a dick…"
"And you don't have to ask stupid questions."

Melody struggles to keep up after I help her off of the breezeway. When we get to the greenhouse, I open it to let them in before me. John goes first and Melody follows. "Thanks." She says pointedly, strutting past me. I move past the ever-thrashing Steven into the main room. "How does it look?" Richard asks. I let out another sigh as I rub my arms and sit back on the table; I don't think I can remember a time when sitting down on a surface this uncomfortable felt so good. Julia trots over, sits next to me, and puts her arms around me.

"You know the expression about shit hitting the fan?'"
"Yeah."
"It looks like the other side of the fan."
"Maybe they cops just aren't *here* yet…" Matt says.
"No way, they're going everywhere *but* here." Ava says.
"I doubt it. There were at least a thousand people here tonight, and we're right next to the cemetery." I state.

I rest my back against the doorway. There is about a minute of silence until Melody sighs. She starts shaking slightly as she pulls her legs closer to her body and sighs again. I glance at Ava, who already looks like she's about to explode. Finally, Melody lights the fuse.

"Oh my god, I'm soooo hungry."

"Bulimic bitch..." Ava mutters.

"You know what? *Fuck* you guys! We've been up here for, like, two hours, and I've gotten nothing but shit from you! What is your *problem?*"

"It's only been *that* long?" John asks with a smile.

"I don't want to hear you bitch about a problem *you* created." Ava says. "We're all hungry, cold, terrified... do you hear anyone else complaining? Know why? Because they know there's shit-all we can do about it!"

"I'm not fuckin' *bulimic*... just 'cause I exercise, you fat whore..."

"Spoiled bulimic bitch."

"Leave her alone!" Don says.

"I can handle this my fucking self!"

"Every time you open your mouth you bitch about some*one* or some*thing*..." John adds to the crowd. "And don't take her fuckin' side..."

"What makes you think you can get away with saying that!?"

"Gym, two years ago... I'm surprised you and your gym class harpies had time to *breathe* with all the bitching you did..."

I roll my eyes as everyone starts to join in, except Richard and me. "KNOCK IT OFF!" I shout at the top of my lungs, making everyone fall silent.

"What is this, the domestic breakdown scene? Shut *the fuck* up! Let's *pretend* we're on the same side."

"...what!?" Don asks.

"It's us against them, not each other, so knock it off."

I put my head in my hands, push my hair back, and end up staring hard at the floor. With everyone quiet again, it's possible to hear scattered traffic in the street. I lift my head after a few seconds. "Look, we're all tired. Let's try to get some sleep." In the next few seconds of silence, no one moves. After looking around the room, Melody speaks again. "Why can't you band people be nice like him?" Ava rolls her enormous eyes and starts to talk, but I cut her off. "The only thing keeping me from getting pissed is patience, and it's wearing thin. When you start showing courtesy, they'll do the same." I get up off the desk and walk past Steve, who is now sleeping on the garden. I flick my toothpick at the left side of the greenhouse and walk up to Melody. "Can I have my coat back please?" Once she's handed it over, I walk back to Julia and wrap it around us.

I lay on my side, resting my head on my forearm, and she wraps herself around me. I drape my arm over her and she clutches my hand in hers, holding it tight around her. I watch Melody retrieve her jacket from the corner and curl into a ball by the door while everyone else tries to get comfortable. Richard stands up and walks over to the light switch. "I was sleeping all day, in a dumpster..." He clicks the light off, shrouding the room in darkness save for the ambient light bleeding through the windows. "I'll stay up and keep watch." I close my eyes and pull Julia closer. "Thank you, Richard."

"Most welcome." I can almost feel the smile through his scraggly, reddish beard. When I readjust myself, I wait a moment and blow in Julia's ear. She grips my hand tighter and I can hear her lips pull back over her braces as she smiles. Keeping my one arm around her, I prop my head up on my hand and look over to see Richard illuminated by the light of the stars and the moon on one of the greenhouse rows. After I've stared at Richard for a few minutes without him noticing me, I look around the room and my eyes start to lose focus as I stare into the corner of the ceiling.

"Hey." Julia whispers, pulling me back into consciousness. "Hey..." I whisper back. She cups her hand over my ear and speaks so softly I have to hold my breath to hear. "Think anyone can hear us?" I return the favor by repeating her motion. "*I* can barely hear you." I hear her smile as she cups my ear again.

"What do we do tomorrow?"

"I'm open to suggestions."

"I think we should check Steve, call 911, find food, get clothes and blankets, find weapons, get a TV, move your car, and have people keep watch outside incase anyone comes."

"…where have you been all night?"

"I didn't want to say anything."

"Why not?"

"Uh… I don't know if I can get them to listen…"

"They would've if you'd said that… man, now I feel like I haven't shut up all night and you've been sitting here waiting to get that out."

"I've been listening. Besides… *you* can tell them."

"…you want me to take all the credit?"

"I don't care… they'll listen to you."

"I motherfuckin' love you."

"I motherfuckin' love you too."

I kiss her a few times, let out a heavy yawn, and watch someone lying against the wall turn over restlessly in the darkness. I can't stop myself from focusing on the low, distant drone of traffic that is only occasionally punctuated by the soft hissing of squealing tires and the muffled crack of a rare collision. None of it is loud enough to wake or stir anyone else in the room, and it clearly does not bother Julia, because I feel her breath shallow and her muscles relax as she passes out. I might be jealous of the plan she put together if she weren't so damn selfless, and if she weren't so damn right. I spent all night talking and she spent all night listening. I'm a lucky, lucky man, and tonight's events absolutely prove that.

Now that she's said that, though, I can't stop thinking of contingencies. I've spent a lifetime writing stories about the undead and watching Zombie movies, so I have to stop myself and refocus. Naturally we're going to need new clothes, blankets, pillows, food, weapons, and all that other stuff, but to gather it now would be pointless. Everyone has to rest, and it would only make things worse if we tried to mobilize now. We're above ground in a big structure with two stairwells and dozens of exits scattered across the roof. I've told them everything I know and placated them the best I can.

I realize that the undead could break in at any second; any moment I could be jolted awake by the sound of rotting fists being banged into one of the two doors, and if one set of fists is doing it, there's bound to be hundreds. I accept, absolutely, that this is beyond my control and convince myself that the only things that matter are the factors that I *can* control.

I allow myself a few minutes to think about all the things that I might never be able to do in my life, like see my parent's faces on my wedding day, or know the potent bliss of cashing my first professional level paycheck, or plant my first newborn down in the safe confines of their crib. I accept, categorically, that everything about my life has been forever changed by the night's activities. I cry quietly for about ten minutes, but I can't really be sure how long it lasts. Suddenly I realize I've lost track of time and my eyes have gotten heavy.

10-10-04, SUNDAY

The sun stages an aggravated assault on my eyes, and I turn over to face the wall restlessly as I ignore some ambient noise in the background.

My total lack of comfort wakes me again, and I roll over to face Julia. Julia... full consciousness painfully wraps its way around the inside of my skull as I squint and yawn again. I sit up to find everyone sleeping, even Richard. I spend a few moments trying to figure how I can move without waking Julia, but when my hand comes off of her, she wakes instantly. I look down and smile, lean over and kiss her. As I start to stand myself up, I realize just out of shape I am; there's a moderate pain in my left shoulder that I can't work out despite rotating the joint, my back feels like a drying patch of cement, my leg muscles are warm, tingling, and tighter than a snare drum. The pain in my neck is about the dullest and most manageable I've ever felt, but I can't tell if it's because the rest of my body feels so awful.

My stretching, it seems, is a call to arms, and despite my best guesses, everyone's morning ritual does not begin with them questioning whether they're still dreaming. Some scratch their heads, some smell their breath with disappointing results, but most of them look at each other accusingly, wondering what these strangers are doing in their sleeping space. Melody is the first one to attempt conversation.

"What time is it?"
"Don't know. Anyone else feel like their body was just put through a meat grinder?"

My comment doesn't seem to register, so I figure I'll ask again later. Don follows Melody's lead by standing up and doing some lazy stretches, followed by John Squared, then Ava. Jake hasn't moved, but he's clearly alert. No one seems particularly happy to be awake and they seem to regard their surroundings with sorrowful disdain; Ava's eyes pierce Don as he continually and annoyingly rubs the back of his head, and I see some of the muscles in John Squared's face twitch as he looks back and forth across the floor. I last come across Melody's eyes; warm globes sheathed in a water that reflects the light, her face shadowing the shock and sorrow of someone who is watching their house burn to the ground. Finally, I follow her gaze to see that her eyes are locked on Steve.

I stand, causing the trench coat to slip off my shoulder as I stare at the faded gold light glazed over his limp form and the hard, contrasting shadows he casts across Richard, who still lies sleeping on the garden row next to him. I lean down to pick up my gloves and slip them on. His head is turned toward Richard, away from me, so I anticipate a sudden jerk as I approach... but it doesn't come. His chest isn't moving.

I carefully position my fingers to grab the tape, then rip it off in one quick motion and leap back. The tape drags his head over to face me, showing me the wrinkled lumps his lips have become from a night trapped by gray tape. A foamy stream of drool pours out of his mouth as though he were a statue hovering over a pond. Maybe the cut was worse than I thought. Maybe he bled to death. Maybe his nose was congested and we suffocated him by putting the gray tape over his mouth. I glance over at his arm to see a sizable brown stain on his green uniform sleeve. "Jesus Christ, I killed him..." His lungs quickly fill with air, causing Melody to let out a quick yelp that she stifles with her hands. At the end of an exhale, his head rolls toward the ceiling.

I edge forward. "Steve?" His eyes lilt open to reveal a thin glaze. Though his eyes are open, there is positively no focus or recognition in them as he stares up at the ceiling. His head gently falls over to the right, facing me, and he continues staring as if I'm not here. "Steve." His head snaps up with a growling sound as he begins gnashing his teeth at me. "Oh shit." I say. "He turned. He's..." I step back.

There's a muffled clatter behind me, so I turn to see everyone focused on Jake as he leans back on one of the old teacher's desks, his eyes red and swollen with black bags beneath them. "Jake..." Ava says from my right; a tear frees itself from his left eye before he gruffly shoves his wrist across his eye socket to clear it. He hastily turns back to the door and shoves his body into the desk to move it away, but Don is immediately on top of him. Jake thrusts his elbows out behind him and catches Don's lip, causing Don to reactively poke at his own face and swipe some of the blood away before going back after Jake, but John Squared pushes himself between them.

Ava, Melody, and Julia all stare on horrified, trying to murmur for them to stop. I leap across to stop Don and Jake from coming to blows, and as Squared holds Don back, I cover Jake. "Jake..." Squared starts whispering something to Don as he grips the back of his shoulders; Don turns away, gritting his teeth and pounding his fist into the wall. I take a few steps toward Jake to find that he isn't crying; in fact, he looks furious. "Jake, talk to me." More tears follow the paths of their predecessors down his face, negating my previous verdict.

"Just tell me what's going on..."

"Fuck you."

"Jake, if you want out... I'm not gonna stop you..."

"What do you care?" He spits. "You've got Julia... you don't give a *shit* about the rest of us. You don't give a shit about anyone..."

"That's not true..."

"Isn't it!?" More tears glide down his cheek, his chin quivering as he tries to grunt through a sob. "My girlfriend was out there..."

"Jake... we both ran because we were scared, right? I know how you feel... all that frustration, anger, sadness... guilt." I happen to glance back and catch a twitch in Julia's lips, and I think I hear Melody sobbing in the corner. "Take it as hard as you have to... and we'll be here. No one wants you to get hurt, and that's all that's gonna happen out there. Okay?"

He nods, takes a deep breath, and exhales. I turn back to see Don standing against a wall. "Don?" He turns to face me.

"Is your lip okay?"

"You tell me."

"You're bleeding... are you okay?"

"Yeah, I'm fine."

"Can you let it go?"

"What the...?"

"I'm not challenging you... I'm asking, is it possible for you to let it go?"

"Yeah, yeah."

"Good. Okay... now... is everyone else as stiff as I am?"

They all subtly shake their heads or mutter in the negative.

"Guess I'm just the lucky one..."

"Do you exercise?" Melody asks.

"No, I guess I don't... you?"

"I run every day, go to the gym at least once a week..."

"...oh shit, and the rest of you are in marching band... god dammit, I need to..."

I look around the room and get the sinking feeling that we're one short. "Uh... alright... are we missing someone?" I watch Julia as she looks around the room. "Matt." Unsurprisingly, she's the first to volunteer this information. Upon her confirmation, I notice that the desk by the observatory door is in a markedly different position than it was before. We've already had our first runaway, and it hasn't even been a couple of hours. I can only hope, for our sake, that he doesn't try to come back, accidentally bringing hundreds of Zombies with him.

I look around and let out a sigh. "Okay, Squared, I'm gonna ask you to hang out for a second. Jules, come with me. Everyone else... stay put." I get a few complacent sighs in response as everyone sits back down. I walk quietly past Steve, who is still gnashing restlessly at the air, and open the door to be greeted by yet another burst of cold air. "I hate mornings." I say as Julia pulls the door shut behind us. I rub some of the crust out of my eyes and take in the stale condensation as I straddle the fence and climb over, helping Julia after me. We walk cautiously across the damp roof until we can see over the edge.

A few sparse and spread out clusters of the undead silently traverse the fields and the parking lot through the wispy fog that has settled just over the ground. I put on my glasses to see that the amount of blood spilled on the main field is visible even through the fog, but nearly nothing remains on the football field, apart from the motion-less brown pile of corpses I watched the officer take out last night. If I squint, I can see yellow lights flashing on West Chester Pike through the trees to the northwest and red lights flashing on the telecommunications towers in Manayunk to the east. "Okay..." Julia and I walk quietly across the roof and go back into the greenhouse. Only now do I notice the musty, chunky air, ripe with the scent of fermented BO, unclean mouths, and flatulence. All eyes are on me, and Ava speaks first.

"What do you know about this?"

"...Zombies? Books, movies, and video games."

"So you don't *know* anything?"

"No one does, I'm making educated guesses..."

"Can they run?"

"It doesn't look like it."

"Why would they go slow, they're human beings who are like, sick or something, right?" Melody asks.

"Rigor mortis? That's my best guess..." I wonder if they can detect how impatient this tangent is making me.

"What's that?"

"When you die your limbs get stiff... guys, we need weapons and food."

I shoot Julia a pointed glance and wink which she returns.

"Cafeteria..." Ava says. "There's... granola bars, canned fruit and stuff... but where the hell are we gonna get weapons?"

"A two by four, a metal pipe, a table leg..." John Squared offers.

"Cafeteria's an excellent idea, but I'll tell you this much... I've got some pretty wild stuff in my trunk." I say.

"Your trunk?" Don asks, seeming agitated.

"Yeah. I have weapons in my trunk."

"Like what?"

"A katana, a baseball bat, a crowbar, a hockey stick, a bull whip, uh, uh... steel pipe..."

"Why?"

"Does it matter?"

"Yeah." Ava says.

"Why?"

"'Cause it makes you look like a psycho."

"Fine... I write Zombie fiction, and one night I got so worked up, I put all that stuff in my car. Okay?"

"Yeah, okay."

"There's no way we're gonna be able to do this without everyone." Julia says to me quietly.

"Good point. We're all in on this, so we're gonna have to start dividing up tasks. I already have a few ideas..."

"Wait a second." Don says. "Since when do you get to lead us?"

"...I'm not."

"I don't buy it." Don says.

"...fine. Since there are eight of us, well, seven of us awake, we'll put it to a vote. Who wants to hear me out me?"

The hands of Julia, Ava, John, Jake, and Melody go up. "And who doesn't?" Don's hand goes up, prompting Ava to cast her daggers.

"What?" I ask her.

"Does that mean we're gonna get this stuff and he's just gonna stay here?"

"It would seem so. But I'd say that relieves us of any obligation to bring anything back for him."

"Jesus..." Don spits.

"Look, Don... If you don't like it here you can just go... wherever. If you want to listen to me, even just this once, everyone shares the risk and the benefits. Okay?"

The room falls silent. I wish Anderson were here with his training, weapons, and marksmanship. I could trust him with authoritative decision making, but he's undoubtedly off fighting the horde. People like him in the military are the best chance we have to put an end to this quickly.

"Okay. We have to split up more than I'd like, but we can do this. Jake comes with me out to the car, we'll be hauling some of my bags inside and getting weapons."

"What's in the bags?" Ava asks.

"Clothes... uh, a few toothbrushes, mouthwash, deodorant, sheets, pillows... I figure we just bring everything in... John, you and Melody to the cafeteria, but first you're gonna find backpacks to carry food."

"There's a bunch of backpacks in the lost and found down there." John says. "Plus, we are in a *school*..."

"Right. We need non-perishables, especially bottled water... nothing from the tap, can't trust it. Jules, Ava, you're going to the band room. You're gettin' a change of clothes, and see if you can't find some weapons while you're at it. Now, I can't stress this enough... if you see one of them, anywhere, *do not fight.* You turn around and you run and you go back to the greenhouse... but make sure you aren't followed."

"Maybe we shouldn't come back here..." Julia adds. "Incase they follow us up."

"Excellent idea. Uh... we can..."

"Meet up in the lobby?"

"Perfect..."

"What about me?" Don asks.

"You tell me."

Don sighs as he looks at his shoes.

"There might be some... blankets, pillows, and other clothes in the theatre loft."

"All right then... Julia, Ava, hit that before you go to the band room. Don, stand in the auditorium lobby and watch what Jake and I are doing. If you see anything suspicious, you yell out. Okay?"

"Alright... can I have something to defend myself?"

"Sure, take my cane... wait, no, I'll probably need it..."

I throw on my trench coat and pick up my cane. "Okay everyone, we're about ready to go. *Do not* split up for any reason, and don't drink tap water, just in case. If something happens where you get bitten or scratched, tell us." I bend over to Richard and shake him. He wakes easily. "What is it?" I stand up.

"We're going out, we need someone to stay and watch Steve."
"You comin' back?"
"As quick as we can, we're goin' for supplies."
"Is Steve...?"
"Yeah. Actually, can you watch us from the roof?"
"Watch you?"
"You know... survey... tell us if you see something we don't?"
"Can do. Which side?"
"Out front."

I stand up and open the door to the back stairwell. None of the fluorescent bulb glass has been disturbed from last night. "As soon as you're done, get back up here. If you must, go to the bathroom. Everybody ready?" They're scared shitless. So am I, but if my gambit pays off, it'll have been worth it. "You guys are a nervous wreck." They all let out anxious laughs. "We'll be fine. Okay?"

I jump up on the first desk and run down the stairs; the pain in my legs is instantaneous and unmistakable as the footsteps of my compatriots clap into the steps behind me, chasing me down to the double doors on the second level. We run down the next two sets of stairs and out the door to the ground level. When I stop, the group is at my back. "Okay, Jules, Ava, use the breezeway, don't go outside." Just as they start to run off, I pull Julia back and look into her eyes. "I love you." I say, and kiss her. She smiles back. "I know." The two of them branch off.

"Come on!" I say as we run down the English hallway, turning right at the end. The muscles in my legs now feel sublimely tight, like I can run the strain out of them, and for some reason, I can't get *Animal Waves* by Can out of my head. Melody and John split off to the left, going into the cafeteria. "Don't forget the teacher's lounge!" I say, still running. Now it's only Jake and Don behind me. Once we arrive at the main entrance, we hang a right and run down the language hall until we make it to the auditorium lobby.

"Anyone got a watch?"
"It's... 9:45." Don says.
"Damn."
"What?"
"Shadows..."

I step into the first set of doors, then out of another before I'm outside. I can't see any of the undead in the street or on the grass, but I was correct in surmising that the trees and buildings are casting long shadows toward us.

"Okay, Don, we're counting on you to open this door when we get back, because it's probably locked."
"They aren't."
"What?"
"They aren't locked, none of them."

I think back to last night, recalling that I walked into the auditorium with no impediment. "Yeah, you're right. Just be our eyes and ears. Actually, do you know how to lock the doors?" He nods. "Good, lock all but one, and be ready to lock the last one when we get inside." I look over at Jake to find him shaking. "Just stay close to me, and keep your eyes open." Jake nods, still shaking. "Ready?" I ask as I grip my cane and pull off a rubber cap to reveal a copper tip. "Yeah, ready." I'm about to open the door, then I stop. "Wait... here." I pull out my toothpick dispenser and give him a mint toothpick, taking one for myself as well. He glances at me before he sticks it in his mouth. "Don't you feel more prepared?" He lets out a nervous giggle as I open the doors and the cold air pours in.

Holding the cane in both hands, I sprint across the driveway, making sure I don't overexert myself as Richard's voice drifts down from above. "You've got six on your left spread out, three on the right." I'm still running. "Are we clear to the corner?" I look back to see Jake hunkered down, looking back and forth with his eyes gaping wide. I can hear the distant moans of the undead echoing off to the left of me as our feet slap into the moist grass. "Yeah!" He shouts.

I raise my hand up in a wave but do not turn around. I look to the right, spotting a few members of the undead wearing formalwear, covered in dirt, and probably hunting with sound and smell from about thirty feet away. My heart accelerates as I again consider the break in reality provided by the existence of the undead, and for a moment, I feel like I'm in a video game. "Oh my *god!*" Jake yells, prompting the dead to start stumbling toward us. "Shh!" As we hit the street running, I look to the right to see if there are any beyond Richard's sight line; a woman, wearing regular clothes, is ambling around in circles slowly, apparently not paying us any attention.

Someone slammed into the back right side of my car. "Are you *kidding* me?" I hit the car wheezing and panting, hop in, and put the keys in the ignition as Jake gets in the front seat. Music starts playing, but I turn the radio off. Three of the undead hit the back of the car together, causing me to shove my foot into the accelerator and fire the car in reverse to send two of them under the tires and one flipping off the bumper. "Jesus, he hit head first!" Jake says as I swing the wheel around, knocking over a stop sign. I spin the wheel again and turn back toward the school, looking in the driver's side mirror to see one of the corpses in a crumpled heap with blood pouring out of his cracked skull.

"Did you see that, did you see that!?"
"Yeah, I saw it... shut up for a second..."
"No, no, cop car, down the street!"

I didn't see that. I accelerate again, driving over the grass before stopping right in front of the auditorium doors. I turn off the car, pop the trunk, put the keys in my pocket, and jump out.

"Come on Don, Jake... get the shit out of the back!"
"What about the car!?" Jake asks.
"We'll deal with it later!"

"They might be *gone* later, let's check it out *now!*"

Don holds the front door open while Jake starts throwing him the bags.

"What car?" Don asks.

"A cop car!"

"There's a *cop* car down the street!?"

"We'll *deal* with it!"

"Jeff! I-je-look out!"

Two of the undead are within twenty feet of the front of my car walking toward us. Others are further away, but also heading our direction. "Oh god, OH *JESUS!*" Jake screams. "Keep throwing him stuff!" I yell back. I clutch the top of my cane as my pulse races. "I'll handle this." I jump up on the hood of my car and look down at each of their faces; one has eyes and normal clothes, and one is without eyes and wearing formalwear. I raise the cane over my head and freeze. This is not a human being. He isn't going to scream, and I'm not going to get arrested for hitting him. I don't know if I can do this. Can I do this?

Before I let my adrenaline subside, I swing the cane down, thumping the top on the weak skull of the one wearing formalwear. I can't stop my mouth from wrenching open as a pop in my shoulder enhances the pain from moderate to pure, stinging wrath, nearly causing me to drop the cane. "Are you alright?" Jake shouts. I look down at my prey to see his head cracked open on the blacktop, the blow having exposed his desiccated, graying brain and sending up a waft of musty, putrid air. I channel my pain into anger as I kick the approaching woman in the chin, sending her backward, her skull hitting the pavement with a low crack.

Still nursing my shoulder, I leap down off the car, choke up on the cane with my right hand, and swing the top one-handed into her skull repeatedly until I can feel that I've gotten through her skull. I spin the cane and spear the copper tip through her eye hard, causing it to snap through the back of her skull into the pavement while blood and vitreous leaks out of the socket like a crushed egg. I pull the cane out with a wet sucking sound.

I turn my attention to the other one and lift my cane up in the air. "Via con dios." I slam it down into his eye socket; he jerks once, then stops moving. I let out a hard sigh through a half smile as I try to slow my pulse and calm myself down. I lean down and use the woman's shirt to clean off the end of my cane. Knowing there are more in the area, I run to the back of the car to find Jake and Don just standing there.

"What is it!?"
"There aren't any weapons." Jake says urgently.
"Sure there are, you just…"

I look into the back of my car, finding nothing but a gray carpet, my DVD player, and a plastic trash bag containing a blanket.

"Someone cleaned it out, my mom or my dad or… FUCK!"
"Jeff, what are we doing about the car?" Don asks.
"Hold *on* a second!"

Before I can finish my sentence, Don takes off across the driveway. "GET BACK IN… STOP!" Jake starts hyperventilating like he's going to run too.

"Jake, don't even think about it… get inside, lock the door, and *don't* open it until I come back!"
"B-you… you can't…!"
"Calm down…"

I turn back to see Don clear across the grass, almost to the street and about halfway to the flashing lights. "I'm coming back." Jake bangs his fist into the glass and slams the door shut behind him. I slide back into my car, back up, and pull out across the grass. "Unbelievable… stupid motherfucker…" I slam my fist into the head rest a few times, stopping when I realize how much more important it is for me to focus on the road. The few undead between the car and me are now pulling toward Don like water flows to a drain. "Son of a *bitch*…" He's at the car now, looking in the windows and running around like a de-capitated chicken. I pull up a few feet shy of the car and jump out, leaving the engine running.

"What are you doing!?"
"There's no one inside!"
"No shit…"

Before I can get out another word, a choking sound comes from our left. We both turn to see a woman's corpse with bruises all over her face and neck, her lower lip quivering as she emits a staccato gur-gle. Her stumbling steps are probably being caused by the big chunk of flesh taken out of her left ankle. Don has frozen. I step in front of him, brace tip of the cane under my armpit, and swing the bulb at the top into the left temple of the approaching woman with my right arm, sending her stumbling to the right. Before she can regain footing, I slide the cane out to choke up and hit her again. She lands face up, so I kick her over and start landing blows at the base of her skull until she stops moving.

The next one is a few feet behind her, a man in his boxer shorts and a wife beater. I run up to him, knock him back with a blow, and spear him through the eye with the end of the cane, twisting it back and forth, scraping his head against the pavement until I'm convinced he's dead. I take a moment to catch my breath and turn around to see Don backed up against the car with his hand hovering over his mouth. "Well?" It takes him a moment to look up at me.

"What?"
"Do you hear anything… or see anything?"
"I saw the car, I…"
"Ehht- stop! Look around. I'll ask again, do you *see* anything? Do you *hear* anything?"

He takes in the silence, his hands quivering up in front of his chest. He looks up and down the street, at all the houses, and finally back at me. I raise my eyebrows.

"No…"

"It's quiet. If there were a rescue, you'd see it. If the police, SWAT, military, anyone came, you'd *hear* it."

"…yeah…"

"Do you see why I didn't want to come out here?"

"…yeah."

"…are there any guns in the car?"

"No."

"Then let's go."

Don quietly walks around to the passenger door and gets in. I look up the block to see if anything else was following him, but as if to make my point, the streets are now vacant. Our drive back to the school is brief, quiet, and uneventful. Before I can stop in front of the doors, Jake is back outside, fortunately looking more composed. When I get out and shut the door behind me, I think about the weapons that were supposed to be in the trunk. The katana, the bullwhip, and the steel pipe were laid over the carpet, but the other weapons were beneath it. I open the trunk and lift the gray carpet to reveal a crowbar, the car's lug wrench, an aluminum baseball bat, and a sawed off hockey stick with a hose clamp affixed on the end. "Alright, let's go!" I sling the last bag over my shoulder, slide the lug wrench in my pants, take up the hockey stick and toss Jake my metal cane. "Pick it up! They're coming!" Richard shouts. I turn around.

Despite the visual yield of my earlier glance up the street, the four on the left haven't gone, nor have the three coming up the street, and they're being joined by another six coming from the back parking lot. "Let's go! Let's go!" I slam the trunk door shut and we run back inside. I watch the progress of the undead while Jake and Don sling the bags over their shoulders. We run along the front of the auditorium and back into the main hall, but I stop at the sign that reads *Band Members Only.*

"Come on Jeff, we have to go!" Jake says. I take off my overnight bag and hand it to him. "Check on Melody and John, I'm checking on these two. Give me the crowbar." He throws a bag over his shoulder while handing off the crowbar. "Hey, no one goes anywhere alone!"

Don says while I start running down the hall. "Shut up and go! GO!" I can hear them take off down the hall as I run toward the band room with the two weapons in my hands. Sure enough, I quickly find Julia and Ava toting black uniform bags that are apparently full of clothes. They look surprised to see me.

"What are..." I cut Julia off. "You find any weapons?" I ask. They both shake their heads. "We've got incoming, so let's get moving, now..." With that there's a slam on the back door to the band room, followed by a dry, gasping moan. "Come on!" I bark. I lead the two of them back into the hallway, up the four steps, and turn left. I open the door to the staircase next to the hallway aligning the auditorium, catching a quick glimpse of the dead scratching at the glass on the door that leads outside. I look back as I'm running to make sure that Julia and Ava are right behind me, but they're not. I shudder with fear as I run back into the hallway to see them slowly dragging their heavy bags behind them. With a hard sigh, I run over to help pull them up the steps. We stop at the first landing so I can pass off the crowbar to Ava and the lug wrench to Julia.

I turn where the stairs loop around to see a walking corpse strolling in the upstairs hallway, just outside the doors. Ava sees this and looses the kind of high-pitched scream I could only imagine hearing in a '70s horror movie. "Get back!" I shout. When I kick the door open the corpse skids backward and I slam the hose clamp end into his skull, making a dent. I slam his skull again and again until I'm convinced he's dead and that one more repeated motion with my left arm would cause it to simply fall off. I stand up straight over my kill and look down the hallway. "It's clear, let's move!" I wait for them to get into the hall before continuing with the bags dragging behind us. We hang a slight left in the upstairs hall, go straight for a few hundred feet, turn left at the end of the hall, and pull the bags until we reach the second floor staircase that leads up to the greenhouse.

I hold the door open for them and I hear footsteps running up the stairs below. "Run, run! They're coming!" Melody howls. "John, Don, take the bags, girls, upstairs... go!" I scream at Julia and Ava. They run up the rest of the way to the greenhouse while Jake and Melody both run past me as I start to feel the asthma set in again. Once I see John and Don on the steps, I grab my bag and drag it through the thick patch of broken glass before making it to the greenhouse landing where Julia and Ava are at the other side of the desks accepting them. The door opens behind them and Richard holds it there as we drag the bags inside.

I wait so that I can be the last person to climb over the desks before moving inside the greenhouse and finally shutting the door behind me. As I turn, everyone is falling to the floor in exhaustion. "Well, that was fun! Let's do it again!" When they can't help but laugh, I smile at them. "If I was 21, I'd buy you a round... you did great." Julia speaks next through her Cheshire cat grin. "No thanks to you." I smile back. "Okay, what'd we get?" I ask, prompting John to stand up as he speaks. "We got iced tea, bottled water, a bunch of granola bars... and canned peaches!" They spill the contents of four backpacks out on the floor.

"Good, good. If we ration, that should last us a few days. I don't doubt we're all gonna be sore from running and fighting, so we should definitely stay put for awhile. Jules, Ava?" Ava pats the bag. "We got Don's clothes, Julia's clothes, mine, Squared-ston, and Jake's. We also got a few blankets and some warmer coats from the loft... and Julia's bag is full of water." I look over to see her unzip the vinyl bag only to have four bottles of water roll out from the teeming, crystal cluster within. I try to estimate how many are in the bag, coming away with the figure that could see each of us having one bottle a day for a week. "Okay, we did much better than I thought. Me and my boys got hygiene stuff, clothes, blankets, two pillows, and a couple weapons. Now I'm sure everyone's hungry... John, Melody, you get first dibs."

They both smile. "We already ate downstairs." John says, pulling some more granola bars out of his pocket. "Brilliant." I mutter, watching as each of them empty their pockets and Melody empties her pocketbook. I think about trying to tell everyone to ration their food, but before I can open my mouth I consider that, if we do end up rationing, we're better off weaning ourselves off of a large diet. Strangely, as I think that, I notice people limiting their consumption. With some food finally in my stomach, I feel better about popping open the bottle of Ibuprofen in my overnight bag and swallowing four pills before I pull out a dirty t-shirt from my hamper and wipe the blood off my hockey stick and cane. "...we make it out of this, we'll all be a lot skinnier."

"Not Melody." Says Ava. I smirk and hold my mouth closed so I don't spit out my peaches when Melody furrows her brow. "Just a joke..." I say, swallowing my food. Melody smiles half-heartedly while Ava continues to eat, oblivious. "What time is it?" Melody goes for her cell phone immediately. "Yeah, it's, uh, 10:32." I shake my head. "Good, now I can set my clock radio... holy shit..." Clock *radio*. I quickly fumble toward my bag, fleecing out soap, shampoo, deodorant, toothpaste, and a hand towel before I get to it.

I quickly find an electrical outlet on the wall next to me, hook it in, and pull the antennae out. I switch it over to radio on the AM dial and go through the channels until I reach the local news station. Once I settle on a human voice, I go about setting the time.

"...hours... have passed since the first reports and no one group has come forward to accept responsibility for the acts, only prompting further questions. Early this morning the President was asked to comment, only saying that the situation was being monitored and proper steps were being taken to respect the rights of the protestors as well as the rights of the town's residents, though to this point there has been no reason to make any distinction between the two. The time is 10:34, giving you breaking news on perhaps one of the strangest occurrences in Delaware County history... starting last night and continuing throughout the day today, a surprising amount of seemingly unmotivated protestors have been wandering through the streets and neighborhoods in the small town of Broomall, Pennsylvania. The exact purpose of these protests seems to be undefined, but it is clear that the protestors are going from door to door and listlessly patrolling major roadways, holding up traffic in every direction. While property damage appears to be at a minimum, the police have reported several casualties in major roadways... particularly a car accident on Route 3. Now, early reports are still vague at best, but it's also being reported that some of these protestors are attacking those they encounter. It is strongly recommended that these protestors be avoided... we've just received a report in the last few minutes that some are reporting the protestors as manic, even possessed, and that those coming in contact with them have reported clawing and biting. Those bitten have been taken to medical centers and there is no reason to believe the protestors are sick as was previously reported... no sign of infection has been found. Anyone who has been bitten is urged to seek medical care immediately, as normal

bacteria is enough to cause serious staph infections and septicemia. Those re-
ceiving medical treatment for their wounds have shown no ill effects. The
Broomall Police department, in conjunction with other departments in the
area, has begun setting up a perimeter on all the major routes out of town
and the National Guard has already begun setting up road blocks at the wid-
est points..."

"Yes! Army! That's great!" Melody blurts.

"Shhh."

"... on route 3 across 476. It is strongly recommended that citizens stay in
their homes until otherwise notified. If civilians located in the Broomall and
Newtown Square city limits must leave, they are advised to approach the road
blocks cautiously with their arms in the air, as rumors circulate that deadly
force has been authorized. Law enforcement sources are roundly repeating
that there is no need to panic. Uh... we will continue coverage of this story
when we return..."

I click off the radio, making sure to give Don a stern glance.

"Why'd you turn it off?" Jake asks.

"We can turn it on later... so, did everyone hear that? We're being
quarantined."

"What? We-wait, what does that mean?"

"They're probably setting up blockades to stop us from getting
out... which is good..."

"That's *good*!?" Melody scoffs.

This starts a quick burst of terrified voices that I manage to silence
with a hand gesture.

"Guys... if they can keep this contained, they're gonna pool their
resources right here, and when they get organized, they're gonna
come through and wipe 'em out..."

"What if they just drop a bomb on us?" John asks.

"They won't do that. But I am worried about what they missed..."

"What?" Melody asks.

"That we're fighting Zombies? And didn't they say something
about... people recovering?"

"Yeah..." Richard responds.

"Well, nearest I can figure, people die when they're bitten, then they revive, hence being the living dead. It sounds like some people aren't dying."

"You say that like it's *bad* news..." Don starts. "What if you can be cured?"

"That's... very possible..."

"But?" Melody starts.

"...but conventional wisdom, to me, says that you don't recover from a Zombie bite. The fatality rate is 100%."

"Yeah, but you're just going off... books and movies..."

"Look, I'm trying to be realistic about something that isn't... what do we know about these things? They rise from the grave..."

"...we haven't exactly proved that one..." John Squared interrupts.

"Given the tuxes and embalming, we'll call that an educated guess. So, we've got that, people who get bitten turn into them, and we know that you can only kill them with headshots... that, to me, goes by everything I've seen in a movie or read in a book."

"So what are you getting at?"

"Well... I'll be honest, my first thought was how stupid it is for anyone to think these are protestors..."

"I read something about some woman in Toronto doing a Zombie parade last year..." Jake says.

"...seriously?"

"Yeah... maybe someone else scheduled an event and they think this is part of it?"

"Christ... well... considering that, I can't say I'd deem any of the information dealing with the undead in that newscast factual... but if people get bitten and don't die, what happens?"

"They get better?" Melody asks.

"What if you still turn without dying?"

"By definition, don't you sort of... have to?" Squared asks. I sigh.

"So, it affects the brain, right? What if that's all that happens? If you don't actually die, there's no reason for rigor mortis to set in."

I look over to see Steve squirming and making dry gasping noises through the tape.

"What are you getting at?" Richard asks.
"If they don't go stiff..."
"You mean, if someone was an Olympic sprinter..."
"Or a bodybuilder..." Melody says.
"Right. That's worst case scenario." I say.

I slap my hands together a few times, knocking the crumbs off. "Thanks for bringing me with you." Richard says suddenly, smiling. I realize now that he's been starting at me.

"Huh?"
"Up here..."
"...no big deal."
"No, no, it is. Most people in this town would piss on me if they got the chance, but you *invited* me..."
"Richard, it's okay."
"Julia, hang on to him."
"I will." She says, beaming.
"I've had enough things go wrong in my life to know a good soul when I see one."

I smile and take a deep breath, masking the fact that what he said was quite awkward and there is no way for me to respond to that.

"Okay, we have one more errand to run today... weapons. One of the physics rooms has a bunch of steel rods for pendulum experiments... they'll do. This time, I'll take Richard and... Ava with me."
"You can just call me Rich."
"Oh. Sorry... Rich it is."

The three of us stand, arm ourselves, and head down the back stairwell. Ava's still wearing her band uniform, minus the jacket. As I walk behind Ava, I think about how I thought she was more attractive than Julia when I first met the two of them, at least until she opened her mouth. I stare at the back of her head as she descends the steps in front of me, and when I stop by the door, I turn to her. "Good to see you up here." I say. She looks back slightly puzzled.

"I *have* been up there since last night, you know."
"I know, but... we haven't really talked."
"Yeah, you're too busy with Julia."

Though that comment doesn't distinguish itself as a prime example, I've always felt Ava's speech was marked by tactlessness. I think she falsely prides herself in honesty when, in fact, she lacks discretion.

"That's fair. So... what made you follow me?"
"I was following Julia. Jeff, why is that slut up here?"
"Jules!?"
"No, you idiot... Melody. Why is she here?"
"She *followed* us."
"I know, but I *hate* her. She's just gonna make everyone miserable with her stupid bitching. Do we really have to keep her around?"

I stop for a moment, questioning her seriousness. Rich stands a few feet behind us and pretends not to notice we're talking.

"Are you suggesting we throw her out?"
"No, idiot, but you're in charge..."
"Don't call me that. I'm not in charge, and she's not my favorite person... but I'm sure as hell not gonna throw her out... she has every right to complain."
"At what cost?" Rich asks.
"Huh?"
"Well, you said last night you didn't want infighting. If she keeps arguing and complaining, what's gonna happen in the long run?"
"Yeah, you're afraid we make too much noise... when someone gets her going it's like pulling a fire alarm." Ava adds.

"Let's not split hairs... we can discuss the minutiae of group structure when we're all together."

"Well you're making all the decisions..."

"Well, would you rather be sitting up there wondering what we should do, or have food, weapons, and a radio?"

"The second one."

"The second..." I take a moment to stifle my rage. "I'm *not* in charge. If you have any suggestions, go right ahead and offer them up."

I pray there won't be any further conversation and I'm rewarded with silence. We keep walking and make it to the one physics room with which I am familiar. I smash the glass on the door with my hockey stick and unlock it, entering. Sure enough, the steel rods I was talking about are in the far corner of the room.

"That's it. Take a bunch."

"*You* take a bunch..." Ava retorts.

"I can barely move my left arm..."

Ava rolls her giant eyes and Rich grabs an armful while I guard the door. As they pass by me to exit, I count seven in their arms, which should be more than enough unless we get a lot of company. We walk back to the greenhouse and throw the poles down as soon as we're over the desks. I take four of them and go back in the door. "All right, these are your weapons. We've got more if we need 'em." I sit down and breathe out heavily, opening my overnight bag to grab another pair of socks, my pair of boots, and a pair of boxers. Once I've finished changing into them, I return to my bag and start looking through the pockets. The first thing I happen to pull out is a bottle of liquid mint for my toothpicks. "Anyone hear that?" Julia asks suddenly. In that moment, when everyone else falls silent, I can: it's a helicopter.

There's nothing to stop eight people trapped on a roof in the midst of a crisis from running like crazy when something as eminently life-saving as a helicopter flutters overhead, so in moments we're all on our feet and rushing for the door. "No sound! No sound! *Quiet!*" I shout as Don pushes the door open. Shockingly, everyone has the presence of mind to listen, so they begin jumping up and down and waving their arms, an activity I cannot stop myself from partaking in as well, even if I can't see the helicopter. Finally, I manage to follow their looks to see a parallax view of the chopper as it appears to rise above the edge of the school's south face.

The waving and jumping intensifies as it grows closer, and Melody starts to scream. Instinctively, I grab her shoulder, simultaneously realizing the opportunity we're missing. "Do you have a compact!?" I shout. She stares at me for a second, and then vigorously nods her head. "Get it so we can *signal!*" She squints at me as I point to the door and finally obliges as the helicopter flies off to the northeast. As it passes, I can see the news designation painted on the bottom, but it doesn't stop, slow down, or circle.

When Melody reappears at my side, I rip the compact out of her hand and angle the mirror toward the helicopter to no avail. I watch as it quickly disappears into the distance, taking the thumping heartbeat of the blades with it. "Did he see us?" Jake asks. I close the compact and hand it back to Melody before going back inside. Don bumps into me as he reenters, causing me to drop the bottle of mint. It shatters on the floor. "Christ..." I mutter, leaning down to start pushing the glass fragments into a small pile. "Jeff..." John Squared says; I try to ignore him, but quickly remember our situation. "What?" He doesn't respond, so I look up to see his eyes fixed on Steve.

I stand slowly to see his nose pointing toward the shattered glass on the floor. I lean down, dab some of the mint on my finger, and rub it off along a sliver of the greenhouse row right next to his head. Rather than bite at me, he stays fixed on the mint like a curious dog. I turn my head to the left slowly, not taking my eyes off him. "Jules, Don... with me on the roof." I drop my hockey stick and take both remaining bottles of liquid mint.

We run across the roof toward the front entrance to the back lot. There's a ten foot drop that separates the classrooms, cafeteria and auditorium from the gym, the pool, and the library. Using one of the school's maintenance ladders that Mursak, Anderson and I once pulled up on the roof to assist our frequent efforts to climb around and satisfy our teenage desire for hijinks, we climb down to a lower section of the roof.

Once we get to the roof of the gym, we look over the side of the building with the entrance to the parking lot. There used to be a ten-foot wide strip of blacktop with grass on either side, the far side meeting a chain link fence that separates a row of houses from the school, but cars have filled seemingly every square inch of space between the fence and the school as far back as the parking lot, and they're jammed together so tightly that it doesn't look like any of them can move, especially since most of them are sitting on their rims thanks to the treadles. I pull out my bottle of mint and pour half its contents on the corner of the building.

I look over the edge as I stand; the undead that were formerly in front of the building are gone now, perhaps having found more victims in the surrounding residential area. No sooner than I have that thought, a car rushes up the street and squeals to a stop a few feet shy of the cop car. It sits idle for a moment before the driver slowly advances around the cruiser, eventually screaming off again down the road. I realize only after we turn away that Don is heeding my advice; he didn't try to signal them or start screaming like an idiot. Once we arrive at the rear of the building, facing the football field, I notice that many of the undead appear to be milling around as though they've officially given up on getting in the back door.

We next go to the front of the building on the side of the parking lot exit. Once again, the cars are jammed in so that no one could have escaped in a vehicle. "Jules, go to the other side of the building, the back. See if they react to this. We'll meet back at the greenhouse." She runs and I watch, and while she's in motion, I take out my glasses so I can actually see her signals from the distance. When she gets there I get a thumb up, so then I toss the bottle over the side and it shatters, blasting its contents on the blacktop. I quietly make my way to the other side of the building to meet Julia at the greenhouse.

"Darling, do you have a change of shoes?" She nods and smiles. "Good, mind giving me one of your marching shoes."

"Why?"

"Well, do you get the first part of the test?"

"To see if they're attracted to strong, exotic scents, and see how much height plays a factor?"

"Precisely. And now I'd like to see how well they respond to sound."

She reaches down and takes her shoes off. I watch for a moment as the undead in the back lot try to navigate the cars before throwing one shoe over in the middle of the parking lot. They immediately start gravitating toward it. "Okay," I say. "Let's say we check back in an hour or so." As I turn and go back, I catch sight of Julia carefully stepping across the roof, staring at her feet.

With a big smile, I walk back, pick her up, and carry her back to the greenhouse as Don continues to follow silently. Unfortunately, I can only carry her in front of me for a few seconds before my left arm reminds me of its earlier threat to fall off, so I let her down and carry her instead over my right shoulder. Once we return to the greenhouse, I let her down gently. It's quiet inside, almost as though everyone has been sitting in silence since we left.

"Rich, we have any more tape?" I ask. Rich goes into one of the drawers of the desk and throws me another roll. When he tosses it, I catch it and pull out a big strip, then tear it off with my teeth. I hand one end of the tape to Julia. "Here, we're going to put Steve's head down on the garden. Stay far back, come down slow, and when the tape hits his head, press it down quickly to the sides." We do exactly as I said and Steve's head is pinned down to the table. "Good, Rich, staple the tape down, just in case."

As I hear Rich liberally bang away with the stapler, I grab a pair of old socks from my laundry. "Tape." Rich stands up and tosses me the roll as Steve looks over, loosing a throaty growl that sounds like it should have come from a big dog. Holding the sock in my right hand, I ease my left hand toward him until his mouth opens fully, then let go of the sock, which lands between his teeth. I find a rusted wrench behind me on the table and use it shove the sock in deeper, and in an instant, his jaw snaps shut, cracking all of his front teeth with a wet crunch. Having never grown accustomed to the sound of teeth on metal, I turn to the side and gag as Rich turns away wincing.

Without looking at the pool of blood and shattered teeth in his mouth, I shove the sock in and push another behind it, keeping his mouth wrenched open. Finally, I take two strips of gray tape and place them over his mouth. "Why are we keeping him in here?" Rich asks. "Can't risk moving him. And he might tell us if these things can starve to death." I stand up, pull off my gloves and throw them down, pulling a toothpick from my fob.

"Okay, a couple more things... first, we should spruce up a bit... move all the stuff we don't need into the staircase and assign sleeping areas. It looks like we have enough pillows and blankets for each of us... if we don't, and you can stand it, you might want to buddy up with someone to stay warm at night."

"What about the bathroom?" Melody asks.

"What did you do before?"

"Go to the bathrooms?"

"In groups?"

"Yeah."

"Good. Well, two people go at a time. I think from this point forward we should have two people on the roof keeping watch. When we go anywhere, at least two people stay up here. Every time we'll rotate. We're gonna try to get a 24 hour watch going outside... maybe there'll be a convoy, another helicopter, or more survivors... everyone takes the compact with them..."

"Do we really want more people up here?" Don asks.

"You want to abandon anyone outside?"

"What if that happens to one of us?" John asks. "Just, devil's advocate."

"Well, the first thing is stay quiet. I'd say try to stay out in the open, but don't get yourself out in, like, a giant field. You want room to get around them, but you also don't want to be seen at a distance. Of course, you'll always want to move toward the school, or the last place we were. If someone gets separated, some of us'll stay behind and some'll go out looking."

"What if we meet up with other people," Ava asks. "Should we go with them, or bring them with us?"

"Eh... that's a tough one. I don't want to paint too bleak a picture, but you can't trust everyone. I mean, at this point, we can trust each other. Out there, though... well, situations like this always bring out looters and... opportunistic psychos."

"...what?"

"Well... like Ted Bundy. He'd hang around college campuses with his arm in a sling, struggling with carrying something until someone came along to help him, then he'd walk with them back to his car where he'd either handcuff them or bludgeon them to death, sometimes not before sexually assaulting them..."

"Jesus, you'd think people would be smarter than that..."

"Smarter? Than what? Bundy was attractive, intelligent, charismatic, and manipulative. He escaped from jail twice. He had a degree in psychology from the University of Washington and was liked by his professors. At one point, he was in two serious relationships with two young women despite the fact that he exclusively killed young women."

"...how do you know that?"

"I read The Stranger Beside Me. The point I'm making with Ted Bundy is that sometimes people aren't what they seem, and, you know, I want you to be aware of that. Especially now. That even goes for police and military. Unless you want to end up like Rachel Dobowitz."

"She's just missing... besides, how will we know?" Don asks.

"That's my point. If you come across a cop or someone in the military walking around alone, without a car..."

"So now that we've alienated everyone that we could possibly meet outside," Ava starts. "What's our next move?"

"I..." I sigh softly, restraining myself. "Well, for starters you should change out of your band uniforms."

"Hey, we can hang them outside." Julia says.

"What, darling?"

"The uniforms. Once we take them off we can tape them all to the side of the building... let people know we're in here."

"Not bad. Maybe if we get some more we can write something on them in tape. Anyway, you guys can get changed in the observatory. Don, we're goin' downstairs to change the sign."

The next two hours pass with unreal regularity. After all the band members get changed into their street clothes, we go to the band room and get all the spare uniforms we can find, which is unfortunately not many. We tape letters to them, spelling out *HUMANS INSIDE*, and once they're ready, we hang them over the words *THOMAS MASSEY HIGH SCHOOL* on the front roof section of the auditorium. I put on a fresh pair of socks and put the old ones overtop, and then put my boots back on.

After a couple of bathroom trips are made with three people each time, we decide that the roof patrols should rotate every hour, so we start at 1:00pm even. First Rich and Jake go out, and in that hour Julia vigorously massages my shoulder and back. I feel like most of the massages I've gotten in my life have been cosmetic, just quick sessions of slightly sexual contact, but this time, I notice a marked difference in the amount of motion available to my left arm. When the first pair return, Julia and Ava go, and when they return, the massage continues. I'll have to think of something nice to do to repay her for this. When Don and John return, Melody and I go out for the rotation starting at 4:00pm by her request. She starts talking to me as soon as we walk out of the greenhouse.

"So… why did you come back?"
"Huh?"
"To the Mass… I mean… you're in *college*…"

I help her over the metal divider. "Bandrome, and Jules." We reach the edge of the roof above the breezeway; both of us turn and hang down, then drop to the breezeway roof.

"She's so much younger."

"I did notice. But, I mean, sixteen and nineteen may seem like a big gap, but once you get up to twenty-four and twenty-seven, it really doesn't matter. I guess that starts at college."

I climb back up to the roof of the front section of the building and help her up.

"What brought you here?"
"I live here..."
"I meant Bandrome."
"I got ditched." I pull her up all the way and she brushes herself off. "Thanks. I was supposed to go to a party, but none of my friends told me where it was and they wouldn't answer their phones. I ended up... driving around, until I saw the lights in front of the school."
"I guess it piqued your interest?"

We have a seat near the edge of the roof, she takes out a cigarette and lights it.

"Uh, no, not really, but if I don't have anyone to hang out with I like to feel like I'm at least doing *something*."
"Helluva night to swing by the high school, huh?"
"For sure."

She offers me a cigarette.

"No thanks. I guess when Mass went on you saw me running across the field?"
"What? Nah... there's no way I was gonna pay to get in... I was just waiting for someone to call back. I was in my car when I saw you guys run past."
"And you got out instead of driving away?"
"I don't know... I had no idea..."
"Did you happen to see that kid... and the car?"
"Chris."
"Sorry... I can't believe that happened."

"You know, with all the stuff that's going on, it's weird that you can't believe *that*."

"Well, no one's ever accused me of being normal."

She seems to snicker at that, but I wonder if she's just being polite. "In any case, I guess you're glad you didn't go to the party..." She continues a long puff of her cigarette and stares at me for a few seconds, her hanging jaw allowing the smoke to escape her lungs. "...what?" I ask finally. She continues staring.

"Does this bother you, like, at all?"

"The smoking?

"No, numb nuts, *this*."

She motions to the air around her. I try to contain myself.

"Is there some practical reason you say that?"

"What?"

"I can't imagine why you talk to people that way. Idiot, numb nuts... did I insult you or something?"

"Jesus, take a pill."

"...is it a defense mechanism?"

"What?"

"Do your friends talk to you like that?"

"Duh, it doesn't mean I think you're stupid..."

"Then why say it?"

"It's just a dumb question..."

"...you light up a cigarette..."

"Jesus, are we still talking about this?"

"...alright."

She keeps looking at me, but I resolve to stay quiet until I hear some kind of apology. She looks away, and I think I see her subtly shaking her head. She mouths something without making any sound, and finally looks away. "It's just the way I talk, okay?" Is that the best she can do?

"Alright, fine, I'm sorry..."

"Thanks..."

"That's a total girl move..."

"...what?"

"Being quiet until I apologize."

"Sometimes not saying anything is the best way to resolve an argument."

"Who told you that?"

"My dad... and he's right. I don't know if you've noticed, but if someone argues with you and you get them to keep talking, they start to reverse themselves."

"Never noticed... how does that work?"

"If you're quiet, they don't know what you're thinking. Not knowing is hard to digest... and if you feel guilty, you project those thoughts on the other person."

"Huh."

"I'm not trying to teach you a lesson or anything... I just despise insults."

"I wasn't trying to..."

"I know. But when you talk like that, it's hard not to feel that way. Insults just wind people up... it's just better to say what your thinking. And just ignore Ava... she's a bitch."

She manages to laugh. I feel a vague sense of psychological discomfort leak into my brain as I stare off at the houses across the street. After a moment, I think I see something move behind one of the ground floor windows.

"...I'm sorry." Melody says suddenly.

"Don't worry about it."

"...so, does it bother you?"

"...not really. Like I said, I read about it and write about it, so it's at least something I've thought about. In a way it's kind of exciting."

She takes a long drag from her cigarette.

"So what you're doing... it's the kind of stuff you write about?"
"More or less."
"Why?"
"Like I said, it's interesting to me."

She edges a little bit closer to me. I feel her eyes on me, which now helps me put a finger on that psychological discomfort I felt minutes before. I'm probably exaggerating. I decide not to let it go.

"You okay?"
"Yeah... s'nothing."
"Sure?"
"Yeah."

She just keeps looking at me, maintaining a half-smile. I glance over at her thin, glistening lips. She can already see that I'm looking at her, so I turn my head completely and, as if driven by animal instinct, she puts her hand on my neck and begins probing my mouth with her tongue. My first thought is that Julia's inside, which is followed instantly by the observation that Melody is a good kisser. I pull away first to see her looking into my eyes and smiling. I look back into her brown eyes and take in her body, instantly feeling suicidally guilty. Feeling my mouth hanging open, I shut it. She moves in for another and I snap my head back.

She tries to kiss me again, but I keep my head away. She doesn't give up though; in one swift motion, she grabs my fly and unzips it. "Whoa!" I say, standing up and zipping myself back up. "What?" She asks, cocking her head as she looks at me. "No, I... no... just... not." I can't seem to find the right words. "Don't worry, I won't tell." Melody says, coming in again. "Stop!" I sit back down about three feet away from her; she slides closer and licks her lips, causing a sensation of tightness in my pants. I swat her away.

"Don't!"
"Why not?"
"I'm not into it..."

"*Why* not?"

"I... are you not used to people turning you down?"

"No one ever has." She says with a smile.

"Ugh..."

"...what was that?"

"No, I... ugh, I just... never mind."

"No *what*? You don't think I caught you staring at me?"

Shit.

"I wasn't... *looking* at you..."

"You think I'm retarded? You don't thinkI know *every* time a guy looks at me? You want me..."

"No I don't... I *have* a girlfriend. I mean, even if I didn't... no, I wouldn't..."

"Do you think you're better than me?"

"...where do you get that?"

She stares at me as though she can read my mind.

"What?"

"There isn't a word you wanna call me?"

"...*what?*"

"You thought it..."

"I didn't *say* anything..."

"Because I'm *not* a slut."

"I-you... ugh, it doesn't matter, I love Jules. Besides, you're *acting* like a... slut."

"Excuse me?"

"I didn't mean... I mean, if you..."

"...how *dare* you say that!?"

"What-uh... you're... coming on to me... you *barely* know me..."

"Maybe I *kind of* liked you..."

I'm floored, and somehow angrier than before.

"Look, if you want to screw someone, go ask Don, or Jake, or fuckin' Rich..."

"You're still a virgin, aren't you?"

"Yes."

She laughs.

"That's funny?"

"It's *pathetic*... you're like 20..."

"It's a *choice*..."

"Only virgins say that!"

"Look, just because I didn't tear up the first girl who made eyes at me..."

"Please, you don't know anything about it."

"Clearly you're the authority."

"More than you, buddy."

"Except when I do it, it'll actually mean something."

"Hah, only virgins talk like that!"

"And I'm certainly not gonna use her and treat her like shit..."

"You don't know *anything* about it. You couldn't handle me."

"I wouldn't if I had the chance..."

"Oh, and that makes you *so* much better than me..."

"Yeah, it does. I didn't start this. *You* came on to *me*; I turned you down, now you're attacking my non-existent libido to feel better about yourself."

"Chicken shit, fuckin' dickless douche bag."

She gets up and swaggers quickly to the greenhouse, but it's a long walk. From the breezeway roof she shouts, "Fag!" There's nothing I can say to that, partially because I don't want to attract any more of the undead. Melody walks all the way across the roof and inside the door, and in a few seconds Julia comes out. "Oh great... god knows what she... god dammit." Julia is still at a distance.

"Calm down. She knows you better than that. But you've lied to her before..." I shut my mouth as she gets within earshot and sit quietly until she comes over to find me with a huge frown on my face.

"Hello darling." I say weakly. She sits down next to me, putting her hand on my back.

"Are you okay? What happened?"
"She didn't say anything?"
"Nope, she just stormed in and said someone else had to go out."
"Well, she... she was coming on to me... and... ah... she... kissed me. She... unzipped my fly too..."
"Oh my... what did you do?"
"I made her stop."
"What else?"
"That's it... we fought about it... I'm sorry."
"Don't be."
"Leah, I can't... I don't... she's not... she just..."

Julia's expression is flat. I only call her Leah when I'm being totally serious, at which point she calls me Ef. Her lifeless responses suggest that she's upset and doesn't know what to make of it. When I smile at her she looks over and smiles back. I lean in to kiss her and when I pull away she's still smiling. "You know how much I love you." Julia smiles bigger, exposing her braces.

"Tell me again when you brush your teeth."
"Heh..."
"You sure she wasn't using your mouth to put out a cigarette?"

I lean in closer and tickle her. She giggles and playfully fights back.

"Alright?"
"Don't worry Ef."
"Are you sure?"
"Yeah..."
"... Leah..."

She buries her head in my shoulder. "It didn't mean anything... she's just so... not you..." She's listening, but even to me, the words don't sound like anything but cold, empty lines. I take a moment.

"I hadn't told you this... but sometimes, when I look at you... I get this feeling like I can see what you look like in twenty years... a friend, a lover, a wife... a mother. It's not something I expect anyone to understand... but for me... to know I'm looking at the person I'll spend the rest of my life with... am I talking too much?"

"God I love you..."

She grabs my neck gently and pulls me in for a kiss. She smiles again and wraps her arms around me, so I put my arms around her too. I tilt my head down and blow in her ear, and she lets out a little moan of delight. She clasps my neck and lifts her mouth to my ear. "Just please brush your teeth when we get inside." We both laugh, and her smile now is untainted. Arm in arm, we stare out at the street quietly for the next forty minutes.

Melody and Jake are the next people up on deck since she abandoned her previous stint. Once I've brushed, I feel the first pangs of being tired despite the fact that it's only five. Since we're going to be taking shifts all night and through the morning, I lay down with Julia. We're on the floor where we were the previous night, laying out perpendicular to the observatory door. The fact that it's light outside and I'm this exhausted reminds me of when I used to get home from high school, try to watch a movie, and pass right out.

I sleep for... I don't know how long I slept because I don't know when I fell asleep exactly. I get woken up by Rich. "Hey, hey Jeff." His voice is raspy and soft in an indistinctly familiar way, like a former teacher whose personality I was too young to retain. I don't know why that connection seems important when I'm waking up. "Wake up, man. It's your turn." I sit up and take a deep breath.

"What time is it?"
"8:55."

"8:55? You let me skip a shift?"

"Well yeah, Julia pulled a double, so now you can go out together."

His breath smells like an unattended dumpster packed with feces, and it takes all of my olfactory fortitude not to wince. I lean over Julia, softly running my hand over her face. "Julia, my love, time to get up." I whisper. Her eyes blink open as she gives me her adorable half-smile. I throw on my trench coat and gloves before we head out to the roof; the arm is starting to ache again, but at least it doesn't feel like someone's digging out the socket with a broken bottle. As I straddle the gate surrounding the greenhouse exterior I remember the experiment I had attempted, so I take off toward the back corner of the building.

Once there I look over to see that the dead previously at the back door are now trying to get around the cars again, but not showing a lot of initiative; regardless, I can still hear a group of them clawing at the back doors beneath me. I lean over the side and look to where I threw the bottle to see the undead circling; they *are* attracted to strong smells. Julia's at the other side of the school, maybe 500 feet away, looking at the dead. I look at the shoe I threw to find the area clear.

With that, I quickly make my way to the other side of the school, over bumps and ravines in the structure, down the ladder, and another 1,000 feet or so to the corner where I poured the mint. It's still there in a little puddle, but the undead are not. "So they can't smell up here, but they can smell us when we're downstairs. Interesting." I walk back over to the front of the building facing the street, near the band uniforms. Since Julia and I have nothing to do and since I can't even see past the grass line, we decide to make out for a while.

It's about 9:30 and I have one hand up her shirt when I hear some pops in the distance. We both pause for a moment, hearing silence after the report of a tiny explosion dissipates. Then I hear overlapping waves of rapid pops. I stand up quickly and pull my hand from underneath Julia's bra, prompting her to get up and fix it. "What's that?" I stare out into the vast, dark expanse. The dead are still wandering around the mint puddle. I soak in the silence until it's interrupted by another rapid series of dull pops.

"It's... southwest? Gunfire, maybe?"

"That could be good though, right?"

"...I don't think so."

"Why?"

"Shots that close together... sounds like... panic."

I put my arms around Julia and hold her close. As the sounds continue, they turn into a dull roar, like a thousand firecrackers amplified through bassy speakers. Both of us look down to see some of the undead on the front lawn start shuffling in the direction of the pops. The eruption of noise declines slowly over the course a minute, finishing at another cold moment of silence. Finally, there is a single suspended string of about thirty rapid pops followed by silence. "Stopped."

"You think they'll come for us?" Julia asks. I take a deep breath and continue looking in the direction of the shots. "Maybe. I almost hope they don't." We each smile at each other as she wraps her arms tighter around me.

"Where did your parents go again?"

"Bermuda, I think. I'm not... oh Jesus. My mother must be having kittens."

"I can only imagine."

"What about your mom and dad?"

"Maybe still in the area. I'm not worried. Oh my, that doesn't sound too cold, does it?"

"Nope. I mean... I barely know them..."

"I'm more worried about your parents. Let's just leave it at that, shall we?"

"Sure. Nice, though, considering you've never really met mine."

"Had the situation permitted..."

"Yeah, I know. It's okay. I did *want* you to meet them."

"I wanted to as well. There may still be time."

Another distant pop echoes from the distance and we both instinctually look out, our vision stunted by a black mass of trees that extends endlessly in all directions. I look at the ground between us as it falls silent again.

"You wanted this to happen?" Julia asks.

"…that's not an easy answer. You know I love to obsess over details… but I never thought about it like this."

"Like what?"

"…about what it means for the future when myth becomes reality. How much you can miss something as fundamental as sleeping in a bed, or eating two meals a day. Stuff like that… the things you have to feel to understand."

"We always talked before… I still have high school, and then I'm going to college. We'd have to wait until I was out of college to start a life together. Yesterday we had to wait the rest of our lives. Now… we're together. No school. No work. No bills, no responsibilities, no money… just us."

I look into her eyes intently.

"What you said earlier… meant a lot to me. Let's just say… I want the same things as you. Even if we fight. I've always felt safe with you, and I'll always love you… you can understand how much more important that is now. What I'm saying is, even if my parents are still okay, even if they come for me… you're the one I want to be with. And if it never gets better… the rest of our lives start today."

I hug her gently and warmly for what seems like an eternity. It's a relief to me that she can comfortably acknowledge the fact that this crisis might never end. I look past the top of her head to the highest branches of the tree line and see the limited expanse of stars in the night sky. The cold air carries the silence from the distance as the feet of the undead shuffle steadily and quietly beneath us. She's the first one to break the silence.

"Do you hear that?"

"I don't hear anything."

"No one's going to help us."

Before I had a slight feeling that I'd like to see another car, or person to walk down the street, but I am completely content sitting here quietly until it's our turn to go back in again. When it feels like ten we return to the greenhouse to find most of our group awake. It's 10:07, we still have the lights on. From what I can see, the only ones sleeping are Ava and Jake. Julia takes to the bed. "I'd never thought it would feel so good to lie down." She says.

"God, I have to piss so bad my teeth are floating." Don says from the desk, hugging his knees against his body. "I have to go too," I say. "We might as well." I get up and stretch, then pick up my hockey stick. Don picks up one of the steel rods and we make for the door. Melody stands up. "Aren't we supposed to go three at a time? That's the way you wanted it." I look back at the group to see that John and Melody appear to be the next up for outside rotation. That leaves Rich and Julia in the greenhouse with the sleeping people.

"Whoever is on rotation goes out, the other two stay in the greenhouse. We'll be fine... we're just going down to the second level and back." I turn to the door again, but Melody stops me. "All the bathrooms up here are locked... remember, we had to use the first floor?" I bite my lip and then shrug, avoiding a verbal response, causing her to overemphasize her steps in a little strut as she walks to the door with John Squared in tow; before exiting he gives me a half-humorous look that tells me how much this next hour is going to hurt. "Good luck." I say softly, turning away.

On the way to the door, I put a toothpick in my mouth. Naturally it occurs to me that, as men, the world is our toilet; Don and I could easily piss off the side of the roof and return in seconds, but rather than address this, I'd prefer to set a precedent for bathroom trips that will also function as a method of following what happens inside the school. We exit to the landing, go over the desks and ceiling tiles, down four sets of stairs and stop at the bottom of the steps. Once there, I look past the edge of the stairwell to see a door that leads out to the rear parking lot. I approach cautiously, but it doesn't make a difference as a fresh corpse slams against the glass and starts clawing at the door. The suddenness makes me jump back, and Don looks like he's about to have a panic attack.

"Don't scream, don't yell, don't say a word... you'll just draw more. He can't get through." I walk backward and push Don slightly toward the exit into the English hallway. We walk straight out thirty feet and turn left toward the bathrooms. "All right. I'm gonna go in first... you wait outside for a second." I enter to find that the lights are already on. I quickly go to the urinal and pee, and then go to the mirror. I take off my gloves, lean down to wash my face, and then I stop; can't trust the tap water, paranoid prick.

My reflection shows me a young man who doesn't look so good. There are dark bags under my eyes and the skin on my face looks tighter than before. Suddenly, I hear the sound of breaking glass from somewhere inside the building. I step back, hearing another shattering sound. "Don! Don?" I run out into the hallway, and he's not there. "Don! DON!!! Where the...?" I look back and forth; most of the hallways are lit, but there's no sign of him. "Tell me where you are Don!"

I shove my hands through my hair, reach into my trench coat pocket to retrieve my leather gloves, and then grab my hockey stick with both hands. I pinch my eyes shut for a moment as I try to develop a mental picture of the school; almost none of the windows in the school are accessible from the ground, all the door glass is tempered... the offices in the basement have huge windows that look up toward the grating above, and there's a set of steps that lead right down to them. I turn right and start running as fast as I can down the hall when I hear two loud crashing sounds behind me, causing me to stop and nearly fall over. I set my hand on the ground to steady myself and run back the way I came.

As I'm running, I remember the new wing of the high school; attached to the history halls, it extends out to the back lot exit, meaning it's the one place in the school where there are windows on the ground level. Worse, there are cars there. If the beasts got on top of them, they could easily break the large glass panes just above the small opening slits below. I turn right toward the steps, and then make a left. I run straight through a set of double doors to the new wing, finding it sheathed in darkness.

Thud. Thud. Thud. "Don?" The toothpick falls out of my mouth. The noises are emanating from the closest room. I take ten steps and almost throw up when I turn to the right and see a figure in a white t-shirt slamming a steel rod into another body. "Don!" There are ten in the room lit only by the light sneaking through the windows. "Don! God dammit, get out of there, start backing up!" Don takes a step backward and swings again, hitting another one across the face, sending a spurt of blood four feet across the room. Two that I had not seen before get up off the floor.

"MOVE IT!" I move into the room and slam my hockey stick into the head of the nearest person. We're outnumbered and overpowered, and this realization makes me think back to all the movies and video games where the undead always win with superior numbers. I make a continuous figure eight with my stick, hitting skull after skull, exerting all my force, ignoring the lingering ache present in my left shoulder, and when I take notice of my surroundings, I see blood dotted across everything nearby. My eyes get more used to the light in enough time for me to spot a figure crawling quickly across the floor toward Don's leg. "DON, YOUR FOOT!"

It's too late. Drool pours out of the creature's mouth as it grabs Don's ankle and his eyes shoot open as he trips backward, falling into a desk with a clatter. The undead are drawn instantly to the downed body. I nearly trip, slipping through the school desks so I can get to him, and when I do I barely clasp his sleeve with my fingertips and start pulling him toward me as I lean my back against a desk. I look around quickly as the fear of vulnerability washes through my veins. Once my eyes fall to the floor, I see one approaching my dangling feet. I swing as hard as I can with just my right hand on the stick, knocking the beast over, creating a domino effect that knocks over two more.

That's when I look over to see black liquid pouring out of Don's calf. I let go of his sleeve and push back, causing the desk I'm on to flip backward and slam into the floor, knocking me over as I kick my feet wildly. I kick a desk into one of the creature's legs, causing him to fall on top of me. I can hardly see anything that's going on and it feels likes arms are coming at me from all sides. Still kicking, my hands come off the floor and grab the beast's neck. Before he can react, I slam his head into the side of a desk, cracking his temple and causing him to go limp.

I kick harder, pushing the corpse away, gaining precious inches across the cold classroom floor when Don lets out a scream that will surely haunt me for the rest of my life. Backing up wide-eyed, I can't see what's happening to him; I can only see his face contorted in pain, tears running down his cheeks, and the undead piling on top of him. Steam rises up from his body as the smell of urine fills my nostrils. In a few seconds, I'm up on my feet again, backing up. "HEEELP HELP ME!!!" His screaming is so high pitched and pained it makes me nauseous. I look over at the teacher's desk, which is five feet from Don's head and come to a grim conclusion.

I slide my hockey stick across the floor behind me and get behind the teacher's desk, close my eyes and flip the desk as powerfully as I can manage so that the surface lands on Don's head with a loud, wet crack. All at once his screaming stops and I gag again. I look down to see the undead slowly pulling wet, stinking pieces out of his stomach as he wiggles and writhes. Shaking from the adrenaline, I drag the desk across the floor, bringing Don's body behind it. Once I'm at the door, I quickly handle the locking mechanism on the inside, pull the desk against the door as best I can, and yank the door shut. I land on my ass in the hallway and look up at the window, but I can't see anything. They're too busy eating to bother with me. I pick up my hockey stick and kick myself away.

I stare at the door for a moment as I catch my breath, then look to my right to see another one standing in the hall with a set of muddy footsteps behind him. We freeze each other, or at least he freezes me. I look the other direction to see just the dark hallway, and the hairs on the back of my neck stand up. I shiver as I look back to see him slowly advancing toward me, letting out a moan that makes me instantly grateful I just went to the bathroom. More footprints behind him lead into the school, and despite the knowledge of how good they are at cutting off escape routes, I stand up and run toward the opposite end of the hallway, skidding to a stop at an intersection and turning left through a set of doors.

This hallway is just as dark as the last one and the possibility of even one of them hiding in a shadow forces my heart up into my throat. I'm reminded of the times I've paid to go through haunted houses; I've got a simple set of directions, and the hallways in front of me look innocent enough, but I know that the chances of something lethal popping out of nowhere are high. I wiggle my fingers before slinking toward the doors twenty feet away, feeling naked as I free myself from the doorway.

I look back and forth at the next hallway intersection; I still don't see anything, so I go through the doors, walk quietly up the steps and head through the breezeway. I look frantically through the enormous glass panes aligning either side, but the courtyard beneath is empty. I don't know exactly what I'm going to do when I get to the other side, but vague ideas begin forming in my head.

I know that the one I saw in the hall is following me, and I'm sure there are at least a few inside now. With my heart pounding, I step through another set of double doors, head down the steps, and run through another set of doors into the hall where the main entrance is visible. I look to the left and see a shadow shuffling down the hall. Suddenly, a wave of shock shoots through my arms and legs and I start running into the lobby, making a slight diagonal left down the hall toward the nurse's office.

The doors to the library, which are close to the end of this hall, are miraculously open. I run inside, reaching into my pocket to find the last bottle of liquid mint. I open the top quickly and pour it out in a line, then throw the bottle against the wall, right next to a glass door that leads outside to the driveway. I then fill my lungs with air and scream, praying that they'll hear me and congregate in the library.

I run right back out the doors only to feel the swift kick of asthma as I look down the hallway behind me to see one walking corpse three hundred feet away. The door to the gym is immediately parallel to the library, so I go inside. I run across the gym floor, which turns each of my footsteps into a percussive slam that signals my position better than a war drum might. I run out the doors on the other side, twisting and turning through the halls until I'm back on the main hallway, right next to the cafeteria. The one that was out here before is gone.

Now I run to my right, turn left at the doors to one of the staircases, run up two sets of stairs, come out, turn left, and run. Once in the science hallway, I turn left and run to the other staircase that leads up to the greenhouse. I barrel up the steps, slip on the fluorescent light bulb glass, and I am lucky enough to not cut myself. I swing around and run the rest of the way until I reach for the ceiling tiles at the top step, and I watch my hand extend from my body as it if were someone else's.

I notice my body shaking, and suddenly I lose the ability to move any of my muscles. With my eyes still open, my body skitters back down the steps and I'm able to watch like a spectator. When I breathe in, my chest sounds like a motor. My left arm starts to twitch awkwardly as I try to reach the handrail, but my vision is covered with an effervescent purple cloud, highlighted by blurry multicolored dots upon which I cannot focus. Fear washes over me again as I remember my vulnerability, but there's literally nothing I can do.

A door opens somewhere in the stairwell. "Oh god, Ef, are you all right!?" Julia asks, dropping her steel rod. I can hear rabid scrambling, and suddenly someone's holding my head, but I grab her arms and hold them out while breathing heavily. "Check... me... bite... marks." I let out several heavy, hacking coughs that culminate with the induction of my gag reflex. I suddenly forget how I got up here. I feel hands all over me, checking my legs, my arms, and my stomach. "You're fine, now tell me what happened!" I'm still panting, gasping for air. "Inhaler." I wheeze. I can hear her run upstairs. Rich stays with me.

"What happened, where's Don?" Rich asks. My eyes are closed, so it feels as though his voice is omnipresent in the blackness of space. I swallow and try to explain, but I can only cough up snippets. "Dead..." I churn out a hacking cough. "I... had... to..." Rich pulls away. "Are they inside?" He asks calmly. Still wheezing, I hack again as a plastic ring pushes into my mouth.

Julia fires a jet of albuterol in my mouth and I breathe deep, struggling to find the device so I can introduce more life-saving sulfates into my lungs. I hold my breath for a moment, and then breathe out through my nose and resume gasping for air. "Ef, please, what happened to you!?" I grab her head and kiss her on the lips, then pull away.

"Love…" She strokes her hand across my face and that's the last thing I see or feel.

"Oh god, is he dead? He's dead!"
"No he isn't, his eyes just opened."

Blackness again. I don't know how long it lasts because I don't remember my dreams. I can only perceive darkness, that hazy purple-black void between when I sleep and when I wake. The void is nothing, almost impossible to comprehend, and with my brain running on low power, time loses all meaning. I could be sleeping for years or minutes.

10-11-04, MONDAY

I can feel the oppressive weight of a muddy sky before my eyes even open, perhaps worsening the strangely unnatural feeling of remembering exactly where I am and in what situation I'm currently waking up. My eyes curl open and dart toward the greenhouse, confirming the sensation I had about some forthcoming inclement weather; dense cumulonimbus clouds are bottoming out on the horizon, but they're not close enough to significantly blot out the rising sun. I take a deep breath in to confirm that I can breathe normally now, and as I finish exhaling I slide myself away from Julia so as not to disturb her.

The events of last night have been committed to my brain with a nearly mythic quality, allowing me to recreate the situations in third person to the point of editing out the incidental bits. I shudder as I recall the sound accompanying Don's death, bringing about feelings so deeply mixed that I am unlikely to attempt to summon them in detail again for some time. I take stock of the remaining people in the room to discover that Melody and Rich are missing, likely on roof patrol.

Standing up presents me with weakness in my knees and tightness in my groin and leg muscles before I grudgingly welcome a dizzying headache. The shoulder still hurts, but it's in good shape considering I haven't had any painkillers in more than a day. Finding no one else awake in the room with me, I quietly find the Ibuprofen to kill what little sting remains and pray I can get the kinks worked out with some light stretching. I go out the greenhouse door, cough immediately, and start the trek to the other side of the building.

As I walk over, I reach into the inner pocket of my trench coat to find my inhaler. That must have been Julia's handiwork. I can hear some voices mumbling on the roof above the auditorium, so I make my way over and calmly scale the thirty foot ladder. Rich and Melody both lock eyes on me as I ease my body over the edge. "Oh my god! You're okay!" Melody rushes over and hugs me, so I hug her back hesitantly. "What time is it?" She rummages through her bag and pulls out her cell phone. "It's 6:43." The sun will be rising in about 20 minutes. "Jeff... did you *kill* Don?" I stare at Rich quietly for a few seconds.

"I... I guess... sort of..."
"Sort of?"
"He... ran off... I..."
"What was he doing?"
"...I didn't have time to ask... he... he got bitten... and... I did what I had to do."
"...you didn't help him?"
"...you weren't there..."
"But why, why..."
"Rich... I didn't *want* to. I mean... did you want me to bring him up here?"

He stares back at me.

"What were *we* gonna do for him?"
"Would you have wanted him to do that to you?"
"*I* wouldn't have had a... wait, what?"
"... I know you and Don didn't get along..."
"...what the..."
"I'm just..."
"You think I *killed* him?"
"Jeff, I believe you..."
"Go downstairs and see for yourself..."
"No, no, no... I understand... all the same, I'm saying he should have had a choice..."
"He didn't..."
"I know... I'm saying we should all have a choice in what happens."
"... Rich, he..."
"I know, I know... I'm asking... if you were bitten, would you have wanted to pick how you'd go?"
"...yes. Yes, I suppose I would have..."
"So... if it happens again, we let them make their own choices."

Without another word, Rich walks toward the edge of the building and looks off. I pull at my shirt as the condensation clings to it. Out of the corner of my eye, I can see Melody staring at me with her mouth hanging open. Ignoring her, I walk over to the stone ledge, kneel down, and look out to the east. I spend the next twenty minutes watching the sun rise up under the clouds while fighting with Rich in my mind. When I finally manage to subdue his arguments, I put my arms out on the raised ledge and rest my head on top of my hands.

With my head down and my eyes closed, sound becomes the only thing I can take in from my surroundings, and I hear nothing but the sound of scuffling feet. In fact, I can pick out how many of them are out there: ten or twelve out back, one in front of the school in the driveway, two in the grass to the left, and I think one out in the street, coming from where we heard the firing the previous night. I lift my head to find Melody leaning over the edge, squinting to see the walking corpse, but when I look, I see a person in military camouflage, and he isn't scuffling around like an undead person. I put on my glasses.

He's hunched over, his arms dangling down as he takes jaunty, lumbering steps. He looks as though he's been stuck in the rain despite a total lack of precipitation. I can't tell if he's human or not. "Hey! You! In the BDU!" He instantly drops his head and dives into the bushes alongside of the road. The three of us wave our arms wildly. "Hey, *hey*! Up here!" He then responds without us being able to see him. "How do I get in?"

Everybody points in a different direction; I point to the doors below, Rich points to the back, and Melody points to the greenhouse. "Uh, come in through these doors down here. Head upstairs until you find the greenhouse door." He waves and darts between two bushes. "I know where it is." He says. I watch him for a few seconds while he zigzags between bushes, behind cars, and behind the enormous generators that remain on the front lawn. He manages to do so in silence, not attracting the attention of the undead.

After carefully descending the ladder, we run and climb our way across the building to greet him. Glass breaks behind us; I suppose he elected to smash the glass of one of the auditorium doors rather than have us unlock them. But how does he know how to find the green-house? Even people who have gone to this school don't know how to find it.

"Jeff?" Melody asks.

"What?"

"What's BDU?"

"Battle dress uniform."

"Okay... so, camouflage?"

"Camouflage isn't descriptive... a pile of sticks can be camou-flage... the uniform he's wearing is a BDU."

"Okay... but was there anyone else out there wearing one of those?"

"...no."

"So why does it matter?"

"At this point, I was hoping you could explain that to me."

When I rush back inside, Julia wakes up immediately. Her eyes light up as she sees me and jumps out of the comforter to hug me. "Are you okay?" She whispers. "Yeah, I'll be fine. Listen, someone..." On cue, I can hear him tugging at the greenhouse door, but it won't open. He got up here fast. "The door won't open! How do I get up?" He calls from the other side of the door. "From the door, take a left, then a right, another right, and head up." I hear the distant sounds of boots running in the hallway. His voice is familiar. It's not déjà vu, but he sounds vaguely like someone I know. I walk out to the landing, closing the door behind me as I catch him trotting gingerly up the steps, stop-ping at the edge of the landing below to look at the fluorescent bulb glass before looking up at me. His piercing blue eyes connect with mine. I do know him.

"That's a really good idea..." He says, and trails off. "Jesus, Ander-son?" He looks just as shocked as I probably do. He runs up the steps, climbs over the desks, and shakes my hand. "You didn't die..." He says. Without another word, I hug his solid body against mine.

"Where the fuck did you come from? And all that firing we heard last night, did you have anything to do with that?"

"You heard that? We set up a check point at 252 across the reservoir, didn't you get that message I left you?"

"What message? Oh... I left my phone at Temple..." I now wonder what other kind of messages I could have gotten.

"Shit. Well, we set up a check point at the reservoir and we were supposed to hold up there..."

"Yeah, yeah... they mentioned that on the radio, but they said the army was still trying to figure out where to put a rescue center."

"Well, you can expect about a week before that comes out. I'm just fucking glad you didn't get the message."

"What happened?"

"Well, the Marple cops held things down and got chewed up holding the line. We set up a tent for the wounded in the back and defended the choke, takin' 'em out... sometimes someone'd come looking to get through, we'd tell them they either had to get behind the line or stay in town... most of them kept moving. Then it got dark. So we're all just sittin' there when people start screaming behind us... half the guys turn to see what's going on and the other half keep facing forward. I turned around... we didn't have lights yet, so we could just see the cops runnin' for it... and we're all shoutin', tellin' 'em to get down... there was this yellow... flashing... traffic sign, you know, turn ahead or some shit... they were infected."

He sees the blood drain from my face.

"We didn't know they could run... I opened fire, emptied my clip... the rest didn't catch on until they hit. After that... Jesus, I don't know if you'd believe me if I told you. I... *what?*"

"I didn't know they could run..."

"Shit..."

"...where's the rest of your unit?"

His expression says it all. We stare at each other for a few seconds of awkward silence that he finally breaks.

"So who else is up here?"

"Jules, obviously..."

"Obviously."

"Ah, Ava, John Squared, another band kid, a homeless guy, and a raving bitch. Oh, and me, obviously."

"And this was your idea?" I nod. "Fantastic. I'm hungry, and I stink."

"Ha ha, uh, you look like you've already had a shower... I'm not sure we can trust tap water yet, incase it's contaminated..."

"I swam in the reservoir last night."

"You're kidding."

"Nope. So I think the water's okay."

"...how did that happen?"

"Later."

"Worst part of your night, I'll bet."

"Damn right... my cigarettes got wet."

"So, uh... fire showers in the science halls?"

"It's a date."

"Hang on..."

He shrugs as I turn to open the door to find Julia, Ava, Rich, and Melody trying to look behind me. John Squared is sleeping on the floor. "Some of you band people might know this fellow..." I enter the room, and Anderson comes in directly behind me. Julia runs over and hugs him, Ava does the same. After enduring a few minutes of them getting caught up, I break up the conversation. "Okay, so if anyone here feels they need a shower, we go to the science rooms in groups of two. I suggest finding someone you're comfortable with." I grab a towel, pick up a bar of soap, get a container of shampoo, and find some fresh boxers and socks. Anderson takes some of my clothes as well. Melody stops us before we can get to the door. "You're going *together*? Are you *gay*?"

Anderson stares hard at her as I engage in some eye rolling. "Cunt." Anderson says flatly, dropping Melody's jaw as he turns to the door. I can hear the rest of the group struggling to contain their laughter before I attempt to deliver the final blow: "He's never at a loss for words." Admittedly, it was funnier in my head. The two of us run downstairs and around the building to the science room across the hall from the greenhouse stairwell. The door to one science room is luckily open, so we just walk in and I shut it behind us. "I'm going first." John says, disrobing immediately. He tosses me his belt, somehow I missed that he had two Beretta pistols attached to it. "Wow, holy shit!" I say. I pull one of them out and look at it.

"I've never actually held one before..."

"Knock yourself out..."

"These aren't... standard issue...?"

"Nah... pulled 'em off some dead lieutenants."

I look up to see him walking toward the back naked and stepping immediately beneath the giant orange faucet attached to the ceiling. "Can you slide the soap and shampoo down here?" He asks. I place the items on the towel and slide them along the counter top to him. "Thanks." He yanks down on the chain and water pours out. "GOD DAMN! This shit is *cold!*" He jumps, cringes, and lets go of the chain. "Well, you're dirty, and you stink..." I offer, smiling. "Yeah, fuck you." He says, pulling the chain and recoiling as I play with the Beretta.

He laughs as he rubs the soap in his hands, producing lather. "You have a razor or something?" He asks while soaping his face. "Pssh, you know I don't need to shave." I depress the switch at the bottom of the handle and the magazine slides out. "Mind if I beat it?" He asks, laughing. "Seriously? Sounds like that thing is spraying ice cubes at you." He laughs hard, probably more from the cold water than anything else. "Besides, I'm sure you could get Melody to do it for you..."

"Who?" He asks. I slap the magazine back in and yank back on the action. "The c-word?" Anderson spins in the shower, washing the lather off. "No thanks. Still haven't laid any pipe yet." I point the gun around the room; it's tempting to pull the trigger, but I keep my finger off it. The statement finally registers.

"Wait, really?"

"Well... yeah... what about you?"

"Yeah... but I figured by this point..."

"Nope... been close with Shar once..."

"Shar... Antosky? You still hang out with her?"

"Yeah, but that's fucked. You ever meet Adam?"

"Who?"

"They were going out for like two years. She started bitching about him right before they broke up..."

"High tension wires?"

"Damn straight. But you and Julia haven't, uh...?"

"We're going her speed."

John reaches over, firing me a knowing smile as he lets go of the shower handle. He yanks the chain again and lets out a yelp as the water hits him. A few more seconds and he's convinced he's clean enough. He steps out and dries himself off, then wraps the towel around his waist and walks over to me. "You know I need that, right?" I ask. He stares blankly and pulls it off, handing it to me. "Thanks."

I take off my clothes and walk to the back, yanking down on the chain and being struck by the only liquid form of hail I've encountered in my life. "God dammit! It *is* fucking cold!" When I turn back toward him he's in boxers and one of my Pink Floyd t-shirts. His fatigues are laying on one of the tables, still damp. I lather my hands individually and use them like a wash cloth over my body, and despite the cold, the feeling of cleanliness is instant and fantastic. Yet another thing I took for granted before this happened.

As I let go of the chain, I notice my skin now feels like rubber thanks to the hard water. "Man, there is a testicle ascension factor of ten in here." I say, Anderson laughs. I towel off and step into my new boxers. "You got a pen on you?" I ask. He steps over to his fatigues and pats the pockets, finding nothing. He pauses for a moment, then looks at the teacher's desk and finds a pen in one of the drawers. "Why?" I ignore him for a moment as I stare at the phone on the wall.

"Grey?"

"There's a red light flashing at the top of the phone... doesn't that mean there's a message?"

"Who cares?"

"Who would call *this* phone in an emergency?"

"All right, check it."

I lift the phone to my ear and dial the voicemail. *"Please enter your password and press pound."* I hold the receiver to my chest. "Password, we're screwed." Anderson pushes himself between the wall unit and me and enters five digits. When he steps away, I press pound. *"You have. Five. New voice messages..."* I hold the receiver to my chest again.

"How did you guess that?"

"44678. Ghost. It was the password for everything when we went here and I knew they'd never change it."

"Clever."

"...press 2. You have. Five. New voice messages. To listen to your messages, press 1..."

I do.

"First message. Yesterday. Seven. AM."

"This is an automated call from the Delaware County Emergency Services Department. A mandatory evacuation order is now in effect. The following townships are to be evacuated: Broomall, Bryn Mawr, Edgmont, Newtown Square. Please evacuate immediately and in a sane, orderly fashion. Please do not attempt to gather personal effects. Please remain on major roadways wherever possible. For further information, please tune your radio to your local AM news, or call the Pennsylvania Emergency Management Agency at 1-888-973-2397. Do not stay by your phone or turn on your television for further updates."

"To erase this message, press 6... message erased. Next message. Yesterday. Nine. AM."

"This is an automated call from the Delaware County Emergency Services Department. A mandatory evacuation order is now in effect. The following townships are to be evacuated: Broomall, Bryn Mawr, Edgmont, Newtown Square. Please..."

"Message erased. Next message. Yesterday. Eleven. AM."

"This is an automated call..."

"Alright, all the same thing... evacuation order."

"Not surprised."

"The first report said they were protestors…"

"We never got that… they didn't call 'em protestors, anyway."

I tap my fingers against the wall.

"I didn't think this was possible." I say, finally.

"What?"

"Zombies… getting the upper hand. It didn't make sense to me that they couldn't be contained. Depending on who you ask, you get a different answer on what to do. People are confused, frightened… that's how they do it."

As Anderson nods solemnly, I walk through the door and head toward the greenhouse. "Put your name on the door and change the date. Oh, and uh, cross out Don Mason." I say. He doesn't even look at me when he starts scratching off the name and the date. "By the way, I locked the auditorium door behind me." He adds, apropos of nothing. "Don do something stupid?" I shift a bit and look at the floor. "Technically…" He stops writing and looks up.

"Well?"

"Let's just say… I don't feel great about it."

"You killed Don?"

I give him a hackneyed serious expression. After staring at me blankly, he subtly shrugs and returns to writing. "He was an asshole anyway." Once again, he has me laughing. While the arising isn't yet a full-blown crisis, I sort of assumed that I wouldn't see most of my friends again. Now that Anderson is here, I feel complete. He's gotten a few steps ahead of me, so I take a few quick strides to join him. "So, yeah, uh… Don was… getting eaten…" He cuts me off so quick I forget what I was saying. "You don't need to explain shit to me. It happens."

We avoid the fluorescent bulb glass on our way back up to the greenhouse, and as we make it through the door, I catch a glimpse of Steve. "Oh shit, I forgot… check this out." I wave him over to the row, making sure I stay in front of him so I can give him a proper reveal. As I step away, Steve violently thrashes to no avail. "Jesus!" Anderson shouts, leaping back and flailing his arms. "And you haven't even been properly introduced yet. John, Steve." Anderson cautiously leans in, holding his hand over his mouth. As he looks him over for the first time, I notice that Steve's eyes seem paler than before; I remember thinking they were brown, but now they look hazel, or is he developing cataracts?

Anderson seems to be genuinely disturbed by Steve; it's a look I don't see often, but all of his face muscles are relaxed and his eyes look totally lost. "You found him like this?" He asks in a quiet, terrified tone. "Of course not... oh shit, I haven't told you anything... do you know what happened here?" He shakes his head, keeping his hand perched over his lips.

"Well... they came out of the cemetery..."

"Well... *I'm* having nightmares for the rest of my life."

"Right in the middle of Bandrome... I *had* to be the first person to see it... there was at least a hundred... I ran out into the field for Julia right before the crowd panicked, and I wanted to get out to my car... but we ended up here. Yesterday we went out for food, blankets, and weapons... last night I killed Don, so that brings you up to date."

"You killed Don?" Julia asks, terrified.

"I thought you heard that?"

"No..."

"Well, yeah. I had to..."

"So wait, I thought you said there were more people?" John asks.

I look around the room to see that Melody and Julia are awake, Rich and John Squared are sleeping, so Ava and Jake must be out on the roof. "Nope, everyone's accounted for." Anderson looks out the window and finds Ava and Jake easily. "Oh, I see. You have a rotation, that's smart. They can't smell you out there?" I shake my head, and he nods. I take notice of the dark bags beneath his eyes. I snicker, morbidly amused that his blank, frightened expression, married with those bags, kind of makes him look like a Zombie.

"You look like shit."

"Then I look just like I feel."

"Get some sleep..."

"I will... first, we need to talk."

"Sure."

"...outside?"

"Oh, duh, alright. Uh, everyone just hang out, we'll be back shortly."

I wrap myself up in my trench coat and lead the way out the door. He walks around the outside of the greenhouse and climbs up a metal ladder attached to the side of the building while I follow closely. As I come up to the top, I see him looking off in the distance. He turns when I get to the top.

"You know what escape and evade is?"

"Nope... but if the name is any indication..."

"Probably... when you get separated from your unit, you have to get back to a point of troop population by any means necessary. You stay covered, avoid threats, and fire only when necessary. So I have to get back as soon as possible."

"Understood."

"Now, the procedure on home turf wasn't confirmed, but it's pretty well assumed that civilians go with you. Usually you avoid outside contact on E and E, but I think it's a safe bet our Zombie friends won't be tapping comms. So, I have to get to the next check point, but I'm beat to shit and if I don't crash, I'm gonna fuckin' die. This looks like as good a place as any."

"Agreed, and we have food."

"And I need to dry my fatigues..."

"I see where you're going. Dude, get as much sleep as you can, eat up, and talk to them. When we get to the check point, we'll back whatever play you make."

"Alright, and the other thing is, we don't go looking for survivors. That includes Dave and your parents."

"Dave's in Penn State, my parents are in Bermuda."

"Lucky. Well, tell everyone else about that if you get the chance. Man what I wouldn't give for a cancer stick."

"I don't think anyone else smokes."

He turns to the side and squints as he looks at the top of the tree line to the northeast.

"What are the chances of us actually running into each other like this?" He asks.

"About the same as Zombies existing?"

"…good point."

"Karma."

"It's probably a coincidence."

"Maybe… a few days ago I told Jules you wouldn't have to go to Iraq if there was such thing as karma. We still have power, water isn't contaminated, and they can't seem to figure out how to get inside. Sounds like a good balance to me."

"Dude… I'm about to fall over."

"Enough said."

Once inside, I select a blanket and a pillow for Anderson. "Pick your sleeping spot. You can skip watch shifts… you earned it, soldier. We'll put your fatigues by the heaters to get dry. There's food in the backpacks and water in the uniform bags if you need it." I place my hand on his shoulder. "It's good to have you with us." He gives one of his trademark low, extended laughs as he walks over by the observatory, next to where Julia and I sleep, curls up into a ball, and passes out immediately. I look over to see Julia half covered by the sheets, propping herself up with one arm. When we make eye contact, I smile. "How are you this morning, my love?" I ask softly. She smiles back. "Don't think I could be much better." I get on my knees and crawl into the sheets with her, putting my right arm around her immediately.

"Seriously?" Melody mutters as her words descend into incoherent mumbles. We both sit up and Julia speaks for me. "We never get to spend this much time with each other." Melody raises an eyebrow and gives me a sarcastic smirk. "Have you two even *slept* together?"

We both shake our heads. "Not before a few nights ago." I say as she lets out a little laugh. Julia smiles and shakes her head, prompting Melody to force another laugh.

"No wonder you were too chicken shit to make a move..."

"You know," I start. "Chances are that I've given at least one of your boyfriends advice on how to do it..."

"That's some shit, right there..."

"...maybe they didn't have any rhythm..."

"...shut up..."

"...or they were too small... so they asked you to hold up your legs and put a pillow under your ass... or hold your knees together while lying on your side..."

"Shut *UP!*"

Satisfied, I look back behind me at the clock; it's now 8:05, which means it's time for a shift change. I'm going to be up most likely. Sure enough, in the next few seconds, Jake and Ava walk inside. "Okay," I say. "I'm obviously up. Who else needs a shift?" Jake looks around as Melody stares at him. He points to John Squared. "He's the furthest from a shift." Julia smiles and raises her hand. "Well I guess we have a volunteer." I say, hugging her. While she's close, I sniff her hair and pull away.

"Or would you rather have a shower? We'll get plenty of time together, and you're better off going while it's still light out."

"...I'll take a shower then!"

"Watch out, the water's freezing."

We both stand up and kiss, then I go over to John Squared and tap his shoulder.

"Come on, Squared. We're up."

"All right, I'm up." He says immediately, startling me.

"Wait a second," Jake starts as he points to Anderson. "Who's that?"

"Anderson."

"Holy shit, how'd he get here?"

"Luck."

I grab my cane and throw on my trench coat, stopping halfway out the door.

"By the way, there's a phone in the room with the showers... feel free to call anyone you want while you're down there... but remember, Anderson was adamant about us not collecting anymore survivors... so don't lead anyone here or leave unless you're not coming back."

"How can you..." Ava starts, immediately reversing herself. "*Anderson* said that?"

"Like I said... he's adamant."

"I'm Adam Ant." Anderson grumbles from the floor.

"...dial nine to get out."

With that, John Squared and I step outside amidst some soft chuckles. It's quite cold, but neither of us says anything about it on the way to go sit on the raised ledge of the roof's highest point above the auditorium. It strikes me as funny that I've been prone to leaving out silent gaps like these in my writing. In my mind, Zombie fiction has always been an entertaining mixture of gritty suspense and human drama, but rarely do I find the time to mention that characters have to go to the bathroom.

I suppose calling those moments uninteresting is simply an excuse. I've tried, in the past, to imagine what other people think about when they're alone and have nothing else to do, particularly when they're on trains or buses. For the life of me, I can never dive into their heads and figure out what keeps them motivated. Just because I always end up dwelling on my thoughts and enter into an existential quandary doesn't mean everyone else does. Sometimes I feel that transcribing these thoughts might be useful. The rest of the time, they strike me as sensationally boring.

"What's next?" John Squared asks suddenly.

"...huh?"

"Well... what you said got me thinking... about our parents."

"...I'm... not convinced that's such a good idea."

"No offense man, but your parents are in a different country."

"Excellent point..."

"I don't know. It's hard to sleep in there... people keep... crying."

"Yeah, I've heard it."

"Ava, for sure... Jake... Melody too."

"I don't know... it's just so... dangerous. And I guess... I don't understand why you didn't go after your parents in the first place..."

"Some did... you probably didn't see how many people were behind you. I think... Gary said something about his parents and turned back. Guess whose parents weren't there... Ava, Don, Jake, Julia, and me."

"And Matt, too, I'm sure... your sister was down there?"

"Yeah... Lisa..."

"...you didn't...?"

"I understand why you'd ask... but I don't want to talk about it. I feel like more people should have come in, though..."

"Most of the doors were locked... and you're right, by the way... my parents being in Bermuda... actually..."

"Huh?"

"Well... everyone seems to be looking to me for answers. I can't justify going out to find people's parents because half of us won't make it back. Besides... could you imagine having to deal with your parents as Zombies?"

"Yeah, well... you never know."

"...what?"

"...you know how some people like open caskets?"

"Yeah... not something I'd ever do..."

"Me either... I'd rather remember them alive."

"Definitely."

"Open casket people need closure... some people can't stand wondering if their parents *might* still be alive..."

"Well, Anderson said we shouldn't be look for survivors."

"Shit, he did. Well, you've convinced me... what else did he say?"

"Once he's rested up, we're gonna head out to the other check point."

"Where's that?"

"Hell if I know. But when he leaves, we're going with him."

We're both quiet for about a minute.

"So... you wrote about this?"

"Heh... I was just thinking about that... how I didn't account for things like showers."

"I used to shower twice a day. Glad I got away from that."

"Right. There's about a hundred things like that... having a bed, eating a warm meal, or any meal. I think the worst one is that there's no afterward."

"Like, it's not going to end?"

"What I mean is... when I'd write, I could ellipse. I could take breaks. When I was done for the night I could go to bed and pick it up whenever... I could *control* it. Now, there's about a million things I never accounted for. Like what happens if I get bitten."

"Or when someone else does."

"Right."

We share a reasonable pause.

"You seem to be taking it okay, though."

"Haven't been thinking about it."

"...are you okay?"

"Hmm?"

"I mean... it's not eating you up?"

"Not really."

"Well, that's how we're gonna make it through this. I'm... sort of religious..."

I can't stop myself from turning to him.

"You didn't know that?" He asks.

"I guess I never thought about... I guess..."

"What?"

"...nothing."

"You assume smart people are Atheists?"

I break into a heavy chuckle before I stifle myself with my hand.

"Guilty."

"Nah, I... get the mindset... I mean, I don't think any less of anyone being an Atheist..."

"Oh, no, I certainly don't think less of you..."

"Well, it wouldn't matter if you did... it's not like I care what you think."

We both stifle our chuckles.

"Anyway... I'm not going to tell you this is God's judgment... but I have to wonder. The Rapture comes after the Tribulation... that's New Testament. I don't remember the Bible being very clear on that..."

"There wasn't a bulleted list?"

"Heh..."

"Well, I figured with the ten commandments the lord liked to keep things itemized..."

"Less than you'd think... anyway, this fits the build."

"Resurrection?"

"Not... really. But depending on how you look at it, Jesus was a Zombie, right?"

I let out a laugh.

"Seriously, though, I think the Rapture and the Second Coming happen at the same time after the Tribulation. That's when everyone, living or dead, is supposed to be judged."

"What about the ones in between?"

"Limbo's the in-between, so this makes sense as the Tribulation. The dead return to... well, not *quite* life..."

"I follow, but where does science come in?"

"Well, I don't use science to enhance religion or the reverse... they're mutually exclusive."

"But we've reached a dividing line. This can't be entirely spiritual, and it can't be entirely biological."

"Why?"

"I'm no scientist or doctor, right, but from the looks of it, they came from the ground."

"Yeah."

"There's no oxygen in a coffin. It can't maintain a person for more than a few minutes. That means biological death. No heartbeat or pulse."

"They still eat, though... isn't that feeding an impulse?"

"Is it true hunger, or just instinct? They have no heartbeat and they don't breathe, so how do they use their muscles? How do they not feel pain?"

"Got me... I mean, best guess, some experimental drug to restore dead tissue leaked into the ground... or it's some bio-weapon... a virus..."

"Or prions..." I offer, after a moment.

"Prions?"

"Mad cow... anyway, on the other side, you destroy the brain, and that's it. They don't need a heart or lungs, but they need a brain? Is that where you keep your soul?"

"...voodoo?"

"Voodoo Zombies are just like people. They have emotions, feel pain... it's more like a trance... what if it's Gaia?"

"Gaia?"

"You know, the theory that the Earth is almost a living creature... something like 99% of all life on Earth has gone extinct, what if nature figured we were too wily to be wiped out by a natural disaster and threw this at us... like some weird evolutionary control?"

"Yeah... the planet doesn't need to be saved by us, it can save itself... did you hear the theory that SARS came from a comet tail? What if this is some weird interstellar affliction?"

"...I don't think it can be explained."

"What worries me is that Zombies were fictional, maybe even mythic just a week ago. If they're on the table... what other impossible things got set with it?"

"I don't think it matters."

"I guess the big question is... did this happen for a reason?"

"Some things happen for no reason at all."

He nods as I assume he considers the dizzying abyss of comprehension suggested by that statement. Just when I think we're done...

"Why'd you have us run?"

"What?"

"When we were going to get food and stuff, we *ran* downstairs..."

"Did it give you a rush?"

"Yeah..."

"That's why. When your adrenaline is jacked, you react on instinct. Instead of freezing up, you roll with the punches, and I'll take alerting the dead over scared kids ready to shit their pants if they hear a pin drop any day."

His nodding confirms that we are officially at a stopping point, so we both start walking in opposite directions to get a look around the roof. I can't get food out of my mind. Provided that we are unable to connect with the National Guard, we're eventually going to have a serious problem with food supplies. We can only eat packaged food for so long until it runs out and we have to eat plants, and I'll never be satisfied by the cleanliness of things I know aren't out of a package. If the outbreak originated in this town, it follows that people were either overtaken or evacuated fast enough that there won't have been much looting, and few if any will make the determination to willingly push through this area. Of course, it's also quite possible that our forthcoming attempt to surrender ourselves to the National Guard will end in disaster a few hundred feet outside of the school.

I sit down on the edge of the auditorium and stare out at the street. One by one, we'll all die somehow, we have to. One of us will get sick and not get treated, or get bitten and be cast aside, or get an infected paper cut. Can we even survive long enough to grow old? If Julia and I get to a point where we want to have children, could we bring them up in a world like this? Otherwise, what happens if we die? There probably won't be any people younger than us still living, so if we manage to survive and don't procreate, the human population could die with us. But how would we deliver a child?

There could be light shed on the situation, which could come in the form of the military containing them and battling them back. Then, depending on the spread of the infection, we could either start over or just get things going again. Maybe it won't spread that far and life will continue as normal. The other potential light on the situation could be thermonuclear. A few hydrogen bombs would be enough to eradicate all life in the five state area. I shake my head heavily and begin walking around. The image of a nuclear weapon exploding overhead is not a pleasant one because it would likely be centered on Philadelphia, which is not far enough away for us to escape its wrath. Next thing I know I've killed fifty minutes of my rotation with my combination of thinking, pacing about the roof, and talking.

I go back inside along with John Squared, and they've already woken up the next two, who look to be Rich and Melody again. As I'm looking at them, tired and shuffling like the living dead, I can't help but think about the conversation John Squared and I had about the parents and protecting our people. We have the band clothes hanging up on the wall outside with our message if anyone important passes by, and Anderson said he would have us moving on in the near future, so watch duty should be optional until we leave.

"Let's ditch the roof rotation."

"What?" Rich asks.

"Well, if we're tired, what shape are we gonna be in if we need to run? Besides, I don't know about you, but I'd rather sleep."

Melody sits back down. I drop my trench coat and climb under the sheets next to Julia, who is clean and smells amazing. I wrap my arms around her. "I think there should be a shift in power." Rich says carefully. Melody takes a deep breath in and Jake squints, giving him a coy smile.

"I, uh... what?"
"The soldier should be in charge."
"Are you insinuating that I *was?*"
"I think if anyone asked who was in charge, we'd all say you were, even if you deny it."

He aggressively points to Anderson, who is lying on his side, snoring loudly with one arm dangling loosely over his face to block the light. There could be no worse portrayal of a group leader.

"I think it should be Jeff... he knows his shit." Melody says.
"Yeah." Julia agrees.
"I don't know what the game is here... I'm sure Rich doesn't want to take orders from a kid, but I'm actually older than Anderson..."
"Whoa whoa whoa," Rich holds up his hands in protest. "That has *nothing* to do with it. I just think he's the best option."
"So, is there, like a second in charge or something?" Melody asks.
"No. Everyone's on the same level except when it comes to tough decisions."
"Not necessarily. I was gonna wait to get everyone together to tell you, but he wants us to move on to the next check point." I reply.
"Where?"
"I don't know, but it doesn't matter. It's his duty to rescue civilians, so wherever he goes, we follow."
"Fine by me."
"May I make one suggestion?"
"Yes?"

"If something happens where we can't join the army, I suggest co-leadership. I nominate you, myself, and Anderson… an adult, someone who knows about the situation, and someone who has military training. If we have three people we always have a tiebreaker."

"What if just everybody leads the group?" Melody asks.

"True democracy? Doesn't work."

"Duh, we *live* in a democracy… that works…"

"Does it?" Rich asks with a smile.

"No, it doesn't." I add, building on Rich. "Our government's technically a democratic republic. If true democracy is the will of the majority, then the majority can vote to execute the minority. In that case, the minority doesn't have a say. Majority rule encounters biasing and politicking, so someone's always gonna be unhappy."

"Okay, we'll ask what he thinks when he gets up. But in the meantime, you want to trash *your* watch system?" Rich asks.

"Not for a lack of trying… after all, I just finished my shift. Besides, we should be awake at night."

"Why do you say that?"

"If you're tired and there's low visibility, you can make mistakes. That isn't as easy in the sunlight."

"Does that really matter?"

"If we need to leave… can you imagine waking up and running like hell on only a few hours of sleep?"

"Let's hope we don't. For now, I'm going out to keep watch."

"Keep us posted."

"Will do."

Rich walks past Steve, who tries to shake his head at him; thankfully, the tape is holding. Jake goes out on the roof, presumably to talk to Rich, as Melody slumps back in the corner and closes her eyes. Both Johns are sleeping. I pull the comforter tighter around Julia and myself and squeeze her. She's warm, and my mouth is magnetically drawn to her neck. She lets out a little satisfied sigh as I kiss her. "I love you so much." I whisper in her ear. She smiles and kisses back.

"I *really* hate that guy…" Ava says from the other side of the room. I bite my lip and look at Julia to see that she's biting hers. I raise my eyebrows insistently and after a few moments of indeterminate head wiggling and blinking, she finally gives me a gentle shrug of resignation. Here we go.

"What do you hate?" I ask.
"Rich. He pisses me off."
"Why?"
"He talks down to everyone, like *he's* smart... and he smells horrible, but he won't take a shower."
"Well, that's kind of unfair, isn't it? I mean, he *is* homeless."
"Yeah, well, *I* took a shower."
"He probably doesn't think he needs one."
"Well someone should tell him he does."

I lean over so I can look at her.

"Why don't you?"
"Why should I?"
"Because you're the one pissed off..."
"And it doesn't bother *you*? It's *nasty.*"
"I haven't noticed."
"How could you *not!?*"
"I'm not paying attention to how he smells... if it's bothering you, either say something to him about it or... focus on something else."
"You can't miss it though..."
"No one else has said a word about it..."
"Because they're too scared to say anything."
"So are you."
"No I'm *not...*"
"Then why haven't you said anything?"

She's silent for a moment.

"It's only gonna bother you if you let it. Just focus on something else."
"Easy for you to say." She snaps, looking at Julia.

"…I don't know what else to tell you. If it's bugging you, tell him."

"It's not bugging me…" Melody starts.

"No one asked *you*, fucking concubine."

"And stop *that*." I say, finally sitting up. "I'm not kidding."

"What the fuck is a concubine?" Melody asks.

"Don't ask."

"Why should I?" Ava starts. "You can't tell me what to do."

"*Hey*! What'd you just call me…?" Melody starts.

"Melody, don't…"

"Why shouldn't I? This bitch's been steppin' on my shit…"

"You didn't seriously just say that…" Ava responds.

"Jesus, what is your problem!?" I interrupt.

"You! Fuckin' annoying…"

"And you're… what? Just being honest?"

"Yeah."

"Fuck that. I'm tired of your passive-aggressive bullshit, you're an inconsiderate *bitch*…"

"And you're a pussy… just because *I* tell the fuckin' truth…"

Now we've all elevated to shouting.

"The *truth*? You're an even bigger pussy than me and a *bitch* on top of… *you* couldn't tell Rich he stinks, *you* couldn't tell me you were annoyed, *you* couldn't tell Melody you wanted to throw her out…"

"What!?" Melody shouts.

"Now you're putting words in my mouth, retard… I said she was being a bitch and I let her know about it… and what about you? It's not like I'm surprised you're saying this now 'cause it sounds like you've been fuckin' rehearsing it…"

"Because I try to tolerate you…"

"…to lie…"

"…look who's puttin' words in *my* mouth! I wouldn't be polite if I didn't feel like you deserved it…"

"Oh grow up, you don't *actually* care about me, you wanna be on good terms 'cause you don't want Jules takin' sides again…"

"Don't you *dare* bring Jules into this…"

"I want my fucking *friend* back! We always have to invite *you* to hang out with *our* friends because you've got her on a leash..."

"A *leash*!? That's what this is about, isn't it? You don't care if she's miserable, as long as you can be friends."

"Well if she's miserable, it wouldn't be the first time..."

"What the *fuck* is that supposed to mean!? You think she's happy right now? If I were her, I'd be pissed at both of us, and unless the two of you are the same person, you can STOP *FUCKIN'* TALKIN' FOR HER!"

"You think you know her well enough to say that..."

"What did I say? You and I are the ones fighting, so stop bringing her into it."

"Stop talkin' about her like she's not here! She's right FUCKIN' next to you!"

"And you wonder whose side she's on?"

"Fuck you, Jeff... you're trying to... change the subject because you don't know how to fight back..."

"*Wrong,* I refuse to involve her because she's *my* girlfriend and *your* friend, *NOT AMMUNITION!*"

"Right, and you've always been in her corner..."

"I'm there now, aren't I!?"

"I've fuckin' had enough of this..."

She rips herself off the floor and for the first time I get a look at the stunned glances of Melody, Jake, and John Squared. Somehow, Anderson is still sleeping.

"Too ashamed to admit defeat?" I ask.

"No, idiot, I'm not gonna fight about taking sides with a fuckin' *cheater!*"

With that, she slams the greenhouse door shut behind her. For some reason, I notice that the floor is cold beneath Julia and me. "Ef." She says softly. "Yeah?" She grips my hand.

"Thanks for standing up for me..." Melody says from across the room.

"It's alright. If you can... just ignore her. We can't keep doing this."

"I'll try."

Rich suddenly blows through the door.

"What the fuck was that about!?"

"Oh Jesus, Rich, I'm sorry..." I mutter. "We... we just... that fight's been boiling over for like two years..."

"Is that why she slammed the door?"

"I... yeah... you didn't hear us fighting?"

"Just the door... well... don't fight anymore."

Rich pulls the door shut and we all snicker. I look back down at Julia. "Do you think they'll get up here?" She asks softly. I close my eyes and rest my head against hers. "I hope not." Silence. "Do you *think* they will?" Between speaking we each take long pauses to think.

"I don't know."

"I'm afraid."

"Of?"

"That I might lose you."

"I know... but you can't dwell on it."

"Easy to say..."

"Well... try to be optimistic."

"You've never been optimistic, love."

"I've been hiding it from you."

She smiles. I'm so used to waxing poetic with her online that this conversation seems surprisingly straightforward.

"Jules... I'm sorry..."

"Don't worry about it."

"I know... but the way she said... I... like, maybe you hadn't... forgiven me... or that I don't love you."

"I know you do. *Don't* worry about it. I love you more than any-thing..."

"I know, Leah..."

"No. *Anything.*"

She's referring to Ava. I smile and kiss her neck, then hold her close.

"I can feel you thinking." She says finally.

"Remember when we talked about... how stupid people and smart people make the same decisions for different reasons?"

"Of course."

"Seems like the stupid people'd look for survivors out of fear and loneliness... in the middle, people think saving others'll just slow you down..."

"And smart people see the necessity of codependence."

"Exactly..."

"I'm lucky to have you."

"No, I'm the lucky one."

"Why do you say that?"

"Because I only need you to survive... and I have you."

We both close our eyes, and though the sun is somewhat harsh, I reach into my overnight bag and find a pair of sunglasses. She takes the cue and pulls her own sunglasses out of her pocketbook.

"Jeff?"

"Yeah?"

"Are you okay... after what happened with Don?"

"Yeah."

"Do you not want to talk about it?"

"I'm indifferent. I haven't even been thinking about it."

The silence in the room is still palpable after the argument, and that lack of sound is matched in my brain. I feel as though I'm close to meditation, but as usual, I never see unconsciousness slipping in.

I wake up suddenly in the middle of my sleep cycle, and I am confused. Thankfully, I realize I have been woken up by what sounds like John Squared snoring. I turn my body and see Julia's eyes open. She gives me a funny look and rolls her eyes. I let out a short laugh and roll over to wrap my arms around her again. Now that I know what the noise is, I can go back to sleep without interruption. As I'm drifting off, I can softly hear what sounds like pouting. I ignore it and pass out.

My first recollection in consciousness is that last night's dream featured Don. It wasn't a nightmare, as I certainly don't feel guilty, but I have a lot of difficulty pinning down what it entailed. I think I might have been kicking him in the ribs? I open my eyes to find Julia grinning down at me. I slide toward her and kiss her, then look at the clock to find that it is 3:34pm. I marvel that I could have slept so long, especially after a night of good sleep. Anderson and Jake are absent and Melody is sleeping, as is Rich. John Squared is sitting on the garden row across from Steve, just staring at him, and Ava is sitting across from me, staring as well. "How long have you been up?" I ask.

"An hour, maybe... did we wake you?" Julia asks. I shake my head and yawn before asking my question. "You know where John went?" They both shake their heads. Jake is missing too. I hope he's off doing something useful with Anderson. Then again, have *I* been useful in the last 24 hours? I lie back for a second and let out a deep sigh, staring at the ceiling. "Jeff." Ava says softly. I sit up and look at her.

"I'm sorry."
"So am I."
"Really... I'm *sorry*. And... I just wanted to tell you I apologized to Melody."
"Thank you."

I lie back down with a sigh. Julia runs her hand across my chest. "Are you okay, my love? Is your arm better?" She asks. "Yeah, now that you mention it... but god, what I wouldn't give for a cheesesteak." The image of an Amoroso roll filled with steaming browned meat, fried onions, ketchup, and melted American cheese slides into my mind. I imagine the grease running down my throat as I tear the meat away from the rest of the roll and swallow, and when I open my mouth again a fresh pool of drool looses itself from my lips and runs down my cheek. I wipe it away, hoping no one noticed.

"Oh no!" Julia says in a playful voice, as she is a vegetarian. "Wait a sec, so are you no longer a vegetarian now that we're in the midst of a crisis?" She cocks her head like a confused dog. "You said your problem was the mass slaughter of animals, so if we learn to hunt, you wouldn't mind eating some hunted deer, unless you're a charlatan!" I smile at her and she smiles back, I pull her close and hug her.

"Seriously though, I want a cheesesteak."

"Geno's, Pat's? Tony Luke's?" Squared asks, still staring at Steve.

"Jim's."

"Ah, never had it..."

"You get a good cheesesteak pretty much anywhere in Delco. Pinocchio's, Doc's, Drexel Hill Pizza, Joe's..."

Though mildly entertaining, I recognize that our conversation had limited potential. I stand up and toss my hair around my head a few times, stretch, then observe the room. I throw on my trench coat and adjust the collar, then lift up the bottom of my corduroy shirt to clear the sleep crust from my eyes. "Squared, want to take a walk?" Squared jumps off the garden row, making sure to stay away from Steve. "There's something coming out of his mouth." John Squared says. "What?" I ask. He points to Steve's head. I walk over to find a white crust around his mouth and in little puddles next to his head. The tape and socks are still secure, but it seems to have seeped out around it.

"Maybe he wants a cheesesteak too." I say absently, staring at the puddles. They're all dried up, not like they've seeped into the dirt that is below them, but like the liquid has turned to dust. I liked to write in stories that the virus, or whatever substance makes the undead convert the living to their ranks, would concentrate in the salivary glands of the infected to improve the chance of passing it on, so I imagine that's the culprit here as well. I walk out the door with John Squared in tow and go directly toward the back lot. Once there, I drop to my knees to see over the edge.

There are still roughly twenty undead clawing at the back doors, banging, trying to get in somehow. Fortunately, their depleted motor functions don't allow them much force, but given time, they will find a way in. Some of them, probably about five, are already downstairs, but we needn't worry about them so much. There's something apocalyptic yet calming about the cars in the back lot; by now each that previously had a running motor has fallen silent, and seeing them motionless, plowed into each other, floods my brain with the sort of adrenaline fueled panic that caused their drivers to fail in their effort to save themselves. I can't shake a sense of underlying beauty in this stillness that makes their actions seem totally unavoidable.

"It's really something, eh Squared?"
"What's that?"
"Now that you don't hear the noise... you miss it."
"Yeah... they're still trying to get into the school."
"Maybe they smell us."
"Or Anderson and Jake downstairs."
"Is that where they went?"
"Yeah, Anderson wanted to check the lockers."
"I'll bet they don't find much."
"Unless someone was planning on taking out the school and left a bunch of guns."
"I don't think we're that lucky."

We're silent for a few minutes as we look at the hundreds of corpses both lying on and walking around the football field. I take notice of the fact that most of the buses are gone, and now that I think of it, many of them are missing from out front, which probably means that my worst case scenario prediction will come true; if the buses are gone, that means at least a few visiting band members were able to get back to their home town hospitals.

"Jeff?"

"Yeah Squared?"

"Think we'll get out of this alive?"

"You know… I don't know… united we stand, divided we fall."

"What?"

"Buddhist philosophy in a nutshell."

"…huh?"

"My professor said that one day and it stuck… I don't remember what he said before it… probably should have listened."

"Sounds like it… besides, you'll always have Julia. You know… she never talks about you…"

"That sounds about right. We both despise people who don't shut up about their loved ones. Do you have a girlfriend?"

"Not now."

"….consider yourself lucky."

"Dude, seriously?"

"Yeah… what if something happens to me, or her? What's the other one gonna do?"

"Say we never get evacuated, or this doesn't stop… what's the point in living if you don't have someone?"

"I wouldn't waste any opportunities… as far as we know, you only get one shot at life."

"Two shots."

"Touché."

We look out over the undead and the cars again. Nothing has changed in the past few minutes, though I notice it's awfully dark for 4:00, or however late it is. I look skyward to see the morning's cumulonimbus clouds ruffling like a dark gray blanket overhead. I roll my eyes and look down at the array of cars, snickering to myself when I see all the SUVs in the mass.

"What is it?" Squared asks.

"SUVs."

"What about them?"

"Suburbanite's useless vehicle."

"I doubt that'll really change if we get through this."

I smile at him. "If." He smiles back and holds out his fist, which I nudge with mine.

"God, it's great to know someone else is thinking that."

"Honestly," I continue. "How do you bring that up in conversation?"

"For now, it's our secret."

"Well... *if* it works out... I'll treat you to a cheesesteak."

"How about a Flyers game? I guess this season's done."

"It's locked out anyway. You know the last game I went to? Game 6, Tampa Bay."

"Jesus..."

"For three beautiful rounds, Keith Primeau became a god. When he tied it with two minutes left... ugh... I thought this was our year. Oh well. At least the Sabres'll never win the Cup."

A silent war of attrition begins as I slowly amble toward the greenhouse, the endgame coming when John Squared straightens up and brushes past me to get inside. "How are things outside?" Julia asks as we enter. I shrug. "How are things inside?" She shrugs back. With more useless chatter out of the way, I make my way to the food backpack for two granola bars and a bottle of water, tossing off my trench coat. When I'm done eating, I smack the crumbs off my hands and look at Julia. "Yes?" She asks.

"Did we hear where the military checks are?"

"...are we leaving?" Ava asks.

"Anderson's taking us to his check point... they announced it, but I missed it."

"Assuming it hasn't been compromised." Rich offers. "Where else could we go?"

"I've got nothing. We're not staying in a house, though. We need someplace big, open, and defensible with a lot of exits."

"Does this place exist?" Julia asks with a chuckle.

"Haven't the foggiest. I don't think we can get too comfortable here... it'll just make it harder to leave. If we could find some place with a safeguard... a mall maybe..."

"That's too much like Dawn of the Dead though." Anderson says, walking in. I jump back startled.

"...you scared the shit out of me."

"Remake or original Dawn?"

"Original, of course. How'd it go?"

Anderson holds up a few jackets, including a trench coat. He's wearing his fatigues again, which I hadn't expected would dry that fast. I insert a toothpick in my mouth.

"A few jackets, some hard candy, and $38. You didn't tell me they got in."

"I told you about Don..."

"Yeah, I assumed you took care of it... there were still like, ten inside."

"Shit... sorry."

"I took care of it... you just have to tell me that shit... anyway, I was hoping someone was gonna go psycho and shoot up the school..."

"I thought the same thing. Who's the trench coat gonna fit?"

"John Squared, probably. The other jacket's for Melody... Jake said she needed one."

"She *was* complaining about the cold..." I glance over to make sure she's still sleeping. "Well, since you found it, the hard candy's yours."

"Hate the stuff."

"Well, then that sucks."

"But the money's mine."

"Right. Oh, uh, Rich wants you to be in charge since you're in the military."

"...I *am* in charge. But we'll call you my subordinate."

"If we don't link up with the Guard, I suggested you, me, and Rich."

"Don't worry, we will. There's another check point like the one we set up at the reservoir on the 476 interchange at route 3. You'll be safe there, and they'll put me back in circulation after I debrief."

"How do we get there? Walk?" Ava asks.

"I have a car. It'll be a squeeze, but it beats walking." I respond, drinking some water.

"When do we get going?" John Squared asks. "Tonight?"

"No, no." Anderson says. "We'll wait for daylight... no unnecessary risks. Tonight, we hang tight, relax, and listen to the radio... and talk about what happens if we need to walk."

"And contingency plans..." I add. "...just incase it's abandoned."

"Right."

I let a smile escape as I think that Anderson and I are infallible leaders. Well, so far no one has died because of my actions, since Don's early exit was as a result of poor judgment on his part. I slide myself under a big comforter and Julia joins me in a few seconds, nestling her back against the front of my body. After removing my ragged toothpick, I tighten my right arm around her, pulling the comforter tighter as well. She always smells wonderful, so she must keep some perfume in her handbag. I wonder if Steve smells her as well.

I can't see his head, but it looks like Steve's simply not moving and his eyes are closed. Not even struggling, like maybe he's sleeping or something; we would be lucky indeed if the undead need sleep, luckier still if they die of thirst in a few days. I run my hand down Julia's chest to her stomach and put my hand beneath her shirt, working my finger underneath her bra, encountering a wall of warm, soft skin.

I hear her take a deep breath in as I slide my hand underneath the wire completely, and I let out a sigh of relief. I crane my head down and start kissing and biting her neck softly. I'm immediately distracted by a soft patting noise on the grimy glass of the greenhouse, a noise that signifies rain. Just after I realize how dark the room has become, Jake hops out of bed and turns the lights on, causing Rich to rocket out of bed wide-eyed. He looks around the room as he settles his breathing, and then locks his eyes on Anderson. "Oh, John's up."

"I didn't get your name." Anderson says to Rich, and Rich immediately extends his hand forth. "Richard McKnight. Just call me Rich." Anderson accepts his hand and shakes, nodding, and as he steps back toward the corner, I notice the pistols are fixed in holsters on his thighs. "You clean those, Anderson?" I ask. He turns and pulls one out of the holster, then spins it once on his finger so that he's gripping it by the barrel and holds it out to me. I look at him for a moment, puzzled. "Take it." He says.

I slide my hand carefully from underneath Julia's shirt and accept the weapon, looking at it for a few seconds. "Yeah, I guess you did." I say. He sits down on the desk. "If it gets wet, you have to. We've gotta oil 'em every two weeks." I nod while examining it, and then hold my hand out to give it back to him. Now he looks at me puzzled. "What?" I ask. "It's yours." He says, and I feel heat within my chest. "Really?" I imagine I sound like a little kid at Christmas as I examine the gun again.

"Yeah, what am I gonna do with two pistols?"

"Star in a John Woo movie?" I say, eliciting a look of confusion. "John Woo, the double gun guy... Face/Off?"

"Oh yeah... someone had to make that up?"

"Had to come from somewhere. The Criterion Collection put out a version of The Killer that I wanted bad... guess I lost my chance."

"Come on Jeff, it's not *that* bad yet." Squared says with a wink.

"Just give it back before we get to the checkpoint." Anderson says.

I can already hear the rain plodding down harder on the glass. I roll over to look at the clock/radio. It's 4:25 on the dot. "Shall we see what's on the radio?" I ask. Everyone awake says yes in some form or another. Despite turning on the lights, Jake has fallen asleep again. I click the radio on and make sure to keep the volume down.

"... insofar as the dissemination of the infected, it, uh... was not expected that they should spread at this rate. The president announced at a press conference today that there is believed to be no terrorist involvement, however, the office of Homeland Security has raised the threat level to red. As of now, the Canadian government has shut the border and all monitored flights have

been grounded until further notice. The news wire tonight brings us reports of infection breaking out within several local high schools, including Penna-wanee, Rockhaven East, and Poquessing."

"Jesus, you were right." Rich says. I hold my finger to my lips.

"Recapping our continuing coverage of the crisis for those of you just tuning in, the time is 4:27, once again we ask you to bear with us, but it would appear that in Delaware County, Pennsylvania, the dead... the dead are returning to life and have been committing acts of murder as far south as Chester and as far north as Willow Grove. Reports are still scattered at best, but our latest epidemiology shows that the outbreak began near a car accident on Route 3, West Chester Pike, and the Thomas Massey high school, both locations in Broomall. It has been confirmed that the dead are eating the flesh of the living in some cases, but often leave the bodies intact enough that they will remain mobile when they revive. It has been confirmed that those bitten are considered medically dead before they revive and begin attacking the living. Uh, it has also been confirmed that those who receive medical treatment for their wounds still die from their wounds, contrary to earlier reports. It is absolutely vital that you avoid the infected and the risen dead. They will be visually prominent via their blank stare, listless strides, and low moaning. Even close family members that are infected will not respond to emotional stimulus of any kind. In some cases, where the infected have been seen running, this may be even harder to judge. As such, we have been asked to recommend that you avoid running wherever possible in open ground. If you must, please do so while waving your arms, and if you encounter anyone else, make it known verbally that you are not infected, as it appears the infected are incapable of producing any similar forms of verbal communication. The infected and risen dead have been shown capable of infecting others with bite wounds, scratches, and contact of their blood with mucous membranes and the inside of the mouth. We cannot stress enough that any contact with the blood of the undead or infected may result in infection, which has proven and irreversible effects. As of 1:15pm this afternoon, a martial law is in effect in Delaware County, the... curfew is in effect from 6:00pm to 7:30am, anyone outside during those times is subject to arrest. It is suggested that those surviving no longer seek occupancy in private residences, no matter how safe or well guarded they may appear. Those surviving in private residences are urged to make their way to the nearest rescue center..."

"Rescue center!" I spout, hushing myself immediately.

"...Broomall Police Station, Broomall Pa. Lima Mall, Media Pa. Uh, it was reported earlier that the Mercy Community Hospital was to be an emergency rescue center, but there has been no contact with the personnel since the beginning of the crisis. The military is attempting to set up further rescue

centers as time presses on, but... uh, resources are being concentrated on containing the infection. More reports on the subject as time presses on..."

I click off the radio and instantly join every set of eyes in the room pointed at Anderson. He takes a deep breath and stands up.

"Okay... martial law means the military's in charge, so here's what's gonna happen... Grey and John Squared, at dawn tomorrow morning we're pullin' recon... everyone stays here while we scout out a route to the check point. If we can make it there and back in one piece and verify that it's still operational, we're all headed back, at that point they're gonna put me back on duty and you guys are gonna get evac'd. If that's not working out, we're headed to the station, and if that doesn't work out, the mall. It's gonna be a tight squeeze but we're all going in Grey's car."

"Why can't we go with you?" Melody asks.

"It's just recon... if everything else is totally fucked, we at least have a foothold here."

"What happens if we can't go anywhere else?" John Squared asks.

"Look, right now we have three options. We can start revising the plan once we've exhausted one. Once we're done recon, we're all sticking together, so don't worry."

I'm immediately impressed by the effect his words have; maybe it's the fact that everyone knows he's in the military, or perhaps it's the authority of his delivery, but it's great to see everyone calmed down for once. Never one for sitting on my hands, however, I go back to thinking about what they said in the broadcast, skipping over the bits that were seemingly ripped from every Zombie movie I've ever seen. Mercy hasn't been contacted since the beginning? "Shit." I say softly. Melody, who is apparently just waking up, yawns as she asks her question. "What?" I am stoic, but I manage to prop myself up as I organize my thoughts.

"Jesus Christ..."

"Spit it out!" Ava barks.

"God, I... it's like everything was planned."

"How do you mean?" Rich asks.

"Well, notice how they managed to trap everyone on the field?"

"Yeah?"

"The hospital's out of commission... there's that car accident on West Chester Pike..."

"So?" John Squared asks.

"It's like a surgical strike."

"Huh?"

"Well, the accident was going to require the assistance of cops, firemen, and EMTs, and it cut out the most obvious route for people to leave, I mean, 476 is the best way to get anywhere around here. Then there's the hospital, the place where everyone would go if they needed medical treatment, then the school..."

"What's the connection?"

"Well, there's no direct connection, but it's as if someone made these strikes with the intention of cutting the town off."

"You think it's, like, a terrorist attack?" Melody asks.

"Can't rule it out."

"You do make a decent point all the same." Rich says.

"Well, whatever. The police station isn't too far to drive. We can leave and be there in a few minutes if we have to."

"Uh, have you ever been there?" Anderson asks.

"No, why?"

"I have, and it's really not that big... if a lot of people have already gone there, we could be out of luck as far as space goes."

"Wait, why have you been there?" Melody asks.

"I was arrested."

"I guess that's a risk we have to take." I interrupt.

"We could go to the mall." Melody says.

"Oh, you'd just love that, wouldn't you?" Ava responds.

"Ava?" I say crossly.

"Jesus, listen to the rain..." Jake says.

As he says that, I realize we've been shouting over the pounding rain. I climb out of my comforter and throw my trench coat back on.

"What are you doing?" John asks, and I shrug, pointing to the green-house door. I throw my bowler on and open it. "Anyone want to come with?" I ask. It would appear everyone wants to stay dry. I look back for a moment to see Julia, Ava, and Melody get up and exit, presuma-bly to go to the bathroom. As soon as I get through the door, the rain begins collecting in my bowler rim; is this storm the remnant of some hurricane I didn't hear about? I carefully climb over the guardrail around the greenhouse and take a few steps before nearly slipping; the spill serves as a good reminder to stay far away from the edges of a wet roof with zero safety features.

Keeping my center of gravity low, I stop five feet from the edge and look down to see the rain carrying dark streaks of miscellaneous trash and body fluids toward the low points where they gather as pud-dles. The damp bodies, cluttered all over the field and parking lot, become giant lumps of clothing and flesh through the glistening haze. The sky is black enough that I momentarily mistake it for night; in fact, the only light I see comes in the form of a shrill white glow ema-nating from several light posts. The only thing I don't see is the undead.

I look off at the bleachers around the football field and remember that Mursak and I used to sit about here, smoking a cigar and looking off at the vague outline of sparse traffic on West Chester Pike. He was on the bleachers on the big night. I imagine him traversing the crowd like a hyped-up spider monkey, finding a safe spot and hunkering down in silence. The reality, I know, must be far grimmer than that. Maybe John Squared had something when he mentioned closure. I have to wonder, though, can one truly get closure from seeing the un-dead? Wouldn't that be the opposite of closure?

If I were writing about this at home, I'd have written that down and worked it into my next story somehow. I sigh as I imagine going back into the greenhouse and writing it down; what would be the point? Maybe I can use that concept to convince someone not to find his or her parents. Something moves to my left, derailing my thought train as I crane my head over to see someone running out of the cem-etery gates. I restrain my urge to call out to them, instead taking a few steps forward. He continues running as if possessed, crossing the parking lot while completely ignoring any doors or vehicles, and as far as I can tell there are no undead in pursuit; it must a runner.

Watching him run as though his lungs have infinite capacity makes me feel winded, but more than anything, I'm curious as to where he's going in such a rush. He's not chasing anyone, unless the sound and texture of the rain somehow confuses the undead. He runs all the way to the other side of the parking lot and climbs up on the car at the back of the mass of stopped traffic plugging up what should be the entrance to the rear lot, disappearing without a sound. For a moment, I pretend this is okay.

I imagine Julia in the bathroom, hearing footsteps and naïvely sticking her head through the bathroom door, only to have... she's on the first floor. I have to know where it's going. I turn and walk back to the greenhouse, barely able to restrain myself from running. I get a brief mental image of how many horrible things could have happened while I was out here looking at the rain, things I wouldn't be able to hear with the ever-present precipitation and thunder. When I make it back to the door Julia has already returned from the bathroom, so I breathe a sigh of relief. I step back inside, and immediately all eyes are on me. "Anderson, John Squared, you're coming with me." Anderson cocks his head and raises his eyebrows. I throw off the bowler.

"Nothing major." Anderson's glance suggests he sees through my ruse as he takes a holster off his leg and throws it to me. I go to the desk and pull out gray tape, taping it to my belt loop first, then around my waist. When I remember that my trench coat has a belt on it, I remove the tape and replace it with a real one, and then adjust the holster. I fix the strap to tighten it around my thigh, and then pull the Beretta from underneath my pillow. I yank out the magazine, look at it, then slap it back in. To complete the move, I chamber a round by pulling the top back, then put the safety on and slide the Beretta in my holster.

"Why do you never want me to go?" Rich asks. I turn back and look at him. "It's not that I don't want you to go... I think you make everyone else feel safe." Rich nods, apparently buying my line of crap.

I grab my hockey stick and leather gloves, Anderson takes the crowbar, and John Squared takes one of the steel rods. We take the stairs, avoid the glass, and exit on the second level. I stop for a moment and look out into the hall before running toward a perpendicular hallway. We run down the math hall until we get to the doorway that leads down to the breezeway. From here, I can see the corpse I dispatched the previous day when I was coming up the steps with Julia and Ava.

"Clear so far... so, why are we doing this?" Anderson asks.
"I saw a runner headed to the front."
"From where?"
"Back parking lot."
"So shouldn't we be checking the gym?"
"I figured we'd start as far away as possible and work back."
"...I don't get it, but okay."

Rather than argue, I walk down the rest of the steps and walk into the hallway that leads from the auditorium to the main lobby. Anderson and Squared leak out of the opening behind me with Anderson peeling back toward the auditorium while Squared looks into the doorway across from me. "Shh." Anderson stops us suddenly. We all freeze, forcing ourselves to listen to the rain as it throttles the building. "It's quiet." Neither Squared nor I can restrain ourselves from snickering as I start toward the gym, trying to suppress the manufactured image of a single member of the undead, silhouetted and unmoving in one of the school's hallways. Is there some reason why a single, unmoving one seems more terrifying to me than a pack of them running?

"Basement?" Anderson asks. I turn back, unable to debate him. We enter the stairwell and descend into the basement, where the only light is barely able to streak through the watery windows, leaving every color washed out to a nauseating gray. A flash of lightning shows me that there is nothing else in the hallway before me. I try to walk confidently down the hall with my associates in tow while Anderson sidesteps quietly behind me. The generator in the next room over is whirring loudly, not allowing me to hear anything else. I choke

up on my hockey stick as I look through a doorway to one of the basement level classrooms; I can't see anything aside from a few scattered
desks, so I squint and press my face up against it, preparing myself
from something horrible to flash in front of me.

I jump when the lightning flashes, and before the light subsides I
manage to catch a glimpse of six undead standing on the opposite side
of the windows and another one coming down the steps to their left.
Shuddering with a sudden burst of adrenaline, I rip myself out of the
doorway and press my back against the wall. "What, what!?" John
Squared squeaks. "S-six… at the windows." Both of them instinctively
look through the door glass, and a sinking feeling in my stomach tells
me to peek out of the door alcove and look toward the opposite end
of the hall toward a fire exit that leads directly to where they were
standing. I can't see anything, which makes me more nervous. Lightning flashes after a minute, illuminating the empty hall as Squared and
Anderson leap back from the window.

"Maybe they chased someone down?" Squared offers.

"That would somehow make this *better*?" I ask.

"There's eight now…" Anderson starts. "We should get the fuck
outta here."

"We've got guns…?" Squared hesitantly counters.

"No." Anderson and I promptly whisper. I allow him to continue.
"You don't want to fire off a gun and tell the next hundred out on the
lawn where they can get in."

"I didn't see any out on the lawn." I manage to choke through a
catch in my throat. Before I continue, I have to wipe a tear out of my
eye. "Let's just go."

"Wait… before we go, everyone just take a deep breath and calm
down." Anderson says.

We do so, making a painfully slow exit to the steps even though I
can feel sparks of electric energy snaking around my shoulders and
putting in my legs spasm, no doubt telling me that I should be running.
Once at the top of the stairwell, at the second floor, I feel a bit more

relaxed and I can walk comfortably. When we arrive at the green-house, I see that Julia has fallen back asleep, as have Ava and Jake. "Find anything interesting?" Melody asks. I shake my head, throw off my trench coat and crawl back into bed with Julia. I feel uncomfortable with the gun holster on and wearing boots. I've never been comfortable sleeping in regular clothes. I'm not in bed more than a few seconds before I get out and sit on the garden row, across from Steve.

On the other side, Jake is asleep on a row and Anderson is talking to Rich. Melody appears to be listening intently to Anderson while he drones on about something having to do with his missing sniper certification by only one target. I look past them, back at Jake, and finally at Steve. Fear wrings another wave of shock up my spine as I see him staring up at the ceiling; despite three people being almost within arm's reach of him, he's not even agitated. I close my eyes and again take a deep breath. It doesn't mean anything.

"…used to work for the bus company, but they laid me off when the damn Republicans took over the school board, cut back four bus drivers, and set the routes longer and earlier… it only got worse from there." Rich says.

"How long until you became a…?" Jake starts.

"Bum? A few weeks…"

"Why, though?" John Squared asks. "Didn't you have any friends, or family?"

"No family… not in this state anyway… that doesn't matter. Everyone I've met knows someone crying out for help… they help out of pity, and that becomes scorn. You talk about it with friends, you know… 'it's always something new with Rich'. You hate people that rely on your sympathy… you stop giving them things because you feel *obligated*… that's no way to get what you want. Some people can do that… I couldn't."

"And your wife just…" John Squared stops immediately.

"So you live at the school?" Melody asks.

"Well, you find places to sleep where no one bothers you… where you won't be seen in the light. Stay someplace where people throw out lots of food."

"Eww…"

"You'd think donut shops would be the best, you know? They tend to throw out whatever they baked that day when they close, but it's still fresh… can't stay there, though…"

"Cops." Anderson offers.

"Exactly." Rich says with a scoff. "Cop in a donut shop…"

"Are you the bum that people said was living in the school like three years ago?" John Squared asks.

"No, that was Jay Wegman." I say.

"How do you know?"

"He told me."

"I never slept in the school." Rich says. "I stole one of the fire blankets to sleep and sometimes I used the bathrooms. The one door near the gym sticks open at night…"

"Fire blankets? That's smart." Anderson says. "Terrific insulation."

"How long you been living here?" John Squared asks.

"Four years now."

"I can't believe we haven't run into each other." Anderson says.

"Why's that?"

"We climbed the roof a lot."

"That was *you*? Oh wow… small world… god I hated you guys…"

"Really!?"

"Well yeah… cops come through here every once in awhile… and I could hear you climbing around and talking up there… someone'd call the cops and they'd stick around 'til morning trying to find who it was, and I'd have to hide."

"Well, I hope we're making up for it now." I add.

"In spades, my friend. You know, I truly feel we're through the worst of this… I mean, even if it goes on for months. The first few days have to be the worst. If we can make it somewhere safe, like a rescue center… oh, they'll treat me the same as everyone else…"

"That's an interesting perspective." Anderson adds after a moment.

"When you live in a dumpster, equality doesn't sound so bad."

"Don't you get… food stamps or something?" Melody asks.

"Don't want 'em. I don't want money I didn't work for. I've heard people say my tax dollars paid off the money I'd be taking, that I could pay it off again when I got back on my feet... but I don't want to make my problem anyone else's."

"That's why I signed up..." Anderson interjects. "Good way to go to college and make some money."

"Every once in awhile I go somewhere to look for work, but that's been tough since Bill got remarried."

"Bill?"

"One of my friends from the depot. We kept in touch after I got laid off, he used to let me spend the night when it was really cold... stop in for a shower, or borrow clothes for an interview... his second wife had kids, so... can't blame her for not wanting me around. He was a saint to keep it up as long as he did. He's one of the few people I worried about when this started... him and Nancy..."

"Your wife?" Melody asks.

"No, Nancy's homeless too."

"Did you ever have any kids?"

"Being homeless wouldn't have changed that."

"What?"

"You phrased it in the past tense, did I *ever* have kids? It wouldn't matter if I was homeless or not, I'd still have 'em. Anyway, it's been awhile since I've been around high school kids... things have changed a lot since I used to drive a bus."

"How do you mean?" I ask.

"Well, just listening to you. Cell phones, computers, sex, and I haven't heard any of you mention anything about drugs."

"They used to talk about drugs on the bus!?" John Squared asks.

"Not directly, but you don't need a college education to figure it out, if you know what I mean..."

I remove the holster and my boots, tuning out the continuing conversation as I lie next to Julia and close my eyes. I grab my bottle of water and take drink as I pull Julia closer to me, causing her to loose an unconscious sigh of relief. I lay there and look at the back of her head, listening to the pounding rain, and even if I've gotten enough sleep, my body's exhaustion overtakes my mind and I pass out in a few minutes.

I often sleep when I'm not tired. I've done it during all of college so far, and usually when I do, I wake up several times and try to go back to sleep. Eventually I get up, but I'm not accepting that this time. The only thing to do when I'm awake is wait to go back to sleep, so I toss and turn with my eyes opening and closing involuntarily until I get comfortable enough to allow my brain to shut down for a while. What dreams I have are all short and don't make sense, yet somehow they manage to tie into reality. At least once in the few seconds that I'm awake, I snicker to myself about how people used to say I had potential. I roll over and eventually pass out again.

I estimate I've been out for roughly half an hour, but a quick look at the clock reveals that it's now 11:30pm. I glance over to see that Julia is awake, then look to see that everyone else in the room is lying down like they're sleeping, but their eyes are open. It looks like my plan to keep everyone awake at night worked. I look over and see Anderson's spot vacated, so I quietly make it known to Julia that I'm awake. "Evening, my love." She turns around to look at me already smiling. "Hello darling." I put my hand on her cheek and kiss her, then pull away. "Did you see where John went?" I whisper. "Roof. How did you sleep?" I pull out of the covers.

"Okay, but now I'm probably going to be awake for like, 20 hours."
"Maybe not." She responds.
"Oh?"
"You haven't eaten much... that's why you're tired. Everybody else has been taking their rations except you..."
"...good point."
"Here..."

She reaches into the food bag and pulls out a can of peaches. "Thanks love." I pull open the top, drink the juice, and then start eating the peaches. I've never much been a fan of peaches, but given that or nothing, they go down quite well. When I nudge myself around a little more I feel like I have to piss again. Rather than chance the bathroom, I opt to step outside. It's still raining, so I put on my trench coat and bowler. "Where are you going?" Julia asks. "Piss. Be right back."

I realize as I'm exiting that I broke the laws of horror films by saying the infamous last line. On my way out Anderson brushes past me, not saying anything. I make a subtle nod and he returns it, then I circle around to the observatory and relieve myself. There's a flash of lightning, followed almost immediately by booming thunder. I think nothing of it until a few seconds later when I hear what sounds like thunder again. I've never heard of two separate thundering noises accompanying one lightning strike. The second thunder sound probably belonged to the strike I just witnessed, and the one before belonged to a previous strike. I toss this into my mental recycling bin and go to put a toothpick in my mouth, but the container is empty.

I come back in feeling relieved and return to my bed after disrobing my outward articles. It's quite dark outside, almost as if there is no moon. I sit up and look around the room, noticing the scant reflections of light off the open eyes of my compatriots. Ava, Rich, Julia, and both Johns are awake, but no one is speaking, perhaps because they think everyone else is still asleep. I rest my head on my pillow again, and when I get comfortable, I sort of half notice my pillow vibrate softly. I lift my head up and look around. Not hearing anything out of the ordinary, I rest my head back down on the pillow, prompting Julia to face me. "What's wrong?" She asks. "Nothing, I just... felt like my pillow was vibrating."

"I felt it too." She says. I prop myself up on my elbow and look down at her, and then I hear a squeak somewhere below me, followed what sounds like someone falling over beneath us. With this, Anderson snaps up out of bed and John Squared follows suit. "What is it?" Julia asks. I shush her. "Are we all up here?" I ask. "Yeah, I took a head count." Anderson immediately responds, getting up. My eyes dart needlessly in little circles as I concentrate all of my senses toward listening. When I realize that all I can hear is the sound of rain smacking against the glass, I get the horrible inertia feeling of being in a car moments before an accident, promptly accompanied by a sharp wave of dizziness. "Feel that?" Anderson asks. I didn't hear that. Nothing just happened. Nobody felt or heard anything.

"Feel what?" Rich asks. I reach over, open a toothpick box, and stuff some inside the minuscule container a moment before I hear a glass pane breaking within the building. There is a heavy slam beneath us and everybody jumps. Shakily, mechanically, I reach over grab my boots and start ramming my feet into them. I notice that, upon seeing this, tears have begun to pour down Julia's face. I try to ignore the quick, distant footsteps, but I can't ignore the shallow gagging noise, followed by another loud slam. Somehow, I can feel my brain pass through a threshold that sees me standing up and walking through the door to the stairwell. "What are you *doing*!?" Anderson spits from behind me. As I step toward the railing, I can't help but get the feeling I'm watching a movie, or that someone else is controlling my body.

Someone runs up to the landing and immediately slips in the broken glass, falling in a way that allows me to see a thick green gash across his pale and swollen face a moment before he's up and running again. I throttle backward, pulling the door shut as I see at least seven more come up the steps behind him. "UP! GET UP NOW!" Anderson shouts over the sound of flimsy metal school desks clattering down the steps. The light switch is flipped on in the same moment that one of them slams into the door, and I feel like every molecule in my body explodes. "HELP-HELP-HELP!" I bellow, shoving back into the door. "GET THE DESK!" Anderson shouts. I look back to see everyone scrambling in a mess to gather things together, and behind them, I see Steve thrashing maniacally at his bindings.

Another heavy slam comes and pushes the door open a crack, pumping a quick burst of air that smells like rotten meat into the room. Suddenly, my fear fuels my muscles into getting the door shut again, and this time I let go of the handle. "MOVE!" Anderson shouts, prompting me to leap away from the door as he and Rich shove the desk up against it. "WHAT DO WE DO?" Melody suddenly screams. "I DON'T KNOW!" I shout in return. Feverish clawing accompanies a dissonant chorus of moans as John and Rich push against the desk harder. "THE STEPS!" I shout, pointing behind Melody. She gets up quickly, opens the door, and looks down. I turn away, hearing a tinny clatter. "NO NO NO!" Anderson screams.

Melody looks down confused for a moment, and then I see every muscle in her upper body contract over the course of two seconds. "OH *MY* GOD!" She burbles, shaking so hard she can barely shove the door shut. "WE'RE TRAPPED!" Jake screams. No we're not. "Get a weapon, now! Roof, roof, roof! HURRY!" Suddenly, my brain is overtaken by unmistakable and unexplainable clarity as I throw on my trench coat, grab my Beretta holster and belt it back around my hips, then pick up my hockey stick and gloves. Julia grabs my cane, Anderson already has the crowbar in his hand, Rich has the bat, and everyone else gets steel rods. "As soon as I move, they're gonna get in!" Anderson shouts urgently.

Something slams into the door that Melody just closed; she jumps back, howls in fright, and immediately starts crying. I pat my pockets quickly to check for my wallet and my car keys as I try to formulate a plan. "The loft! Above the auditorium!" I head for the greenhouse door and look back at Anderson and Rich to find their eyes wide with fear. "Get *OUT!*" Anderson screams with such authority that I swear I feel myself start to lose bladder control.

Everyone files out of the room as I stand by the door watching him and Rich, and as I watch, I yank my inhaler out of my pocket in self-preservation. Anderson and Rich look at each other, nodding heavily. "One, two, THREE!" As though it was rehearsed, they leap away from the desk and bolt past Steve through the open door as the desk starts squealing against the tile floor.

I slam the door shut, turn, leap over the railing and starting running into the freezing rain as the door glass shatters behind me. I turn to see the undead spill out of the greenhouse with surreal organization before allowing themselves to be momentarily contained by the railing, and when I turn again I can see Anderson already far ahead of me with several people just behind him; they're already jumping onto the cover that separates the shop hallways from the band room. "ANDERSON!" I scream through the rain. There's no way he can hear me. Just beneath him, a swarm of undead cast gesticulating shadows as they desperately try to reach up. "DON'T SPLIT UP!" I shout as my voice cracks.

Julia and I get to an overhang where we are able to see inside the science rooms across the courtyard, and when lightning flashes I can see that the undead have filled the rooms. Before I jump down, I look over toward the auditorium roof to see our separated comrades about 200 feet away, standing in front of a set of metal doors that lead to the loft as Anderson picks the lock. I turn back mid-stride to see that John Squared and Melody are right behind me as I continue to shove Julia in front of me.

Anderson quickly gets aggravated and pries the doors open with a crowbar, causing three walking corpses to fall into the group. I grab Julia's arm and turn around. "Come on! COME ON!" Julia, John Squared, Melody and I start running back in the opposite direction as screams, thudding noises, and two gunshots fight the rain and the distance to get to us. I don't stop to look back. "WHERE ARE WE GOING?" Julia screams. "Come on!" As we run back across the roof toward the breezeway, I look back to the overhang and seven of them spill over the edge, making hard contact with the roof but instantly getting up.

"Breezeway, breezeway!" I shout. I watch my three compatriots run across the breezeway roof to the other section of the building, terrified that one of them is going to slip and fall to certain incapacitation followed by what will surely be the most terrifying and excruciating final moment to their life that they could have imagined; when they begin helping each other up to the higher segment of the roof, I turn to face the rear and start backing up, trying hard to keep myself directly in the middle of the breezeway. Four walkers fall off the higher part of the roof onto the breezeway, revealing a dozen or so behind them. Another gunshot emerges from the loft, only distracting me for a moment. That could be good, bad, or both.

Suddenly, a runner parts the undead and falls on the breezeway roof in mid stride with a sickening crunch; his foot has broken at the ankle and now appears to be only attached by skin and sinew. Unabated but for a hobble, he keeps running at me, and as he draws closer

I channel the latent anger of Anderson's possible demise into a combination of three swift blows with my hockey stick, sending the beast flying off the roof into the courtyard. "Jeff! We're up! Come on!" I turn and run, stepping on a metal chair and having them grab my arms to pull me up. Once I'm up, I take off toward the roof of the gym. I keep my eye on the greenhouse, which is now across the courtyard.

When lightning flashes again, I can see dozens walking in a scattered line across the roof and a few running away from the greenhouse. In another hundred feet, they'll be able to flank us by making a simple right turn. I take the group to the edge of the roof, staring down a fifteen foot drop down to the next segment. "Grab the edge, hang down, and go limp when you land. NOW!" I shout. I'm the first to drop off once every else is hanging off the edge, allowing me the first look into the bank of dark windows parallel to everyone's dangling legs.

A quick flash of lightning reveals a dozen faces inside the classroom. "Down! NOW!" Melody and Squared drop immediately, but Julia stays hanging just long enough for one of the undead to punch through the glass, grab her leg, and start pulling it toward the broken shards and a pair of lips chapped to the point of laceration. Without hesitating, I rip the pistol off my hip, shove it through the glass and pop off a round, sending a spurt of blood from the darkness as my arm flies up into the window frame from the report. While letting a groan of pain slip, I swing my left arm around Julia's waist, falling back against the roof with her on top of me.

"Are you okay?" She mutters. I nod, and then quickly wiggle her off me as I remember what's happening. "Quick, go, go, go!" I spit, stumbling to my feet as I push Julia in front of me to catch up with Squared and Melody, who are already running. I struggle to shove the gun back in the wet holster on my hip, looking up to see Melody and Squared headed toward the front of the school. "Left, left!" I shout, prompting them cut swiftly toward the roof of the gymnasium. I look back toward the broken window to see one of the runners stepping off and falling fifteen feet, landing with an audible crack. Two more fall down on top of him, in effect shielding their fall. All three of them are wearing hospital gowns. When they get up and start toward us, I push Julia ahead again. "Stop that!" She shouts back at me. "JUST RUN!"

We finally catch up to the others at the maintenance door that leads into the top of the gym. I try the handle, but I jump back when my fidgeting is returned by heavy slams from the other side. "Up on the roof! Climb!" I shout. Squared and Julia get up quickly, but Melody struggles, so I put my hand on her ass and give her a hard shove up. I grab a hold and kick myself up, hearing the quick splash of running feet behind me. "Oh GOD!" Julia shouts, grabbing my arm and pulling me the rest of the way. "What now, you fucking idiot!? There's nowhere else to go!" Squared shouts. I've forced us up onto a curved section of roof where the only place to go is down.

Down. I look at my feet to see a raised panel on the roof, so I slam the hockey stick down hard and it instantly caves, landing after an instant in the ceiling compartment just beneath the roof. "WATCH OUT!" Melody screams, and I instinctively push Julia out of the way as I spin around holding out the hockey stick. "Behind me!" I order, watching a hospital-gowned runner slip on the roof as he approaches. The moment he pitches forward I bring the stick up, crushing it into the under side of his jaw with a wet snap hard enough to knock him back.

"Inside the roof, now!"

"Jeff, look out!" Squared shouts.

"Watch your feet, stick to the crossbeams!"

Julia and Melody ease themselves down through the roof, which drops down to above the ceiling of the actual gym. Three more runners pull themselves up on the roof as my heart hammers against my sternum. Feeling convinced that I'll miss with my bravado, I make two massive sweeps with my hockey stick, first on my left, then my right, knocking down two of the beasts, then I step forward awkwardly with my left foot and land in a forward squat, ramming the end of my stick into one of their chests. John Squared leaps over to the one on the left and starts beating his head in, producing a thick blackish liquid that mixes with the rain water as it streams down the roof.

I kick the Zombie in the abdomen, sending him back as the other one gets to his feet. I swing my arm out hard, letting the stick slide through my hand until the knob hits the bottom of my palm. I swing it over my head once for momentum and throttle it into the cheek of the first one, snapping his head to the left as he trips over his feet and falls back again. The next one gets up and comes at me with both arms flailing. Keeping the stick close to my body, I swing it up on the left and right to knock his hands up, then slap one side into his ribcage hard enough to crack a few and belt him across the left side of his face in one continuous motion. I spin around and smack the next one in the rib cage and my vision starts to go purple as the asthma finally gets the better of me.

I run my foot along the roof until I find the opening, and when something grabs my leg, I immediately thrash my feet. "Stop!" John Squared shouts as he guides my legs down to a support beam. Inside, Julia and Melody are leaning across a heating vent. "Careful!" I welcome the opportunity to slow down and catch my breath as we slowly make our way across the support beams, trying to avoid the tiling spots in the ceiling that represent the only thing between us and a fifty foot drop to the gym floor. I hear footsteps across the roof and one of them jumps into the hole we came through, falling right through the ceiling tile and smacking into the ground below. I kick out one of the tiles below me to see that the gym appears to be empty. One of the walls of the gym is a few dozen feet ahead of us, as is an exposed ventilation shaft that leads directly into it.

I ease my way across the beam and move carefully around the others as they grab my waist so I don't fall. I grab two of the beams across the ceiling and kick out a section of the ventilation shaft. "Come on!" They climb into the shaft behind me and we start crawling toward the maintenance room. I start sneezing wildly, and somewhere in the back of my head, I can hear my mother telling me that I forgot to take my allergy medication. "Are you alright?" Julia asks. "I'll live." I shoot back between sneezes, but as a headache settles in, I wonder if I will.

The bottom of the shaft starts giving less as I reach what I assume must be the wall. Just in front of us, the shaft turns sharply downward; in my mind's eye, I can remember seeing the opening to this shaft against the wall on the ground floor. "Down." I spin myself around to go feet first, ease my legs down and spread them to retard my descent, then drop my hockey stick down and press my arms against the walls. The inside of this shaft is concrete, which allows for good friction on the way down.

The instant I hit the floor I slide out and pick up my hockey stick, looking around the enormous, dark gym, which is totally empty and silent save for the one unmoving corpse on the floor. "Come on, be careful." I shout up the vent as I hear the others descending. I look to my feet to see water marks on the floor leading to the open doors next to the vent. I run over and slam them shut as I see Julia's legs come out the bottom of the vent.

"Pick it up a little!" I shout, immediately hearing Melody's voice from the top. "I can't do it!" She says. "Get *down* here! Don't forget what's coming after you!" I hear a little squeal from her as she presumably slides herself into the shaft. "Jeff!" Julia shouts, I spin and press my back against the wall as a runner comes at me, but I can't react quick enough to lift my stick and hit it. Instead, I see the thick head of my cane come up and strike it in the jaw as it gets close enough to grab me, causing it to fall back. Julia jumps at it on the ground and repeatedly smashes its skull with the cane as John Squared squirms out of the vent. A chunk of skull flips over my shoulder and clicks off the wall beside him.

The sound of multiple shattering glass panes emerges from the hall followed by the terrible, off-key, harmonizing moans of the undead. I look across the gym to the opposite side to see two undead entering the gym from the girl's locker room door. "Melody!" I shout. With that, I hear a slipping sound and a scream from within the vent before she hits the bottom, having fallen about five feet. "Are you okay?" I ask instinctively. "I can't see, I can't see!" She squeals. I grab at something of hers inside the darkness of the shaft, I think her shirt collar, and drag her out to the gym floor. She immediately begins dusting herself off and making general noises of disapproval as I look around. There is a loud bang at the gym door to my right, and just now I notice the sound of at least a dozen scuffling steps. I drop my head and sigh, attempting to ignore my lungs and my headache.

Julia leads us across the gym as the doors fly open and rotting corpses pour into the spot where we were just standing. Once at the other side, I throw the doors open and jump out in the hallway, looking left to see at least twenty of them spread out and pressing in from the end of the hall, then right to see a dense group of probably a hundred coming from the front doors. We're trapped on both sides. I go to turn around, but more of them are coming through both sets of doors on the opposite side of the gym. "The office!" Julia shouts. We run across the hall to the main office door, but it's locked. I step back and pull out my Beretta. Holding it with one hand, I point it at the lock and fire, causing the gun to jerk back as I let out a yelp of pain. I then hit the door handle with the butt of the gun and it falls off.

I look over to the right to see John Squared holding his steel rod in both hands and using it to push the undead back in huge groups while Julia swings wildly at the undead on the opposite side, landing head shots that knock them down; between the two of them, John Squared is doing a better job of keeping them back. Melody is standing behind me, squeezing either side of my coat. I kick the door open and step into the frame, holstering my pistol. "JULES! COME ON!" Melody turns and runs past me in the door, followed immediately by Julia. "SQUARED! COME ON! LET'S GO!"

He turns his head for half a second to look as he sends his steel rod through an undead woman's skull before getting it lodged in her eye socket. As he tries to pull it out, another walking corpse staggers forward to John's right and crumples behind him, taking the rod out of his hands. "JOHN!" I don't think he can hear me. "JOHN!" He starts gasping and letting out short, stressed moans as his hands come down together and start smacking at something.

I can't see what's happening because of his trench coat, but I do see and hear what looks and sounds like five pounds of raw, wet meat slapping to the ground in a steaming pile, followed by about a gallon of blood. His greasy, membranous innards spew forth as he struggles to push the undead away at the same time he tries to pull his intestines back into his body. He's not screaming, but letting out grunts of excited pain that are quickly getting louder and closer spaced as he no doubt begins to understand the futility of this attempted reintegration.

As he falls over, I can see the fresh hole torn in his abdomen as the undead greedily consume his organs. He looks directly at me, wincing as one of them tears his liver free from his ribcage.

I scream as I slam the door shut and push the girls in further. "But John!" Melody says. "He's DEAD! RUN!" I can't believe that just happened. I turn to push their soggy bodies down the hall, my hand landing on Melody's breast as I push hard enough to knock her over. I grab her hand and pull her up as I rush Julia forward, stopping with both of them and pulling open the door to the conference room. I thrust them inside, looking back at the door we came through; it blows open with the bloody hands of undead as they stumble in and crawl toward us, dragging Squared's body with their feet.

I look to the other side of the office to see at least four more pressing in on us, so I push the door shut and take in the conference room. Julia is already pushing the center desk toward the wall, so Melody and I join her as the wall bulges from the assault of the undead. We all back away slowly until we make it to the opposing wall. "Oh god, he's dead, he's dead..." Julia mutters, sobbing slightly. I hug her against me. I want to say something, but I'm staring wide eyed into the wall. Did that really happen? Is John Squared really dead? I kiss the top of her head and snap my head over to the windows, which start at waist height and stretch to the ceiling.

"Now what do we do?" Melody asks softly as the banging continues. The walls are flimsy and will undoubtedly give at any second. I drop my stick, grab a chair and throw it over my head into the window glass, which shatters about the same time the necrotic hands of the undead start to rip though the panel walls. I grab the stick and hop up on the heating unit, looking out the window; beneath the frame is a sheet of grating that separates us from the basement windows. I look back and forth, finding no infected on the grating. "Come on..." The two of them hop up behind me and come out. Looking down again, I see nothing but water collecting over an orgy of shattered glass. They went through the basement after all.

I jump up on the concrete edge of the grating and look over; the front doors of the school are swarming with undead, but the driveway for the buses is largely unoccupied. Most of the ones by the door are just standing there, apart from a few who are gravitating toward us. I grab Julia's hand and we jump through the bushes onto the grass, making for my car. I don't see any runners outside, but it appears the walkers have every exit and entrance covered.

When I get within distance of my car, I unlock it and jump inside, starting it up immediately. "What about the others?" Julia asks as Melody squeezes into the back seat. I look up at the roof toward the doors Anderson and his group were trying to go through, then roll down the window and look to the left of where we hung the band uniforms. The doors are hanging open; there is nobody up there, but thin wisps of pinkish fluid run over the edges along with the rainwater. The undead near the auditorium doors are turning toward the car, so I slip it into gear and start driving. "They're still in there!" Melody shouts from the backseat. "I'm *not* leaving." I say flatly. I click on the high beams and emergency flashers, pressing my hand into the horn.

I drive out of the school's driveway the wrong way, where one is supposed to enter, drive through the vacant street, and pull back in the alleged exit of the driveway, pressing on the horn repeatedly. "Come on..." I mutter. The dead are now gravitating toward the driveway.

"Come on..."
"They're coming... turn off the *lights!*" Melody sputters.
"Good..."
"Good!? B-..."
"If they're still in there they might be able to get out..."
"But..."
"Just SHUT *UP!*"

I cruise through the driveway entrance again, pulling back into the street as I try to look past Julia to see the front of the school. I pull into the exit again and go slower, still laying heavily on the horn. I scan across the gathering hoard, knowing that I won't be able to make another pass without having to plow through them. "Look!" Julia shouts, trying to draw my attention to something I saw the moment the word came out of her mouth; twenty of the undead fall over like dominos, spreading out in an arc as a cluster of people rush through the small opening toward the car. Julia and I both open the doors, and when I hear banging on the back, I open the trunk as well. Rich squeezes through my side and Jake gets in behind Julia, forcing Melody into the middle seat; immediately I consider that Ava will argue she belongs there.

"Go, drive, NOW!" Rich shouts from the back seat. I slam my foot into gas as I roll my window up, following a curve in the path to the street only to see two seamless clusters of bodies on both sides of the driveway slowly closing the gap that represents our exit. "Hold on!" I shout. I grind my foot into the floor, pushing everyone back and producing a loud thump from the trunk. Out my window, the waves of bodies are close enough to touch, and in a flash my driver's side mirror disappears as a corpse goes rolling over my hood. A moment later, I see myself speeding toward the street and slam on the brakes as I jerk the wheel hard to the left, bringing the car to a stop just inches from the curb as another loud slam emerges from the trunk. "Is everyone okay?" I mutter, looking back. Rich, who is still trying to catch his breath, nods as he swallows.

"Anderson, Ava?"
"Trunk." Anderson mutters angrily.
"Ava?"

Julia and I turn simultaneously to see Jake and Rich look dejectedly at the floor. Jake bites his lip to stop it from quivering. "Oh no... oh no..." Julia's voice catches like her heart stopped beating and tears instantly come down my face. "Oh my god. So stupid... so... fucking... stupid!" I manage to spit out before I try to stop myself from crying. "We couldn't do anything." Rich says softly. "I would have... I'm sorry." I bang my head into the steering column and slam my fists against the wheel, causing the horn to beep. Seemingly out of my control, my fist repeatedly slams into the top of the dashboard. "I watched... I watched him *FUCKIN'*..." I bury my head in my hands on the wheel.

"Honey, honey..." Julia says, tugging at my arm.

"What do we do now?" I gasp through tears.

"Police station." Anderson says from the trunk.

"How, how can you be so calm about this? John and Ava are *dead!*" Julia finally starts bawling as well.

"Jeff, calm down." Rich says.

"How!?"

"There's nothing you could do…"

"Even if we make it out of this, what am I supposed to tell their families!?"

"Jeff…" Jake says softly.

"It's my *fuckin' FAULT!*"

"JEFF!"

"WHAT!?"

Jake points toward the shambling dead outside the window. A runner breaks out of the pack and slams into the side of the car. As everyone screams at once, I gun the engine and fire us down the street toward West Chester Pike. "Jeff, don't torture yourself. It's not your fault." Rich says quietly. I begin weeping.

"I can't blame anyone else…"

"You don't blame anyone."

"I'm sorry…"

"Don't be sorry, it's not your fault."

His voice is surprisingly calming. I take in a deep breath and exhale slowly. "I'm sorry." I look back at the group to see Jake staring forward stoically, Melody with tears in her eyes, and Rich looking at me sympathetically. Suddenly all of their eyes go forward; I turn as well and slam on the breaks, causing the passengers to lurch forward and Anderson to slam into the back of the seats. "What the fuck was that about?" Anderson shouts from the trunk. "You're not seeing what I'm seeing." I say softly.

I have to imagine that everyone is gawking at the cars packed bumper to bumper as far as the eye can see in the eastbound lane of West Chester Pike. "What is it?" Anderson asks from the trunk again.

"We can't take route 3." Jake says into the trunk. Every car down the line looks abandoned, but it's tough to be certain; despite the torrential downpour, a fire still burns bright from beneath the hood of one car, casting shadows from the few undead milling around and reflections from the shattered glass. "Go to the station." Anderson responds after a moment.

One of these shadows appears to be dancing closer to us, and I only realize it's running toward us the second before it jumps on the hood of the car. With everyone else screaming, I shift the car into reverse and screech in the opposite direction, tossing him off the hood. "Hold on!" I shout. As I drive backward I let off the gas, and let the wheel list slightly to the right before jerking it over to the left, causing the car to spin and hydroplane in a circle as I press hard on the brakes, jerking Anderson around some more in the back. "STOP IT!" He shouts.

Once we've turned around I even the car out and turn left on the next side street while driving close to seventy, but an attack of conscience causes me to ease off, dropping the car to fifty. I switch the windshield wipers to their fastest setting and squint, wiping the tears out of my eyes. With no traffic, traveling at sixty, we are at the police station in less than three minutes. Every other building along the block is pitch black, making the only light a discomforting clash of green fluorescent street lights and the orange tungsten bulbs outside the station. Without a word, we file out of the car; Rich runs past the rest of us to take out one of the undead, first skewering him through the eye, then beating his skull against the pavement.

I look to the end of the street that intersects with the main road we are on now; there appears to be a police barricade set up toward the end before it intersects with West Chester Pike. An ambulance appears to have plowed through the barricade line and crashed into the hoard of cars. The gate to the EMT station positioned toward the center of the street is still open. As we walk toward the station, I again become aware of just how soaking wet I still am. While I awkwardly paw at my upper chest in discomfort, my eyes lock on the broken glass of the station's front door and the blood spots on the floor just behind it. "Oh god." Someone says from behind me. "Grey, up front with me."

Anderson says. We both pull out our Berettas and hold them up by our heads, setting our melee weapons against the door on the outside.

We both move up to the door as everyone else stands back and watches; each of us takes a side and Anderson nods toward the station, but I just stare back. He does it again harder and I get the idea. He slams into the door, throwing it open, and turns the corner to the right as I follow behind him, bringing us face to face with the front desk to see a man sitting in a chair behind it with a massive hole in the middle of his head and blood on the wall. He doesn't appear to have been infected.

Again, we look at each other. He points to his chest and points to the left, then points to me and points to the right. I nod, and then we both jump out into the next room turning to the left and right respectively while holding our pistols out. There are cubicle dividers in front of each of us, so we strafe along them until we can see the walkway that stretches out in front of the desk in either direction.

There are two more corpses, one on either side, both of which clearly shot dead. "One over here." He says. "Same." I say. "Guys..." Anderson shouts back at the door. The rest of them enter and cluster by the doorway, shaking from the cold rain. Melody stays toward the back of the group and looks around nervously. "Jesus, what happened?" Anderson gets down on the ground and looks at the dead police officer. "His gun's gone." I look at the one on my side, also without his belt, and I quickly put it all together.

"Looters."
"What?" Julia asks.
"No way. No way!" Rich responds.
"What else could it be?" Anderson asks.
"We have to get out of here..." I respond immediately.
"Not before we check for guns and ammunition..." Anderson says.

For a moment, everyone is quiet, leaving only the sound of the soft rain in the background.

"They could still be here."

"If they *were*, they're gone now. They don't stick around, you know, they take and then they go."

"Well if they've taken what they need, then this place should be cleaned out."

"Rich, what do you think?"

"I say we take a look around."

I breathe in and sigh. "All right, but let's make it fast." I say. "You, Jules and Melody go that way. Rich, Jake, with me." Anderson says. We each go the direction of the dead officers we just spotted. As I turn the corner to a new hall, I look back at Julia. "Watch our ass." I open a door to find an office. I walk inside and open the desk drawers to find a Glock. I pick it up and examine it, but apparently, it is only a replica paperweight. Wondering if I'll encounter more apparent references to Zombie video games from my youth, I drop it and go to the next room. Two doors later, I come away with nothing. At the end of the hall there is another door on the left, leading to another dead police officer, also sans belt, sitting inside. Down the next hall we find four jail cells on either side of the wall. I look in the first one on my left but there is no one inside.

I turn to the opposing cell, finding the gate shut with no one inside. The inside of the cell on the left is obscured in shadow, so I sidestep carefully over to it, and the moment I get within sight someone jumps at the bars. I fall backward startled, pointing my gun up at the head of my attacker while Melody screams. I slide myself away, shaking when my back hits the opposing cell and a set of arms immediately grab my trench coat. "GET IT OFF!" I scream, pulling my arms out of the sleeves and jumping back toward the other cells.

I reach out and pick up my Beretta, which I dropped during the struggle, and holster it. "Jules, check my back! Check it!" I shout, shaking my shoulders. I feel Julia's hands gently stroking across my neck and back. "It's okay, you're okay." I breathe out deeply and grab the end of my trench coat, pulling it roughly away from the undead person holding it. There are at least seven crammed together in one cell, and only one in a police uniform adjacent to them. I take a closer look inside to see his belt on the floor toward the back. I reach in my trench coat pockets and pull out my leather gloves, slipping them on.

"One of you got a belt?" I ask. Melody takes a moment before removing hers and handing it over. I close the loop, lasso the dead officer's arms, and yank hard until he's anchored to the bars, then hand the end of the belt to Julia. "Hold it tight." With the officer incapacitated and apparently displeased, I grab my cane off the floor and stick it in the cell, using it to pull the belt toward me. The undead officer wriggles, but he can no longer reach me.

Once I get the belt through, I examine the contents: two magazines, a Glock pistol, handcuffs, a radio, pepper spray, a baton, keys, latex gloves, and a flashlight. I rip the gun holster off my waist and put the belt on, taking out one of the gloves to wear as I wipe off my cane. Once I've finished, I hand it back to Julia.

"Why'd you wipe it?"

"Just a precaution."

"So, can we, like, get the fuck out of here?" Melody asks.

We go into one of the offices and clean the cane off with a bunch of tissues and some disinfectant kept in one of the desk drawers. I pause for a moment and play with the radio on my belt, hearing nothing but static on all the channels. The two ladies follow me back out to the front desk where Anderson is already waiting.

"Find anything?"

"Police belt. Rich, Beretta's all yours. Find anything?"

"Beretta mag, no bullets... still warm. So let's move."

"Wait, where are we going?" Rich asks.

"Check point."

"What if it's not safe?" Melody asks.

"Mall."

"And if that's overrun?" Jake asks.

John stares blankly, and I shrug.

"We... I don't know." I say.

"I've got an idea." Rich responds.

"Let's hear it."

"School bus."

"Huh?"

"High ground clearance, plenty of room, they take diesel, and I can drive one."

"That's a great idea." I say.

"Well, it's not exactly efficient now, is it?" Anderson responds.

"Huh?"

"Think about gas, the noise it makes, maneuverability... it's not exactly a dirt bike."

"We'd at least be safe if we had to sleep somewhere."

"True, but what happens if we wake up surrounded?"

"Run them down... like I said, high ground clearance..." Rich mutters.

"Christ, what time is it?" Jake asks.

"Uh, 1:30." Melody says, checking her phone. "Shit, the battery's almost dead."

"Melody, try 911 again." Julia says.

"Oh, okay."

She dials and puts her hand against one ear, holding the phone to the other. It's ringing. Expecting that Melody will ask me what to say, I motion for her to hand it off, which she does. Once it's against my ear, it rings for exactly fifteen seconds. A woman answers.

"911, what's your emergency?"

"There's six of us in the Broomall Police station, we're being chased down..."

"Who's chasing you down?"

"Zombies."

"What?"

"Ugh... protesters, infected, whatever you want to call them, they're fuckin' Zombies, and we need *help!*"

"Are you safe in the station?"

"No, everyone's dead."

"There aren't any police there with you?"

"No, everyone's *dead*. There's six civilians here and if possible we want to live through the night. What should we do?"

"You should stay in the station."

"...that's it?"

"I don't know what else to tell you."

"How about, we're sending a unit over, we should go to the nearest safe house..."

"Safe house?"

"Rescue center, for Christ's sake..."

"You're in a rescue center."

"Are you not hearing me? Everyone here is dead. What are we supposed to do, barricade the door with their bodies? If we stay here, will someone come get us, or will more cops show up...?"

"...I'm not sure."

"What is the point of keeping this number connected?"

"Incase of a fire, violent crime, theft..."

"...those are all happening here right now."

"Sir, we simply don't have any units to dispatch in Broomall or Newtown Square."

"Why not?"

"The area is under quarantine."

"So what you're saying is... we should just stay put."

"Yes, if you..."

"Fuck this."

I hang up and toss the phone back to Melody. "They said we're under quarantine, so they're not sending anybody." Unsurprisingly, I get some pretty disappointed looks. "Is this really happening?" Melody asks. Despite the simplicity of the question, everyone present has a moment of pause. Of all the things I thought possible in an undead outbreak, I never considered that I'd be in this position. I close my eyes and open them. Anderson pinches himself. "I think so." He says finally. "So can we go to the bus depot and drive to the motherfucking checkpoint?" No one proffers any disagreements, so we immediately disembark. Taking the only route available to get to the bus depot includes passing near to the high school, and when it is in view, I stop the car.

"Guys, look out your windows..."
"What are we looking for?" Rich asks.
"See how spread out they are around the school."
"Still a lot of them, but they *are* spreading out."

I nod and pull away, driving the next quarter mile to the bus depot. As I get out of the car, I hear the drone of the distant undead milling around in the shadows by the enormous traffic standstill. Anderson walks up behind me as I stare up into the dots of rain streaming through a pillar of light. "Not what you expected?" He asks softly. I glance back at him and shrug despite the feeling that this is exactly what I expected. Any further thought is frozen by the sound of someone's feet splashing through puddles to my left. I turn to see the one we hit with the car a few minutes ago running toward me. "Anderson, Rich!" I shout as he approaches.

They stand beside me and hold up their weapons as I kneel down and hold my stick out like a spike, watching him run full speed while making dry, stomach-churning gasping noises. I position the butt of the stick tightly to the ground and he impales himself right through the stomach, which is accompanied by a putrid sucking sound. He moans in pain, I assume, and when he hits the ground Anderson swings the crowbar, striking his temple with the hook. Liquid spews out the opposite side of his head and then Rich smashes his skull with the baseball bat, sending him off the stick.

"Anderson, get the lock." I say, as Rich and Jake beat the corpse on the ground. "Hang on a second." Rich mutters. He walks over to the lock, lifts it, and tries a combination. Rich smiles as he pops it open on the first try. Anderson lifts the inner latch as Rich and Julia push the twenty-foot barb wire laced gates open. "Too rusty." Anderson says, softly banging his crowbar into the gate. I hand him the police baton off my belt and he stares at me blankly. "You know I can't kill anything with this, right? They're designed to *not* kill people." I shrug, dropping it. The entire bus yard is surrounded by barbed-wire fence and holds about two dozen buses. When lightning flashes, I see five or six undead clawing ineffectually at the fence along the back. The back side is cut into a hill, which makes the top of the fence only eight feet off the ground. I look back to see slow moving undead walking toward us from the crashed cars and shut the gates, latching them from the inside.

Rich runs over to the small building within the enclosure and breaks the glass on the door to the office, unlocking it from the other side. I hear a short scream and look over to see him back out as an undead woman steps toward him. I step forward with my hockey stick, but Rich holds his hand out to stop me. "No, no. She's mine." I squint, vaguely recognizing the undead body approaching him.

Several years ago, I was headed home from school for winter break and the bus was rowdy. If I recall correctly, someone threw a cheese curl out the window and the bus driver turned the bus around and took it back to the station. Some woman got on the bus and yelled at all the kids, then singled out one specific kid and hurled curses and threats of bodily harm such as I have never seen. I remember our bus driver had a look of pure satisfaction on his face as she berated this poor adolescent, and this was that very same woman. I didn't like her, and if Rich worked for her, I can only assume he hated her.

I see Rich lift the bat over his head and bring it down hard and fast, slamming it into her skull repeatedly, even when she falls over. When the lightning strikes I can see his hair shake violently as aggravation and anger fuel his assault on her corpse. He lifts it over his head one last time and puts everything into the final blow, which produces a low, wet crack. He slowly stands up straight and steps away from the backlighting so I can see the puddle of thick red liquid combining with the rainwater.

"Sorry." Rich mutters, heaving as he wanders in the office and turns on the light inside. "What are you, a misogynist?" I ask with a smile. "What's that mean?" Melody asks. "It's a man who hates women." Rich responds after a moment. "And I just hate *that* woman." After about a minute inside, he opens up a garage door facing away from the street and walks out holding a set of keys.

"We'll take the '98, 84 passengers."

"What about gas?" I ask.

"They fill these suckers up every Friday afternoon, after the final run. That way they're full for Monday morning."

Rich walks over to bus 77 and opens the door, which I take as a good omen because 77 is my favorite number.

"What kind of fuel?" John asks.

"Diesel, which is good."

"How so?" Asks Julia.

"Efficient, plentiful... besides, look how much fuel we have right here."

Rich holds his arms out in the presence of all the buses, then points to an isolated diesel fueling pump just inside the opened garage.

"Wow that's lucky..."

"Why do you think I wanted to take a bus?"

"So, do we siphon too?" I ask.

"They have some empty tubes in all the buses just in case, and spare fuel containers in the bus station."

"Well, we better fill them all." Anderson says. "As much as we can afford to take. If everything is abandoned, we'll be driving around for a while."

"The buses have crowbars, so we can dump the metal sticks."

"Awesome."

"Okay, so like, what do we do while you're siphoning gas?" Melody asks.

"*Everyone's* siphoning gas." Rich says.

"Jeff? Do we have to?"

"Unless you're walking."

"A 'yes' would have been fine."

Rich instructs us how to siphon gas, which is actually as easy as it looks. Take a hose, stick it in the gas tank, suck on it until it comes up through the hose, and the atmospheric pressure takes care of the rest. We each take keys to open the bus fuel doors and within fifteen minutes each of us has filled three one gallon containers with gas, giving us eighteen extra gallons, equaling about one fifth of the bus' tank. Rich says we'll need to find more empty fuel containers to get the most out of the diesel pump, but I doubt we'll be coming back. As a group, the six of us share a water bottle to wash out our mouths. By the time we're done, the rain has slowed even more. As I finish, I see Anderson's face twist up in confusion.

"Grey?"

"Anderson?"

"How bad do you think this is?"

"On a scale of one to ten? Probably about a five."

"Huh?" Melody offers.

"We're looking at more than a thousand undead, most likely... government and military response hasn't been anywhere near what I'd hoped..."

"Don't knock 'em... they mobilized us pretty quick." Anderson says.

"Yeah, with shitty information. Hence the military intelligence paradox."

"Watch it, civilian."

He and I chuckle. "Well, you're probably leaving your car here, at least for a while." Rich says. "Get what you need." I look at my car for a moment, accessing my photographic memory. The back has my DVDs and my player, but I wouldn't need that. On second thought, the bus has a lot of room, so I might as well. I paid a lot of money for my collection of well over 200 DVDs, and the ones in the blue vinyl case are my favorites, so I might as well take them.

"Yeah, let me get a few things." I open up the car and the glove box, pulling out the license, registration, and other assorted papers. Behind them is electrical tape, a box of solid fuel tablets, six small boxes of matches, two lighters and a folding knife. I shove them in my trench coat pockets, and then grab the DVD case. I open the trunk and grab my DVD player out of the back. After a moment, I notice that my mini DV camera is in the back, so I take that as well.

"A DVD player? What do we need that for?" Jake asks.

"We don't *need* it for anything..."

"But we don't even have a TV." Melody states.

"That's hardly a scarcity..."

"Guys," Anderson cuts in. "We're going to the check point..."

"Alright. Well, if the check point is abandoned we can stop back at my place to shower and get changed. Oh, and the supermarket. Just incase we get stuck."

"All the same, let's plan for the check point." Rich says.

"We need backup plans..."

"You guys realize..." Melody starts. "They said this place is quarantined..."

Though I don't feel that changes anything about our intended plans, the thought never really sank in. The military's probably set up at every major road out of here, and depending on how bad it gets, they might shoot first. No one could blame them as the imperative is to contain rather than save the few remaining civilians. Even if we were to survive an encounter with itchy trigger fingers, we're very much stuck here with few options.

"Yeah... so we head to the check point." Anderson says forcefully.

"And after that?" She asks.

"The *other* check point... then the Lima Mall."

"So..." Jake offers. "Basically, we're following the Zombies out of town."

"I'd rather be chasing them than have them chasing us." I say.

"Okay, well, we're gonna need more than a few crowbars if we're gonna make it anywhere..."

"Gordon's!"

All eyes are on Melody after her explosive outburst reminding us that Gordon's Sporting Goods is just up the street. Julia's eyes light up with excitement. Though I know she hates guns, it's clear that this is the time and place for them. Anderson and I both scoff.

"Yeah, sure. That hasn't been looted." Anderson says sarcastically.

"Is it or is it not worth a shot?" I say, with no intention of pun. "Rich, John?"

"I say check it." Rich says immediately.

"Well... here's my thinking. I don't wanna show up to the check point armed to the teeth with stolen weapons..." Anderson replies.

"Depends on how serious the situation is... they might want a helping hand."

"No way... unless the check point was completely overrun, they wouldn't let you help, and at that point they'd be trying to evacuate you anyway."

"How about this..." Rich starts. "You ran into us and we already had the guns, the bus, everything. If they have a problem with it, we'll take the heat and they'll take the guns away. Simple as that."

"But do you want to face the repercussions?"

"Well, either everything is okay and we end up in jail, or we keep the guns... I don't see a downside."

"I like where he's going." I say. "Besides, the gun store is just up the street... the longer we wait, the better chance there is of it getting knocked off."

Anderson stares at me.

"Dude, if we don't go now, and something went down at the check point, we won't live to regret it."

"Alright." He sighs.

"Alright then, let's go. We'll take my car. Who's staying?"

"Is it wise to split up?" Julia asks.

"We need the space. So who's staying here? Anderson?"

"I go; Rich stays here with Julia and Melody. Get one of the buses ready. Rich, time us. If we're not back in twenty minutes, leave. If you hear screams and gunshots, wait five minutes and leave. If you hear us fire, listen, we'll shout 'clear' if we're okay." Anderson says.

"Gotcha. We'll start the bus after fifteen no matter what. Good luck boys."

I nod and get in the car, immediately thinking that those screams and gunshots could easily be all Julia ever hears of my death. I pass my finger over the magazine catch on the Glock handle, letting the clip fall into my hand. The bullets inside are in fact lead, and are also hollow point rounds, which means they will shred whatever they hit on contact. Anderson, in the passenger seat, looks over in mock anger. "You asshole with your hollow point rounds." I hand him the knife out of my pocket. "Here. Carve crosses into them." I say. He looks nonplussed. "What are we, conducting a crusade? These things aren't satanic."

I shrug. "You don't know that. Besides, carving a cross in the top makes it a dum-dum." He shrugs back, takes the knife and starts on a magazine. Rich waves and closes the gates behind us as we head out of the station. I see undead headed toward the station and beep the horn repeatedly to draw them away. "What are you doing!?" Jake shouts. "Baiting the hook." I pull in at a small deli, driving across the sidewalk and the street simultaneously. The store's parking lot is filled with cop cars, none of which are on or have lights flashing.

I instantly get a bad feeling when I drive up to Gordon's and see the door open and the light on. I've been to this place many times in my youth, and the door has never once been open. I hop out of the car and see an undead walker closing in fast, arms outstretched in the usual fashion. With insufficient time to react, I pull out my Glock and plug two rounds in his forehead, which causes a purplish cloud of thick liquid to squirt out the back of his skull. Anderson and Jake each dispatch one as well. I look back and forth to see two on the right and one running at us on the left. "CLEAR! Jake, John, take him. I've got these two."

I look back and holster my Glock, taking up my hockey stick and charging at the walkers. I spin it in a butterfly motion on either side, cracking the temple of the one on the left followed by the one on the right. When they fall over, I stamp hard on each of their heads in the order I hit them on the ground. I thought about this briefly in between

REM cycles one night; a hard shot to the temple could create a weakness in the skull and the hard stomp to follow could exploit it.

This apparently works like a charm because their skulls snap and crumple in the middle beneath my boot heel. I glance at the undead closing in on us from either direction and determine that we have a few minutes until they get to us. "Clear!" I shout. I take a few steps toward the building and nearly lose my footing. "Are you okay?" Anderson asks immediately. "Yeah, yeah, I'm..." I look at the ground, which is covered with bullet casings. "You've gotta be kidding me."

Anderson helps me up, and then holds me back before I can get to the door. "We're not looters!" He shouts. "We're coming in, don't shoot!" I step in with my hands up, relax, and then tense again. "HOLY SHIT!" The carpet is lined with corpses, both undead and human. There are bullet casings everywhere, the room is foggy and smells heavily of cordite. After a moment, I hear what sounds like labored breathing from the back of the store and begin to step cautiously over and around the blood soaked corpses until I see a man leaning forward over a glass display counter in the back.

He is almost completely bald, wearing a red flannel shirt beneath a Kevlar vest. I can't stop myself from gagging when he pushes himself up and takes his hand away from his neck for a moment, producing a thick blurt of what looks like tomato soup that splatters on the glass counter. He falls forward again, his right hand clenched in a fist as he tries to reach for something across the counter. There's nothing there. "Sir?" I ask softly. He looks up slowly, revealing an exquisite pain on his sweaty face and tears in his eyes. "Get... out..." He sputters, failing to sound aggressive through his weakness.

His right hand goes back and comes forward, his elbow banging on top of the counter as he holds a revolver in the air; this maneuver seems to have been calculated to scare me just as much as it appears necessary for his balance. I take a step forward and the next thing I know the gun is pointed at me. I can almost feel my body pulling me to the left, but I can't move my feet. His arm then gently falls limp as his body finally refuses to cooperate with his will and slides off the counter. I can't stifle a big sigh, but my eyes quickly return to the floor. One corpse in front of me is wearing a police belt and a Kevlar vest over a pair of slacks and a dress shirt. Another one close by is dressed head to toe like a cop. "Must be the guys that took the station." Anderson says, before I can think it. How the hell did they get so organized so fast? Jesus, what a battle this must have been...

Hearing footsteps on the sidewalk outside, Gordon eyes the door. Surrounded by his life's work, a collection of firearms almost too perfect to sell, he clutches his rifle tightly enough that his damp skin might fuse with the wood. He knows how to operate and clean every one of these firearms. He knows how much ammunition he has and how the casings marry to each barrel. He has enough of each to outlast every walking corpse and thief that might think to enter his domain. "Let them come... any minute they'll..."

A gunshot pops me back into reality. "Jesus, what the f..." Anderson is standing behind the counter holding the man's smoking revolver. He releases the cylinder and hits the ejector rod, sending six empty bullet casings into the air. No further discussion is necessary. "Clear!" Anderson shouts. We all scan the corpses again to see if any of them are still moving, but this task is almost impossible due to the overwhelming number of them. "Let's get the gear and get out." I grab the shotgun next to the dead man behind the counter and break the case behind him as Jake admires my handiwork.

"Ooh, shotguns!"

"Don't get too excited. You need something versatile, like a rifle, something for long range and short range. Preferably lightweight, not too loud, with ammunition that is mainly common, yet has good stopping power."

Jake looks at me like I just told him to shit out of his forehead.

"What should we take?" Anderson asks.

"You're the expert, but preferably a good mixture of bolt or lever action and semi-autos or carbines. Maybe one shotgun, and as many pistols as we can lay our hands on."

"I've got three hand guns, a few more mags... the bodies on the floor are clean... any gear loose behind the counter?" Anderson asks.

A cursory glance reveals nothing out of the ordinary. That would have to mean someone came in and took their things, but didn't interrupt the counter...

No one's getting my bullets unless they pay. Fair and square, even if they take the money off a corpse and hand it to me, I don't care. It's only legal.

That would explain why the gun case is still mostly full. "Take the pistols and round up as many bullets and empty clips as you can." Something moves in the store, but I lose it too quickly to identify what it was. I walk around to the other side of the counter, seeing nothing through the racks of clothing and displays. I turn back to see Anderson pointing his pistol at me, supporting it with both hands.

I freeze, not knowing whether I should duck or speak. My brain feels as though I'm corkscrewing through a roller coaster. When he pulls the trigger, I think it's all over, so I close my eyes. If I were alive, I'd like to think I would have heard the gun go off, but I hear nothing. The internal balance mechanism in my brain has been offset, so I hit the ground thinking I'm dead. Once on the carpet, I realize I've retained my ability to move, so I turn back behind me to see an undead corpse with a wealth of spoiled blood flowing out of his forehead.

"Gotcha. Jake, get the bullets and the clips." Anderson says. "Good thing you're a crack shot." I say softly, rubbing my ears with my shaking hand. "Good thing you didn't move..." I look at the corpse behind me. "Clear!" He shouts. We walk over to the rack that extends like an 'L' behind Gordon, or whoever the corpse currently resting against the glass counter may be. "Anderson, this guy sell any silencers?" I can't hear his mumbled response.

"Speak up, I can barely hear you..."
"No."
"Illegal?"
"...Actually, I'm not sure. You need to submit to a background check and pay a huge fee for owning it, and obviously there are regulations in the states you *can* use it..."
"Just... see what you can find."

He says something else quickly as he looks at the dead man behind the counter. I didn't hear, but it seems like he was talking about the vest.

"Huh?" I ask.
"What?"
"The vest? Dude, how many zombies are gonna bite your chest? They go for the arms and the neck."
"Good point. Not taking the vest... wait... never mind, he's been shot, can't take it anyway."

I look at Jake's collection of pistols and my eyes nearly pop out of my head. "Is that a Colt .45? I have literally wanted one of those all my life..." I say, dropping my Glock on the table and substituting it for the .45 pistol. Anderson smacks the glass with his crowbar, causing a single pane to shatter. He then shatters the next three as I look at the guns.

With a good idea of what I want, I go to work looking for a rifle; it should be easy to reload, lever action, relatively lightweight, have a large round capacity, and be chambered for high caliber bullets. I grab two lever actions, one is black, the other is camouflage, but neither feels right. I pick up another and it clicks; blue steel, walnut stock, two foot barrel. I snap the lever and turn into the store, aiming it. I pull the trigger and the hammer snaps.

I check the tag on the bottom. .45 caliber bullets, 12 round magazine capacity, 24" barrel. I flip the tag over to see the word 'nominal' written next to specifications. It weighs just less than seven pounds. Anderson drops a large camouflage duffel bag on the table. "Amazing." I state proudly. I look at the tag again to get the name. "Winchester 94 Legacy. You've got to love this fucking country." He nods at me, and then goes through the display cases and cabinets behind the counter while I continue marveling at my rifle. I barely catch the sight of his arms waving and look up.

"Well?" He asks.
"What? I still can't hear you."

"Can you work that thing?"

"Yeah, spend a few dozen summers at the rifle range in Indian Guides... not this model, but I can shoot."

"Son of a bitch..."

"What is it?"

I realize I'm not sure that was what he said when I recognize that my ears have been ringing. "I've got my gun." He says, smiling as he jumps over the rack and grabs a huge black bolt-action rifle with a scope and a bipod.

"That gun is so... Andersonian."

"And heavy, just like I like it." He checks his tag and reads the specs. "Winchester .308."

"Aren't those rounds hard to come by?"

"Nah, .308s are popular... based on military 7.62 51mm NATO rounds. You know what that means?"

"No..."

"If we come across any mounted weapons, like M60s, I can use those rounds in this."

"Really? I'd figure the difference..."

"Nope. It's not a perfect interchange, but you can use one in the other."

"Isn't 7.62 what you use in most military automatics?"

"5.56. But snipers still use it, and like I said, M60s take 7.62 51mm. But the interchange and the weight aren't the only reasons I'm taking it. Look what I found."

He holds up a thin metal cylinder that I recognize as a sound suppressor.

"Made for .308s. It's the only one he has, so someone must have special ordered it."

"Jesus Christ... You've *gotta* love this country."

I look through some more rifles while Anderson gets ammunition. He asks me a question I can't hear, so I turn to face him and he points at my rifle. ".45 Colt. Same as my handgun." He shakes his head and I miss what he says. The gun I'm holding now is similar to the last one, but much lighter and shorter; perfect for Jules. 9 round capacity, .357 bullets, just over five pounds. "Anderson, .357." Despite the ringing, I can hear lots of bullet boxes going into the bag. Jake picks up a semi-automatic and aims it. He appears to like it.

"You want that gun?" I ask Jake, he nods. "What's the make, capacity, and bullet caliber? It's on the tag." He looks slightly confused as he does. "I got it. Benelli R-1 magnum, uh, seven pounds, holds three rounds, .300 win mag." He rips the tag off and sets the gun down. "Jake, keep the tag. Anderson, .300 Winchester mag rounds." Jake breaks the glass with his gun, pulling out magazines to throw in the bag as well. Anderson appears to be almost done taking the bullets we'll need.

"Um, shouldn't we take guns that have all the same bullets?" Jake asks us. I look at Anderson to run the idea, but he shakes his head. "If we stop at a place and they're out of only those kinds of rounds, we're all screwed. If we cover a bunch of different types of rounds, that won't be a problem." Again, I nod in concession to the resident military expert. "This guy has a Remington 870 Marine Magnum. We should..." I can't hear the rest as Anderson turns away from me to grab buckshot shells and slugs. "Perfect. Then we've got the shotgun for close encounters, my Winchester for mid-range and your super gun for long." I hear Anderson muttering something about the fact that Remingtons hold seven rounds as he grabs the gun and sticks it in the bag as well.

"All we need now is an idiot proof gun for Melody."

"Do they sell sticks?" Anderson asks.

"Here. Ruger PC9, plenty of magazines. Doesn't get more idiot proof than that. Anderson, could you get some straps? Holsters too."

He nods and quickly finds several, two of which are bandoliers for rifle bullets, another is shotgun suitable.

"Now this is movie military." Anderson says.

"Toss me a box of the hot stuff." I reply.

Anderson sets down a box of .45 ACP rounds, so I eject the magazine in my Colt and begin inserting them. "Jake, how many more?" He goes through the bag and hands out two empty mags, which I fill with ACP bullets as well. I remove the 9mm mags from my belt and put them on the table with the Glock, slipping two extra Colt mags in the now vacant holes on my police belt. Once I've finished loading all of my magazines, I chamber a round in my pistol, remove the clip, and load an extra bullet. Anderson stops me before I can load my rifle. "Different bullets." He says, hunting around in the bag.

"But they're both .45s..." I protest.

"Yeah... the pistol takes ACP, *that* takes .45 long... can't just pop ACP rounds into that..."

"Jesus... thanks..."

"Not a problem."

After loading twenty .45 long rounds in my bandolier and loading twelve rounds in my Winchester, I chamber one round, slip in one more, and slide the box in my trench coat pocket. "Does anyone else not feel okay taking these?" Jake asks suddenly. The question freezes me, but not Anderson.

"Like Rich said, if there's anyone left in town who has a problem with it we'll turn ourselves in and face the consequences. I'll take an inventory, and once this is over we'll have the guy send us a bill, though money's not gonna do much good where he is."

"But... this is still stealing..."

"Do you think there's a difference between a starving man taking a loaf of bread for his family and a guy who holds up a gas station?"

"Yeah..."

"We're the ones taking the bread. The alternative is we leave the guns and ammo here where they'll stay until someone else comes and takes them. See those corpses on the floor?"

"Yeah…"

"More people like that are probably already on their way, and if they get the guns, they'll use them to raid *another* police station. We're using them for self defense."

Jake looks at the floor while considering this. "Look, if you're still unsatisfied, you can go through the pockets of these dead guys and put the money in the register. The next group that comes through is gonna take that money, and the guns, and won't think twice about it." Contented, Jake finally nods and we return to work. Just as I begin to strap the rifle to my back, I see one of the undead stepping through the front door. "All right boys…" Anderson's head snaps to the door, but he stays down. I lift up the gun and hold it tight to my shoulder.

I wrap the strap around my left hand to tighten it and hold my breath halfway. I squeeze the trigger and allow myself to be surprised when the gun goes off; the kickback is heavy, the gun makes a cutting *pak* when it goes off. A splatter of blood precedes my would-be assailant's final fall. "DAMN that's hot!" I shout, working the lever to eject a smoking cartridge. I pull another round out of my bandolier and slip it in the loading port.

"Wait, wait, let me try mine." Jake says. He holds up the gun after wrapping the strap around his hand. "Hold it tight, hold your breath." Anderson says. He obeys and points the gun at the next undead coming through the front door. He jerks on the trigger, but there is merely a click. "You forgot to *load* it?" Anderson asks. Jake silently curses and goes into the bag for bullets that match his gun. I can't see Anderson's lips mutter his response as he lifts his super gun. He eyes up the sight and wraps the strap around his left hand.

When he pulls the trigger the muzzle flash burns one of the orange hunting jackets on a rack in front of him, the shot lands in the center of the attacker's nose, and the bullet explodes out the back of his head. I've never seen one hit the ground that fast, not even in movies. "A more perfect shot could not be fired." I say. "I missed… I was aiming forehead." Anderson admits dejectedly. "Yeah, but you want to aim for the spinal stem, cerebral cortex area. That shuts down motor functions instantly." He shrugs.

"CLEAR!" Jake shouts. It's a good thing he remembered, because I completely forgot. Now he's got his gun loaded up. Unfortunately, it's a semi-auto and he can't chamber a round manually because he wouldn't know how. "All right boys. Let's strap it on and get outta here." Jake grabs the bag, which is apparently quite heavy. "Wait! I've always wanted to try something." John says, reaching into the bag. I again notice that my ears are still ringing from the shot he fired off next to my head. He pulls out the shotgun.

He jams his rifle into the bag and holds up the shotgun, pumping it once. When he does so, he slides another round in the side. We look at the door to see an undead woman entering. Anderson walks up, and when her arms extend he stops and lifts the gun, pulling it snug against his shoulder and pointing it at her nose. The explosion makes me instinctively laugh and the woman's head literally disappears in a mushy cloud of gray, red, and purple that shoots straight back to the doorway and splatters on the walls.

One slab of unscathed flesh left over from her face falls down limply like uncooked steak as her body goes limp. I give Anderson a brief ovation. "Clear!" Anderson shouts, but it breaks down into a laugh. "Clear!" He manages to get it all out this time. Still smiling, I walk toward the door and look down at the corpse's leaking neck and can't help but be a little disgusted. Wiping the image out of my head, I run out on the front porch of Gordon's, hearing *La Caccia* from the *Dawn of the Dead* soundtrack in my mind. Anderson and Jake come out behind me. I run around and open the car, Anderson jumps in shotgun. "Open up the sun roof!" He shouts, so I oblige him. He stands on the center console and aims out the back. "Hold on." I slip the car into reverse and pull backwards.

A shot rips out above me and the car jolts as I hit something. I stop and look back to see what it was. "Straight back!" Anderson screams. Assuming that I don't want to see what's behind us and interpreting his statement as direction, I slam on the gas and we lurch backward until I can turn around and take us back several hundred feet to the bus station. Anderson and I can't help chuckling at each other as Melody and Rich close the gate. "That was fun." I say with a smile. Rich's expression suggests I shouldn't be smiling. "Uh... Jeff... Julia's been bitten." He says.

Normally it's hard for me to imagine my facial expressions, but I can actually feel the color draining from my face. If my bladder were full, it would have released at that moment. My heart sinks down to my lower chest despite its quickened pace. "She... she... what?" Rich motions to Julia, her right hand clasped tight around her left forearm. I can't see any blood. "When... I'm sorry." Rich mutters, turning around. "How bad is it?" I ask, reaching out for her arm, but she pulls away. She seems more bitter than upset.

"Oh no... oh god... Leah, I..."
"Jeff..."
"We..."

My voice cuts off before I push my hand over my mouth to shut my sagging jaw. I don't know what to feel, and it makes me sick. I try to force myself to feel as horrible as I should by careening into all the memories I have of her, but I feel nothing. In a few hours, she's going to die. And come back. "What do you...?" I can't finish, instead looking at my feet and letting out a deep sigh. I look in Julia's eyes. It's not hitting me properly that I'm going to be without her. Tears begin forming in my eyes as I speak.

"What do you want us to do?"
"What do you mean...?"
"We can... we have to... *something*."
"...what?"

I feebly shrug.

"Oh god..."
"What?" Melody asks.
"We gotta take care of her." Anderson says quietly.
"You're just gonna *shoot* her!?" Melody moans. "How could you!?"
"Jules... we don't have a choice..."

"Oh Jeff, I'm so scared..."

She starts to crack a smile. "What?" She chuckles in response to my grave question. "I'm sorry... we just wanted to see what you'd say." She takes her hand off her arm to reveal that there is no bite wound. She's smiling, as is Rich, and I can't see Melody's face. It takes a moment for the haze grief to wear off, or perhaps it doesn't wear off as much as it is simply replaced by a rush of slowly boiling rage. When I take a step forward, Julia steps back and her smile promptly disappears. I throw back my arms, causing her to jump, but the action merely causes my trench coat to slide off my shoulders. I grab her in a massive hug and hold her against me as she wraps her arms around me as well.

I kiss her neck softly, and then bring my lips up to her ear. "Never do that again." I whisper softly, causing her to break into sobs. She buries her face in my neck, wiping the tears away as she turns her mouth toward my chin. "I promise, Ef. I'm sorry." I can't be certain that's what she said, but I know it's something to that effect. I kiss her once more, steadying her head as I massage her tongue with mine, then pull away softly, putting my trench coat back on. "Let's hit it." I hear Anderson and Rich talking about where we should go next, I go to take my gun out of the car along with the duffel bag. When I pull the bag out and turn around, I see Melody standing behind me. I feel like she just asked a question I couldn't hear. "What is it?" I ask evenly.

"Are you gonna hit her...?"
"*Hit* her?"
"Yeah..."
"Why would I *hit* her?" She says nothing. "I... you've been...?"
"Yeah..." She says, as if it couldn't have been more obvious.
"Jesus..."
"What?"
"...no, I'd never hit her."

Melody looks back at Julia humbly. "But you!" I say looking at her, smiling, and poking her ribs. "Jesus, I thought *I* was bad. Now you're gonna get it!" I lift her shirt to start tickling her stomach and she immediately squirms to avoid it. When she straightens out, I put my arms around her, glancing over to see Melody uncomfortably moving away. Julia taps the bag. "What'd you get?" She asks. I smile back. "Toys. Let's hit it." Anderson is standing in my way when I turn around. "Grey, Rich and I think we should drive to the check point first, then hit up the supermarket, then your place, then the mall... you know, *if* the check point is abandoned."

I nod, watching Anderson board the bus as Rich starts it. Hearing that sound at night and standing beside a yellow school bus reminds me of all the band competitions I used to attend in high school. As I look back at Melody, Jake, and Julia with a cloud of diesel smoke billowing out behind them, I'm reminded of a dozen old movies with departure scenes, the most prevalent one being *Casablanca*. It makes a speech seem appropriate. I look back at Anderson and Rich to make sure I have their attention as well.

"Everyone, listen up... I know we barely made it out of the high school... so I just wanted to say... don't give up. Something may happen where you don't think... you'll make it... I'm saying don't let yourself get beaten. We get one chance at *this* life... so don't waste it."

I suppose I picked the right moment and the right words, because they all smile and nod in approval. Anderson jumps out of the bus before I usher them through the door, waiting until Anderson has the gates open to board. "How long is this gonna last?" I ask, pointing at my ear as I stop in the doorway. "It'll get better soon. A day or so until you're 100%." I nod. "If I go deaf I'm making you pay for my hearing aid." He chuckles dismissively as he waves Rich through the fence, walking alongside until the bus is clear, at which point he closes and locks the gates. Anderson takes up the weapons bag as Rich peels off down the street.

"All right, we've got guns for everyone. Rich, you got shotgun. Remington 870, 12 gauge rounds, six shot capacity, seven if you keep one chambered."

"Thanks." He takes the gun and puts it next to his seat.

"Jules, Winchester, don't know the model. Holds nine rounds and another if you chamber a round, .357 magnum."

"Thank you."

"Melody, Ruger PC-9 with 9mm rounds. It's real simple to load, just pull out the clip, press new bullets in, stick the clip in, yank back on the action, and fire it again. We left the tags on so you'll know what we need if we find more ammo." Anderson hands it off. "All right, me, Jeff and Rich each have a side arm, then we've got a Glock, another Beretta, and a .38 special, who wants what?"

"Glock." Melody says, I assume simply because she's heard the name before.

"Beretta sounds fine." Jake says.

"I'll take the other one." Julia adds.

"Okay, we've got a couple mags for the Berettas... it's not like the movies where you can just keep sliding out mags and leaving them on the ground..."

"What's a mag?" Melody asks.

"Magazine. Ammunition clip. You can switch them, as long as you get the old ones. To reload, just press the bullets down and in. You can probably fit more than it says, but you don't want to wear out the spring. Once it's in, yank back on the top to chamber a round and stick in another. The .38 has a cylinder, here's the release catch, flip this and the cylinder comes out, hit your palm on the ejector and the shells come out. Jake's and Melody's rifles are semi-autos, they load automatically. Once you run out, do the same thing as with the Berettas. Always keep your gun loaded and within arms reach. The shotgun is real easy, it's got a round chambered, and you might want to slide some more in, but once you shoot, pump it and shoot again. Don't go pumping it every eight seconds like in the movies or you'll have wasted shells all over the place."

"Sounds easy enough." Rich says.

"I took a bunch of cleaning kits from the gun shop, a few for rifles, handguns, and one for shotguns. We'll need to clean and oil these suckers at *least* once every two weeks. Now, when you fire, hug the butt tight to your shoulder or you could dislocate your arm, especially Rich. Wrap the front of the strap around your non-dominant hand to steady your aim more, close one eye, and hold your breath before you shoot. Aim small, miss small. Try not to flinch, and never shoot it from your hip. Accuracy is less of an issue for Rich, he just has to point at a general area and squeeze the trigger. Never jerk back on the trigger, always squeeze it until it releases. Rich, don't try to do any shooting from more than twenty feet or you'll waste the shot. As far as using your weapons for hand to hand combat, only do it if you're out of ammo for the handguns. For the pistol, hold it up next to your head and smack the bottom of it down on the attacker's nose. For the rifles, keep your finger out of the trigger guard, hold the gun tight, and snap the butt of the rifle away from you real fast, aim for the nose. Never, *ever* put your finger in the trigger guard unless you're gonna fire. Always point the gun in a safe direction unless you're about to fire. Now, if you're down to your sidearm, I want you to keep something in mind... if they're within 20 feet of you at running speed, you won't have time to pull the gun and aim before they get to you. When we get a chance to stop, we'll practice so you get an idea what I'm talking about. Most importantly... just try to remember all this crap. Clear?"

The group murmurs a series of positive responses.

"Good. What time is it now?" Anderson asks Melody.
"Uh, 5:10."
"Sun's up in... two hours?"
"Jeff?" Julia asks.
"Yes?"
"How do I load it?"
"Simple. Lift this, put the bullets in here... this way... then that lever on the bottom? Work it in and out. It's not loaded. Anderson, can we get the .357s?"
"Sure." He goes through the bag and tosses them back. "Here, everyone get your bullets and load up if you haven't already."

For the next few minutes, I help Julia load her gun. I hear the sounds of bullets entering guns and magazines being loaded, but only softly through my still ringing ear. Anderson has to help more than a few people, and I can tell he relishes the opportunity. When everybody is finished, they throw their boxes back in the bag. I look at Anderson. "How many boxes of each do we have?" He goes through the bag and shakes some. "Not counting the boxes everyone just loaded up from, uh… ten boxes of 9mm with fifty rounds each. Seven boxes of ACP with fifty, five boxes of .45 long with fifty, seven boxes of .308 with twenty, four boxes of .38 with fifty, twenty boxes of 12 gauge buckshot with five and ten boxes of slugs with five, two .357 magnum with fifty apiece and four boxes of .300 with twenty. We'll keep the ammo boxes in this bag, except the ones everyone loaded from… screw it; we'll give everyone a fresh box. We need backpacks."

I nod, thinking I understood that properly. It seems strange that it's harder to hear people indoors. I look to my right to see Anderson tossing the bat, the crowbars, the cane, my hockey stick, and some of the poles on one seat. I sit back and rest my hand on my forehead. Looking out the window and up I can see the moon and some of the stars in the sky, almost as though it had never been raining in the first place. My hand moves off my forehead to my side, brushing over the back of my Colt. When I touch it, I'm unable to stop my mouth muscles from exposing my teeth.

Rich takes the back roads to get out to the juncture of route 3 and I-476. After roughly fifteen minutes, he pulls out on the main road, which warrants me the opportunity to look at the massive crash again. It would appear that the entire building has burnt up, with each store front missing and the interiors gutted and ashen. More cars have fanned out over the sides of the median; presumably people tried to escape when the undead came, but most of said cars have their doors open, glass broken, or both.

As Rich straightens out on the road we can see heavy sandbags and barb wire set up across the overpass of 476 south, and hundreds of corpses piled up in front, giving the troops behind them a visually impressive tally. A cheer goes up throughout the bus, but my attention stays fixed on Anderson, whose self-satisfied smile disappears as he stands up and walks to the front. The murmuring cheers continue as I stand and follow him, immediately understanding why he's no longer excited by the prospect of approaching the barricade. Rich, seeing what we see, slows the bus to a stop.

At first there appears to be too much visual information to glean anything useful; corpses, a barricade, blood, shells, and tents are the first things I see, and though there is a wall obstructing me, it would seem there are no gun mounts, no helicopters pending takeoff, and most importantly, no people. Stranger still, and despite the fact that I can practically smell the putrid bodies from behind the windshield, I don't see a single insect. The bus falls silent.

It takes a moment for me to divert my eyes to the string of traffic lights flashing yellow as far as I can see down the overpass, extending to where the downward slope of the road bottoms out before rising and curving slightly to the right, disappearing into a mesh of trees and buildings. Just to the right, as far ahead as I can see, is Mercy Community Hospital. The undead are also scattered along the road, well past the overpass, wandering east toward Philadelphia. "Rich... open the door." As Anderson makes his way down the steps, I shoulder my rifle and join him.

"Stay on the fucking bus."

"No way... no one goes anywhere alone."

"...fine, but everyone else stays on the fucking bus."

The smell is immediate as the door swings open and Anderson leaps out; while I instantly pinch my nose, he fixes his eyes on the barricade and he marches forward into the faint light preceding the rising sun. While he stays fixed on some central location I may not be seeing, I look at the on and off-ramps on either side of the bridge interchange; each is plugged up with chest-high sandbags, forcing anyone who approaches into a funnel, or bottleneck, in a line across the start of the bridge proper. Each body seems to be riddled with at least twenty bullet holes, and judging from the damage, they figured out they needed a shot to the head pretty quick.

There has to be at least two hundred undead corpses in front of the barricade, but luckily they're far enough apart that we can safely walk between them. The only thing I have trouble figuring out is the construction of the primary barricade itself; stringy, densely layered, unpatterned carpeting in multicolored jewel tones? "Any of this look like panic fire to you?" I ask. Anderson keeps walking and doesn't respond, eventually climbing over a bare spot in the center of the barricade revealing a line of highway k-rails fortifying sandbags. Now it becomes clear: the carpet I was looking at is a thickly packed slough of flesh, organs, and clothes hewn from the bodies of the undead by razor wire.

Immediately behind the dividers rests a trio of gun mounts with the weapons suspiciously absent, and the number of corpses does not abate, though the amount wearing camouflage increases dramatically. I quickly notice there is not a single firearm to be found, just enough casings to melt down into enough metal for a two story building and enough corpses to fill a cemetery. I look up again to see that nothing stirs on the entire bridge, save for the loosened flaps of a communication tent halfway across.

I look over to Anderson to see him standing still, staring off into space, restraining his desperation through his emotionless eyes. He doesn't want to say anything, and he doesn't want me to either. "Jacoby." The word takes a moment to register. "Behind us, about two meters... face down." I turn around, take three steps, and find the corpse in question immediately. He's missing everything but his clothes, and judging from the bullet hole in the middle of his buzzed black hair, there's probably a good reason for that. He doesn't have a single bite mark.

Jacoby turned his head swiftly as another wave hit the sandbags, hearing a cacophony of rifle fire behind him as he watched one of the crawling infected lose almost all the flesh on his torso on the razor wire. Jacoby grimaced and tightened his M-16 to his shoulder and shot three rounds into the crawling one's head, blowing it apart like meat filled piñata. Some of the screams were supposed to be orders, but most of them were surely precipitated by someone else getting bitten and gored. Keeping the fire selector fixed on one shot, he patiently loosed two rounds into each undead head he saw. Just as he paused to change his magazine, he felt something hard press against the back of his skull. He turned slightly, but the last thing he heard was a bellowing noise that shattered his eardrum. The report from the pistol matted and

seared the back of his hair and the bullet sent his pinkish brain flying out a
newly formed hole in the front of his head.

"...you knew him."
"I knew most of 'em."
"Anderson, I don't..."
"There's nothing you can say. I'm serious. Don't try."

With that, he turns around, hops back over the barricade, and grabs one of the sandbags. I look around at the rest of the bodies behind the barricade and most of them have gunshot wounds, civilians and military alike. Thinking about guns again reminds me of the ringing in my ears, so I ineffectually massage my pinkie into my right ear canal as I look at the ground. I can only imagine there was a standoff. I consider asking Anderson for his opinion, but he's already halfway back to the bus toting a sandbag.

"What's that for?"
"Block up the steps on the bus... so they can't get in."
"Do we need anymore than two?"
"Two's fine."

I finally take my fingers off my nose and try hard to breathe through my mouth as I lift one of the heavy sandbags and follow Anderson back toward the bus. Rich opens the door as we approach, and just after we slide the bags in the door, Anderson snaps swiftly back toward the barricade. "Did you hear that?" In my silence, I indicate that I did not. Anderson promptly rips the rifle off his shoulder and swings around the front of the bus toward the onramp attaching to the westbound lane. Taking his lead, I pull the rifle off my shoulder, gripping it in both hands as I follow him over the pile of corpses.

I have no idea where we're going or what's going on until I hear a muffled scream that is definitely not coming from one of the undead. I look past Anderson to see a few of the undead gathering around a car stopped behind a row of sandbags, trapped on either side by massive hills of grass. Anderson, gaining ground much faster than I do, shouts ahead. "GET DOWN! GET *DOWN*!" I barely have a second to see a woman's head drop below the view of the windshield before Anderson has his rifle up and a wet mess of blood splatters on the glass. Anderson works the bolt on his rifle as I run past him. "Stay back!" He shouts. "I can't get a shot!" I yell back at him as I pass, prompting him to obligingly chase after me. The shouting riles them up enough to turn them off the woman in the car and advance on us from twenty feet away.

When I stop a few feet shy of the sandbags and fire, I let off a round that wildly misses every one of them, although the muzzle flash does allow me to see ten walking corpses shuffling out of the shadows. Before I can work the lever, Anderson fires again and another one of them drops ten feet away. I kneel down, settle the gun on my knee and take aim again, this time popping one of their heads like a melon. I pump the lever again as Anderson makes yet another perfect kill. My next shot hits one of them in the neck, spraying blood out as his head falls forward sickeningly limp and the body collapses five feet away. I must have severed his spine with the shot. The rest of them, six from my count, are now tumbling over the barricade toward us. Anderson puts down another, then I follow suit and stand up as I work the lever.

I turn to Anderson to see the gray, sinewy fingers of a corpse stretching out to reach him from behind the sandbags as he works the bolt on his rifle; with an enraged grimace, Anderson belts him across the temple with the rifle butt, knocking him back. When he hits the ground, Anderson fires a shot into his head that tears through his skull, ricochets off the pavement and hits another undead in the knee. I try to take a step back as they approach, but the ground is too uneven and I can't take my eyes off them to secure footing, so I shoulder my rifle, yank out my .45, and suddenly it's hard to look at the bodies as targets.

My finger stops on the trigger as I look into the eyes of the undead woman stumbling toward me. Though anyone else might look at her expressionless face and see nothing, I can't help but notice what looks like the remnants of a smile on her face, like her lips were pulled up as she died. Her arms move exactly like a normal person's should. For a moment, I question if this is what a real human looks like.

"Shoot her!" Anderson screams, waking me up. Gripping the gun tightly with both hands and preparing myself for the recoil I'd so often experienced in videogames, I pop off a round that kills the woman and another person right behind her. I quickly shoot the other two in the forehead before Anderson can take out his Beretta. I'd never fired a pistol before today, and I can definitively say that, short of an orgasm, there is no more cathartic feeling I have experienced in my life. Anderson takes in a deep breath through his nose and secures his sidearm. We both look at each other for a second, his face still a granite, unreadable relief. "I'm 100 percent on accuracy." He mutters, and it takes a moment, but the humor sinks in and I scoff. He starts to walk toward the barricade as I stand there.

"So am I." I say, following him again. "Bullshit... you missed the first one." Though his voice is still dripping with bitterness, I can sense jest. I climb over the bag behind him as I respond. "I got two with one shot." He shakes his head back at me. "You're full of shit." We get up to the window to find the woman cowering against the other seat, covering her head with her shaking arms.

"Look at that." Anderson says.

"Take anythin' you want! Please... don't..." She screams.

"Uh, miss, we're not gonna hurt you... but we're gonna have to ask that you come along with us now."

"I... what? No... I just... I can still get home..."

"Unless this is actually an ATV with anti-slash tires, you aren't going anywhere but back." Anderson says.

She finally looks up at him, and I can see her muscles relax as she sees his uniform.

"Do you know what's happening?" Anderson asks.

"Jesus... they were tryin' to break into my car..."

"I realize that..." Anderson says with a groan. "What I meant..."

"...do you know why?" I ask. "Can you roll your window down ?"

She obliges. "Okay, tell me..." Anderson awaits my answer as I find the best way to phrase it.

"Zombie apocalypse."
"You have two choices." Anderson interrupts. "You can come with us… or take your chances alone."
"How do I know I can trust you?"
"Either come with us…" Anderson continues gruffly. "…or don't."
"I… would you let me handle this?" I say.

Anderson steps away, not-so-silently cursing as he does. I lean into her window and she recoils.

"I'm Jeff."
"…Karen."
"Karen. That's John. As you probably guessed, he's in the military… so you can imagine he's having a shitty day. On that bus…" I start, pointing. "There are two women, including my girlfriend, and two other men. We're just trying to find someplace safe. And we're not gonna force you to come."

She thinks it over for a moment, looking toward her blood covered windshield. "Okay." She quickly unbuckles her seatbelt and opens the door. As Anderson starts back over the barricade, I stand behind her. "Do I really have to leave my car?" I turn around to see another two of the undead coming up the onramp toward us. "Do you really need it?" I assume she looks past me, because when I turn back, Anderson's already helping her over the barricade. Once she's over, I follow suit.

"Is it possible… can you just get me back to Upper Darby?"
"Upper Darby is fucked." Anderson says gruffly.
"Oh god…"

She's just seen the piles of corpses. It didn't occur to me at first, but she's actually quite attractive; fair skin, light brown hair, and blue eyes with a petite physique. More than anything, she seems like she could pass for a friend's young, painfully cool mom. Rich opens the doors and stares down at her. She looks back at him before Anderson gets her attention. Apparently he's cooled down. "I'm Anderson..." He says, extending his hand.

"Karen DeMarco."
"Jeff Grey."
"Rich McKnight."

It's going to take me a long time for me to get over her surname. She freezes when she's standing next to Rich, who looks her up anddown before settling his eyes on her face as she stares off into the bus. Coming up behind her, I take the initiative. "Karen, this is my girlfriend Julia... Melody, and Jake." When Rich closes the door, she swallows and nods, touching the tops of the seats as she makes her way past the weapons and into the seat in front of Julia as Rich and Anderson force the sandbags against the door. "Now, could someone please tell me what's goin' on?" As she speaks, I look over at the cross-hatched design on her beige suit jacket, immediately noticing a small patch of blood.

"Did any of them get you?"
"Huh? Oh, it, uh... splashed on me."
"Did any of the blood get in your mouth? Eyes?"
"What's that got to do with anythin'?"
"Well... you know what Zombies are, right?"
"Doesn't everybody?"
"Maybe not. They bite you, they infect you. If you die, you either reanimate before or after rigor mortis... let's just say we've done our fair share of running to this point. As far as we can guess, the blood's contagious... one bite, one scratch, and you're done. Get it in your mouth, eyes, mucous membranes, you're done. Do you understand the risk of getting infected?"
"Yes."
"Good. So, uh..."
"Supermarket?" Rich asks.

10-12-04, TUESDAY

I look out the window to see the orange sun cresting on the opaque horizon just as Rich flips on the radio; as far as I'm concerned, a new day has just begun. Even after a moment of fiddling with the dials, all that can be heard is static. "What time is it?" I ask quietly. "7:00." Melody responds after a moment. While I pretend to pay attention to what's happening outside the window, I replace the three spent rounds in my .45 magazine, chambering one. In less than ten minutes, Rich has us out front of the local supermarket. There is only one car in the entire lot and only a few undead, none of which appear to be runners.

Rich flips a few switches on the dashboard before standing and making his way toward the back. "Turned off the alarm... go ahead and open it." Without another word we climb out the back of the bus, but our group's latest addition is absent. I climb back in and find her sitting in the same seat near the front of the bus, staring out the window. "Karen?" She turns back, her forehead ruffled to signify she's listening. She's holding a cell phone.

"You coming?"
"Do you mind if I stay ...?"
"Uh, not really... would you mind keeping an eye out?"
"...uh, sure."
"Jules?"

She walks to the back bumper, looking up at me with a slight smile. "Mind if we loan your rifle to Karen for a bit?" She shrugs indifferently and pulls the Winchester off her shoulder. I walk back up the front of the bus and hand it to Karen.

"Can you handle one of these?"
"I think I can manage."
"Okay, just breathe easy, aim carefully, and squeeze the trigger... shut the door behind us, and lay on the horn if anything happens."

She turns away, nodding as she holds the gun to her chest. After I climb out the back she walks to the rear door, pulls it shut, latches it, and plops herself in one of the seats. As I turn to face the supermarket, I'm suddenly reminded of Phil, one of the store's regular customers and something of a folk figure in the Marple area. No one was ever certain if Phil actually worked at the store or not, all that was known was that he was almost always there and seemingly never had aspirations for shopping or working. It was clear that he was mentally deficient in one of the most benign iterations; he used to walk up to everyone in the store with a vacant smile on his face, shake their hands, ask their name, and tell them his. If anyone ever got irritated or aggressive with him, he would shrink away like a scared kitten. Tears quickly build behind my eyes as I consider that Phil didn't stand a chance against the undead.

"Grey, you alright?" Anderson asks.
"Huh... uh, yeah..."
"...what are you doing?"
"Nothing, I just... had a thought... it's not important."

Anderson nods, and then throttles his crowbar into the sliding glass doors, causing me to shudder. The lights are still on and the store is totally unoccupied. "I've always wanted to do that..." Anderson mutters as I steps over a shard of glass. "I can't believe there was no alarm." Jake says behind us. "I've always wanted to do this too..." Trying to put an undead Phil out of my mind, I run straight for the back of the store into the milk aisle, pull a gallon out of the refrigerator and launch it across the room. It explodes with a satisfying snap, sending white fluid all over the walls.

I look back down the aisle to the front door to see that my compatriots have already fanned out. Maybe the idea of throwing a gallon of milk across a supermarket never appealed to them. "Remember, everyone, essentials! Canned food, foil packages, medical supplies, bottled water, vitamin water, flashlights, fuel..." Anderson shouts, his voice turning to static in my weakened ears. I find an abandoned cart a few feet away, jump on the back, and ride it into the medicine aisle.

Before letting myself go ballistic, I close my eyes and take a moment. There are things we need, and things we don't.

I open my eyes and start by taking the full stock of every basic pain reliever available. I then grab every kind of cold medication I can find, including gallons of cold-relief sleep aids. Bandages, braces, gauze, alcohol, antibiotic ointment, and splints go into the cart next, followed by cough drops, throat lozenges, throat spray, decongestant pills, sleeping pills, and caffeine pills. I grab bismuth subsalicylate, laxatives, and anti-diarrheal pills before I start running out of ideas, so I just grab whatever looks helpful and head over to the meat aisle.

Some of the expiration dates seem too soon or expired already until I find the pre-cooked bacon which expires in two weeks. I think back for a moment to what my mom told me about meats going in the freezer at college, and I'm almost positive that she said if you freeze meat, it never goes bad. With that in mind, I find a bank of freezers currently being used to store frozen pizzas and empty them. In several trips, I take every kind of decent meat I can find and pack it in there, then turn the temperature in the row down to zero degrees Celsius. It may be impossible to transport the meat around without it going bad and the power could go at any time, but if we get a chance to come back, we'll have some meat of reasonable quality.

I then move on to the row with foil sealed cereal bars, energy bars, and granola bars, taking dozens of varieties. I next make my way over to the toothpaste and brushes, taking enough for everyone. After grabbing a lot of mouthwash, I go for shaving cream, razors, aftershave, shampoo, soap, antibacterial hand soap, and deodorant. Finally, I make my way over to the toothpicks and take the entire supply of round toothpicks before making my way over to the spice aisle to take all of their liquid mint. I next make my way over to the section with disposable plastic containers and empty both caches into a sealable pot. Then I place the lid on most of the way and pour no less than three containers of liquid mint inside, snap the lid shut and toss it in with my groceries. As time passes, each of us ends up going through the dozen aisles twice.

I hear a gunshot from somewhere outside and I can immediately hear everyone running up the aisles with their carts. When we get outside I can see a bunch of the undead approaching the bus from the opposite side. I put my hand up near my mouth and pull my glove off with my teeth. By the time my glove is off, I hear a soft click and see one of the undead fall out of the corner of my eye. We all stop in a line, almost synchronized, and we let our shopping carts supersede us. There are twelve of them against the bus. The weapons all open fire within a few seconds of each other, and five of them fall instantly.

As we move on to the next round of shots, Jake strafes to the side so he can shoot them from the back, but Anderson grabs his shirt. "Side shots only... don't want to hit the bus." We reload within a few seconds, but Julia keeps firing with her pistol, grimacing as the recoil pushes her arms back. When the firing stops, there are twelve corpses, and I get the impression that Anderson and I got most of them. Somehow it hadn't occurred to me that no one else knows how to shoot. I look up at the windows to see Julia's rifle poking out of the back window. "Everyone okay?" Anderson asks. Everyone murmurs their agreement as I start pulling bullets from my bandolier to put in the loading port of my weapon. Julia is shaking her hand hard, the pain she's feeling visible only in her face. I look over at Anderson.

"That normal?" I ask, referring to Julia.

"38's got a hell of a kick... snub nose, file grip... it's like trying to hold on to belt sander when you fire. She'll get used to it."

"Get anything good?"

"Yeah. Cigarettes."

"Oh, great, bare essentials first, right?"

"Also, we're in luck... they have 5-Hour Energy."

"What's that?"

"Energy shots... never heard of it?"

"...one of those bullshit herbal supplements?"

"Not bullshit... remember how when we did plays at the Mass we'd pound a ton of high-caffeine soda?"

"Of course..."

"Fifty times better... trust me; I've tried everything on the market."

"Shame they won't be around to see the profit windfall... if we make it through this, you can be their spokesperson... 'When I'm trying to ward off the pangs of sleep in the midst of a Zombie crisis, I turn to 5-Hour Energy...'"

"Uh, guys... we better get going, like, *now*..." Jake says.

I turn my head up toward the main road, which sits up on a forty foot hill three tenths of a mile from us, to see five of the undead running along the guardrail with the sun as a backdrop, surely coming after us with even more undead in tow. Rich is the first one on the bus and the rest of us follow while Anderson and Jake throw our supplies on board. When we finish, Rich pulls the door shut and speeds off before they even make it into the parking lot. "Where to now?" He asks of either Anderson or me. "My house. It's the next turn after where Bryn Mawr intersects with West Chester Pike."

After helping Julia reload the cylinder of her .38, I let my head fall into the clustered fake leather material of the bus seat. When my head goes back, I feel a hand on my rib cage. I smile as Julia's other arm goes around my back and pulls me closer as she brings her head into my chest. I put my left arm around her and play with her bra strap from the surface of her shirt. Behind me I can hear Anderson discussing something with Karen; he's probably teaching her how to shoot or maybe explaining what we're going to do. It only seems like we've been driving for a few minutes when Rich makes the turn on to a street that leads to my house. "Where do I turn?" Rich asks. I let go of Julia and move up to the front with Rich.

"Does the traffic end?"

"No, but there's enough of a break between West Chester and Bryn Mawr. I went through the shopping center to get here. If you notice, we're on the wrong side of the road." He says with a smile.

"Wonderful. Turn left on Bryn Mawr, and you're going to make another left on the first full fledged road you see. Follow that one until... you know the routes, head toward St. Alban's and I'll tell you where to stop."

"You sure we can make it?"

"What do you mean?"

"If there's one car crash, it's gonna be hard to turn back."

"I hope so. Do what you can."

I go back with Julia and continue hugging her; she buries her head in my chest as I stare out the window, occasionally watching the odd corpse patrolling the street, attracted innately to the bright yellow bus. Each medium sized suburban house has trees that either conceal the lawn or provide a hefty backdrop, and each lawn is reasonably maintained save for the fallen leaves. Halloween decorations litter many of the lawns. Some of these people had children. I'm thankful now, more than ever, that we only moved to this house a few years ago, allowing me to know none of my neighbors.

Rich gets us close enough, so I flag him down and provide the necessary directions until he turns off in front of my house. "Okay, everyone, we're stopping here. We can all get a shower, but we need to limit the time we spend inside or else they're gonna find us. If that happens, I know what to do, but there is a good chance we won't be able to make it back out. We clear?" They nod, we arm ourselves, and Rich opens the door so we can filter out of the bus. I run up to my house, reaching for my keys.

I run in the side entrance, the breezeway, then open up the door to the body of the house and let everyone inside. Once inside, I refuse to let familiarity overtake me as I run up the steps to the second floor and open the doors to both bedrooms, entering my own on the left hand side. Green paint and green velvet drapes adorn the walls and windows, a thirteen foot desk that has more than once been the site of network gaming is against the back wall, a mini fridge and the rest of my enormous DVD collection are tucked in a corner to my right. The only thing missing is my computer, which is still at school. In spite of only one missing element, my room has never felt so barren.

I turn on the substandard computer that stays in my room and sign in to my instant messenger service immediately out of habit. "What are you doing?" Rich asks. "I'm getting online... see if anyone else is on." My eyes instantly lock on the dozens of people online as shown by my buddy list and my heart races. Upon closer inspection, I discover all of them have either their away messages up or have been idle for several days. I expect that if anyone is still at their computer, they'll talk to me.

I look down the list in detail to find the screen name of my friend Drew. Drew was a close friend during a time when I had few, specifically no more than he, Alan Taylor, Jack O'Connor, and Anderson. The five of us had endured nearly half a decade being completely unable to attract members of the opposite sex and forged an intensely close and emotional bond hinging primarily on our frankness when it came to our feelings and highlighted by geeky activities of stark contrast, the most noteworthy being the gratuitous playing of network computer games and regular viewings of Flyers games. Every weekend we used to hop into Drew's car, scream and yell at the tops of our lungs, sit down and talk about how vindictive women could be at the local coffee shop, buy DVDs at TLA Video, and go home to watch them. Apprehensively, I rest my mouse over Drew's screenname and wait for his status to pop up:

Looking for a bomb shelter. No, I'm actually serious. I am looking for a bomb shelter, and after I find one, I'm locking myself inside. I'm not coming out for at least a year.

"That's a relief... who wants a shower first?" Everyone calls for it except Julia. I smile at her. "Jules, you're first. I'm next. After that Rich and Anderson. Try not to take too long, my love." Julia kisses me and goes into the bathroom. The shower turns on immediately.

"I'm gonna get some more towels... some of you might have to double up."
"In the *shower?*" Melody asks.
"I mean share towels."
"Oh..."
"There's toothbrushes and toothpaste in the bus if you need it."

Jake accompanies me downstairs where I go into the linen closet as well as my parent's bathroom for more towels. I tear the sheets off of their bed and throw them into the living room.

"What's that for?"

"Winter's just around the corner..."

"Oh, duh..."

"Do me a favor and unplug the TV in the living room?"

"Makes sense."

By the time everyone is done picking out towels, Julia walks out of the bathroom with one wrapped around her. "You can get changed in there." I say, pointing to my brother's room. I take great relish in pulling off my stinky, soaking corduroys, socks, shirt, and t-shirt. Once inside the bathroom, I take off my sweat encrusted boxers and toss them on the floor. When I sit down on the toilet, I evacuate my system. Once finished, I take a good long shower. I wash my hair and condition it. I wash my face down with some anti-bacterial rinse. I rub every inch of my body with hands coated in soap. I enjoy the heat of the water with almost tantric glee, and when I'm done I clip my fingernails and toenails. I grab my electric razor so I can cut down the sparse hair on my face. I manage to accomplish all of this in fifteen minutes.

I cover my electric toothbrush in toothpaste and exit the bathroom to allow the next person to go. Once finished, I return to my room, marvel at my supply of boxers, and pick the most comfortable pairs. When I've finished selecting my wardrobe, I lie down on my bed and stare at the ceiling. When my eyes start getting heavy, I pull myself up and sit on the edge. Julia joins me on the bed and we both lean back and stare at the ceiling. She's never been in my room more than a few minutes before because her parents wouldn't let her over my house.

Rich asks for a razor, scissors, and shaving cream before he goes into the bathroom and comes out shaved with a haircut, looking a bit like Robin Williams might if he were lanky from decades of malnourishment and had been born with dark red hair. I strip my bed, the trundle bed underneath it, and both beds in my brother's room. Between my clothes, my brother's, my parent's, and the older clothes we'd intended to give to charity, we manage to find a new set for everyone, though Melody apparently dislikes hers. I follow Karen as she goes through my mother's closet. Finding something quickly, she takes off her jacket without any warning, so I turn to find myself looking at the pictures on the mantle.

I then run out to the kitchen where I find a note on the counter, giving me all the information I'll need to call my parents in Bermuda. Ignoring the beeps that indicate what must be a wealth of voicemail messages, I dial the number for the hotel and someone immediately picks up.

"Pompano Beach Club Southampton, how can I help you today?"
"Room 26 please."
"One moment."
"Hello?"
"Hi mom, it's..."
"JEFF! OH MY GOD, You're okay, are you okay?"
"Yeah, mom, I'm fine."
"Oh god, I was so worried about you!" She's already starting to cry.
"Hey, mom, what did I tell you? I'm the *last* person you need to worry about in a Zombie crisis."
"Oh god, I'm so glad you're okay, are you okay?"
"Yes, mom, I'm fine."
"You haven't been answering your phone..."
"I left it at school... sorry."
"We've been trying to get back for two days now..."
"You shouldn't do that."
"What? Why?"
"Well, I mean, you're safe in Bermuda."
"But what about you and Dave?"
"Mom, I told you, I'll be fine, I'm doing fine already..."
"Jeff..."
"Mom, I'm 19 now. I can handle myself. Besides, we're already on our way to a safe house."
"We? Who's with you?"
"Uh, Julia, a bunch of people you don't know, and Anderson."
"John's with you?"
"Yeah."
"Well that makes me feel better."

"If there's anyone you should be worried about, it's Dave. Did you get a hold of him?"

"Yes, yes, he's fine..."

"Thank god. When you get a hold of him again, tell him to head west, as far away from Pennsylvania as possible, if he can."

"And you're going to be okay?"

"Yeah mom. I guarantee it, I'll be fine."

"I want you to call me every day so I know you're okay."

"I don't know if I can do that. I'll... *try* to check up when I get the chance..."

"Oh, don't say that..."

"Mom, it's not gonna be easy... and you can't call me either... god forbid we're trying to hide and a cell phone goes off... we've been on the run today, and I've been up since... like, seven last night?"

"What happened?"

"Don't worry about it, we just had to leave someplace in a hurry. We're all okay."

"Jeff, please tell me what happened?"

"Like I said, we're fine. Since then, we've armed up, and I'm at home right now."

"Please, please just stay there."

"It's not safe..."

"How are we gonna find you?"

"Mom, I told you, it's not safe for you to come back."

"I know but... your father wants to talk to you."

She hands off the phone, and then I hear my dad's voice.

"Jeff?"

"Hi dad."

"Are you okay?"

"Yeah dad, you know me, I'm fine."

"What happened?"

"I think you know as much as me. It had to start around here 'cause things went to hell fast."

"I'll bet. Mom said you think it's a good idea to stay in Bermuda?"

"Yeah, I know you guys want to be with me and Dave but we're better off apart."

"Why's that?"

"What if something happened to… it's just easier if we're apart. If you're in Bermuda, I know you're safe and I don't have to worry. I hate to make *you* guys worry…"

"I…"

"Look, the best thing you can do is talk to Dave. Have him call me if you get a hold of him."

I put my hand over the receiver. "Anderson, go get Melody's cell phone number, Karen's too." I take my hand off as Anderson runs upstairs. There are three undead outside the window approaching the house slowly.

"I'm going to give you the cell phone numbers of two people in the group. Don't call us, we'll call you. If you get a hold of Dave, tell him to call… we'll leave the phones on silent and call back when we get the chance."

"We talked to Dave, he's okay, he's just in his apartment. Jeff, we're gonna get the first flight we can out of here. I don't care what it costs…"

"Dad, I know you want to be here… but you have to stay put. Even if you somehow made it to the airport, is it open? Is it overrun? Could you get a car? Are the roads blocked? Could you find weapons? Could you get a plane back? You *have* to trust me when I say I can handle myself, no one knows more about Zombies than me."

"Philadelphia's overrun."

"What?"

"Your mother just heard it on the news."

"Oh god. Dad, there's like a million people in Philadelphia."

"Probably a million and a half."

"Jesus, there were only thousands before, but now…"

"Jeff, I want you to pay attention to the news. Do you hear me?"

"Yeah."

"And I'll tell you why. You can bet the military is trying to take care of it, but there's a good chance that they're gonna start using bombs if it doesn't go well…"

"I hadn't considered that…"

"Look, if that happens, you have to get as far away as you can. Some churches have bomb shelters, and that's the best place to stay."

"I know dad. I'll be all right. Just trust me. If I know you guys are okay, I won't have that clouding my judgment."

Anderson rejoins me.

"Here, the numbers you can call are 610-649-8482 and 610-733-8100. Remember, only call if you really need us, if the power goes out we'll need to conserve our batteries... besides, like I said, I don't want a phone ringing when we're hiding. I'll try to contact you when I can."

"Jeff?"

"Yes?"

"Be careful, my son."

"I will. Put mom back on."

"Oh wait a minute, Jeff, are you getting whatever you need from the house?"

"All we can think of."

"Take the katana."

My eyes light up as I managed to forget about that. I hear the phone switching hands as I respond to him.

"Thanks dad, I'll keep that in mind."

"So dad says you want us to stay here?"

"I just can't imagine any plan that could safely put us back together."

"Don't forget to take your allergy pills and bring your inhaler with you..."

She lets out a small sob as one of the undead outside scratches at the window.

"I will mom."

"And remember to try to balance your diet, eat plenty of fruits and vegetables..."

"I *will* mom, I..."

"Okay, okay. Please, please call me."

"I have to go mom, I have a thing here..."

"I love you."

"I love you too mom…"

Anderson fires a shot that instantly blows out the window the moment I hang up. "Jesus!" I shout, staring at Anderson disapprovingly. He shrugs back before pulling up a crowbar, shattering the rest of the glass out of the fractured pane as he starts to beat down one of the undead through the gaping hole in the side of my house. Hearing the thundering of footsteps, I turn to see Jake and Rich barreling down the steps. Before I can think to say anything, I pick up a permanent marker and write the hotel and room number on the back of my hand. As I finish, I can finally concentrate on speaking again.

"Did you have to break the fucking window?"
"Yeah… what do you care? It's not like we're coming back… Rich… gimme a hand!"
"Shit…"

This is my house. Waves of terrifying energy begin coursing through my veins. This *was* my house. It isn't an asylum, it's not indestructible, and it's not even remotely safe. Every possession that had importance to me is in this place, and though my familiarity with the surroundings due to daily traverses during breaks from college give me the ability to move through the halls and rooms with autonomous ease, each step conjures a different memory. Each direction I look carries an image loaded with information and emotion.

The dinner conversation when my mom and dad shamefully went to work on my brother for the fact that he didn't have a summer job. My mom and I talking awkwardly about when I first began dating Julia. As I stand there, the words and phrases play in my mind in a continuous loop, as if I need to see each of them multiple times for the memory to have the right impact so they don't fade with time.

"Grey, you alright?" Anderson asks, startling me.
"Yeah, is Melody done in the shower?"
"Yeah, everyone's done."
"Okay… I just need to round up a few more things."

I go into the medicine cabinet for my allergy pills, praying that I'll eventually be able to wean my body off of them. "Anderson, there's camping supplies in the garage, see if you can find anything we might need..." I say, hearing Karen go through pots and tea kettles out in the kitchen. When Anderson nods back at me, I rush up the stairs and go into my closet. I load up a backpack with the other things I need, including my army jacket, my pocket flashlight, two more pairs of glasses, a disposable camera, more gloves, another inhaler, my Leatherman, my boxes of bullets, a change of clothes, and a change of shoes. The single most important thing I take is the bundles of books and papers that make up my writings.

I quickly load my DVD collection in a huge plastic foot locker and use the extra space to store a few random personal effects, including two of my stuffed animals I've had since infancy. As a group, we take all of my socks and whatever jackets, hats, scarves, and gloves we think we will need. Just about everyone has sheets wrapped around their bodies for transportation. Rich volunteers to put my television in the bus while I insist upon carrying my DVDs.

Finally, I run into my dad's office. Attached to the wall, above a picture of my father, brother, and I wearing white uniforms and black belts is a black katana sheath with silver fittings. I reach up and pull it down, fixating the sheath to an empty spot on the left side of my police belt. Once in place, I yank it out of the sheath at examine the beyond-razor-sharp blade. This was a gift for my father by one of his Tae Kwon Do instructors so he could begin taking katana fighting lessons. When he did so, I joined him, but we didn't keep up with it for more than a few weeks because it didn't seem practical. We were both cautioned that fighting with a katana can take decades to master, but fortunately I won't have to fight any of the undead since a clean stroke through the neck could hardly be considered a fight. I sheath the katana and find the sharpening kit.

"All right, everyone ready?" I ask, walking out into my dining room. Once I get their gestures and grunts of approval I throw the door open and slide the metal stopper into the pneumatic device that holds it there. The first wave of gunfire rips past my head before I can even look outside, and after I've ducked and covered, I watch several bodies fall. The sound produces an instant and sharp pain in my ears. Anderson, Jake, and Melody come forward and strike the temples of the next wave with their crowbars. Once one on the ground gets close to me I pull out my handgun and fire a shot into the center of her head. The weapon kicks back and slams into my shoulder, forcing a dull shriek of pain out of me. Julia steps forward and drops her gun, running into the scores of undead swinging her crowbar, knocking them over.

"Come on!" She shouts. I must admit the authoritative way she defended me was pretty hot. I get up off the ground holding my right forearm against my body as the group runs to the back of the bus. I glance back and forth around my front lawn to see the undead scattered throughout the little suburban neighborhood; the largest group, about ten, are on my front lawn between the bus and me. Holding my right arm in pain, I stare at the group as they close in toward us, and for the first time I realize how much more difficult maneuvering is when they have their arms stretched out. Panic taps the base of my spine with enough force to see my extremities shake with terrified adrenaline as I prepare for one of them to stumble forward and take hold of me.

Julia holds both ends of her crowbar and uses it to push some of them back, and she narrowly misses a violent swipe as backlash. "Watch out!" I shout uselessly. Rich opens the back of the bus as we get ahead of the group and cut off swiftly to the right. "Load it up." Anderson says passively as he steps out and unleashes a baseball swing that snaps the fragile neck of one assailant, leaving his head to hang off his baggy neck skin as the body hits the ground. He swings again, but even as he knocks another two back, I can see the rest closing in on him. "JAKE, HELP HIM!" I shout, realizing the futility of my struggle to push my box of DVDs into the back of the bus. "LOAD THE BUS!" Anderson shouts back.

I turn around and start pushing beneath the box, finally lifting it up to the walkway and shoving it in. Someone hands me the TV and I concentrate on that next, limply pushing at it with my sore arm as Julia pushes it in for me. That's when I become aware of the silence behind me. I take a moment to brace myself before I turn around to see Anderson and Jake standing over a group of motionless corpses. Anderson has a lit cigarette dangling between his fingers and stands as though he was in the midst of a coffee break.

Perhaps noticing my terrified expression, Anderson gives me a droll thumb up. Once we all make it inside the bus Rich takes off and easily finds his way back to West Chester Pike, then heads off back toward the school, which we must pass to get to the mall. I move my shoulder to get a better look out the window and instantly get a little shock of muscle pain, which makes me aware of the debilitated state of the rest of my body, giving me the undeniable urge to lie down. The pain I received in my ears a few moments ago is gone, but the ringing is still present. I reach into the aisle to grab my box of DVDs and slide it up to bridge the gap between us and the seat across the aisle. Once it's in place, I grab a few more small square items from the seats around me, lay a comforter over top, and just like that, Julia and I have somewhere to lie down and sleep. Everyone else sets up gear in a similar way after seeing what I've done.

As we pass the strolling corpses on the street, the central theme from *Dawn of the Dead* pops into my head, the combination of bass and drums simulates the persistence and pace of the undead too perfectly for me to ignore. As we prepare to turn onto a larger road, we pass by a preschool. I expect to see infants patrolling the insides, clawing at the fence. Luckily, I see no such thing. I then look to the front of the bus to see Anderson already asleep with his rifle at his side. Everyone else seems to be staring ahead or into the backs of seats while I stare out the window with morbid curiosity, half lying across my makeshift bed with my shoulder propping me up on the window frame.

I look down to see Julia sleeping and chuckle; her mouth is hanging open slightly, her one arm is up across my chest and the other is absently placed against the window frame, making it look like she's reaching out for me. Unsettled, I carefully place her arms back against her body and straighten up. Taking a moment to assess the situation on the bus, I realize that Rich is alone at the driver's seat, so I get up and try to approach him casually.

"How you doin'?"

"Just fine, just fine. How's everything back there?"

"Fine. Jules is asleep."

"That's happenin'."

"...what's happening?"

"The two of you. You know, happenin'?"

"Oh, yeah, thanks."

"How long you been together?"

"Year and a half."

"Wow, at this age..."

"What makes you say that?"

"The way you look at each other. I mean, I used to drive a bus, so I seen plenty of kids going out... after long enough, you can tell who's gonna last and for how long."

"Interesting."

The silence that follows is painfully banal, and my acknowledgement of this fact leaves me with no avenues to explore in conversation.

"So, you want the story?"

"Excuse me?"

"It's not a problem for me to go into it, I'd just like to know if that's why you came up here."

"...what story?"

"Why I turned to the streets."

"It, uh... hadn't occurred to me to ask."

"Never mind, then."

"Well, now you've got me curious."

"Sure?"

"Absolutely."

"Well... I'd say it started with my parents. My father... good man, a hard worker... loved his job... home heating. It was what my grandfather did, so he really wanted me to be my own man. My mom... well, I suppose they fought about as much as anyone else. She was always in and out of work... neither of them was around much. Dad never seemed... he was anxious all the time, wound up. Sometimes when I asked about mom he'd to snap at me. Then, one night, she was gone."

"...what?"

"Just like that. No note, nothing. I took it a lot easier than my dad. A week later, we found out she took everything out of our bank accounts... even what they'd been trying to save for me for college. Ever seen your father cry?"

"I have."

The ringing continues fading from my eardrums as we stare silently at the road.

"He didn't say much... you see expressions and know what people think and how they feel, but most of the time you're so caught up in the moment you gloss over it..."

"I know *exactly* what you're talking about..."

"So I saw everything in the way he opened a cereal box or... shined his shoes. He never got any explanation, not that I heard anyway... can you imagine what that does to a man? It was all he could do to keep us alive. Ever had to live on one meal a day?"

"Never."

"Sometimes I'd come home praying that'd be the night for dinner. You knew as soon as you walked through the door when it wasn't. I didn't see my father those nights... anyway, when I got out of high school the money wasn't coming in fast enough... I wanted to go to college, and he wanted me to, but I couldn't make that choice. He supported me for 18 years, so it was my turn."

"That's when you took the job at the bus station?"

"Right. So for almost twenty years, I was the 'good' bus driver."

"What year did you stop?"

"'93."

"Shit, I wasn't in the district yet. I had Harry when I was here."

"Maplewood? He was a soggy shit sandwich."

"I'm sorry, so, you were the 'good' bus driver..."

"Right. I played the radio, talked to the kids, let 'em do whatever they wanted. The first two years were rough, since I was fresh out of high school... they recognized me."

"Kids can be such dicks."

"It's even worse when they know how to take you down a peg... that's how I found out my mom was into coke. I wanted to kill my father for letting me find out that way... but I'd get home and remember what he was dealing with... the happiest I saw him was asking about my day... maybe he just needed a break from being stuck in his head... anyway, I couldn't let him have it..."

"And were you saving up for college?"

"What I could spare. It was living a dream, though... every other Friday I felt closer to college. Dad and I used to take turns paying the bills, and then the other would pay for a decent meal once every two weeks. Every dime that came out of our paychecks was split evenly, and whenever my dad couldn't quite pay out something with his paycheck, I'd chip in mine. Sometimes I'd just give him my paycheck to pay him back for taking care of me. He told me later that he used to just put those straight into our joint account."

"Sounds like you have a great dad."

"He was a good man."

"Was?"

Rich's half smile stays the same, but his eyes go cold.

"Don't imagine you know what it's like to spend every day talking only about the good things... and watching someone you love take fifteen years to self-destruct because they never talk about the bad ones."

"I don't."

"Ten years went by where I barely noticed how much worse he looked. He hid all the family pictures... I guess he didn't want to see them but couldn't live without them. When I saw the picture of us at Christmas the year before she left I knew something was wrong. At first I was able to tell myself it was just stress, until he started coughing up blood. Lung cancer, for someone who never smoked... as if that would have made it better... I used my college money to pay for chemo. They can only manage it for so long, though... it's like watching someone drown in an inch of water."

"God. Rich, I'm... I'm really sorry."

"It's okay."

I search for somewhere else to look and my eyes land on his left hand. He is wearing a wedding band. For a moment, I fight the urge to ask. "Married?" He looks up at me, and then glances down at his left hand.

"Was... used to hang out at Casey's on Saturday nights when I got old enough to drink. Met a girl, fell in love... you know how it is."

"Yeah... why her?"

"When you try to pick up girls at 25, they're so... it's like all anyone cares about is money... or college. When you tell people you're a bus driver who lives with your dad they stop being interested. She didn't ask, and didn't care. When she got the full story, she didn't try to console me... that's when I knew."

"So... was she your... escape, or something?"

"We just didn't have to talk about it all the damn time..."

"Shit... I'm the same way with my friends..."

"They ever hate you for that?"

"Nah, of course not... you?"

"Eventually... I always found myself not wanting to talk about what was bugging me, even if it was an elephant in the room. I thought she accepted that... turns out she just tolerated it. I didn't know when I was doing it... you get caught in the moment."

"Is that why you ended up splitting?"

"I didn't *leave* her..."

"I meant why the two of you split..."

"Oh, well... I've never heard a single case where it's just one thing... you need that last straw to break the camel's back. We were married after five years... just before that I got my dad's life insurance money, so I sold our old place and bought a new one. Turns out the old man had saved up a bunch... so we'd be okay for awhile. We moved in together and it was just..."

"...just?"

"...when you something like that gets taken away from you, the only think you can keep is what you felt. I remember the first summer in that cramped little apartment behind St. Alban's... people listening to the Phillies games on the radio in the courtyard, resting on the grass. A warm wind blows in the window and it's like poetry in motion... the smell of the grass and the Sam Adams you just cracked open, the static of insects, the triumph of having just assembled a cabinet... and I remember sublimely missing Ally. Thinking I couldn't wait for her to come home."

"Sounds familiar..."

Our eyes shift to the road ahead simultaneously as he navigates a bend in the road which leads toward the adjacent Springton Reservoir. "I never get tired of this." I say softly. Rich turns back to me, and I motion to the road in front of us. On the left side, we are flanked by countless trees that mesh into an ocean of green, red, orange, and yellow, and on the right, an endless, flawless expanse of glimmering water; the palette of treetops runs from the sky down to the impeccable surface where the sun streaks along the middle in a golden haze that is only interrupted by the bleached, skeleton branches of trees that lie dead at the rocky shoreline. The road is bordered by gorgeous stone walls, and in the middle, a bridge extends out to a cylindrical observation hut that I've been told was constructed for a watchman to oversee the reservoir affairs in the mid-forties when the water source was ripe for poisoning by potential Nazi spies.

Now, the bridge, which is over a third of a mile long, is cut off by sand bags and razor wire, and not without good cause; this road is the only major outlet from the Marple area for at least a mile in any direction. "There's no way we can pass that." Rich says. I turn back toward the group and wake up Anderson. He gets up and follows me to the front of the bus to look out the window. "Great... it took twelve guys three hours to get that set up." I sigh and roll my eyes. "All we need to do is clear a path for the bus on both sides. It couldn't take *that* long to do it..." I look out the windows on both sides, not seeing the undead.

Anderson looks at the sand bags and shrugs, strapping on his rifle. He stops for a moment and looks at Rich. "There was a check point at Bishop Hollow and Providence... is there another way around?" He asks. Rich just shakes his head. "Not nearby. This is the most direct route." I get my rifle as well, and then Rich gets up with his shotgun. Anderson wakes up Jake and talks to him while I go back to Julia.

I'm about to shake her, but I decide not to. I run my fingertips up the sides of her rib cage to her armpits and back down again. Her sensitive spot is on the other side of her armpit on the front, just above her bra, so I softly knead my thumbs in there. She lets out a smirk and her eyes open. "Darling, we have some work to do. Can you stay on the bus and cover us?" She nods while yawning. I smile and lean forward to start kissing her neck, her arms come around me. I kiss up to her ear and whisper. "I love you." Then I kiss her on the lips and she gets up to arm herself. I throw my trench coat and gloves on and step outside the bus. Exhaustion hits me like a tranquilizer to the neck and my head falls limply forward, bringing my body with it. I manage to right myself before hitting the ground, but not before my vision clouds over in a fog of effervescent purple. I shake my head and stand up.

"You alright Grey?" Anderson asks. I nod in reply, walking purposefully over to the bridge as Rich and Anderson follow. There are two razor wire fences, each formed by large metal Xs and poles through the center, which take up the entire width of the street. "Grab an end." Anderson says. He and I move to the ends of the one on the right; like the barricade across 476, the barbs are covered with chunks of shredded camouflage fabric and flesh. I'm glad I have gloves. I look over the sandbags to see three corpses torn down to the bone, left only with the shoes and socks which identify them as military. The only meat remaining is inside the skull and the joints, making them look as though they've been licked clean. Once again, the weapons and ammunition are strangely missing from the site. There is a triple thickness of sand bags on both sides of the bridge up to a man's chest.

Rich, Jake, Anderson and I start moving the bags, each one weighs about a hundred pounds and we're all weak from malnourishment and a lack of sleep, so it's two to a bag. I'm somewhat surprised to see Anderson smoking almost the entire time. The work goes slowly and our presence attracts several undead that the girls manage to take out. Anderson eventually goes back and tells them to cool it with the firearms so we can cut down on our bullet consumption. They opt to wait outside the bus with their melee weapons.

When we've finished clearing the right lane, I feel a tremendous surge of accomplishment wash over my tired body. I start heading back to the bus when Anderson loudly clears his throat behind me. "Can it wait? I am *extremely* tired." I take his silence as meaning he's not prepared to negotiate his position, so I turn to see him pointing at the far end of the reservoir road. "We're not done yet." After a collective sigh, we trudge along for what feels like an hour while the others stay behind to guard the bus. Once again, we go two men to a bag until we've cleared out the right lane.

"We're just about out of daylight." Anderson says after another hour. "We should probably find someplace close to bunk up." I look back at the bus as we start walking back. "We can sleep in the bus." Rich offers. Anderson and I take a moment to consider the suggestion, but he beats me to the punch of negating it.

"Yeah, we'd probably be safe, but if the shit got thick, where would we go? How would you like several hundred of those things outside when you wake up in the morning?"

"Just pop it into drive and run them over."

"Have you ever run people over before? I sure haven't. I know this thing has high ground clearance, but they'll get stuck in the wheel wells. We don't want to run that risk, because then we're *really* boned."

"What do you suggest?"

"Could try for the mall." I offer.

"Just incase, I think we should stay close. We're tired... if we head there and it's a clusterfuck, that's it."

"You know... when you say it like that, it sounds like you're talking about a videogame... but you mean there's a good chance we could actually die."

"The preschool is back up there..." Anderson says, partially ignoring me. "It's on a hill, a lot of exits."

"Only one level though. The community college is right up the street. It's big and isolated from the street." I say.

"Sounds good to me."

"I don't have a problem with that. It'll give us some time to eat." Rich sighs.

We board the bus, drawing the women inside to inform them of our plans. Rich turns the bus around to take us back down the road about a half mile, turns into the Delaware County Community College entrance and takes us through the winding parking lot to the main building, which is made of brown brick. The series of structures is quite square and plain, surrounded on all sides by dense woods. The enormous parking lot is segmented into several rows and every set is separated by a grassy knoll that travels down toward the school. As we get closer I notice that there is some light emanating from the tinted windows. We'll have to turn those out before we go to sleep.

We pull up out front and I feel like a student on a field trip as we prepare to exit the bus. We gather some of the food, weapons, blankets and pillows, and one of the coolers with drinks, all of which assist in making it a long walk from the bus to the main building. The outside of the building looks like the kind of college that would be reserved for movie sets, and the iconic imagery is not abated when we enter; just across the hallway from the front doors is a small computer lab whose ceiling is four stories high, and each wall of each level is comprised entirely of windows so one can see what's happening on each floor.

We walk to the right once we enter and quickly find the stairwell enclosure. I lead the group up three flights of stairs, and then we exit out to the hall. As with the first level, the center of the floor is cut out, allowing an unobstructed view of the ground floor. We walk to the right, go into a hallway and stop inside another computer lab with tiny interlocking cubicles for each computer. I remember taking a course on the Internet here when I was young, at a time when taking a course to understand the Internet was still something one might do.

In ten minutes, we've set up a barricade so that only one door opens and our sleeping area is only accessible via a maze of cubicles. Once we're set up, Rich finds a bathroom and fills a pot with water to cook hotdogs. Since I haven't eaten anything close to a cooked meal in several days, the idea of boiled hot dogs is simply amazing. Unsurprisingly, Julia has brought along a stash of vegetarian hot dogs. "You know," Rich says while cooking. "Even hotdogs seem like a luxury." Jake looks up at him. "That's gotta suck." Rich doesn't even look up at him when he responds. "You do get used to it." Jake leans back, stretching.

"I don't think I could."

"You'd be surprised."

"I'd like to think I couldn't accept it for myself."

"…unless you've got no choice."

"Well, I'm just saying, I don't think I would be above begging."

"Then you're just making it someone else's problem, when it's really yours."

"Didn't you say it wasn't your fault everything happened, back in the greenhouse?" Anderson asks.

"I said it wasn't my fault, not it wasn't my problem."

"What about welfare?" Melody asks.

"Like I said before, I refuse to make my problem anyone else's. That includes taxpayers."

I wrap Julia and myself tighter in the Flyers blanket I took from my house. While we eat, Anderson stands silently by one of the windows. "Someone get the lights." He says, as if he noticed that I noticed him. Melody gets up and turns them off as Rich finishes cooking the first batch. "Okay, how many does everyone want?" Rich asks. Anderson, Jake, Karen, and I each want two while Melody and Julia only want one. The buns and ketchup come out, I point out that ketchup is a good source of the anti-oxidant lycopene. Everyone just looks at me, and rather than try to explain I get some fruit punch and potato chips.

When we've finished and cleaned up the night has almost completely fallen. We have ourselves set up to sleep in sort of a square except Anderson, who sleeps by the door from which we will eventually exit. Julia and I are sleeping underneath one of the many computer cubicles in the room, separated from the rest of the group. Behind me, I can hear Rich and Karen talking softly about their families while Anderson repeatedly shows Melody how to user her rifle. I'm lying on my back with my arms behind my head, staring at the fluorescent ceiling lights, wondering how long it will take for the power will go off.

After a few moments, I feel Julia's hand lift up my shirt slightly. She runs her index finger up and down the pubic track underneath my navel. I turn around and wrap my arms around her as I kiss her. She pushes my right arm away and grabs a hold of it; I pay no notice as I continue kissing. She presses my hand against her hip and slides it down, between her legs. I pause for a moment, and then keep kissing her.

Five minutes later she's unconscious, a smile still partially stuck on her face, and I'm more than a little wired. I hear shuffling behind the cubicle. At first, I dismiss it, but then it continues, culminating in metallic jangling. I squint and poke my head around the corner to find Melody going into her purse. I no longer see Anderson. "What the fuck are you doing?" I ask silently. Her head comes up swiftly. "Cigarettes." I slide myself a little further inside the room.

"You smoke?"
"Trying to quit..."
"I haven't seen one touch your lips... ever?"
"I smoked on my shifts... remember?"

I nod and slide back, and then something hits me.

"Wait, you aren't going to do that in here, are you?"
"Where else would I?"
"What if it sets off an alarm?"
"You want me to go outside?"
"No, no. Just... the lobby or something."
"Alone?"
"...I'll go with you..."

Once I throw on my boots and put on my police belt and katana, she and I walk around to the door. As we approach, Anderson wakes up immediately, pointing his pistol at us. "What? What is it?" He asks in a daze. "She's having a cigarette, I'm going with." He squints and lets his head fall back. "Since when do you smoke?" He asks. "I don't. No one goes anywhere alone." He nods and rolls over into sleeping position again.

The two of us walk around the corner where I stop to take the opportunity to look out the large windows, but I can't see anything moving. We walk down the barren concrete staircase to front door; the moment her foot touches the bottom of the steps she pulls a cigarette out of her purse, and in the dark it looks like she lights it before it's even in her mouth. I look into the dark center of the building, then back and forth down the halls. On the far right side from the main entrance are two glass doors that lead out directly into the woods. I walk past Melody to the window and rest my forearm against it, giving my eyes a few moments to adjust to the darkness, but I remove my arm when I notice the giant crack running up the middle of the window. I can see a few blobs of movement a few hundred yards away in the tungsten-lit parking lot. Even though I can't see them that well, I consider how amazing they are to watch.

"Why do you say that?" Melody asks. I must have said that out loud.

"Huh?"

"You said watching them is amazing...?"

"They're just so... human."

"...what?"

"I mean... I almost feel sorry for them..."

"What!?"

"Well... you are aware that they used to be real people?"

"Duh."

I step away from the window and lean my back against the door.

"So... *think* about them as people. They shopped for clothes. They styled their hair. They got married. Had jobs. Partied. Got laid. Had kids..."

"Ugh..."

"They were just... people."

"Aren't they still?"

"That's not what I meant... I remember just about every Christmas I've ever had. I remember my first kiss. Now... what does it really matter? I always used to think about that when I watched horror movies. It's not difficult to imagine them as just everyday people that got sick. They're not trying to kill anyone on purpose... they have no choice."

"You don't know that."

"Well, I guess I don't."

"So... why do you *think* that?"

"...I want to believe that all people are inherently good."

"Hah. Even me?"

I glance at her, and then move over from the doors to the three large panes of glass that look out toward the bus, but in the darkness, I can't see it.

"...sorry."

"Don't sweat it."

"...what was that?"

"Huh?"

"That face..."

She flicks her cigarette into the darkness and reaches for another.

"...it's like you expected me to apologize."

"I didn't... I just... didn't know where the conversation was gonna go..."

"You're not good with girls, are you?"

"I... not really... I mean..."

"If you have that attitude, you're never gonna make it work... you have to be confident."

"I'm not."

"Then you pretend to be."

"No use pretending to be something I'm not..."

"It's not that..."

"It's more like... my personality. I know it's not for everyone."

"Why do you say that?"

"I have a strong personality and strong opinions..."

"Oh, you're one of *those* people..."

"One of... what people?"

"You need to be right."

"No, I just... I mean, if I argue with someone, if I know a lot about something, I'm not going to let it slip by on opinion alone."

"So you need to be right."

"No, I don't *need* to be right..."

"But if you're saying you can't let someone have their opinion..."

"That's *not* what I'm saying. I'm saying if I *know*... when I argue, I *need* to know they know what they're talking about."

"I still don't see how that's any different."

"Okay, so, I argue with people who don't 'believe' in evolution. First of all, it's not something you believe in. It's a scientific theory. You subscribe to it or you don't, belief has nothing to do with it. Second, most people start their counterargument by saying that if man came from apes, then why are there still apes? Apes and man share a common ancestor, we just took a different evolutionary path. Third, some people think Darwin recanted the theory of evolution on his deathbed. It's a myth... Darwin's family was at his side when he was dying. Even if he did, it doesn't matter. Galileo was forced to recant his theories, but that made them no less true. That would be like saying 'I don't believe that I need oxygen to survive'. Where was I? Fourth?"

"Yeah..."

"Right, fourth, the loophole that creationists use to argue is that there are certain macroevolutionary processes that aren't described by classic population genetics... scientists debate the *how* and *why* of these processes, *not* whether evolution is real. Fifth, Darwin was right about natural selection, and there is no debate over that. Sixth..."

"I'm not arguing with you about evolution…"

"I know, I know, hear me out… Sixth, there are two types of evolution, microevolution and macroevolution. Microevolution is directly observable to the point that creationists must concede that it happens. Microevolution is still evolution. Now, I don't mean to talk your ear off, but do you see what I mean?"

"Sum up for me again?"

"Do you get the impression I know what I'm talking about?"

"Well yeah…"

"Right. When I get in that argument, I can't accept that the other person hasn't studied it."

"You could say God is responsible for evolution."

"Indeed, and that satisfies some people. But if someone says that evolution is just a theory, I remind them that so is gravity."

"It is?"

"Yeah…"

"I gotta be honest… I mostly just forgot everything you said."

"That's alright."

"…and I wasn't listening."

"I get that a lot. Some people's brains switch off when I get excited about something… or they just think I'm pretentious. The people who say that aren't even using the word properly."

"That sounds pretentious."

"…I get that a lot too. My friends and I don't just laugh at jokes… we dissect them and talk about every aspect… finding the smallest facial expression or word emphasis that sells it."

"It doesn't bother you that she's so much younger than you?"

"…wha…Jules?"

"Who else?"

"No. I mean, I'm 19, and she's 16. When I'm 43 and she's 40, three years won't mean shit. Besides, if she's younger, she'll stay better looking longer."

"That's shallow."

"…I was kidding. Besides, what a person looks like has as much to do with what you like about them as their personality."

"That makes sense. I mean, if they're beat…"

"Well, I wouldn't put it in such crude…"

The massive glass pane next to me explodes open with the kind of concussive force that compels me to open my mouth to equalize the pressure in my inner ear, and a second later I'm sprawled out on the floor and convinced I've been bitten. If I wasn't struggling to move, I'm sure I would be screaming. The lobby is dark except for a soft yellow streak of light across the exasperated face of my attacker as he tries to sink his teeth in my arm. I push at him, trying to get him off me, and then Melody kicks his neck, knocking him back. Those precious few seconds give me enough time to rip the .45 out of my belt. "DIE MOTHER *FUCKER!*" I scream, unloading four rounds while turning my head and closing my eyes. Blood hits my left cheek, his body goes limp and I throw him off. Then, Melody screams.

She is being pushed back against the railing separating us from the computer lab in the center of the building, moments from being flipped over backward with her assailant. Before they both fall, I run in from her right and reach over his extended arm, grabbing his upper chest and throwing him back before he can try to bite either of us. When he turns to me, I unsheathe my katana and send the blade through the bottom of his chin in one swift motion, shocked at how easily it slides through his skin and muscles. I grit my teeth, scream, and continue to shove the blade in deeper. I slip the blade out and stomp on his skull as hard as I can.

In my peripheral vision, I catch three more running in through the giant hole in the glass, and I also notice another that neither Melody nor I dispatched. Melody pulls the Glock out of her purse and shoots one in the eye. I bring my katana across his neck from my right side as hard as I can, decapitating the first one, then in the same move I bring the katana up and smash it into the nose of the other one, slicing off a section of the front of his face to send him to the floor in a heap. As I stomp him into oblivion, Melody points her pistol at the head of one on the ground and shoots off two quick rounds, the first shot blows a dense puddle of muscular pudding on the floor, and the recoil sends her arms back, wasting her second shot on its leg.

Suddenly, a bright light reflects off several of the windows and for a moment I have no idea where it's coming from. "What the…" Both Melody and I hold our pistols out in front of us as I watch the light narrow in the hallway ahead of us to the right, and suddenly a man with a shotgun adorned with a tac light runs out. "Human, human!" I shout insistently, pushing Melody's arms toward the ground. I realize at this moment that I have my pistol in my right hand and my katana in my left, so I holster both as the light shines up in my eyes. When he brings the light down, I have to laugh despite the situation.

This man is wearing a bullet proof vest and has what looks like a Benelli shotgun with a small flashlight attached to the front, but aside from that, he looks pretty pathetic; he's a tall, chubby, in his late twenties, and has a flashlight taped to the top of a helmet that looks to be part of police riot gear. From the neck down, he's wearing flannel pajamas and unlaced boots. He mutters something I don't understand: *it's not donetti's shoe?* "Is everyone okay?" He asks audibly. Three more people come out behind him, one of them has a hunting rifle and the other two are carrying baseball bats. "Everything okay Dave?" A woman asks. "We're fine. Are you okay?" He asks us. I hold up my hand to block the flashlights, prompting them to shine them away.

"Was I bitten?" I ask.

"…you look okay… what are you doing here?" The large one, who I assume is Dave, asks me.

"We're passing though…"

"We? This your girlfriend?"

"No, my girlfriend's upstairs." I shouldn't have told him that.

"How many are you?"

"Eight, including us."

"You can't stay here."

"Relax; I said we're just passing through. We'll be gone by tomorrow." Their weapons look stolen. "You guys looters?"

I realize immediately how stupid that question was.

"What makes you say that?"

"Just curious."

While they look around, I undo the clasp for the pistol I just holstered. Dave sees the cigarette on the floor, picking it up and holding it out toward us. "Smoking!? Are you insane?" As he talks, I see something move in the door to the stairwell behind them. "What?" Melody asks. "Those things can see a lit cigarette from a mile away!" Dave roars as he stomps out the butt. The door handle works gently, quietly, and the door swings open slowly enough that none of them are disturbed. "Oh. How far away can they see a flashlight?" Melody asks, and I laugh, glancing again at the doorway to see Anderson come up with his rifle tight to his shoulder and Rich right behind him.

I glance over at Melody to make sure she's still holding her pistol, and she is. "Everything okay?" Anderson asks, and all four of them turn in shock, starting to lift their guns. "Don't even think about it." While Rich watches the group, Anderson glances at the corpses, then looks over at Melody and me.

"We're fine. Just... a mistake." I say.
"You *can't* stay here. We were here first..." Dave says.
"Actually, aren't we *all* trespassing?"
"I'm not," Anderson adds. "National Guard."
"Bullshit."
"Spec. John Anderson, HHC 1st and 111th Infantry Division, 56th Brigade, 28th Division. I'm empowered by the United States Government to commandeer this building if I see fit, and since I'm currently on active duty, I can force its owners to provide me with provisions. So I suggest you listen to me, or I'll place you under military arrest. Since Delaware County is currently under martial law, I can detain or execute you if I find you unruly. Any questions?"
"Well, how are you gonna detain us?"
"Let's make this real simple: we've got more guns than you."

Dave's arms go limp and the shotgun goes out at his side. He sort of lifts the weapon out in a little shrug, and then his arm goes limp again. "Good. So go the fuck to sleep." Anderson says. The four people go back to where they came from and we all start back up the steps. I wince as the previously faded pain in my shoulder starts stinging again, and then rotate my arm.

"Christ, is this ever gonna go away?"
"What was that about?" Rich asks us.
"She needed a cigarette, and I didn't want her to go alone."
"And those psychos?" Anderson asks.
"I have no idea. The undead came through the windows, then those idiots showed up."
"You see the guy's pajamas?"
"Yeah. Regardless, we should be real careful tonight."
"Yeah, and you should wash off that blood. And take that shirt off."

I look down and see a blood splatter and a tiny chunk of flesh on my shirt. "Jesus..." I now notice the smell, like rotted meat; the dead carry with them everywhere, and I'm just starting to get used to it. I go to the first bathroom I find and take my shirt off, wipe the blood off my katana with it, and toss it in the trash, knowing I'll have to comprehensively clean the katana later. I thoroughly wash my hands, then my face. As I do so, I curl my lips inside my mouth and pinch my eyes shut, washing my face until I'm sure it's clean. When I open my eyes, my face is red from scrubbing.

I concentrate and look at my eyes, watching my pupils dilate as I stare at my reflection in the mirror and again in my own pupils. The silence makes me notice the distant, annoying ringing in my ear again. I walk back to our room, open the door and walk to my nook. Julia is awake again. "Are you okay?" I slide into bed with her. "Fine." I slowly rest my back against the carpeted floor and let out a deep sigh as I hit the ground.

"Mmm, you look so tough without your shirt on." Julia says with a smile. I let out a laugh. "Stop." She reaches over and grabs my right bicep. "I mean it." I close my eyes and smile. "Anything that looks like muscle is fat." She pulls up closer to me and starts running her fingers up and down my chest. Never one to spend long in the buff, I reach into my backpack, pull out my extra t-shirt and slip it on before I lay down again. I reach over and grab Julia's waist. "Come here, beautiful." She lets out a little laugh as I pull her on top of me and start kissing. "Could you two keep it down?" Rich says in a half-humorous voice.

"Sorry Rich." I let her slide off of me on the ground toward the back of the cubicle so she's on the inside. I put my arm around her waist and put the other one beneath the pillow. She turns around to face me and kiss me again. "You don't give up, do you?" I ask quietly. "Do you want me to?" I smile and blow in her ear, then bite it softly. "What do you think?" I ask her. My head goes limp on the pillow and I close my eyes again. "Are you going to sleep?" She asks, poking my abdomen. "Nope."

10-13-04, WEDNESDAY

Dizziness accompanies the sensation of my eyes having been sucked to the back of my head when I wake up, a clear sign that I overslept. Though my shoulder has finally stopped feeling like a mass of nerve-laden silly putty, my legs are still tingling. Fortunately the idea of running the tension out still feels like it will work. The next bit of good news comes from my perception of a whistling noise that starts low and begins building, a sure sign that my hearing is back. Confused at the sound, I poke my head around the dividers to find Julia leaning over the gas grill with a tea kettle and a bunch of paper cups. "Have I mentioned that I love you?" I ask, prompting her to turn and smile. It would seem that everyone else is awake except Anderson, but I think I hear him shuffling around the door.

Each cup has a tea bag in it already, and I find mine easily by the Earl Grey tag. When she pours the water, I take the cup and start bobbing the bag up and down so it will steep faster. Breakfast comes in the form of a cereal bar and a banana. After I've eaten, I take my pills and get dressed for the day. It is 12:02 when I finally check the time. Before I continue I opt to go through my police belt and see what I need and don't. There's a baton holder, handcuff case, flashlight holder, gun holster, double magazine holder, a key ring, and a radio case. I include my Leatherman pouch, put one of my inhalers in the handcuff case and remove everything else but the weapons and ammunition.

Once we've packed up and the eight of us have gotten down the stairs, I tell Rich to start the bus and ask Anderson and Julia to come with me to ask if the people we ran into last night want to come with us. We walk along the hallway to which they retreated, sandwiched between bland concrete on our left and a wall of windows looking outside on our right. I try the handle of the first door, looking inside to find nothing of interest. The second one we arrive at is locked, so Anderson knocks.

"Anyone in there?"
"Who is it?" The responding voice is appropriately hollow.

"Guess… we're headed to the mall… interested?"

"The mall? What the hell's there?"

"It's a rescue center…" I say.

"Sounds like a death trap."

"Well, do whatever you like," Anderson says. "Good luck."

"What the hell's that supposed to mean?"

"Just what it sounds like… we hope you don't get eaten."

"Is that a fact?" Another voice asks, getting close to the door. "Then what was that bullshit last night?"

"Never mind. Just go fuck yourselves." Anderson says.

He starts walking away, and I run up behind him. "You still don't like it, do you?" Anderson says. "What's that?" He stops suddenly, and I do too, but he pushes me forward.

"Walk in front of me."

"They might be standing there with…" I whisper.

"I know…"

"…wait, what don't I like?"

"That I told them to fuck off."

"Of course not…"

"Why's that?"

"Because… I don't know, it's unnecessary?"

"And because you hate confrontation."

"Well that too. Wait, did I tell you that?"

"You didn't have to. I saw the look on your face at the first check point."

My jaw drops. We reach the end of the hall and Anderson covers himself behind the corner as he looks back down toward the room, motioning for us to get behind him.

"It's okay… you haven't been trained to shoot."

"Yeah, I know, I looked in her eyes…"

"That's part of it. They're not people... they're *targets*. Melody told me you don't think they do anything wrong... well, okay, but it's kill or be killed."

"Don't worry, it won't be a problem."

"As long as you don't let it become one."

He spins around and walks off toward the stairwell.

"Do you see what I warned you about?"

"What? About John?"

"No, not that... those people... they've gone nuts."

"I know, love."

"No, no, no. It's just... if we ever get separated, for any reason... you can't trust anyone."

"Okay."

"Especially as attractive as you are."

She grins at me.

"I *am* lucky to have you, and I'm not just being overprotective. The same goes for everyone, it's just..."

"What?"

"...the guys they'll kill, but the women..."

"I understand."

I take a last look down the hallway before we walk out to the bus. Once on board I explain what I just explained to Julia to everyone, apparently reiterating something I said when we were still at the high school. Rich snakes the bus through the parking lot while Julia and I simply lie in our makeshift bed and stare into each other's eyes. Every few minutes I poke my head over to see everyone else on the bus; Anderson is talking intently to Rich and Jake is talking to Melody, but Karen is in the back not saying anything. She hasn't said much of anything since we've picked her up. I lie back down and look into Julia's eyes again, and for some reason I wonder what kind of effect Ava's death has had on her. I know Julia would sacrifice herself if given the chance, and I would sacrifice myself for Julia. By extension, does that mean I would sacrifice myself for Ava, were she still alive?

I would care about Anderson dying, and I would end up incapacitated by Julia's death, but other than those two, I can think of no one else. My brother doesn't live close enough and I've seen him only on extended breaks over the past few years. I will eventually grow to miss him if he does die, but I've never known anyone who has died that I haven't gotten over immediately. I've always thought that meant there was something wrong with me, but now it would seem that it's a gift, presumably one that couldn't explain my immediate reaction to John Squared.

While my mind wanders, I contemplate my mind wandering. Is thinking about my own survival as the only thing that matters a good thing? I suppose, if anything, it brings me closer to the mindset originated by my Cro-Magnon ancestors. I've read that humans supposedly learn new things every day and forget 80% of it, but if I get comfortable somewhere, I won't do anything but live from day to day. School and work are a good way to learn things, but those obligations are now gone. For some reason, that makes me wonder what happens to Julia's braces. Does she just keep them forever? Will someone eventually be able to take them off?

"Are you seeing this?" Julia asks. I sit up and signify my alertness by widening my eyes. I look out the window across the grassy fields of Rose Tree Park, then pull my window down, stick my head out, and look up and down the road for burning wrecks, screaming people, flashing lights, or thousands of the undead.

"I don't see anything."

"Exactly... the road ... the checkpoint... it's like a ghost town."

"Well, the town near Chernobyl was evacuated 36 hours after the plant blew."

"Yeah, but that was... how do you know that?"

"Did a report on it in high school."

"...that was an explosion... on the news, they didn't even acknowledge they were Zombies."

"Maybe when the check point failed they created a wider perimeter. And the military might have evacuated... who knows?"

"Anderson might."

"You know... that's a great point."

I head up to the front of the bus to find Anderson standing behind Rich. I pat him on the shoulder and wave him into the adjacent seat.

"Jules and I were just talking... did you guys get any orders to evacuate?"

"...I can't tell you."

"You mean you don't know, or..."

"I can't tell you. Listen... just... ask me another time."

"Fair enough."

I lift my head and look out the window to see the familiar amalgam of trees and power lines that signify the mall is just up ahead. I once asked a friend who has lived his entire life in Los Angeles what he thought of when Pennsylvania or Philadelphia became a topic of discussion, expecting to hear about Ben Franklin and the Liberty Bell, but his one word response was 'green'. I disabused him of this notion, describing the tightly packed city full of art, music, and sports franchises. I told him about the gradations of urban, suburban, and rural areas. I told him about our proximity to New Jersey, the beach, and the abundance of local rivers. I spoke of Wawa and the widespread existence of great delis and sandwich shops.

Now, as we drive along the back roads of a typical area in the outskirts of Philadelphia, I realize the setting doesn't betray his notion. Look in almost any direction, and within a few hundred feet your view of the distance will be blocked by a dense cluster of trees, though the colors differ greatly. The area highways are, almost without exception, sandwiched by rich forests on both sides. The lawns are wide and lush. One of the few exceptions to this green-based palette lies up ahead; we dump out on the main road to see the Lima Mall set on a decline, surrounded by major roads on all sides, and lit by the ominous glow of the sun as it retreats behind the clouds.

The two entrances I can see from this side have chain link fences with razor wire at the top and a double thickness of highway dividers with sand bags in front of them. There also appear to be more sandbags within the perimeter of the fence and mounted machine gun posts, but the guns are gone. It was easy to tell that they had once been installed based on the piles of bodies around the barricaded entrances and the massive brown arcs of dried blood. Rich pulls the bus up alongside the fence. I open my window and look for a door of some sort in the fence, but there aren't any. Rich drives to the next entrance to find another unbroken wall of fencing, so we drive around back and ascend a gentle incline that leads up to the smallest entrance of one of the department stores, an entrance which is fenced off like the others with a three-foot high strip of sand bags and another weaponless machine gun mount directly behind it, but there is also a large gate.

"That's it." I say.
"What are those big metal things for?" Melody asks.
"Gun mounts." Anderson and I respond simultaneously.
"Then where are the guns?" Jake asks.

Without warning, Anderson opens the back door, leaps out, and runs to the gates. "Tell Rich to back it up through here." His estimation appears to be correct, as the back of the bus narrowly fits through the chain link gate and the bumper just clears the top of the sand bags, which means the only way in now would be either through the bus or over the top. When we stop, I notice Anderson staring at the ground pensively. When his eyes meet mine, I can pretty much guess what we're about to see. I lean forward to find the pavement caked with dark brown stains accompanied by several moist red puddles. This time there are no bullet riddled corpses. The only things aside from the gated entrance and the gun mount are extravagant, artistic blood splatters on the doors and ground, and chunks of corpses that appear to have been torn apart beyond recognition.

Rich turns off the engine and all of us crawl through the emergency exit with our weapons drawn; I leave the katana behind, opting instead for a crowbar to better facilitate breaking into the stores, and

Julia has permanently loaned Karen her handgun, reasoning that I will always be well armed and never be more than a few feet from her. "Don't slip on the blood." Anderson says gruffly as he steps through the door. As soon as I get inside, I can smell gunpowder heavy in the air, and as I look up, I see a haze of thin gray smoke that stretches the entire length of the ceiling. I almost trip over Anderson, who is kneeling in front of me inspecting bullet casings.

"Please tell me it's not looters."
"All military."
"So where are the bodies?"
"They must have had some time to pull out... probably took the civvies out, cleared the bodies... probably just tossed them in front of the gun mounts."
"Alright... call it, what do we do?"
"Take a look."

We both crane our heads around, scanning the department store we've just entered to find shelves of toys on the right and Halloween decorations in front of a plethora of circular clothing racks on the left. Ahead there is a pair of escalators leading down with stairs sandwiched between them. Blood is smeared across the waxed floor, leading toward one of the aisles in two separate, thick streaks. The next aisle we turn toward reveals the corpse of a soldier who has been literally torn in half at the middle, his skin grayed and bloated with bite marks all over and chunks taken out of various parts of his body. The only thing left sticking out of the limp flaps of meat that formerly made up his chest is his spine, which appears to have been violently torn apart just above the lumbar region, leaving the ripped tail of his spinal cord dried to the ground. There is also a gaping exit wound in the back of his head.

I turn around to see Jake enter the aisle, his eyes shoot open and he pitches forward and vomits immediately. The smell of the body is bad enough, but the sight of it is probably worse. The strange thing is that he's been decomposing for awhile, but it would appear that insects had done none of the work. I see Anderson back away and bite down hard on his lower lip, tightening the muscles in his face as he closes his eyes and hugs his rifle. "Come on." Rich says, leading us into the mall.

"Hello?" I say quietly. Melody draws in a breath as though she's about to shout it, but Anderson grabs her and slaps his hand over her mouth. "Don't scream..." He lets go and takes the lead. "Do you *ever* wash your hands?" Melody says behind him, spitting the moment I chuckle. As I move in farther I can see the stairs moving on the escalators, but my attention is drawn to the blood-smeared handrail for the stairs between the escalators, apparently caused by a string of intestines that stretches down the steps while still clinging to the end of the rail. Anderson peeks over the stairs. "Oh Christ." He says, turning back. It appears as though someone was impaled on the top of the handrail and their intestines got pulled out as they fell down the stairs, splashing blood and bits of organs on everything.

The body jerks forward and tries to stand despite the gunshot wound on his forehead; it must have been too high to impact any section of his brain worthy of shutting him down. Before I can react, Anderson leaps forward and impales him through the eye, the crowbar ripping through his head like a red paint can, producing just about the same effect. When the head falls back, I look over at Anderson. The grimace on his face is enough to tell me how little he's enjoying this.

"Strange..." I offer.
"What?"
"He just revived now."
"...so what?"
"We must have just missed the firefight."
"Engagement... firefight goes both ways."
"Whatever, you know what I meant..."

We turn left and start toward the body of the mall. There are more blood streaks leading out of the department store ahead, but still no bodies. We split into two groups and walk along the two sides of the balcony so we can see the ground beneath the other group. All the escalators are still running, and it's strange to see that just one of the moving steps on one escalator has blood on it. Over the next twenty minutes, we cover the entire top level and the entire bottom level only to find no one in the mall and virtually no signs of struggle. Almost every gate in the place is down and locked, which makes me wonder where they kept the people while the rescue center was still operating. We complete our sweep on the lower level where the department store opens up into the body of the mall.

"What happened?" Jake asks.

"Looks like they were overrun, but you'd think there would be more bodies." I say.

"There wouldn't." Anderson adds. "They would've cleared this place out before it came to that. My guess is they were ordered to a new fallback point."

"Okay," Rich asks. "So what's our next move?"

"Jeff wants to stay..." Anderson states.

"Why would you assume that?" I ask.

"Dawn of the Dead."

"...if it got bad enough that *the military* had to clear out..."

"All the same, John, what do we do?" Rich asks.

"If we can figure out how to work the gates we can probably hold up for the night. It's a lot safer than being on the bus." He responds.

"What's the problem with the bus?"

"I don't want to stay on it unless we *need* to. I don't know about you guys, but I'd like every chance to stretch out I can get."

"Smart..." Karen says.

"Wow! You actually *talk!*"

Everyone chuckles, including Karen.

"Where do we sleep?" Julia asks.

"How about the video store?" I ask. "There are TVs and we can block the doors with the movie racks."

"How about the nature store?"

"Maybe we should figure out where the Guard put people?" Anderson suggests.

"Hot Topic." Melody says. "It's got those huge metal gates."

"...good point."

"Hot Topic it is." Rich says.

"Well, what do we do in the meantime?" Karen asks.

"We're in a mall, aren't we?" Melody says. "Let's get whatever we need."

"Alright, I'm gonna collect some necessities..." Anderson says. "The one thing I need all of you to get is boots with solid bottoms and good ankle support. Find some hiking boots, and get some of those foot pads. After that..."

"Just try to be rational." I add. "Maybe some good running shoes."

"Well, let's stick together for now and make sure we get some of the same supplies..."

"Hot Topic's first..."

I lead the charge to Hot Topic that sees Anderson easily breaking through the chain before we move the racks around to block the doors and set up our sleeping area in the back. After that, the group disperses to go shopping in two groups of two and one group of three. Julia volunteers to go with Karen and try to warm her up to the group while Rich, Jake and Melody make a trip for a new wardrobe. I caution them to stick to warm, comfortable, close fitting clothes in drab colors. Anderson leads me to the second floor of one of the department stores where he picks out a dozen backpacks of the same make and color before deciding on a firm list of supplies for them. He dictates a list, which I copy down before we disperse to collect the items which will comprise what Anderson terms our 'survival packs'. His most ingenious addition is heavy duty flashlights that take C-cell batteries, since C-cells are used with the least frequency.

After dropping the stuff off at Hot Topic, Anderson and I look in the sporting goods store, where I manage to find a pair of fingerless gloves intended for rollerblading in that they have a protective sheet of hard plastic aligning the curvature of the wrist to the palm. I figure if I were to hit someone on the bridge of the nose with it hard enough they would probably die, and the undead couldn't be much different. Anderson agrees and takes a pair as well. We walk downstairs and look at the comic book shop.

"It's tempting to go in there just to rip open the packages of those game characters and set them up on a battlefield." I say, he nods. We turn our attention next door to a chain electronics store. "Walkie-talkies." We both stop. "Do you think they have radios in there?" I ask jokingly. We both laugh as Anderson proceeds to destroy the windows with his crowbar; fortunately, we don't encounter any alarms. We find the smallest radios we can and take seven of them, and then we find the smallest but most expensive walkie-talkies and take six sets.

Anderson fills several backpacks with every type of battery he can find. I go into my backpack, which I hadn't emptied from yesterday, and place the radio holster on my belt, inserting both the radio and the walkie-talkie. Next, we venture upstairs to the movie store. As we stand outside the door, Anderson sighs.

"What's the point?"

"Of stealing a bunch of movies?"

"Yeah... the power's gonna go out eventually."

"Might as well have fun with it in the meantime, and if we get it back, we'll have plenty to do."

"Ehhhhhhh... why not."

Once again, it only takes him a moment to get through the lock and pull the gate up. I run over to the movie merchandise section and take several *Lord of the Rings* school backpacks before beginning my quest. I grab all the boxed sets and special editions I've ever wanted to own and take every television show I've ever liked, and though I know I can take any movie, I only take the ones that I actually like and feel should be in my collection. Anderson mills around the store patiently, only occasionally grabbing a war movie or two. He finally stops me when he notices the surplus of undead movies I've selected.

"Seriously?"

"Why not? I mean, how did I learn everything I know about them up to this point? If nothing else, it'll give us ideas so we can improvise."

"Improvise what?"

"Escape strategies, survival tactics... anything."

We stop by Hot Topic to drop off our supplies again, and then return to a department store where we proceed to invade the sporting goods section. They have no firearms to speak of, but fortunately, they're stocked with ammunition for just about every one of our guns. We get ten more boxes of 9mm rounds at fifty rounds each, two more .45 long rounds at fifty per box, three more .38 boxes with fifty, two .357 with fifty, ten boxes of .300 rounds with twenty, twelve more boxes of buckshot shells and two more boxes of slugs, each at five apiece.

After that, we split up, whereupon I go to stock up on as many Leathermans as I can get my hands on while he goes off to gather some more things from his own list. After taking the extra ammunition and movies out to the bus, Anderson and I return to Hot Topic with our wares for the last time; I load our electronic devices with batteries while Anderson starts sorting out the supplies for the backpacks before we officially load them.

"Okay. Identical black backpacks with leather bottoms... we're putting our names on 'em. I got a shitload of CamelBak packs..."

"Of what?"

"CamelBaks... oh, they're great... you wear it like a backpack, it holds way more water than a canteen, and there's a straw on the shoulder. Standard issue, those go underneath the backpacks. Emergency strobe pins..."

He holds up an orange bauble with a clear plastic dome and switches on an extremely bright strobe.

"Pinned to the shoulder. A decoy if necessary, or a way for us to find you if you get separated... you take it off, flip it on, and throw it on the ground so we know you're in the area. Hand crank flashlights and handheld flashlight holsters on the belts, extra batteries and bulbs in the backpacks. Also, right angle flashlights for the shoulder and a plate compass as well. *You* can figure out how to get all that shit on there..."

"Thanks..."

"You'd do a better job than me... I grabbed some sewing kits. If we can pick up GI gear, we're gettin' M-16 ammo pouches for stuff that needs to be accessible and field manuals for the backpacks. The Leathermen go on every belt. Hopefully we can get some MREs to throw in there. After that, you can put whatever you want on it."

"Sounds good."

I notice that he keeps looking toward the front of the store as he continues lining up the supplies. Eventually he sees me looking at him and gives up on staying quiet.

"Alright... do you think it's weird that the mall is totally empty?"

"You'd think we'd have heard something."

"All those blood streaks and bullet casings, and we've only seen *one?*"

"Are you sure all the bullets are from the army?"

"Yep. 5.56, same make. There were a couple here and there from other stuff, but not enough for a firefight."

"Seems weird that there would be no people *and* no undead. You'd figure one would win out and stake a claim."

"Wouldn't the undead leave if there wasn't anyone here though?"

"You've seen them. Yeah, I'm sure the majority would leave, but there'd probably be at least a few dozen milling around."

"You don't think it's possible they used some kind of nerve agent to wipe them out, it worked, and now they're airing the place out until it's hospitable again?"

He and I stare at each other in desperation for a moment. "Wait, no, outlawed by the UN in the nineties." Anderson says softly. "But it's not possible that they could have manufactured something new for this? What if this is a virus engineered by USAMRIID and escaped somehow, and they know how to kill the infected?" We stare at each other in silence for a long time. "You'd think it'd be quick acting. Besides, they didn't equip us with anything like that." I cock my head to the side. "Maybe it's better if we don't tell anyone else." He says gently.

That effectively ends the first part of our conversation. To prevent the silence from getting awkward, he continues to open packages and blister boards while I start collecting fabric to sew together the modifications to our survival packs. I rip off the logos on the backpacks so we can eventually put our names on them, and then sew nylon straps on the left shoulder to keep the right angle flashlights Anderson collected.

"Didn't figure you for a seamstress." He finally observes.

"Well, you nailed it... I love putting together shit like this... I was thinking, there's gonna be plenty of space in the backpacks, I can rig up the CamelBaks so they're secure inside."

"Sounds good."

"We'll keep 'em uniform. I figure most of us are righties, so the flashlights go on the left strap with the CamelBak straws above it. Strobes on the right shoulder, compasses on the lower right strap, tear off the logos and write our names there... I was thinking brown, so it doesn't reflect."

"...you've got it under control."

"By the way..." I start, getting back to work. "I... well, John Squared and I were talking about this before... I have to ask... do you think there's going to be an end to this?"

"Huh?"

"You know... does it end, or do we spend the rest of our lives on the lam?"

"Oh... probably the second one."

"Really?"

"Well, I mean, the army's gonna fuck shit up, but I don't trust the government. If I did, I'd be off getting assigned to another unit. That's between you and me."

"Like there's any doubt about that."

"I could get in a lot of trouble with where I am, unless they think I was going out of my way to protect some civilians. Then I'll get a medal."

"Awesome."

"Seriously…"

"So, what now then?"

"Well, I guarantee the Guard had another plan… probably head out toward Pittsburgh or something like that. After what happened here… well, what I'm *guessing* happened here… they're probably gonna hole up in a stadium or university or something."

"So…"

"So there's no chance we're gonna link up, and they think I'm KIA. So, I'm still Specialist Anderson, but I might as well be a civvie. Remember that three way leadership thing? You, me, and Rich?"

"Yeah."

"Approved."

I think he expected a more exuberant response from me, but I'm struck by a notion I can't help but share. "I can't imagine how depressing it must be… if you're in FEMA, the National Guard, the CDC, whatever… to reach that point where you feel your hold on the situation slip through your fingers… when you realize there's nothing you can do." We mull this over in silence before we switch back to the previous conversation without missing a beat.

"So, thus endeth the Andersonian military obligation?"

"Yeah… if we run into some other Guard guys, don't be shocked if I just start making some shit up. Just back my play."

"No doubt. By the way, what do you want to do if you get bitten?"

"Uh… shoot me. Like, let me say my last words and shit, but I want to be shot. You?"

"Unless I tell you that the pain of it is unbearable or whatever, I want you to wait until you're sure I'm coming back to shoot me. And don't let Jules see…"

I clam up immediately as Melody swaggers in more scantily clad than I've ever seen her, wearing nothing more than a low-cut spaghetti strap shirt and skin tight stretch pants. "Jesus, I said close, not claustrophobic. Can you breathe in those?" I ask nervously. "I don't get to wear anything like this to school." I assume that rationale is supposed to be in her defense. "Well, out here the only people who want to see your skin are the undead." I tap the side of my nose and point at her before she walks out.

"Silly cooze."

"Dude, where is that nose thing from?" Anderson asks.

"I got it from Twin Peaks..."

"That show's great..."

"I don't know why that reminds me, but back at the college, all that stuff you said about your authority, is that true?"

"Huh?"

"You know, to that guy last night?"

"It's bullshit. Technically, I can do it in, like, Afghanistan. It's funny though... I always had this thought since I joined the Guard... if I went to Iraq or Afghanistan or something, I'd die in this big blaze of glory."

"Audie Murphy style?"

"Well, he didn't die..."

"I know."

"Maybe like that... or those soldiers that jump on grenades. They'd call me a hero. I'd think about all the people that would show up at my funeral, you know..."

"Medal of Honor?"

"Maybe. I thought about that on the bridge... I always assumed my number was up when I was called in for action."

"Well... you'll still have plenty of opportunities for that. Not that I want you gone or anything."

"Yeah. For all I know this'll get cleared up and I'll end up in a court martial."

"Fucked up world we live in, huh? People are worse than the Zombies."

"Huh?"

"Well, take looters for example... when you're that ruthless, it's inevitable that it's gonna turn on you... either you mess with the wrong people or you turn each other. On the other hand, there are guys like us... over a long enough time we can kill thousands of those things. Enough groups like this, and we're killing a few million... in the long run, that might just be enough. Individually, we're weak."

"And they're strong."

"What do you mean by that?"

Karen's presence startles both Anderson and me. She's apparently just entered with Julia, who smiles and waves at me. I motion for her to come over and she sits next to me, putting her hand on my shoulder. "You're really tense," She says. "Want a massage?" I turn and smile at her. "Do you even have to ask?" She smiles back and I kiss her, then she goes to work on my back and shoulders.

"What were you saying, Karen?" Anderson asks.

"I was askin' what he meant when he said they're strong."

"One way to think about it is the perfection of the human machine..."

I squint at him, and then it runs across the cracks in my mind and makes complete and utter sense. "Wow..." Anderson grins and nods at me. "You wanna explain?" I nod and lean forward, letting out a soft groan as Julia works out a knot.

"So, animals develop stability in their environment, given their traits, while we need processed food and electricity. By taking away conscious thought, self-awareness... it makes us animals again. Apex predators, in fact."

"So, how is that perfection?" Karen asks.

"They're perfect killing machines. No infighting, no alpha males... they're the only creatures on the planet that can change you to their side, taking your will out of the process... what happened at the high school proves they're the greatest threat we've ever faced."

"What happened at the high school?"

"That's a good story for tonight."

"Okay. Well, they can't be around for very long, right?"

"Why do you say that?"

"They'll starve."

"We don't know if they need food to survive."

"They have to eat *somethin'*..."

"They're the living dead."

"Okay, good point..."

As the conversation closes up, the rest of the group returns. While Julia and Karen prepare dinner, Anderson and Melody seal the store up, and I continue my work on the survival packs. I give mine a quick test by taking a quick jog around the store; nothing shakes off or makes too much noise, but the straps leap off my shoulders with every step. With that in mind, I take out the stitching in the top and bottom of the pack and feed the snug straps of the CamelBak through before sewing it closed again. As I continue working, each person in the group sets up their beds and gets their food. By the time I'm finished, there's very little left. Julia selflessly offers it to me, but I insist that we share it, and I'm sure we both still walk away hungry. One of these days, I'm going to need to warm up a frozen pizza, or heat up pre-cooked bacon and make myself a bacon sandwich with mayo. As we finish our pasta and shells, the lights go out.

"Is the power going out?" Jake asks, trepidation hanging in his voice.

"Don't think so, or we'd get emergency lights. Besides, the lights aren't off in here." Anderson points out.

"Well what is it then?"

"The mall's probably on a timer."

"Gotcha. We should follow suit."

Jake goes into the back to find the lights, plunging the store into darkness except for the lantern and the fire from the grill.

"Everyone, I got each of us radios and walkie-talkies, belts, holsters... we're going to keep the squawk boxes on channel 2. The range is about two and a half miles, though I don't know how we'd get that far apart. Try to conserve the batteries... we have a lot, but if this goes on for a while we *will* run out, so we only turn them on when we need to, or when someone gets separated. Keep it *handy*; don't just stuff it in your backpack. Same goes for the radios, don't use them unless you have to and keep the batteries out of them so they don't die on latent charge. Everyone cool on that?" I ask.

"Wow..." Karen mutters.

"What is it?"

"Nothing, it's just... you're so composed, you're what, seventeen?"

"Nineteen. Some people were born to command troops or invent new technologies... I was born to survive an undead apocalypse."

"I guess you lucked out."

"I suppose. Um... so, once we're done here, what's next?"

"How about the hospital? That could be a rescue center... it's right across the street."

"No harm in checking it out," Anderson says. "If nothing else, we can get medical supplies."

"Like what? Anybody know how to use anything that we can't get from a medical kit?" Rich asks unenthusiastically.

"Actually," Karen offers. "I was an RN before I got my current job."

"Then we all lucked out."

We clean up after dinner and the group collectively tells Karen everything that happened to bring us up to the check point. Once we bring her up to speed, she inquires about why we had gone to Bandrome and how we got together in the first place.

"My friends ditched me." Melody volunteers. "I was bored, so I showed up thinking there was a game."

"I'm in the band, and I'm sort of friendly with Julia, so I figured Jeff was running with her for some reason." Jake adds.

"Well I know where Rich was, Julia was in the band, Anderson was at the barricade... what about you, Jeff, why did you come back from college?" Karen asks.

"Are you kidding, Bandrome is one of *the* geek events of the year... I wouldn't miss it for the world."

"What did you do for a living?" Rich asks Karen.

"Uh, you ever see that movie *Office Space?*"

"No."

"It's a medical compliance desk job. Pay's good, I guess..."

"...what happened before you met up with us?"

"Oh, we'd been hearin' about this for a couple days... the CDC was sendin' out memos every hour or somethin'... patient's rights, unidentified pathogen, non-transmissible via airborne or waterborne vectors... we knew they'd set up a quarantine in Broomall, but we were assured that was as bad as it'd get."

"By who?"

"The CDC..."

"Hadn't you heard what was going on?" Jake asks.

"We probably knew more about what was goin' on than anyone else, but maybe half the memos were confidential, so we weren't allowed to say anythin' about it yet."

"Wait... do *they* know how this happened?" Anderson asks.

"Last I heard they were still tryin' to figure that out."

"Wasn't the check point up Monday morning when you went to work?"

As the conversation continues, I slip into my bedding with Julia. Once I've settled, she tugs on my shirt. I ignore her, listening to Karen.

"I live in Upper Darby, so I head up Lansdowne to get to work... Anyway, I was at work Monday when they announced martial law. I tried to find out if that meant we were supposed to stay at work or not since we're processin' important medical documents, but no one could get an answer. I didn't want to go home alone, so I took up a friend's offer to stay at his place in Villanova. Next mornin' I took 476 back and one of the lanes was closed down. There weren't many people on the road either..."

"Where were you going at 7:00am?"

"Home, to shower and change for work. I was tryin' to figure out how to get around those sandbags when I got attacked... and I guess the rest is history."

Julia pulls herself up close to me and whispers in my ear. "Can we sneak away?" She asks. I look in her eyes, smile, kiss her, and stand up. "Guys, we're gonna run out to the bathroom, we'll be back in awhile. We'll leave the walkie-talkie on." Without a word, Anderson helps us move some of the barricading away from the door. "So, where are we going?" She takes a hold of my hand and pulls me toward the escalators at the center of the mall. "You'll see."

Once at the top of the escalator, she leads me toward the dim lights of the nature store. As I get closer, I can make out a table on a raised platform in the center of the room that seems oddly placed. Once inside, she sits me down at the table and steps away. After a moment, she sets a champagne glass in front of me along with one for herself, then lights the candle perched in the middle of the table. I smile sheepishly and look at the table as she pulls up a bottle and begins pouring us each a glass. "I didn't think you drank, love." I say, looking up at the flame reflecting in her eyes. "Sparkling cider." Her smile is adorable. "Come here, you..."

"Not yet..." She disappears into the back of the store and I become aware of the smell from the candle; it smells like a beach, more like the Virgin Islands than the Jersey shore. Soft, ambient, spacey music bleeds in through the overhead speakers, backed by the sound of rushing waves. The wall mounted water displays are running, and the lights are positioned just such that I feel like I'm in a jungle at sunset. I open my eyes as she approaches to find her carrying a covered tray. She lifts it up to reveal a small cut of filet on a plate and salad in a bowl. "Oh my god..." I whisper softly. She beams as she sets the filet in front of me. "It might be a little cold..." She says, sitting down. I bite my lower lip to restrain the smile.

"Well this is embarrassing..." I admit. "I feel like I should have been the one doing this."

"Give yourself *some* credit... I wanted to do something nice."

"This is... unbelievable. How did you get this?"

"The restaurant. I had Karen help me make it, then I put it in the microwave up here. I figured we could get a chance to talk."

I cut off a tiny piece and begin chewing it. It's a little cool, but it's been properly cooked at medium rare. I let out a groan of pleasure.

"I don't know what it takes for your vegetarian girlfriend to cook you a steak, but I don't feel like I've earned it."

"Well then I guess you'll have to work it off." She says with a playful wink.

"Cute. Sweetheart, I can't tell you how much this means to me."

"For once I've got you at a loss for words."

She lifts up her glass.

"How about a toast?"

"You've caught me off guard here..." I say.

"Here's to the next toast, and a hundred more after that. Here's to spending every moment at each other's side. Here's to never worrying about money, work, or school... here's to making love the most important thing. And here's to never giving up on each other."

"I'll drink to that..."

It's not as easy to find her glass with my eyes damp, but I manage to do it and take a sip. "Did you try to get me to eat less of the pasta?" I ask as I cut another slice off the filet. Her smile answers my question. I take the bottle of steak sauce from the platter and splash a bit on the meat as I continue eating. She reaches under the table and removes her shoes. Without missing a beat, I follow suit, and as we eat, she begins rubbing her toes against the tops of my feet. I have difficulty concentrating on which is more important, the food or her feet touching mine, and I realize that my indecision is the best part of the meal. She makes sure we finish at the same time.

"Dare I ask if you prepared dessert?" She gives me her patented coy smile, wipes her mouth, and steps over to another part of the store that is obscured from the front windows; there is a square indentation built into the floor that is two feet deep and eight feet wide on either side, and it's covered with blankets. My heart rate skyrockets as I watch her step down and kneel on the blanket. Before I have the chance to say anything, she motions for me to come closer. I feel my breath get ragged as I approach; should I take anything off? How do I touch her? How do I know what she wants me to do?

As I kneel down, she brings her arms up to softly clasp my cheeks, drawing my head in toward hers. She glances between my eyes and my mouth before our lips connect. Her hands slide down the front of my shirt before she pulls it over my head. I fight the urge to ask if I can do the same, reconsidering when I realize how much of a mood killer it will be. She doesn't resist me. When I have it off, I run my hands around her back to feel goose bumps. I pull back for a moment to look in her eyes as my hand goes to her bra strap. No hesitation. I snap it open and she lets it fall off her shoulders.

I've never seen her naked before, so I fight the urge to train my eyes below her neck. My heart throbbing, I can see the rest of her body in my peripheral vision. I slide my hands around her ribcage, finally running my fingers over her naked breasts, kissing her lips first before I work my way down the side of her neck. She lets her hands fall down and rest under the rim of my jeans. My nerves are tingling, necessitating that I consciously force myself to forgo anxiety and focus all of my sense toward touch.

Her breath heaves hard across my neck moments before she starts aggressively kissing me. With astonishing passion, she rips my jeans open, pulling the zipper apart the moment before her hands go into my boxers as my heart continues to throb into my breastplate. Her contented sigh stops me from catching my breath as she tightens her fingers. I wonder, for a moment, if I'm gripping her shoulders too tightly as I bury my face between her breasts, but I find that I must constantly remind myself to remain in the moment. I rip her jeans open as well, sliding them off her hips. I feel her take in a deep breath as I slide my hands back up her thighs and ease her down to the blanket.

I pull my jeans off and remove hers next; she's now breathing incredibly hard. Too hard. Taking a deep breath, I hold her hips close to my face before rising up to meet her. "Not until you're ready." She lets out a big sigh as her eyes roll back in unembarrassed passion; she grabs my face and kisses me once more before I start the path down between her legs. I take some of her inner thigh into my mouth, her animated sighs pushing me forward. I rest my mouth between her thighs, feeling her muscles tense. Sensing a recoil, I approach delicately, eliciting yet another sigh before her body spasms hard against me.

Once I have a sense of her reactions, I fall into a strong, steady rhythm. Her breaths become short, perfectly synchronized with mine. She takes a deep breath in and lets a soft, continuous groan escape through her teeth before every muscle in her body relaxes and she breathes out in a huge moaning sigh. I ease off of her, letting her breath subside before I continue. She doesn't scream, but I've never heard that sound out of her before.

Before she has a chance to catch her breath, she pushes me up and down on my back hard and fast, her head immediately diving to my waist. I look down to see the smooth, shadowy outline of her back, and as her head pulls up, I see her ample breasts sandwiched on either side of me for a moment before looking straight down to her thighs. Tingling waves of previously untapped eroticism blanket every inch of me as I urge her on with body language and soft sighs.

After another minute, I feel the electricity below my waist. My mouth mechanically opens wider as my sighs get more consistent. She pushes harder and faster. "Okay..." I can barely get out one word. I can't restrain a long, heavy groan as all my muscles tense up and release, her head still bucking as wave after wave of concentrated sexual energy heaves out of me. Finally, it becomes too intense. "S-S-stop." She slowly pulls herself off, and I instantly curl up into the fetal position.

"I love you…" I mutter repeatedly, running my hands through my hair and shaking. Her head comes up in front of me and I immediately kiss her. Something looks wrong. "What is it?" I plead. She looks down for a moment. "Would you be terribly offended if I got something to drink?" It takes a second to register, then an uncontrollable snort of laughter forces out of me. "Go ahead." I watch her stand up and walk over to the table, finally getting to see her full body naked for the first time. She takes a long drink from her glass, then wipes her lips and comes back down, wrapping the blankets around both of us.

She and I both giggle softly before we stop in a long, naked, passionate kiss. I look into her eyes, even though there's almost no light. "You know what I love most about you?" I ask softly. "What?" She replies with a smile. I bask in the sensations around me for a moment and watch every muscle relax on her face. Neither of us has to say anything. Neither of us moves.

Eventually we manage to get our clothes together, clean up, and return to Hot Topic. The walk back is silent, but blissful. Anderson is up as soon as we enter. "Everything okay?" He asks sleepily. "Yeah." I say softly, returning to my sleeping space with the pile of blankets. Anderson staggers to his feet and blocks the door off again. Julia and I curl up together with the blankets. Not a word needs to be said before we drift off to sleep.

10-14-04, THURSDAY

The lights come on in the garage of my old house, and for a moment, I wonder if I was the one who switched them on, or if the flicker was because of a brownout. I press the garage door button to find the sky dark, with everything on the ground looking as though it were lit from three feet away with an old lantern. I can sense they're outside, so without hesitation, I reach over the doorway and pull up my old sawed off Winchester and walk out to my driveway without an inkling of where I'll end up or how I'll get there.

Off to my right, a flickering light reveals someone stumbling in my direction, and like in the movies, the heavy, dim backlight keeps me abreast of their position even after the brighter flash has faded. I turn, draw, and fire, knocking over another one coming across the lawn. The trees above him are hanging unusually low and have become undeniably dense. I turn again to find the other three closer. I work the flimsy tin lever and hold the light plastic against my shoulder again, pulling the trigger to feel a dull snap. It's a toy. I've never owned a real rifle.

Aside from the colors, the world around me instantly stops making sense as fear begins to guide my perception. Like I've been caught in an ocean, my retreating footsteps slow until I fall over the corpse. My assailants with hollow, glowing eyes are already on top of me. I try to punch them away, but my blurry arm feebly ascends until my hardest impact fails to make an impression on their momentum. A hand closes on my windpipe hard enough to crush it, forcing my lungs to suck from a vacuum that pulls a pint of blood into them, a sensation as unexpected as snorkeling and letting the saltwater in the pipe.

My head suddenly hurts, my vision clouds, and my muscles become useless. I would be screaming, but I'm too busy choking, coughing, and crying. Then, a feeling that can only be described through thick layers of numbing purple wrapping around my spine radiates through my entire body as my muscles weaken to the point that my hardest scream comes out as a comatose whisper.

My entire body has gone numb, and I can't feel anything beside the quick, nightmare breaths being drawn into my lungs. "Jeff, sweetheart, wake up..." I sit up quickly in protest, grabbing my throat and sliding across the floor. I slam my head into the ground and thrash at the hands about me. "JEFF! CALM DOWN!" It's Julia.

The words actually register in my brain as the fear diffuses out of my body from my head down to my toes. I touch my neck, shiver, and rub the crust out of my moist eyes. I let out a cough and breathe deeply, looking up to see everyone staring at me. I sniff and wipe my eyes with my arm, looking away to let a deep, nonchalant yawn escape. For some reason, I try to mask my racing heart. "What time is it?" I ask, squinting through my teary eyes. "It's 1:15." Melody says from my left. "We should probably get moving." I say, getting up, but it would seem everyone else is ready. Anderson tosses me a cereal bar. "You missed breakfast." Julia hands me a paper cup of tea. "Thanks..." When I see her face, I put down the cup and hug her.

I eat slowly, watching Julia run interference with the rest of the group. I can tell Anderson's not pleased with my late sleeping, and Julia is doing an excellent job deflecting. By the time they finish taking the rest of the stuff out to the bus, it's just Julia and me. She casually makes her way over and sits next to me as I start getting dressed. "What was it about?" She asks as I pull my pants up. "Just horrible. Felt like... dying." She stands up and hugs me again. I rest my head on her shoulder as she rubs my back. I love the way her back feels, the delightful pressure of her breasts pressing up against me, the protrusion of her ribs through her soft skin.

I finally let go of her, slip on the wrist guards, put my walkie-talkie in my police belt, put on my backpack, and strap the rifle over my shoulder. "What's that?" Julia asks. I turn my head quickly to see some sort of movement in the mall. I stand up straight, not seeing anything. An undead man appears from behind the cookie stand in the middle of the mall corridor. "We have company." I click on my walkie-talkie to hear some indistinct chatter from Anderson before he repeats me.

"We have company, over..."
"Copy that, where are they getting in?"

"One of the department stores, did we check all of them? Over."
"I didn't, Jules didn't either..."
"Uh... Melody says they're coming out of the corridor, over."
"What corridor?"
"It doesn't matter; get your asses up here now. Over and out."

I grab a crowbar and run out the doors carrying it in two hands. There are four more in a line behind the cookie stand and another two coming around the corner in the distance. I think about running to the first one I saw to give my gloves a trial, but instead Julia grabs my arm and I turn to see a woman staggering toward us with her hands out from only five feet away. I push Julia behind me and cock my wrist back before slamming it into the bridge of my undead assailant's nose as hard as I can, forcing a dark, viscous fluid out. She stumbles backward, then continues coming at me despite the shattered lump of cartilage pushed against her brain. I suppose it was an urban myth after all.

After removing the gloves, I pull Julia toward me, cock my head toward the entrance where the bus is parked and run to the center of the mall, looking up at the skylight before checking the middle escalators. One walking corpse on the escalator turns toward us, trying to come down while the stairs carry him up; having seen us, he falls over and starts pulling himself down the steps with surprising speed. I take Julia's hand again, start running for a corridor escalator, and let go again. Once we get around a stand in the middle of the floor I can see a few more Zombies on the escalator ahead. I know there are a few ways up to the next level, but I opt against going any farther because I may soon have no way of getting back.

"Anderson, come in."
"What's your 20? Over."
"First floor, they're blocking the escalators, I need a way up, are you by the balcony?"
"Rolling to you... hang on, over."
"Don't come downstairs, I just need you tell me the best way up, hurry..."

Having spun completely around while talking to Anderson, I see them funnel in from behind us in a clothesline with a few stragglers following. The ones on the escalator are struggling to come down as the steps ascend, but they tumble forward when the steps lurch to an unexpected stop accompanied by an alarm sound. One of them must have gotten caught in the escalator. "Alright hun, we gotta buy some time..." Without a word, she pushes back the ones to her left before swinging the crowbar up to the jaw of her closest attacker. I aim for baseball swings at the top of their necks, but when my second shot gets caught in the shirt of the corpse to my left I sidekick the next closest one back into the one behind him.

I look back at the escalator to see the undead getting back up but apparently struggling to get their bearings. "Escalator!" I shout, letting her finish off another one. I look back to see another twenty or so filing in behind our recently dispatched prey. Julia freezes at the bottom of the escalator, and without allowing myself a second guess I grab the leg of the first one on the step and launch him over the side. "Duck!" Julia shouts as I reach for the next one, and as I get down, she swings her crowbar over my head and knocks one against the side just as I push another one over. When it clears the handrail, I whack my crowbar into the head of the one Julia just took down.

"Left!" As she shouts, I know that I can interpret that word a few ways, but I instinctively know to push off to the left, and again her crowbar shoots out, this time hooking a leg and pulling one down; he instinctively grabs the corpse behind him and she falls as well. Julia and I both take a step up and blast their skulls apart with our crowbars. *"Alright, I'm at the balcony, whatever you do, don't go up the escalator, over."* I don't even need to turn around to know that there's no turning back, so I plow up the steps into the last one and knock him over the edge, stepping on the corpse stuck in the top stair as I jump out at the top. A loud slam behind me instantly causes me to turn; there's a corpse at the top with his hand wrapped around Julia's ankle.

"Flat!" I shout, and Julia stops struggling just long enough for me to pull out the Colt and crack off a round into the top of his head. "Can't get his hand off!" Julia spits. "Don't touch it!" I say, looking both ways to see the undead about fifty feet away in both directions as I walk over. I holster the Colt and pull my crowbar over my head, bringing it down hard enough to crack his necrotic wrist. A second hit yields no better results. Thirty feet away now. *"God dammit, Grey, what are you doing?"* Three hits in quick succession, and his death grip continues. "Try the elbow!" One swift blow on the inside of the elbow and his fingers uncurl enough for Julia to retrieve her leg.

With that, we're up on our feet, rushing headlong into the next group. Just as I smash my crowbar into the head of the nearest corpse, something bright reflects across my eye; in the distance, I can see Anderson sighting with his rifle. "DROP!" I shout, and a moment later blood rockets out the forehead of one that was coming up behind us. *"Grey, just push them out of the way and get over here!"* I turn my walkie-talkie off the moment before Julia and I follow his instructions; she seems more content to push them over while I take whacks at them and get no small amusement from hitting them hard enough to send them over the railing.

Finally, we clear a path and just run the rest of the way. Anderson closes up the bipod on his rifle as we approach and turns inside the department store without another word. "Started the bus?" I ask, breathing heavily. "Not yet." Anderson calls back, jogging in front. We swing toward the path aligning the toy aisle and I see the rest of the group collectively breathe a sigh of relief. I can't see clearly through their bodies, but as we swing toward the exit, it looks as though the doorway and the bus are undisturbed. Anderson is the first through the door, and once he gets to the bus he turns back and waves his arms. "Weapons out, weapons out!" Half of the group pulls up their rifles and the other half brings up their hand-to-hand weapons while Anderson boards the bus and runs to the front.

"Melee, melee!" I shout in return.

"What?" Melody asks.

"Hand-to-hand weapons, don't waste any ammo!"

Once I make it through the doors and my eyes adjust to the sun, I first notice three pairs of legs wriggling underneath the wheels on the right side of the bus. As everyone stands around looking panicked, I run up to the fence and look through to see the undead dotted across the parking lot leading back to the main road from which we came. "Board!" Rich shouts, pushing Jake toward the emergency exit. Jake puts his foot on a sandbag to steady himself, and as he pushes off, the bag slops down on the concrete to reveal two rotten, moaning faces behind it. Rich winds up and pops them both in the nose; they recoil for a moment, but start right back at us. "Pull 'em through!" I shout, prompting Jake to poke his head out the back and stick his arm under the bus.

"STOP! DON'T USE YOUR FUCKIN' HANDS!" Rich screams, forcing Jake to cower. Julia steps up, swings her crowbar under the back bumper and drags one of the corpses to the concrete patio, backing off so Rich can pound his skull. After the second hit, Rich's bat visibly buckles in the middle. "Guess I'm done with that..." He throws it over the fence and leaps on the back of the bus. "Jeff..." Karen says, pulling at my coat; I turn back to the glass doors just in time to see a walking corpse slip on the tiled floor, knocking over a clothing rack. I turn back to shout in the bus, but Rich now has it started. "Alright, everyone on board!"

I let everyone go in front of me as I climb up on the sandbags on the opposite side of the bus, looking through the fence at the movie theatre; this side of the parking lot is almost completely empty. "Go, now!" I shout, crawling on the back of the bus. Rich starts forward before I can get the door shut, and two hands suddenly reach up from under the bus and grab my right boot, leaving me scrambling to link my hands to a metal fixture under one of the seats. "Wait, stop!" Jake shouts. "NO, *GO!*"

Rich floors it, bouncing the bus over corpses and producing several loud, splintering cracks as he destroys a few ribcages. The one hanging on to my leg swings out from beneath the bus, the sudden change in weight distribution causing me to lose my grip and slide a little further toward the open door before grabbing another seat leg. I shake my foot hard, trying to keep it tense so he doesn't take my boot with him. As we accelerate, the blacktop underneath him grinds off his jeans in a flash before setting to work on his legs, rubbing his skin out on the road behind us in a dark red skid mark. The sound of bone and flesh getting sanded off by coarse blacktop is something that will never leave me.

Just as he gets his mouth around my Achilles tendon, a black barrel comes from my left and pops his skull like a meat balloon. Anderson pulls me inside and Melody shuts the door. "Well, that was interesting." I say, somewhat detached. "Hospital, step on it." Anderson says, moving to the front. Still sprawled out in a crab-walking position, I look at my right leg. There is a residue of saliva in a crescent arc around my tendon, and though my boots are made of thick leather, there is no way they would have withstood the full pressure of human jaws. I close my eyes and try to refill my asthmatic lungs when a pair of arms wrapping around my midsection jolts me up.

I shouldn't have been surprised it would be Jules. I pause, gazing into those big brown eyes, and a moment later, our lips are locked together. The kiss swallows me up, shutting out everything else around me as my brain starts pulsating with sexual energy. When our lips finally separate, she speaks for both of us. "Wow." I kiss her again softly on the forehead and head up to the front of the bus toward Rich and Anderson. "Are we being followed?" Anderson asks. I look back to see Melody still sitting in the back seat.

"Melody, are we being followed?"

"There's a couple behind us, but they're going slow..."

"There's your answer."

"Good..." Anderson mutters. "No dead traffic between here and the hospital."

"Dead *traffic?*"

"Yeah, you know... people abandoning their cars on the road?"

"Ah, clever..."

I lean over the seat just behind Rich to look out the window, watching a light drizzle emerge from the muddy-gray sky. I stand up and look out the front window to see the hospital already in sight.

"You alright?" Anderson asks.

"Fine."

"Sure?"

"Yeah, I'm good."

"So, Rich and I had a talk with Jake this morning..."

"...did he do something wrong?"

"No..." Anderson scoffs. "We want him to feel more involved..."

"Oh, okay... what about Karen?"

"She can handle herself." Rich says quickly.

Anderson and I look at each other and smile.

"Something you wanna tell us?" I ask.

"...like what?"

"You wanna nail Karen?" Anderson asks.

"Shhhhhut up! We're here..."

Anderson pats him on the back, and Rich channels his resentment into opening the door mechanism. Anderson looks at the doorway, and then turns his attention back to Rich. "Did you bother checking outside first?" Without a word, Rich pulls up his shotgun and trots down the steps. "Alright, everyone... don't forget your packs." Anderson says, following Rich. Opting to leave my katana behind again in favor of a crowbar, I follow them out of the bus smiling and gaze up at the front of the hospital. Suddenly, it all sinks in.

I can't remember feeling overly disturbed by what's happened up to this point. Terrified, exhilarated, depressed, exhausted, sure, but disturbed hasn't factored into my emotions. I'm about to break in to a hospital. Three people I know are dead. It's Thursday, and I'm not in class. I may never eat a decent meal again. I may never see my parents again. I'll never have a career in movies. I might not survive the next few hours. None of this moves me to tears, but I stand, as Thoreau and Pink Floyd once described, in quiet desperation, and I can't take my eyes off an overturned wheelchair in the driveway.

"Guys, are we sure this is a good idea?" I ask, mainly of Anderson and Rich. Anderson nods. "If the Guard are anywhere nearby, it's here." Rich nods while Anderson is talking. "Besides, they have drugs inside." I swallow. "What is it?" Anderson asks me. I shake my head and start toward the back. "Nothing, don't worry about it." Anderson pats my shoulder. "Relax. You almost had your foot taken off... that's a *good* reason to be antsy." It strikes me at this moment that Anderson has absolutely no idea why I'm anxious, and that unsettles me further. He replaces me at Rich's side and starts talking with him about the doors as I walk off.

Everyone loads their weapons if they aren't already filled to capacity. I shake my head and drop my backpack on the floor. "Everyone remember, channel two." I say, picking up my trench coat and throwing it on over my clothes. I sling my rifle overtop, and then put my leather gloves on. Anderson and Rich exit the bus first, followed by me and Julia, then the rest of the group in no particular order behind us.

"Alright, five floors... that's not so bad." I say.
"We'd know by now if the Guard was here..." Anderson adds.
"This place gives me the creeps."

Anderson and I go first through the front doors with our pistols armed and proceed to cover the entrance and lobby the same way we covered the interior of the police station. "It's clear, over." Anderson mutters into his walkie-talkie, and I notice for the first time that he's making use of the extra pair of leather gloves I found at my house. The front desk is sandwiched between two poorly lit hallways and the area behind it is similarly dark. Anderson's expression informs me that we can expect to find no military presence.

"Are we really gonna have to walk around in the dark?" Jake asks. No one answers, but Karen strolls calmly away from us behind the desk. With unparalleled fluidity, Anderson clicks on his shoulder mounted flashlight and pulls up his pistol, training both just behind her. Karen looks back into the light apprehensively before turning a corner and turning on all the lights. Anderson exhales and turns off the flashlight.

"They try to keep the switches away from the patients, so it'll be like this on every floor."

"First priority on each level." Anderson states. "Melody, Karen, you got the list?"

"Right here." Karen responds.

"Alright, get to work. Rich, Julia, you check the rooms before they enter and cover from the outside. Me, Jake, and Jeff patrol the hallways. Stay tight and avoid chatter. Let's keep all conversation on vox."

"What's the list?" I ask.

"Medical supplies. It's ranked by priority, so this should go smoothly."

"Good plan."

I hear a burble of static as everyone switches on their walkie-talkies and goes their separate ways. Anderson splits off to the right, I take the left, and Jake stays behind in the lobby. I ignore Julia and Rich outside the door of the first room on the left as Melody and Karen scour the cabinets. The first thing I notice in the antiseptic hallway is a series of gurneys lined up outside many of the rooms, a few of which are practically coated with blood. Several IV racks have been overturned throughout, and almost all the doors are open a crack, so I take out my Colt before continuing. Trying to remain cautious, I peek in each door as I go, but the hallways seem quiet and the undead aren't exactly wired for stealth. As I approach a corner that veers off to the right, I press myself against the wall and point my gun before my body comes around, finally turning to find Anderson calmly walking toward me.

"You shouldn't lead with your gun." He says.

"Yeah, I know... I didn't figure anyone was gonna take it from me."

"Say there's one standing there, and he grabs your arm first..."

"Point taken."

He continues looking at the doors, then stops and turns back.

"That's the first sweep... you me and Jake should all be going in the same direction now."

"Sounds good. Oh, and about the list… anything I should know?"

"…what do you mean?"

"Well, you made it without me…"

"You were sleeping."

"I know, I'm not trying to… I'm asking what you talked about."

"About what?"

"I'm asking… what do we do when someone gets bitten?"

"…we ask them what they want to do."

"I know, but I'm assuming we're not just getting supplies for cuts and bruises and broken legs. Did you, Rich and Karen talk about what we do if someone gets bitten?"

"I don't understand what you're asking."

"Do we treat the wound, give them something for it?"

"Of course."

"But we understand that… there's nothing we can do for them?"

"…are you saying we shouldn't use the drugs on someone that's gonna die anyway?"

"Of course not. I'm saying there's nothing we can do to reverse the process… we've got a nurse with us now, and I'm concerned she's gonna do everything she can to keep us…"

"*John, Jeff? Where are you guys?*" Jake calls in over the radio.

"We'll be around in a second, and remember to say over when you're done talking. Over."

"…she's gonna do whatever she can to keep us alive. If we do that…"

"Oh, oh, I get it… we don't wanna end up with, like, Jake running around on us."

"Exactly."

"Well we didn't talk about that, but I think it she knows… we'll talk about it later."

"I was thinking maybe we give them something to induce a coma."

Anderson stares at me gravely while we both consider the implications of that. He finally nods, walking past me to go back the direction he came. I wait for him to get ahead and take the same path. Maybe that's what disturbed me about coming into the hospital and I just didn't realize it consciously; being here to collect medical supplies is an acknowledgement that we'll need them, which is something I hadn't really considered. I didn't know Steve, and at that point, I didn't think about the fact that he might die. I can imagine talking to someone about what they want to do once they're bitten, but will we be capable of carrying it out?

What if Jake does get bitten? Aside from Melody, he seems like the person in the group who would be most terrified by that proposition. Would he shoot himself in a fit of pique, or ask us to induce a coma? I can only imagine that Karen would be the best equipped person to handle that task, but will I be able to look him in the eye for the last time before the two of them are alone together? Can I talk to someone knowing they're going to be dead in the next hour? I think about Jake lying in bed in a dark room with Karen calmly talking to him, tears streaming down his face as he considers that his last conscious memory will be of needle entering his arm.

"John, we're at one of the supply closets, we're gonna need help gettin' in. Over." Karen says.

"Roger, rolling to you. Over and out."

"John, do we just keep patrolling? Over."

"Yeah Jake, stay on watch. Over and out."

I grab my radio to say something, but realize I have nothing to add and hook it back on my belt. In keeping with the spirit of the patrol, I recheck the rooms Anderson must have seen. Walking to the left, I peek in a cracked doorway and immediately conclude that he missed something important. I click on the light switch, confirming my suspicion about the shadow I saw; a corpse in a hospital gown seems transfixed by the illuminated x-ray of someone's ribcage on the wall. I check the walls on either side of the door before I enter, finding another one facing the corner on my right side.

I'm grateful that I've opted to bring the crowbar in instead of the katana, as it just isn't suited for combat in an enclosed room. I raise it up over my head, and before I can strike my first killing blow, I think better of it. Just to be certain, I poke him first, causing him to limply turn, favoring his right side. The blood on his mouth and his vacant stare confirms it, so I bash his right temple so that his head also hits the wall. The second hit provides his body with a fatal limpness, so I turn to the next one and take care of him about as quickly, lifting my walkie-talkie when I'm finished.

"This is Grey checking in. Just took care of two walkers in one of the rooms."

"*Copy.*" Anderson responds.

"Jake, make sure you hit the lights in each room you check."

"*We trying to advertise? Over.*"

"None of these rooms have windows that I've noticed, so that shouldn't be a problem, over."

"*Alright, hit the lights, but we turn 'em back out before we go upstairs, over and out.*"

In the next half hour, Jake, Julia, and Rich each end up putting down a walker while Karen and Melody fill their backpacks. After Anderson and Jake escort them out to the bus to empty the supplies, Anderson begins our excursion on the second level by conducting a more thorough sweep of the first few rooms while our quartet of treasure seekers continue their business. I haven't made it past the third room when Jake's voice comes over the radio.

"*Jeff...*"

"What is it?"

"*Do you think the elevators work?*"

"*Don't try it.*" Anderson breaks in. "*If the power goes off, you'll get stuck, over.*"

"Don't hospitals have independent generators?" I ask.

"*Let's not bother.*" Rich says. "*Let's finish this and get out. Over.*"

"*Where exactly do we go after this?*" Julia asks.

"*That's a good question. Over.*" Rich says.

"*Well what about Mercy?*" Melody asks. "*Isn't that a rescue center?*"

"*They also said they lost contact with it.*" Jake says.

"*So what?*"

"*She's right.*" Rich says. "*Just because they lost contact doesn't necessarily mean it's been overrun. Over.*"

"*But there's a good chance it was.*" Anderson adds. "*I don't like it. Over.*"

"Where else are we gonna go and what else are we gonna do?" I ask.

"*Well, I'm outvoted two to one. We check it out when we're done here. Over and out.*"

A few minutes later Anderson radios that he had the misfortune of taking out a member of the undead stuck in a hospital bed, presumably having died of a terminal illness. The radio is silent for the next fifteen minutes while we continue patrolling the halls.

"*What about after Mercy?*" Julia eventually chimes in.

"*When we finish here we chill out and listen to the radio again, over.*" Anderson offers.

"*I second that, over.*" Rich says.

"I third." I say.

"*Let's get movin'...*"Karen says. "*There isn't anythin' here we haven't seen already, over.*"

The fourth floor looks relatively clean and unused and roughly half the lights seem to be working. As I start toward the dark half of a long corridor and see the danger of walking around in the dark, I lift the walkie-talkie to my mouth. "Everyone, turn on your emergency strobes. I don't want two people turning a corner and accidentally shooting each other." I stop for a moment and wait to see a dim flashing light around the corner ahead of me, signifying that someone is near the end of the intersecting hallway. I switch mine on, remembering to keep my head turned away. The flash emits with a dull whir that I presume is only audible to me.

For some reason, watching another strobe flash from around the corner ahead makes me uncomfortable enough to wish there was a louder sound to accompany it. I turn the next corner to see that the light is actually emerging from a left turn at the opposite end of this corridor, which is completely black. I stand still for a moment and wait to see if either my light or the other one reveals something in the depths of the hallway. There's nothing, so I lift the walkie-talkie to my lips again. "Anderson, you seen any up this far?" His response takes a moment.

"Negative. Grey, remember to say 'over' after transmission or I won't know if you're done talking. Have you seen any? Over."

"Sorry about that. I've got nothing here. Over."

"Seems like they didn't use this floor much," Rich adds. *"All the same, it doesn't mean it's empty. Right Karen? Over."*

"They'll have supplies on every level. We're almost done here, over."

Once my radio is back on my belt, I turn to look behind me. The light from my strobe alternatively fills the hallway and fades into the corridor intersection. I watch a light flash as someone, presumably Anderson, retraces my steps behind me. My guess is confirmed when I simultaneously hear his voice around the corner and on my radio. *"Got something here. Over."* When I turn around and resume walking, a couple of voices excitedly sputter through the walkie-talkie in brief snippets, so I lift mine.

"What's up? Over."

"There's a door that's blocked from the inside, should we open it?" Julia asks.

"How's it blocked? Over."

"I can't really see in the window, but it looks like mattresses. Over."

"How many? Over."

"It's tough to see, maybe four? Over."

"Anderson, how many beds to a room on this floor? Over."

"No more than two so far..." He says, catching his breath. *"Why? Over."*

I walk more purposefully into the flashing darkness.

"If there's four blocking a door from inside, there's a good chance that someone moved them to hide, over."

"*Copy. Over.*"

"Jules, where are you? Over."

"*I can see a strobe light in the dark hall to my right. Over.*"

"That's probably me, I'm coming to you. Anderson, Jake, stay on watch. Over and out."

I turn the corner to see Melody and Julia standing outside of a door near a spot where the overhead lights are working.

"Aren't you supposed to be with Rich?"

"We switched... he's helping Karen open a door, over. Oh, duh, that was stupid... sorry."

"Don't worry about it... is this the room?"

Julia nods as I jog closer and look inside, confirming immediately that there are several mattresses blocking it from the inside. I knock. "Hello? If there's anyone in there, we're coming in..." I try the handle, but the blockage is firm. I put my body weight into the door and try again, but either someone is holding it or the stuff on the other side is thickly set. I grab the handle, draw back and slam my shoulder into it, ending up with most of the force being absorbed by my shoulder. I let out a dull groan, step back and let out a side kick to the glass, shattering it. "Is there anyone in there?" I shout. A strobe emits from my shoulder; for a moment, I forgot that I had left it on.

Someone stumbles, and I hear a muffled sound that resembles a human voice. The sound is followed by some scrapes against the mattresses as they start moving from the other side. "We're coming through." I say with a smile, pulling out my pistol to cover. When I push the door, it actually opens as one mattress falls sideways and another perched above the door falls down. A single strobe from my shoulder pierces the darkness to reveal a gray face as an arm flashes out and Julia screams.

Distracted by the scream, I fire off three rounds while the mattress continues to fall, and the third shot lands just above his nose, instantly coating the poorly lit floor in blackish fluid. I stare at his body with my mouth hanging open as the strobe light illuminates the puddle beneath his head and the gaping bite mark on the left sleeve of his OR scrubs. "Fuck!" I hear behind me. I turn around, and the first thing I see is a long, thin incision on someone's left forearm the moment before it realizes that blood is supposed to follow. It's Julia's arm, and she closes the wound by wrapping her arm around it. "Did he scratch you?" I hear. My mouth is hanging open. The words are soft, in the distance almost. She looks up, her face strained. Finally, as if I was struck by lightning, my mind puts it together. "K-... KAREN!" I scream.

I wrap my hand tightly around Julia's elbow and hold it away from the two of us. "KAREN! KAREN WE NEED HELP!" Karen comes running around the corner, sees the blood dripping off her arm from the distance, and starts opening her backpack. She throws on rubber gloves, pulls out a tourniquet, and shoves it up Julia's arm, closing it. "Take your hand off." She says. I hear a tearing sound as Karen opens up a strip of gauze and wipes Julia's arm down. It's Julia's arm. Karen squeezes the wound open, forcing out a lot more blood than I would have expected. "Oh god..." Julia mutters, squinting and looking away as her entire forearm goes red.

Karen pulls out isopropyl alcohol and douses the wound, then wipes it down again. "That's deep, you might need stitches..." Shocked, I stare into the room and begin to wonder what could have made a cut that deep, because it couldn't have been fingernails. I click off my strobe light and take up the flashlight perched on my shoulder, shining it down at the corpse; he has a scalpel locked in the death grip of his gnarled knuckle. "Oh thank god..." I say. "He was holding a scalpel." I breathe a huge sigh of relief as I look back at Julia and Karen. Julia, through her pain, lets out a tiny smile. Karen's lip twitches as she returns her attention to the wound. "Wait, why?" Melody asks.

"I don't know, he was probably trying to defend himself..." I trail off immediately, then pull the door open and push my way across the mattresses to get a look at the scalpel and his hand, finding that both are covered in wet blood, and the scalpel has little dried chunks of flesh on it. "This can't be from Jules..." I look up at his throat and see that I conveniently forgot to notice that he had tried to cut his own head off, evidenced by the enormous, clean gash across the length of his throat and the glossy puddle of blood already coating the floor. I look up at the ceiling to see how far the arterial spray reached, and then look back at Karen's somber expression as she looks at me through the doorway having just finished bandaging Julia's arm.

"No..." I mutter. "No n-n-n-n-no." I spit as I wrestle to my feet. "There's no way, not like that, right? I mean... it happened fast, the blood was dry..." I glance down to see Julia clutching her arm on the floor. I look back at Karen to see her bloody, gloved fingers pinched together like she's holding something. She pulls her thumb across her index finger to reveal several tiny, dark chunks. "What is that... a blood clot?" I look up at Karen, whose grave expression doesn't change. "I think it... came off the knife."

"How fast did you get it out?" I ask quickly. She doesn't know what to say. "HOW FAST!?" Julia sniffles next to me as Karen looks at the ground defeated. My eyes glaze over as Julia raises her head to make eye contact. The corners of her eyes tremble, and when she looks at me my nose begins to hurt as pressure builds behind my eyes. The first tear comes out of her left eye, followed by the second from mine. I see genuine fear, an expression I've never once seen on that beautiful face. I open my mouth, but that only makes the pain in my face worse. I close it, my chin drops, and I bite the insides of my lips, shaking my head. Without moving my eyes from hers I become aware of the people around us. "Leave us alone." I utter softly, holding back tears. Karen nods and pulls Melody up with her.

Julia and I stare intently at each other; her head starts shaking softly in the moments before she can let the drowned words escape from her throat. "I'm... so sorry..." Streams run down my cheeks before she can finish, and after a moment I have to widen my eyes to see her. I lift my hand to run my fingers down her cheeks, and as I touch her I can feel warmth penetrating my nerve endings, snaking up my arm until it makes my heart flutter. It feels like the first time I touched her, and the affectation of this moment now turns the sensation to one of freezing water being injected in my veins.

Our terrified fingers dance gracelessly over each other's arms as we struggle to pull closer. When her head is finally against my chest, I can feel her warm tears piercing my t-shirt while she struggles to keep her head still. I'm startled when she bucks against me, and that's all it takes for me to lose control of every muscle in my face. My head falls on top of hers vibrating as awkward burbles and squeaks start popping out of my cheeks. I can't catch my breath. I try to keep her steady, but I can't stop us from falling flat on the floor.

I've never heard my voice get loud enough to produce this awful sound that unhinges my jaw and rips its way out of my throat. And it doesn't stop. As soon as the air runs out, it starts up again louder, harder, turning my entire body into an unwilling instrument that must torque into itself to produce such a dreadful noise. I squeeze Julia as though she can stop it, but it's of no use. Unable to restore control, my brain purges itself into the type of clarity that is usually afforded to drunks and drug abusers, enabling me to accept that my body and my senses are beyond my grasp while giving some separate part of my mind sanctuary to observe and comment as though nothing is happening.

As my body flails about uselessly, I try to remember the last time I cried, knowing immediately that it would be pointless to try to find a moment as bad as this. It was something innocuous that happened a few months ago, and I was crying so hard that it became difficult to breathe, so I moved myself into the bathroom and cried into the toilet so I wouldn't have to worry about finding tissues. I had a similar moment of clarity then, acknowledging that a good cry would provide exactly the type of catharsis I needed to fall asleep, and that whatever it was would look better in the morning. From this safe vantage, I was able to observe the abyss from which I would eventually emerge to recover.

And in this moment, for the first time in my life, I feel the abyss staring back. I've repeated the phrase countless times, enjoying its cryptic reversal without ever truly understanding what it meant. Now I see the definitive end to the first part of my life, the point at which some essential part of me dies, never to be reclaimed. Julia will now be forcibly removed from me, and in her absence, an empty chasm into which every feeling and fantasy I have hence must eventually drain before the entire volatile mass scabs over. I feel myself change as I entertain the notion that the next stage of my life begins with each moment, each day being worse than the last with no indication of how deep the void goes, and the darkness is enough to make me comatose with fear.

My next conscious thought pertaining to reality concerns the fact that it is now night. Julia's head lies silently against my chest, her breath engaging as one giant inhale and exhale, between which there is nothing in her lungs; she's asleep. Was I also asleep? I don't allow myself to entertain the notion that I dreamt her injury for even a moment, especially since my left arm is touching her gauze wrapping. Having cried myself dry for the moment, I can allow myself to think that this is the last time I will ever wake up next to her, so I give myself a moment to enjoy her breath against my chest.

When enough time has passed, I consider breaking her neck. I'm surprised by how calmly I can process this thought, but I remind myself of my own morbidity, having had a woman's head resting against my body multiple times as I considered how implicit their trust was and how easy it would have been for me to take advantage of the moment if I were a monster. In this situation, I would not be a monster. I would, however, be denying both of us the closure of a final goodbye. I suddenly realize that we may have been asleep long enough that she's changed, and the only thing keeping her from sinking her teeth into me is our moment of placidity. I've heard before of one half of a married couple looking at their spouse and seeing a stranger, but I wager few people have had that effect be as profound as it has been in the last week.

For a moment, I consider the possibility that she's not going to become one of them, but any fleeting hope is smacked down by Steve's encounter with the undead. All it had to do was break skin with its bare bones and he turned in a matter of hours. I run my fingers down her cheek, preparing for a sudden jerk of her gnashing teeth. Instead, I look down at her head and feel a massive breath pull her into consciousness, giving her a few moments of sublime confusion before her breath quickens in trepidation. As I tighten my grip around her shoulder, her breathing starts to normalize. I can feel her about to say something, but like so many awkward social situations I've experienced in my life, neither of us wants to be the first one to talk. Finally, she ends the stalemate by looking up at me, and I instinctually smile. When she smiles back, I have to restrain myself from asking a litany of stupid questions. Her first words seem calculated to disabuse me of this notion.

"How are you?"
"...I've been better."
"Yeah..."
"...and you...?"
"Bitter."

We both sit up, our legs touching as we each keep ourselves propped up with a single arm.

"I don't know what to say."
"For the first time, I've got you at a loss for words."
"Second time."

She looks down, smiling coyly. I don't think I'm capable of returning the gesture, and I don't stop myself from avoiding the big question on my mind. "...we have to talk about..." She cuts me off. "I know." She takes a deep breath, not looking up from the floor. After a long moment of silence, she begins nodding softly, sighing before her head comes up to reveal possibly the first completely serious expression I've ever seen on her face, and I'm struck by the impression that she's aged a decade in a few seconds. "Don't make John do it." And there it is. It's my turn to sigh.

"How..."
"Maybe it's better if you don't know."
"...yeah."
"Can they knock me out?"

I shiver, recalling my earlier thoughts about Jake.

"It shouldn't be a problem."

"There was nothing you could do."

"…maybe…"

"No… it wasn't my fault, and it wasn't yours."

She smiles warmly at me before she stands up and extends her hand.

"You know… you're the one getting off easy." I say.

"…how do you mean?"

"Because I'm the one who has to live without you."

I give her my hand and she helps me up. I take her under my arm as we begin walking down the hallway, and I wonder where my grief went. Just like in the past, sleeping on something depressing enough to make me pass out renders me stronger when I wake, and even if I torture myself with the terrible thoughts that will likely consume me the rest of my life, in this moment, they feel inorganic, inert. Dead. Our walk around the hallway surprises me with how naturally paced it feels. Finally, we turn a corner to find Karen and Rich standing by the stairwell. Keeping Julia's head perched against my chest, I look them over and come to the conclusion that Rich is a mess and Karen is numb, a state likely induced by years of practicing bedside manner. As we approach and Julia looks up, Rich looks down, and Karen fakes a benign smile.

"I want you to knock me out. And I want Jeff to be the last thing I see." Karen widens her smile as she nods, and Rich turns away. He crosses behind Karen, pulling two strips of black cloth from his coat pocket. "Follow me." As we walk away from the stairwell, I can hear Karen go through the door as she says something into her walkie-talkie. Rich takes us up the hall to a door embedded in the inner wall, opens it, and holds it for us. We walk sideways to get inside, and for a moment I don't know what it is he's expecting us to do. "Just… open the door when she's ready." I step away from Julia and pull the door shut, immediately becoming aware that the room is free from any ambient sound and somehow the lights have been dimmed. I turn to face

Julia again; her face is partially shadowed, but I can see my own reflection in her warm eyes, and I'm instantly reminded of the first time we met.

The grass on the football field is drowning in the downpour that began no more than five minutes ago, and while everyone else had already gathered their belongings and run off, I take my time to retrieve the cheesy flags used to mark my positions for the field show. I had never been at band camp to see a night practice rained out, so I suppose it's fitting that it happens in my final year. The generators hooked up to the lights are humming and churning, producing steam as the falling water invades their engines.

Soaked to the bone, I lift my clarinet case and run back to my cabin, again finding myself completely alone. I walk to my bed and strip off my wet clothes in favor of warm dry ones, organize my field show booklet, and clean off my clarinet. I throw myself into bed and stare at the ceiling. It only takes a few more seconds of listening to the rain before I rally myself and stand up to find my green rain suit. I spend most of my free time at home alone, so I might as well make something of my second to last night at band camp. There's no real rallying point I can think of, so I head back out to the field to find Anderson, who is most likely enjoying the rain and doing his best to insert himself into a clique of accepting people. I snicker as I imagine the further implications of that.

The generators on the field are still running, introducing me to the two primary clusters of people animatedly talking beneath the cover of two gazebos on either side of the field. A more intimate group has gathered by the trailer upon which our band director generally stands to shout commands. I walk toward it, quickly spotting a tall figure in camouflage fatigues that can only be Anderson. He's surrounded by mostly girls, which fulfills my expectation.

I run up behind him and place my hands on his shoulders, holding myself up over his head for a moment before I drop down. "Anderson. Ladies." Anderson looks back at me. "Oh, come on, a rain suit? You have to get wet!" I shake my head, disposing with banter in favor of a forthcoming introduction. "Guys, this is my best friend Jeff." I wave slightly. Anderson holds his hand out. "Jeff, this is Ava, Julia, and Natalie." I shake all their hands and say hi. I make eye contact with Ava, quickly thinking she's the most attractive of the bunch. Natalie I've met, so I greet her with a nod and a smile. I turn to Julia.

We made eye contact for only a second and looked away with embarrassed smiles. I didn't understand my feelings in that moment, but

I certainly thought she was out of my league. I didn't find out until months later that she felt the same way about me. Now when I look at her, I find the same expectant face followed by a quick look away. I step forward and drop my trench coat, belt, and gun. I softly place my hands on the sides of her breasts and slowly run my fingers around to her back, then close my arms. As we remain silent, I drop my head to her shoulder and hold the position for a few minutes, stroking my hand across her back. "I'm sorry." I mutter it over and over again as I hold her close. Finally, the familiar grief snakes back into my mind, leaving me barely capable of holding myself back from the abyss.

"I was the one who said we should open the door..."
"Remember what I said?"
"Of course."
"It's not a request, or a demand... it's an order."
"Yes ma'am."

She scoffs. For the next few seconds, I scrape at the right words. She snuggles against me, embracing me tighter.

"Oh, Ef..."
"...what can I say?"
"You don't have to say anything. Sometimes you can't decide if you say too much or not enough... I love watching you get excited. I love the look in your eyes when you don't have the words. It probably sounds stupid... but you always said the right thing. You always *did* the right thing. You never gave up on me. As much as you avoided lecturing me and let me be my own person, you taught me so much about hope... it doesn't come naturally to everyone, that fascination, that desire... and maybe it drives some people crazy. But I never stopped wanting it. I didn't want to borrow it, learn it, or even share it. I wanted to be a part of it. And you're right, Ef... *I'm* the one getting off easy... I got to spend the rest of my life with you."

I stare into her eyes and she smiles. No matter what morbid thought my brain tries to slide in front of me, no matter what subconscious defense mechanism tries to temper me with harsh reminders of what's going to happen, I stay in the moment, and it's wonderful. I feel enveloped by her eyes. Tears come to both of us, but neither of us sobs or frowns, and neither of us breaks eye contact. In this moment, I feel freed from any pessimistic thought I've ever had about her. Though an obvious psychological restriction bars me from kissing her, I don't feel intoxicated by the limitation, and for now, it doesn't seem like an essential expression. What I feel, completely untempered and without reservation, is love.

I open her hand and give her the blindfold without breaking the stare. I step back and open the door, then step forward again. "I love you, Leah." I say softly. "I love you, Ef." She responds. After we both shut our eyes and don our blindfolds, she leans forward to hug me. I turn slowly so she's facing the door. She squeezes once, releases, and backs away. Right before the door closes, I hear a tiny moan followed by an immensely contented sigh. I breathe easily as the door shuts and have an expectation of her footsteps retreating down the hall, but for the first time since I entered this room, I hear absolutely nothing, and my blindfold is dark enough I can't see even with my eyes wide open. Something changes in my heart rhythm and it makes me go cold. I'm in a void. I'm never going to see her again.

"No... no no no NO NO! *STOP*! BRING HER BACK! Please, Rich, LISTEN!" My tear ducts burn as I slam my hands into the door. "Karen, listen, *PLEASE*, I need more time, please! OPEN THE DOOR! Open the door..." I can barely squeak the words out, pressing my forehead into the door as the tears quickly soak through my blindfold. I hold my breath. There has to be something I can do to stop this. I try the door handle, but it's locked. I'm sure that there's something else I can do. The silence is deafening.

A gunshot crashes down the hall. "NO! NO NO NO NO NO NO NO!" I slam my fists into the ground, crumpling into a convulsing heap as my muscles uniformly give out. The screams I unleashed a few hours ago are mere whispers compared to this, and I can feel my face contort into such a gnarled mass that my skin feels like it's tearing off.

My fist winds up and repeatedly slams into the door, no amount of pain stopping the torrent fueled by an anguish that would put an adrenaline shot to shame.

My foot shoots out, furiously kicking at a rack in the room until it falls over, shattering bottles and beakers as it lands. I go limp again as I get the first notion of my face covered with various liquids, either from my tears or the beakers or both. It gathers in a puddle on the floor beneath my head, and I realize that my screaming has continued unabated despite the distraction of several physical outbursts. *Don't play this game.* Julia's voice is in my head.

> *No, that's not you. That's what I want to hear.*
> *It wasn't my fault, and it wasn't yours.*
> *It's not you. If it is, I'm insane.*
> *You are not.*
> *I hear your voice in my head, and it's telling me that I'm not insane.*
> *You're not crazy. You need to listen.*
> *I'm talking to myself. Stop.*
> *You want to hear my voice right now.*
> *... I can't... what would you have me do?*
> *Live for both of us.*

I start breathing heavily, scrambling across the floor until I put my hands on my belt. I pull my pistol out of the holster, my hand vibrating wildly, and hold it against my head.

> *I'd be a lot happier with you.*
> *You can't be with me.*
> *Aren't you going to try and stop me?*
> *No.*

I cry hard again and the gun slips out of my hand. "I'm sorry... I'm sorry..."

> *I miss you... so much...*
> *I'm not Julia.*
> *How do I know that?*
> *Julia is dead.*

Don't say that... please... I need to know what I'm supposed to do... Jules... don't leave me... please don't leave me... please... let this be a dream... I want to wake up...

There was never a time in my life that I urged myself to wake up when I was certain that I was conscious. This realization simultaneously assures me of my consciousness and guarantees me that I will not wake up, making sleep my only refuge. As my body continues to expend its last remaining bit of energy, I know it's not far off.

10-15-04, FRIDAY

The moment I wake up I realize I can't remember what I dreamt about, and I'm more thankful than disappointed. I lift my face off the floor and remove my blindfold to see a caked puddle of tears, mucous, and blood on the floor. I scratch my finger under my nose, watching as a scab crumbles away. I've never had a nosebleed before.

I take a moment to collect my things, then stop and look at my pistol. Finally, I pick it up and pull the top back to reveal that there was a round in the chamber. A cold shiver runs down my spine as I jerk the slide, discovering that it was the last bullet in the magazine. I holster the pistol, put the bullet in my pocket and grab the door handle. The light from the sun is evident in the corridor, cascading off the clean floor tiles. I rub my eyes, which still hurt. I hear distant talking, so I walk toward it. My heavy boots clap into the tiling, announcing my consciousness, but apparently alerting no one. I list to the side, landing with my shoulder on the wall as I look down at my gently shaking limbs. I let out a deep sigh and find the first staircase.

Once through, I walk steadily down to the first floor, and once I make it down a few of the steps connecting the second floor to the first, I find Anderson at the landing below. We both freeze. He looks at me and I look at him, and we don't need to speak. He is not crass enough to ask me how I'm holding up, nor is he tactless enough to ask what took me so long to get up, nor is he probing enough to ask what her last words were. We just stare for about a minute and I know he doesn't want to speak first, so I do.

"What'd I miss?"
"Some of them attacked in the night."
"Everyone okay?"
"Yeah."
"Sorry."
"Nothing to apologize about."
"Did I miss breakfast again?"
"No, I think I'm the only person up besides Rich."
"...did he sleep?"

"No."

I finish descending the steps and follow him to one of the intensive care units to find a room filled with hospital beds and sleeping people. I look back out the door to find overturned gurneys sloppily placed throughout the hallway, culminating in a mass of metal where the hallway dumps out into the lobby, and just beyond that the inside door has been blocked off as well. Back in the ICU, I find Karen sitting in the corner toying with a pile of medical supplies, and I turn as Rich sits up quickly from one of the beds.

When we make eye contact, I watch the light's reflection disappear from his eyes. His mouth drops to speak, but I hold my hand in protest. I sigh again, walking to the middle of the room, trying to find something to sit on while failing in my attempt to silence my screaming brain. Giving up quickly, I sit on the floor and Rich immediately hands me a blanket. A moment later, Karen hands me my allergy pills and Anderson passes me a half pint of orange juice, prompting me to smile and look up at him inquisitively. "We took it from one of the fridges downstairs... Tea?" He asks, and I nod. "Earl Grey." Anderson tends to the tea kettle, and as he does the rest of the group slowly springs to life.

Out of the corner of my eye I watch Melody taking tiny steps, looking nonchalant as she crosses one leg over the other slowly to advance. When she gets close, she kneels down on the ground next to me, her eyes full of pity. I hold my left hand out, then draw it back to my forehead. "Just... don't, please." She masks her grief with a laborious smile and nods as she eases herself away. Anderson comes back over.

"What do you wanna eat?"
"I'm not hungry."
"You have to eat something, if you just have orange juice you're gonna puke."
"Assuming I don't anyway... fine, I'll have a cereal bar."

He hands me one. People slowly come around and take awkward stabs at starting polite conversation with one another, sometimes glancing at me and waiting for an interjection. I continue to drill my eyes into the floor and welcome the background noise. I take my pills and I'm about halfway through my breakfast when I hear someone mention Julia, then everyone is silent again. I bite my lower lip and my left eye twitches as everyone anticipates my forthcoming explosion. "Rich..." I start. "She..." I have to stop for a moment. I put my hand over my mouth. "She had... a ring."

I hear the soft clashing of metal in his pocket, then he hands me the ring. I nod and put it on my left pinkie. I can feel the tears building, but they stop. Karen puts her hand on my shoulder. "Jeff, are you okay?" I shake my head, and then nod. "...let's just get out of here." I finish my breakfast in silence and head upstairs to see if I missed any of my gear. Despite being alone and being physically close to the experience of last night, I manage to stay calm and head back downstairs without incident.

"We brought you a change of clothes." Jake says when I come down. "We all took showers last night... we figured you'd want one too."

"Thanks. Where do I go?"

"Uh, end of the hall, on the right."

"I'll try not to take too long."

Once I get in the washroom I quickly disrobe, turn on the shower and hop in. For a few moments, I'm lost in the warmth, but then that which I have managed to weave around all morning hits me: my last image of Julia. My face starts curling back as I recall my one indelible image of us kissing by my car outside one of her friend's houses, unexplainably recreated in third person by my memory. I had just given her my senior picture with a poem I wrote on the back. She loved the poem. I try to fight the images back by closing my eyes and shaking my head around. I let out little gasps as tears stream down my face and mix with the water from the showerhead.

The first time she told me she loved me in person. I try gritting my teeth and grabbing my forehead, kneeling down in the stall as the gasps draw closer together. When I danced with her at prom for the first time. When I gave her the ring that's now on my left pinkie. Deep sobs come, stressed and cut short by my inability to breathe, changing the tone of my voice to a whine, almost like a sick laugh. The steaming water has washed away the protective layer of dirt that has accumulated, exposing the naked flesh beneath.

I stare into the drain as the memories flood back, like the time I spent close to an hour outside with her last October. I had prayed all night I would get to see her and she called me close to two in the morning, telling me she was staying at a friend's house and that I wasn't allowed inside. I told her that if she wanted me, I would drive over if only to see her long enough to kiss her once. We ended up spending the next hour in each other's arms, lying across the front lawn seeing nothing but the grass coated in a silvery sheen from the moon and the reflections in each other's eyes. Nothing else mattered. We always used to say that we were the cutest couple on the planet. That could be said no more.

The momentary happiness the images brought with them is now swirling down the drain. Crying does nothing to assist me with a catharsis. I really let go when I think of what our future could have been, and what it would have been like to see her in five years. My muscles give out and I hit the tile, losing my concern over how dirty the floor is. I let my naked body go limp and flounder as I force myself deeper and deeper into memory. I gave her that poem in passing, and she insisted that I be there when she read it. She kept it for a week, and the following Friday we were together at her friend's house about to watch a movie when she went upstairs. I remember sitting on the couch disinterested as her friends, including Ava, debated over which movie to watch. When she came back down, she leapt over the couch, smothering me with a hug and a kiss, unable to speak. Later that evening, when I was lying in bed at home, I spent an hour thinking about her as she read it. I didn't see it. She was upstairs alone.

Her hand reached in and pulled out the picture with anticipation. *Is this the right moment? Is this impulsive, or natural? Have I tried too hard to manufacture it? How will I remember this?* Her hesitation only lasts a moment when she takes in the words. And she turns it over to see my face. That hug was the only way she could respond because she couldn't find the words; I made her speechless. Her arms moved, motivated by the love she could not express. She had the muscular power to kiss me. Her heart was beating. Her heart beats no more.

The bioelectricity of her brain has ceased to function, and as I lay here, the cells are beginning to degenerate and every thought and memory she had is irretrievably fading into nothing. We were like phone towers in concert, reciprocating, each useless without the other, and now I feel like a massive star extending its light, heat, and gravitational pull into a radiant and beautiful universe only to discover that it is singularly without planets, only holding down a vestigial field of cold, dark rocks.

I cry to the point of complete and utter incoherence, to where the water flows cold and my body covers the drain. I put my shaking hands on the ground and push myself up, blowing my nose hard into nothingness with the hope that I can breathe through it again. No such luck. I turn up the heat to the maximum setting and manage to squeeze some hot water out of the system. With that, I finish up my shower and quickly get dressed.

"Took you long enough." Anderson says with a smile when I come out. I consider responding with some retort, then wonder if my lack of response will make him self conscious, and finally decide I don't care. I walk past him tightening my rifle strap around my torso. "Jeff." I turn around to face Rich. I can see fear in his eyes. "What do you... want to do with her?" I notice Karen looking around the corner from the stairwell, and as she steps out I get a mental image of a long thin figure wrapped in sheets.

Do I want to leave her for the dead? Put her in the morgue? Bury her? "She comes with us." I turn around and the six of us walk down the wide open, well lit hall. In my mind, I can feel us walking in slow motion. Once we make it through the doors, I stop immediately. Hundreds upon thousands of undead are pushing through the entrance to the shopping mall.

"Why aren't they after us?" Jake asks.

"They didn't put much effort in last night, but they're still after the mall? Why *didn't* they follow us?" Anderson asks blankly.

"We were upstairs in the hospital, but not the mall." Melody says.

"Besides," Rich asks. "They attacked when we were taking showers."

"They were crawling all over the mall when we woke up," Anderson says. "But not the hospital. It *must* have something to do with the levels."

"Where are we going?" I ask.

"I thought we agreed on the other hospital." Karen says.

"...is there anywhere else?"

"We did listen to the radio last night." Rich says.

"...and?"

"They're spread out over the entire state. It's like a brush fire; New York, New Jersey, Maryland, West Virginia, they can't stop it. More than half the rescue stations have gone down."

"They're spiralin' out of Broomall and the other vectors." Karen adds. "They tried to evacuate, but each time they moved people out... it came with them. They've already declared martial law here in Delco, who knows what's next..."

"Don't even joke about that." Anderson says.

"I'm not jokin', I'm statin' a fact..."

"...if they declare any further state of martial law, it's not just gonna be at the state level... it's gonna be the whole country... that means the military calls the shots... they take over water, gas, electric, vehicles, even people if they see fit..."

"All the same, I'm just wondering..." Rich starts. "...how long you figure it takes them to get to us?"

I turn my head from Karen over to the mall to see a dozen of the undead running across the parking lot from different points but clearly converging as they run toward the hospital. They haven't made the street yet, so I figure we've got a little over two minutes.

"Two minutes. Where to?" I ask.

"Broomall." Rich says.

"What? Why?" Jake asks.

"If that's where it started, it'd be the last place they'd go."

"Then what was that attack at the school?"

"You heard the broadcast..."

"So, then we should go back to Broomall?" Melody asks.

There's a moment of silence, save for the dry gasping moans of the undead carried on the cold wind that blows toward us. We're upwind, so they must see us rather than smell or hear us. They must have sharp eyes. They've now cleared the street and continue to run unhindered up the hospital driveway.

"I guess so. Broomall it is." Rich says.

"Let's try the community center..." Jake offers.

"I agree." I say.

"I second." Anderson adds.

"Fine, let's just fuckin' *go*!" Karen says as the runners approach.

We all quickly hop on the bus, which Rich starts. I sit down on my bed to see Julia's pocketbook with her journal that she used to share with her friend Natalie and her CD player on the floor next to it. I can just see her now, staring blankly out the window, shutting out the rest of the world as she absorbs herself in music. I let out a deep, heavy sigh and lay down, staring up at the ceiling. It's hard to believe that yesterday happened. If I think about it like a dream or a movie it's not so horrible. But Julia is dead and I will never see her again.

I hold up my left hand and look at the two rings paired together on my last two fingers. I rub that hand down my face and put my wrists behind my head as a sinking feeling overtakes my spine. I suddenly remember the smell of a fleeting summer hanging in the air, accompanied by the orange and purple sky, when Anderson and I came to the high school for a surprise visit before a trip to my house in the mountains. I stroked my hand across her shoulder, and she turned quickly. The surprise and satisfaction in her face is something I will always remember to the point where it became my goal to catch her off guard, but there was never another moment like that, and there never will be again. I imagine looking at her from the side at school coffee houses and the hugs I got backstage at musicals and plays when we were still just friends.

One of those times, for some stupid reason, I was talking about kissing a girl, something specific about the experience that I felt warranted closer examination, and I looked at her and said *You know what I mean, right?* And she responded. *No, actually I don't...* A few weeks later she told me that she wanted me to be her first kiss. Did she die because of me? Because of herself? Was it something that couldn't be controlled? Was it just chance that the Zombie happened to have a scalpel lodged in his hand before he died and made a wild thrash and cut her? I want her alive, even if it means that she has to leave me.

I had that opportunity. Rather than having her shot, I could have just drugged her up and let her be undead, and in a sense she would be alive. I shake that disgusting thought out of my head. If she turned, I would allow myself to be bitten. Not for want of following her into the afterlife, but out of vulnerability, and that's the biggest asset of the undead. I wonder what Julia would be like as a Zombie. The answer is as obvious as it is immediate: just like the rest. Even if there was a semblance of the person I once loved, even if she was somehow locked in her own mind, unable to act of her own volition, it wouldn't matter.

She would, in essence, be a projection of what I knew, broadcast by me and me alone. She would harbor the virulent desire to spread the infectious seed of the one who spread it to her. There would be no mercy or compassion. If I had allowed myself to be bitten by her, it would have been for nothing. My mercy, compassion, aspirations, and memory would be eradicated in a matter of hours, replaced by her new matrix; the repulsive desire to propagate by infecting someone else. My having nothing left to live for is now only secondary to my desire to expend every last bullet wiping out this penetrative plague, even if it means saving myself from my last bullet.

I reach into my pocket and take out the bullet from my .45 magazine. I only stare at it for a moment before opening the back pocket of my backpack and sliding it inside. Once I've done that, I look at the floor and notice the headphones to Julia's CD player. I slip them on, hit play, and the player resumes the ninth track of the CD she was listening to. It's Radiohead, her favorite band. Her corpse is in the back of the bus with a bullet in her head. Why did this have to happen to me? Is there a god? Is he punishing me for thinking that the undead are actually people? Could I have saved her?

No one could have stopped it from happening.
Jules? Where were you?
You'd like to believe that my consciousness remains somewhere, a mental substance that transcends physical matter and death. I am still alive in you.
People say that all the time and it's usually bullshit.
But I am here now.
Leah, I love you so much.
Don't be sad. Remember what you told me so long ago, that we must be thankful for what the past has done for us?

"Jeff." I sit up to see Rich sitting across from me. "Shouldn't you be driving?" He points up to the front where Anderson is behind the wheel. "He wanted to know how if something happens to me. Jeff... I... are you okay?" I give him an inquisitive look and he responds by sliding his right finger down the side of his face from the eye. I pull up my sleeve and wipe my tears away. "Yeah, yeah, I'm okay." I realize only now that the other people on the bus are talking. "Are you sure?" I nod. "Yeah, it'll take some time..." He nods.

"I came to say... I'm sorry, for what happened, and I'm sorry for what I did."
"Don't be. Someone had to."
"I know, but..."
"Don't do this to yourself."
"...okay."
"...how did it go?"
"How did what go?"

We stare at each other blankly until he gets it.

"Rich... if my curiosity doesn't kill me, my imagination will."

"Well, she... Karen gave her morphine. We helped her down the hall... she was smiling. When we got her inside the room... we gave her more. She sounded like she was falling asleep... contented... she said 'Love is so *beautiful*. Tell Ef I love him...'"

Tears again pour down my face.

"She passed out... and that's when I did it. She didn't wake up."
"I heard the shot..."
"We thought... the only way you'd make it through the night was if you knew it happened."
"...right."
"Last night... was the worst night of my life. I couldn't do anything. About a dozen of them showed up a few hours later, and I... I couldn't help. Oh, I just..."
"Why did you lock me in?"
"...we knew what was gonna happen when we shut the door. As much as you wanted out... well... did you want her to hear you? Did you really wanna *see* that?"
"No..."
"Jeff... I know how you feel. It's bullshit when most people say it... but you know I mean it. What we did... it was for you... both of you... I hope... you can look back and be thankful... someday..."
"Rich..."
"...I know, I know..."
"Thank you."

Rich stifles a sob, holding back his tears. His hand comes out to shake mine, but I hug him instead. As I release him, I realize I have no desire to keep thinking about this. While I know I will spend days, weeks, months, maybe even years dwelling on Julia, I need to talk about something else right now.

"You never finished your story."
"What?"
"About you... and your wife."

"Oh, uh..."

"You were telling me about your first summer in your new house."

"Yeah... apartment."

"What went wrong?"

I know the transition must feel like a needle in the side, but I accept that my state of grief serves as armor against shattering the conventions of social niceties.

"Well... you spend enough time with one person and the romance goes... you see what kind of person you've gotten yourself involved with. Most people do anything to get away from their spouse for a few hours, and part of me thinks that's why people are satisfied with jobs they hate... aside from the money, it's an excuse to get away. But Ally and I never lost the spark. We could just sit in a room without saying a word. She'd sleep with her head on my shoulder after a bad day, and it'd just feel like she couldn't live without me. Anyway, we were both in our thirties and we wanted kids... it was either then or never. That was the first fight over money. They always start in the most horrible way... passive aggressive snipes here and there... when she finally blew up, she told me to go back to college and get a 'real job'. After all those years... that was bad enough. She apologized... but that's not the kind of thing you can take back... she was better at math than me, said we couldn't make a kid work the way it was. She was gonna have to take a leave or we'd have to pay a babysitter. She said we could make it through that okay, but then as we got older it was gonna be even harder on my salary. We'd have a tough time sending her to college. You can imagine how it went from there... turned into a cold war. She'd do all the talking, I'd do all the agreeing... but I wouldn't leave my job. Then, she just comes home from work one day and says no matter what, we can make it work. The district laid me off the next Friday. I started looking for a new job... I swear to god, I worked at it so hard I didn't even see her some days."

"Did she just tell you to get a job so you'd have one?"

"No. Neither of us wanted that. We both agreed I needed a career, but I'd never done anything but drive a bus. I didn't know what I wanted to do besides that, so I wasn't gonna waste our money going to college to figure it out. Things went downhill in the fall and got even worse in winter. New Year's seemed to be a turning point, but a month later she left... and that's when I took to the street."

"What about the house?"

"Apartment. Couldn't keep it. I couldn't support myself, let alone that... and two weeks after she left me, she found out she was pregnant."

"Oh god..."

"And I didn't find out until three months later... she hired a private investigator to find me and serve me with divorce papers. He sat there watching while I filled out the forms. I don't know... you look back... and you remember all the things you did wrong. Try to change 'em in your head. More than anything, I remember those few good weeks... before I got laid off and after New Year's. What else can you do?"

If I had heard the rest of this story when he started it, I might have choked up. I feel as though I can fake it now, but there seems to be no point. All I can do is look at him and nod. Finally he breaks the conversational stalemate by looking to the front of the bus before turning to face me again.

"So... uh... what do we do if the community center's no good?"

"Oh, uh..." I somehow forgot we were talking. "Sweep up the roamers and clear some space on the second floor."

"You think the second floor makes that much difference? They found us at the school, and they followed us into the hospital..."

"Who knows? I like our chances better on the second floor. Besides... at the high school... what if someone was downstairs all along? Or what if someone was chased inside?"

"...for argument's sake, what if the community center is crawling with 'em?"

"Well, we try to find some nice, high place for the night and be quiet."

"Aren't there more rescue centers?"

"I don't think that's such a good idea."

"Why?"

"Hundreds of people boxed in together, talking, whining, crying, complaining..." I start, shaking my head. "They'll be drawn to the activity. If one person manages to get bitten and slips through undetected, the whole building comes down from the inside. Worst of all, they're not gonna stop coming if they know there are people inside. Small groups are the best way to go."

"...so why did we go to the mall?"

"Anderson... he wanted to link up with the Guard."

"Say we run into some more people..."

"We take them with us, no questions asked."

"Well, okay... but you let in two, five, seven people, and suddenly our little group isn't so little anymore."

"I guess we'll cross that bridge when we come to it."

"And what about the high school?"

"What about it?"

Rich stops to think, and as he does I try to put together an image of the building in my mind. There's a bank of ground level windows along the front and at the new wing, but we can easily seal those off if we pull the tops off of some wooden desks, and the rest of the first floor has elevated windows. Even if they get through the windows, they'll be trapped in an exterior classroom we don't need to use, so we can seal off the door. Nearly every entrance features two sets of doors with laminated glass that could be locked easily and the space between the doors could be filled with solid objects to prevent them from being opened. There's a cafeteria that undoubtedly has food stored in the freezer, and we could conceivably grow food in the greenhouse and the courtyard so that we'll have something to fall back on.

Though there may be dozens of entrances for them to get in, there are also dozens of exits for us to get out and plenty of places to go once we do. There's a workshop and a lot of resources to make barricades and perhaps better weapons. There's paint to make signs telling the outside world we're inside. We could even set up a computer with internet access and set up a web cam to show anyone that happened to be online that there were people living in the school. We could take hot showers in the gym.

More than anything, there are unrivaled logistical possibilities presented by the school. First of all, almost everyone in our group knows the building back to front. If the undead ranks continue to swell, the chances of anyone going back there are extremely low. On the other hand, if the problem is contained, some government organization would inevitably go back there to study the cemetery and find us. The more I consider how much we can get out of the school, the more of a viable choice it becomes. "You're absolutely right..." He nods and goes to the front of the bus. When we approach the high school, Rich comes up to the front, and I follow behind him.

"Stop..." Rich says.
"What, why?" Anderson asks.
"No, don't stop here." I interrupt.
"Wait, why are we stopping at all?"
"We're thinking maybe we can fortify the school..."
"Uh..."
"We need to talk about this first."
"We can talk about it here." Rich states.
"It might not be the best idea."

Anderson stops the bus.

"I think this is a three-way conversation."
"Okay, think about the school... you, me, and some of the others know it inside and out. Aside from the front and new wing, there aren't many ground level windows... if they break in, we sacrifice the classroom they're in and block the door... we've got showers, food, plenty of space, we can cut off any one area by blocking a hallway, chemicals, tools, books... more importantly, we know the area, so we know where we can resupply and every conceivable way to get from one place to another..."
"Alright, you've sold me... and I agree, we shouldn't stop."

He puts the bus in gear and continues down the street.

"Why not?" Rich asks.

"It's probably crawling with them. Besides, we've gotta fortify, and that's at least a week's work. Loud work. It's gonna pull 'em in. So we sleep at the community center at night and work during the day."

"Sounds good to me."

The community center used to be the old high school before expansion in the area necessitated the construction of TMHS in 1957, but rather than demolish the building or allow it to fall into disuse, the district transformed it into a location for school board meetings, plays, sports events, and a Friday night recreation center for young teens. The most extreme function for which it was intended was to serve as a surrogate high school if something bad ever happened to TMHS. I've been inside the building hundreds of times without having seen all of it.

I stand on the sand bags and look through glass as Anderson pulls into the parking lot. The community center is right next to the bus depot and I can see that my car is still parked between two of the buses; I suppose my Solara's presence shouldn't be a shocking revelation since I only parked it there a few days ago, but it feels like I've been gone for a month. I also look beyond the buses to West Chester Pike to see the cars densely packed into each other like a junkyard full of new vehicles. Anderson slows down as he begins to drive across the grass, I assume because he'd prefer to enter through the gym. After taking a moment to get my belt and grab my backpack, I walk to the back of the bus and wait by the door until he's finished parking.

"Two people stay behind, and leave the bus running. Radios on."

"I'll stay behind." Rich offers. "Karen, you want to stay?"

"Uh... sure."

Melody, Jake, Anderson and I jump out the back of the bus and try the door, but it's locked. Anderson smiles at me as he smashes the glass with his crowbar. "I don't think that will ever stop being fun." He says. I nod in agreement as I operate the door mechanism from the other side, pulling it open before we enter the darkness. I reach inside my inner trench coat pocket to retrieve my flashlight and shine the halogen bulb around. "Far wall by the locker room." Anderson says, running to the right. I grab my katana handle with the assumption that he's spotted a member of the undead, but I remember that he knows where the light switches are. In seconds, the room's aging fluorescent lights begin burping to life. Anderson runs into the locker room next, so I chase after him. "Melody, Jake, cover us."

Once inside, I have to step over a series of chairs and a ping pong table that has been set against the door. There is a ten foot long wall on the left partitioning us from the rest of the locker room. "You smell that?" Anderson asks as I take in an odor like feces mixed with rotting meat and the taste of cold metal. I nod and pinch my nose shut as I continue to follow him. Anderson puts his left shoulder to the wall and holds his crowbar behind his head as he side-steps toward an opening.

He turns and takes a deep breath as he looks away. I poke my head around him to see a dead girl with a gun in her hand. There is a ludicrous amount of dried blood on the ground that appears to have come out of her mouth and even more is caked into her dark black hair. Crusty chunks of purple matter have been fused into the white concrete brick just above her, stretching a reddish brown streak down to the blue tiling. As I approach, several dozen cockroaches scurry from beneath her. She appears quite rotten, like she's been dead a couple of days.

"Jesus Christ." I say, looking away while covering my mouth and nose. I keep my eyes trained on her for a moment, but Julia springs back in my mind, so I have to look at the wall and change the subject. Nevertheless, I can't stop myself from watching Anderson step forward and take the gun, which looks like a Glock, out of her hand. He removes the magazine and checks it to reveal that there are no bullets left, so he lays it next to her. "Eyes look like dried grapes..." Anderson says softly, causing me to close my eyes again. "She was crying..." I've quickly become used to the smell, but I don't understand how Anderson can sit so close to her. "Why... why'd she do it?"

He doesn't respond, so I turn around with the willpower to distance myself from the corpse. There doesn't appear to be a single bite or scratch on her. I look to my left into the shower area, and then look back; the section where the lockers and benches used to be is barren, leaving a white, tiled room separated from the showers. I look inside the showers, barely noticing the scent of urine. "Anderson, are there claw marks on the door?" He steps back and looks toward where we came in. "Yeah, I can see them from here." The images of what happened begin trickling into my mind.

She pushed the door shut, the lumbering steps of the undead drawing close and echoing in the vastness of the gym. Breathing hard, with little time, she ran into the other part of the room to see a ping pong table and several chairs. She pulled the table into the other side of the partition and pushed it up against the door. She proceeded to do the same with the chairs until there was nothing left to block it.

"There couldn't have been many, or they would have gotten in." I say blandly.

She could still hear them at the door, trying their hardest to get in; their moans were dull and droning, but loud enough to keep her awake. She struggles to open the magazine on the bottom of the gun, finally finding a switch that lets it fall out easily. There is only one bullet left. Knowing nothing about guns, she wonders if one bullet would be enough to kill two of them if their heads are close together...

"The shower's been used, and the stall smells like piss, so she had to have been here a while."

Two days of their moaning and it was all she could concentrate on. More of them had showed up at the outside of the building; she could hear them through the elevated windows, shuffling around on the pavement. There was no meter, no tempo, and no attempt at harmonization. They just kept at it; listless, lazy, hollow, and never ending. They might stop for a few seconds at a time, long enough for you to sit in a dark in a corner and pretend you have the outside chance of catching some sleep, and that's the moment they start up again, exactly as before. There's nothing else you can think about that doesn't have to do with them. Can't concentrate on a great vacation or high school or

a day where you slept in and did nothing. All you can think about is that
rotten meat smell and the fact that your friends and family are dead.

For two days.

She'd tried the windows, but they never got too far away. She could pistol
whip the two at the door, but what if there was a dozen more behind them
now? Strategy doesn't exist at this point, unless it consists of an unending
rumble of emotionless moans. The only thing that could drown them out for
a few seconds of peace was crying your eyes out. She tried running the water,
screaming, and banging around, but it only got worse without ever lessening.
She refused to let go of the gun, somehow knowing that her exit strategy
would revolve around it. With that thought in her mind, and without any
hesitation, she revolved the gun around to the inside of her mouth and jerked
down on the trigger, finally hearing nothing at all.

"She must've been driven nuts by the moaning… Christ, just a few
days."

"Why do you say that?"

"It's only been a week…"

"Yeah, can we get the fuck out of here?"

"You mean the room, or the building?"

"This place gives me the creeps." He says rather flatly and calmly.
One thing that has always terrified me about Anderson is how flat he
sounds when he's legitimately scared.

"We have nowhere else to go."

"Can we just get out of this room?"

Anderson rushes ahead of me as I get up to leave. Once I exit, I
pull the door shut behind me. "Melody, Jake…" When I have their attention, I motion for them to walk toward the halls connecting to the
cafeteria, and then my body goes into autopilot. The girl in the locker
room had a story that was no doubt compelling; then again, so must
everyone who survived the initial attacks. How many of the people
running out of the high school managed to get away? How many people are still holed up in their homes?

Mursak immediately crosses my mind. He was on the bleachers,
probably the worst place to be. For his sake, I hope he was trampled
to death before he could get bitten. I wonder if we'll come across his

assimilated body while trying to clear out the high school and surrounding area. Then again, the girl in the locker room made it that far by herself. How did she get her hands on a Glock, particularly one that looks like a police model? I wonder if everyone surviving to this point has a story as simultaneously exciting and depressing as mine. I mask the grimness of that thought when I cover Anderson and Jake as they take a look in the upstairs bathroom.

I suppose Julia's fate was better than being sucked into a hoard of the undead and torn limb from limb. The thought causes my already itchy tear ducts to discharge. Compared to a lot of scenarios, I was lucky, and so was she. She was able to be knocked out by morphine. *Love is a beautiful. Tell Ef I love him.* I can go to my grave satisfied that she was comfortable enough to refer to me as Ef in the company of others. I think back to the moment I put that ring on her finger at my senior prom and the fact that I wanted her to be with me until the end. Somehow, I figure that I was half right without crying.

I wonder how long it will be until I dissolve into sobs again. I can remember how hard I've taken being broken up with in the past, where I'd spend each night crying myself to sleep and feel okay in the morning. As long as I have something to do, like walk the hallways of an abandoned high school looking for the undead, I'll probably be okay. I wonder how long it will be until I hear her talking in my head again. It's probably best I not tell anyone else about that. "Jeff, this door's locked." Anderson says, interrupting my thoughts. My response at first is merely a shrug, but I can tell by the look on his face that a shrug won't do.

"So what?"
"It's the only one."
"…break it down."

Anderson slams his crowbar between the metal guard around the handle and the door frame. Upon the second slam there is a moment of confusion as wood chips explode from the center of the door, then considerably less confusion when we register the sound of a gunshot.

Anderson throws himself out of the doorway and hits the ground rolling.

"Hold your fire! Hold your fire!"

"H… humans?" A voice asks.

"Yes, humans, you *retard*! Don't shoot unless you *fucking* know what you're shooting at!" Anderson shouts.

"Dude…" I say quietly.

"No, what do we do if someone gets shot, have Karen fish the bullet out with a friggin' hot knife? I ought to shoot his ass just for doing that…"

"Anderson, *calm down*."

"How long have you been in there?" Anderson asks.

"Uh, four days?" The voice is male.

"Well get out here!"

"Is it over?"

"No. But if you don't come with us, we're kicking you out on the fuckin' street."

The young man stumbles out of the room exhaustedly. He's slightly overweight and has dirty blond hair that would probably come down two inches past his ears if it weren't all slicked back. His eyes are blue, but bloodshot. He hasn't shaved in a few days and he looks to be about my age. "What's your name?" I ask. He looks down at his pistol and looks up at me.

"Rob… Robert. Proctor."

"All right, Robert Proctor. We're gonna make sure there's no one else here, then we're gonna go to the bus outside and get the rest of our group. That okay with you?" He nods. "Good, this is Anderson, Jake, Melody, and I'm Jeff."

Robert simply nods in response. Part of me immediately wants to ask him about the girl downstairs, but for some reason, I'm simply not comfortable doing it. Apparently no one else is either, because almost nothing is said in the half hour it takes for the five of us search each room in the structure only to discover that most of them are totally empty. Anderson is too pissed about almost being shot to say anything, evidenced by his grunting of monosyllabic instructions as we clear the building with our new colleague in tow. As I watch Robert trail us in a daze, I have to wonder if he's psychologically fit. He doesn't say much.

With the building inspected, we go out to the bus to grab our gear and introduce Robert to Karen and Rich, then spend the next half hour moving our stuff into one of the rooms on the second level, opting to leave some of our things that we don't need on the bus. This, too, is executed without anyone saying much, until Karen approaches me in the hallway and nods for me to follow her into the bathroom.

As I follow her in, I try to rationally reason what's about to happen. Am I about to find out that someone got bitten? Is this the moment where she tells me she's dying to get laid? Have I been Punk'd? Is her skin about to tear off as she reveals that she's an alien here to save one last pocket of humanity before the apocalypse? By the time she turns to face me, I realize I haven't been rational, but I have prepared myself for anything.

"Is everythin' alright with Robert?"
"Not for long, if we let Anderson off the leash."
"I'm bein' serious…"
"We only just met him…"
"But did you think he was actin' strange?"
"Strange? I mean, he *did* almost shoot us. What do you think?"
"I don't know… maybe PTSD? I don't know. Keep an eye on him."

Just as quickly as she entered, she walks out, and as I follow her, I bump into Anderson. He follows her with his eyes as she walks back out toward the bus. "Everything okay?" For a moment I expect he thinks we've become involved sexually, but the look on his face suggests his concern is that one of us has been bitten.

"Nah, we're cool… what's up?"
"We should make a run at the gun store before it gets dark."

"Oh?"

"Yeah... see if there's anything we missed, and get a rifle for Rob."

"You sure you want to give him another gun?"

"Not really... but we're better off with everyone carrying."

"Yeah... Karen thinks he's got PTSD."

Anderson looks down the hallway to consider this a moment.

"I can see that... he's got the stare."

"Which one's that?"

"Thousand-yard stare."

"He doesn't look that focused..."

"...you've never seen it before. It's not like that movie, where they make it sound bad-ass. The guys who have it look... I don't know, wounded."

"Well... Karen says keep an eye on him."

"10-4."

"What does that mean anyway?"

"10-4? It's ten code. Police use it to signal on the radio. It means 'everything's okay'."

"Wouldn't it be easier to say 'okay'?"

"Well, 'okay' can mean a bunch of things... 10-4 is always 10-4."

"Except when people use it in conversation."

After a moment, Anderson chuckles and starts off down the hall. "By the way..." He turns back to face me. "Can you... give Julia's stuff to Karen?" He nods and continues back down the hall. I go straight to the bedroom, drop my backpack, and lay down on the comforter that is, at the moment, my bed. I don't have a chance to shut my eyes for long. *Breaker breaker...* Anderson laughs into the radio. I wait a moment before I retrieve mine to respond.

"You didn't say over. Over."

"You coming with us to get guns and food, over?"

"Nah, I'm beat, I'm taking a nap."

"Alright... Melody and Jake are staying put, so they'll be up in a minute. Over and out."

I consider turning the walkie-talkie off, but decide against it. When I roll over I feel the absence next to me like a phantom limb. I take notice of the rings on my hand and think about how naked my finger used to feel when I'd take my ring off in the shower, but now it feels just as strange having a second ring on my pinkie. Jake and Melody enter the room. Without looking at them, I can tell they see me lying down and follow suit. Staring at the ceiling, not a whole lot crosses my mind, aside from the fact that it feels odd staring up at a ceiling that is roughly analogous to the one at the high school. Given more than a few seconds to stop and think, I suddenly realize how stiff my shoulders have become. Melody is about ten paces from me in her bed, shifting somewhat uncomfortably every few seconds.

"Jeff?" Melody asks.
"Yes?"
"Are you okay?"

I turn my head slowly to look at her. "Great." She sighs as I turn my head back toward the ceiling and start trying to see shapes in the foam panels.

"...that's a stupid question, sorry..."
"It's okay..."
"I just... I don't know what to say..."
"Nothing. I'm loathe to use to expression... but it is what it is."
"I guess... I really just... want you to know... if there's anything I can do... just ask. Seriously... *anything*."

I squint as I look back over at her.

"Wait, what does *that* mean?"
"Jeff... have you ever... lost anyone close?"
"Not this close."

"I have… sometimes, it's hard to know what you want… sometimes you want to be alone, sometimes you need someone. I don't want you to be afraid to come to me with anything… no matter what it is… and I won't judge you for it."

After a moment, I decide it's a sweet thing to say.

"Thanks."
"Don't mention it."
"Who was it?"
"Who was what?"

When I look over at her and she understands, her eyes fall to the floor. She gives no indication that she wants to respond. "Sorry…" I say finally. "It's okay…" We both stay silent for several long moments. I grasp my left shoulder and try to massage it.

"Jeff…"
"Yeah?"
"Did you really give my boyfriends advice?"
"…what?"
"You know… for sex stuff?"
"Oh… uhm… maybe not directly…"

After sitting quietly again for a few seconds, I can't help but laugh. As I laugh harder, she joins in.

"What made you think of that?"
"That stuff about the pillow… and doing it sideways…"
"You know Jen Meridian?"
"Yeah…"
"Well, I was in a stat class, and I'm terrible at math… so we get handed an equation, and I say to myself it's harder than giving a girl an orgasm. Jen turns around and I think she's gonna slap me… and she just says 'you know, that's really hard'. I was flabbergasted. She asked me if I had any tips… I have no idea why… but I *had* looked stuff up

on the internet... so I asked her what the trouble was, and she eventually admitted that her boyfriend was kind of... small... which was hilarious, because he was sitting on the other side of the room... and I told her basically what I told you. A few days later, she told me it was better after that."

"Who was the guy?"

"Jay Nuvar."

"Oh..."

"Know him?"

"Yeah... we..."

"He tried the pillow trick?"

"Yeah..."

"That's too funny."

"Does your shoulder hurt or something?"

"Huh?"

"You're rubbing your shoulder."

"Yeah, it does."

"I could massage it for you."

"I couldn't ask you to do that."

"Actually, you could."

I look over at her, smirking as I nod. "Why not?" When I sit up and present my back, Melody immediately begins roughly working her fingers into the muscles in broad, wave-like motions. Julia's massages became so regular that I hadn't considered anyone else would merely pale in comparison. Her fingers could reduce the tightest knots into liquid. When Melody finishes I thank her and decide to go for a stroll around the school while she takes a nap. I wish I could talk to Robert, get to know him better, but I'll have to settle for Jake, who comes with me while I patrol the top level. I can tell he feels awkward, and his leap to conversation is equal to this assumption.

"So Jeff, what's your favorite movie?"

"Probably Eraserhead... I can watch it an infinite amount of times and never get enough. Videodrome is a close second, followed by Dawn of the Dead."

"I saw that… it was okay."

"The original, or the remake?"

"There was a remake?"

"Yeah, the original is far superior."

"And you still like it?"

"What?"

"You know, with…"

"Oh, that doesn't affect it at all…"

"Even with what happened to Julia?"

I stop and look up and down his body before my eyes drift to the floor.

"…I guess I'd have to see it again."

"Sorry for… bringing that up."

"No, it's okay. I… shouldn't ignore it."

I sigh deeply.

"Do you regret being with her?"

"What!? Why would I?"

"I don't know… now that she's gone, wouldn't it have hurt less if you'd never known her?"

"I… no! I *loved* her… besides, I may not be alive now if it weren't for her… I might have still gone to Bandrome, but would I have run out onto the field? Would I have gone to the greenhouse, or gotten to my car, or…"

I trail off, leaving a moment of uncomfortable silence that Jake, again, breaks.

"You alright?"

"…I can't answer your question."

"Well, you don't have to…"

"I want to, though… of course I'm glad to have known her, but if I hadn't, would this have happened to her? I thought earlier that it would have been easier if we'd had a bad breakup and I just knew that she was okay…"

"But then you never would have known her. Not like you could be comforted by the fact that this person you never knew was going to be alive."

"You're asking me to put an awful lot of limitations on this. Of course if I'd never known her it wouldn't have mattered. If we put this too out of context we could spend years talking about the variables…"

"Sorry…"

"…but if you're asking me if it was worth knowing her to have her suddenly cut out of my life, then the answer is yes. That's the reason I'm depressed now, not because she's gone, but because of… what we had."

"…so, then you *are* depressed that she's gone…"

"…if I hadn't known her I wouldn't be depressed about her being gone. It's because I miss her."

"I'm sorry, but that sounds like the same thing to me…"

"I don't see how you could call the two synonymous. Take Robert for example. If they came back and told me he was bitten while they were out, do you think I'd be sad about him being gone?"

"No…"

"Wrong, I would. I'd have barely gotten to know him, but I want him alive as much as the next person. I'd be sad about him being gone, but there'd be nothing for me to miss…"

"Besides his presence…"

"Would *you* be sad about him being gone?"

"I wouldn't be happy about it, but I don't think I'd be overly sad."

"And do you think that's synonymous with not missing him?"

"I think so, yeah…"

"So something can be gone without you missing it. Can you miss something without it being gone?"

"I… no?"

"So you've never missed your parents even when you knew you'd see them again?"

He stays silent for a moment before responding.

"I'm saying you miss her because she's gone… you're saying you miss her because you miss her."

"…I'm saying I miss *her*, because I *miss* everything that we used to be. I'd feel this way whether she broke up with me or…"

"So if she broke up with you, you'd miss the relationship. If she died, you'd miss her altogether. Either way, she's gone, and because of that you miss her. If she were still here, you wouldn't be missing her."

"But you're telling me that I miss her just because she's gone…"

"I don't understand why else you would!"

"I wouldn't miss her just because I don't have her anymore! Of course I miss her because she's gone, but that's not the only reason!"

"Then why else!?"

"Because I still *have* everything else!"

Jake is now completely silent. I've turned my back to him, but I can feel him watching me vibrate with anger as I walk into a bathroom. Once inside, I burst through one of the stalls and fall face first into the toilet with tears streaming down my face as I gasp for air. When I try to choke some of them back, I let out a dry heave before crumpling to the floor completely. I pinch my eyes shut and sob hard into the side of the freezing porcelain bowl. A few seconds later I open my eyes and look at the side of the stall, then snap my leg out and start kicking the center of it as hard as I can while gritting my teeth. After several kicks I can't keep my mouth shut anymore and I let out a long, strained scream as I kick harder and faster. When I finally run out of momentum I fall limply on the floor and continue crying. I don't get up for another twenty minutes.

Finally, the sobs die out. "It's all right Jeff. It's all right…" I put my hand on the seat and start to help myself up. "Okay, it's not. But you'll live." I rest my back against the stall, sitting on the back of my feet as I wipe the tears away with one hand. I look at the warped metal of the stall partition and let out a brief chuckle before I pull myself up entirely. Once outside the stall, I walk directly to the mirror and turn on the faucet. My face is totally red, including some freckle-like splotches just beneath my eyes. I run my face through the water and rub it in with my hands, then look again. "You look like shit." I say softly to my reflection. After staring for another few seconds, I walk back to our room on the second floor.

I stand in the doorway for a moment before I enter. Melody is sleeping and Jake is facing away from me on the floor, staring at the windows. Neither of us moves, but I know he's aware of me. It takes a few minutes for him to finally speak.

"I'm sorry."

"It's alright... you heard that?"

"...yeah."

"Well, I wasn't doing it out of anger, just so you know."

"Not just anger?"

"No. Not anger at all."

I step through the doorway and lean against the wall. He still doesn't turn around.

"While you were in there I remembered something about Julia... I wasn't sure if you'd want me to tell you."

"Go ahead."

"Well. You know smile she had, the sort of..."

"Mysterious one?"

"Exactly. I'd see her in homeroom and stuff, and even if it was gone for just a few seconds, it would come right back. We weren't really that friendly, but everyone talked about her... smiling all the time, you know. One of my friends made me ask... and she said it was for someone else, and he always kept it on her face whether he knew it or not."

My smile is maintained only for a few seconds. Jake turns and looks at me for a moment, then resumes looking out the window. I can hear the group approaching from the hall, so I wait for them by the door. Anderson is the first to enter, and I nod at everyone behind him.

"How'd it go?"

"Fantastic, got Rob a good rifle." Anderson says. "But the store was cleared out."

"Huh?"

"We had to settle for getting him a gun that takes twenty-five odd six bullets. There were only three boxes left, and we had a hell of a time finding them."

"Just a matter of time…"

"Anyway, I brought you a present."

"Yes?"

"Stogies."

A smile creeps across my face, Anderson holds up the small brown foil bag. "We'll have to save them for an appropriate occasion." I say flatly as the rest of the group passes us. "Save them? I took about twenty packs. And here's a lighter." He hands me a Zippo, which I then stick in my pocket. Robert comes in behind Anderson as he speaks again.

"Just filled it."

"Robert, how are you?"

"I'm good." He says with what looks like a forced smile. "You can call me Rob."

"Sorry. Rob. I was thinking about having a smoke on the roof, you want to come with?"

"Could we eat first?"

"Absolutely."

"Grey, I was thinking…" Anderson says, kneeling by his backpack.

"Yeah?"

"Well, what about the cabin?"

He's referring to the small compound of three houses that my family owns in New York.

"What about it?"

"Maybe we should go there. It's isolated."

"Ehhh… I don't know. Getting there would not be fun, there's less chance of finding supplies, and the backyard is literally a river. Not exactly a low traffic area, you know?"

"Lower traffic than here, though."

"Yeah, but I mean those houses aren't really gonna hold up. We're better off conserving our resources and staying here."

"What are you guys talking about?" Karen asks.

"My cabins in New York as a place to go."

"My parents have one in western Montana..."

"The idea of a road trip to Montana might have appealed to me before this happened... but now?"

Karen shrugs and hands off a set of sheets and a pillow for Rob. He nods and gives her a half smile, and then I watch as he awkwardly pushes them out across the tile floor of the classroom. After a few more people get themselves set up, Anderson makes use of the oven in the kitchen on the first level to heat up some frozen pizza from the supermarket. The kitchen's silver and white color scheme makes it uncomfortably anesthetizing. Anderson makes note of a massive walk-in freezer behind a tile partition, reasoning that it would be big enough to hold fifty corpses.

As he makes the food, half of us put the perishables in their appropriate kitchen places while the other half look for small, portable refrigerators. Anderson and I know that people actually did work here despite the abandoned high school status and our hope was that they were present enough to require such a thing. It seems we are in luck because two offices on the first floor each have small refrigerators. We cart them up the steps to go into our living quarters for beverages and breakfast foods.

After our pizza and a discussion about drinking stories involving vomiting, I ask Rob and Anderson to accompany me to the roof for a cigar. I can't make out much on the rooftop aside from the normal structural rises and dips, and can see little else beyond it aside from the shadowy outlines of naked tree branches. I strip open the top of the cigar package and pass them around. Rob graciously accepts his. "So Rob... tell me about yourself." I ask while lighting mine, then his.

"Thanks. Well, I was at the high school..."

"Really?"

"How old are you?" Anderson asks.

"19."

"I never saw you at the Mass?"

"I went to Carrell."

"Okay... continue."

"I was close to the gate... and when I heard the gunshot, I jumped off the back of the bleachers. There was a... I landed on a trailer. After that, I just ran."

"Where did you go?"

"The way I came in... I just ran for it... I almost got hit by a car... they were running into each other, the building..."

"You didn't have a car?" Anderson asks.

"...I didn't even think about it until I got to the street... then it was too late."

"Hmm..."

"Then, there was this girl following me... asking me what to do... like I should know. I didn't need to make it to the end of the block before I realized we needed to get inside... so we came in here. Then... for some reason... she hands me a gun and says she trusts me with it."

"A pistol?"

"Yeah."

"After ten minutes she trusts you with a gun?"

"Crazy, right? So, I don't know what to do... I take it and we come upstairs... I don't know how long we were up there, a day or so... and one morning, she's just gone... I tried to look for her, but I didn't get very far before I came back... I was just... frozen. I kinda... lost it. I... I don't even know what I was thinking when you knocked on the door... I'm... sorry..."

"Don't worry about it... so, this girl... what'd she look like?"

"Eh, little shorter than me, black hair..."

"Did she have a gun too?" I ask.

"Yeah ... wuh-did you see her?"

"Nah, just wanted to know if she had a way to defend herself."

Anderson glares at me and I give him a subtle nod. I don't think he understands why I said what I said, being that both of us know that her corpse is downstairs, but he knows based on my look that I'll explain later.

"Go to school?"

"DC cubed."

"Nice, nice... any family, friends?"

"Nah, I don't think so. Not anymore. My dad lives in Raleigh."

"Wait, what time is it?"

As Rob glances at his wrist, I notice a pale patch of skin in the shape of a watch.

"I don't have my watch..." Rob responds.

"It is... 9:10." Anderson says.

"News is on. Come on."

We all toss our cigars over the edge and run down to the collective bedroom to find the members of our group sitting around my television. There are two well dressed men sitting in chairs parallel to each other talking. I recognize one of them instantly.

"... *regularly scheduled news broadcasts temporarily suspended to bring you consistent updates, but tonight we have something different. Experts requested for interviews in situations like these are often bountiful and willing to cooperate, and throughout the week we will be speaking to a few epidemiologists, forensic experts, and retired military personnel. Tonight, we bring you a man who never suspected he'd be taking part in a broadcast of this magnitude; I speak of Dr. Lon Miller, an esteemed CDC epidemiologist whose own fascination with the fictional undead saw him publish the Alomal-137 Epidemiology Case Study, a fictional report about the undead, in 1997 when he was still a graduate student. Lon, it's good to have you on the air with us.*"

"*Good to be here.*"

"*Now, when we researched your report, we found it on a website dedicated to living dead fiction... did this idea previously inform your decision to enter the medical field, or was it the reverse?*"

"Neither and both. I've always thought of Zombies as the most interesting movie monsters, the portrayal in George Romero's films in particular. While I was deep into understanding the specifics of public health reports, it just seemed like a fun departure to write some realistic medical prose about the undead."

"Now, you've been vocal thus far in interviews that many of the aspects of your report are fictional. How did you compile the information?"

"Some of it was common sense, some of it was scenarios I'd been discussing with my friends for years. Arguments about the conditions required to reanimate the dead raged on for days, sometimes weeks, so I contacted a few people about bits here and there and did a lot of research, but a lot of the writing just came from spending a few months throwing stones at it."

"Can you tell us what you know about what's going on?"

"Well, most of what has made it through the news already is fairly accurate. The dead are rising and attacking the living. The cause is the X-factor, and I'm afraid I can't provide any answers there... no one can. One of the first questions I raised when hearing about this was whether the bites of the undead would actually infect the living. Now, it's been well reported by the CDC that the human mouth contains bacteria that can easily cause Staph infections or Septicemia which, if untreated, can prove deadly. As a result, the victim dies and eventually resurrects, not necessarily because of a virus, but because the recently dead are returning to life no matter what the circumstances of their demise. As it turns out, infection makes the most sense because we've proven that those bitten can take two paths. The first is to die and resurrect a few hours later, after rigor mortis has set in, rendering them stiff and slow. The second is that, with proper medical treatment, the patient's mental state declines the longer they are kept alive, and ultimately they will die, but the period of death before... well, before un-death is much shorter, rendering them fleet and mobile. So, without a doubt, a bite or scratch is 100% fatal."

"Say the bite were to occur on an extremity, an arm or a leg, would the chances of survival increase by severing the affected area?"

"Without proper testing it's hard to say. If this were proved to be an infection, I'd say that would help measurably. If not, there's no saying."

"The perspective that this is not a bacterial or viral infection has been drawing a lot of criticism."

"Understandably so. Look, the entire scenario is unfeasible. The world has never seen anything like this before, so we should prepare to challenge both our science and our beliefs. If this were just a virus, I don't think we'd be seeing the dead clawing their way through their coffins."

"So, they are, in fact, returning from the grave."

"...yes. It's a terrifying thought, and, as you say, something that has drawn a lot of criticism. In a standard burial, a cadaver is placed in a coffin generally made of wood which is then encased in a burial vault, generally made of concrete, and buried six feet underground. This combination should make it impossible for even an able-bodied person to free themselves. There are a few theories, as this phenomenon seems to have occurred at one cemetery only, but there has been no effort to investigate for obvious reasons. The first theory is that the area was beset by sinkholes, which could theoretically disrupt the ground enough to make escape easier. The second theory is that the cemetery did not follow proper burial guidelines throughout the grounds... hard coffins replaced with pine boxes, no burial vault or one perhaps comprised of cheap alternatives to concrete like stucco or plaster, or bodies not being buried deep enough. The third theory, which is still in its infancy, is that the undead are the product of some sort of biological warfare and disseminated from a cemetery to create fear and confusion. In any case, it's possible that some of these elements, combined with a lack of need for oxygen and sustenance in the undead, could create conditions for the corpses to free themselves. It seems ridiculous to even question whether or not it would be possible at this point, since the most obvious conclusion to draw from the epidemiology and the old, filthy dress clothes of the undead and the stench of formaldehyde would be that they have, in fact, returned from the grave. The question of how their brains survived is the standing one. Nevertheless, for the purposes of all future newscasts, these slow moving but highly dangerous Zombies have been designated 'walkers' and the faster moving ones have been designated 'runners'."

"What does it take to kill them?"

"Well, the only way to kill them is by destroying the brain... which is an area that should be studied more thoroughly before any official reports are made. Certain areas of the brain may prove vestigial in trying to shut down all motor function, so severing the head of an undead attacker may leave the head capable of attack. Severe damage to the cerebellum and nerve stem appears to stop them."

"A recent question has risen by the apparent surgical strikes of the dead... in your opinion, are the undead working together?"

"In a way. They're not cannibals, as many would suggest, because they are not human in a strictly collective sense. They don't respond to the presence of each other, but somehow they can distinguish between their own kind and humans at very long distances. Even humans acting like Zombies are not exempt. However, they do not fight each other."

"Are they capable to forming a strategy to effectively trap and infect humans?"

"I don't think so. This would require intelligence that they wholly lack."

"Now, is there a basis on which they elect to eat or simply infect their victims?"

"It is not a matter of selection... perhaps merely chance depending on the situation or the fullness of their stomachs. It is true that they act on instinct and that they likely do not digest their food, but they are apparently aware when they can eat no more. If a group accosts one human, it is likely that the human will be picked clean, unable to revive. With a smaller group, they will eat more slowly, and if they hear, see, or smell another human, they will stop and go after them. They prefer the living over the dead, which is curious..."

"So, if I were surrounded by a group of walkers, unarmed..."

"Unarmed? Well, if you're able to kick, I'd say a leg would be the safest extremity to use to make a hole to run through them. Otherwise I would suggest finding the biggest opening, ducking and running below their arm range. If you have an object to strike them, try knocking them back. A gun is the best thing to have, I suppose, in that case."

"As far as firearms, what is the best choice?"

"Any single shot weapon is good... the best choice is probably lever action rifles. Next up would be semi-automatics, but a rapidly firing weapon tends to be a bad choice."

"Now why is that?"

"Military personnel are exempt here because they've been trained to handle such weapons, but even when backed against a wall, a spray of bullets would not deter them. One is better off with a more conservative approach, or even a melee weapon."

"And how about hand to hand combat, 'melee' weapons, as you say?"

"A crowbar is the best choice, since it serves multiple purposes and has a sturdy build. As their numbers continue to swell beyond the thousands, however, such tactics can only be considered a last resort to escape short-term engagements."

"You believe that they are in the thousands now?"

"Tens of thousands, certainly. Having spread throughout the northeast, their numbers are great. If this can be contained... the efforts to restore society to normality will be nothing short of an enormous undertaking..."

"I'm sorry, did you say if?"

"...well, yes, if. I can't entertain optimism for its own sake because doing so would almost certainly leave us unprepared for the rapidly swelling probability of encountering our worst case scenario. I say 'if' because the particulars of this syndrome are still eluding both the police and military. If there isn't some degree of slowing in the near future, it may be safe to assume that they will not be slowed down."

"I understand we are to go to a commercial now..."

"I apologize for not sugarcoating the truth, but we face the very real threat of total..."

The picture cuts out and, much to my dismay, a commercial actually does come on. I turn off the television and look back at the group. "Anyone have any questions, comments, or concerns?" The instant the words come out of my mouth, I consider the last thing he said before the commercial and my blood runs cold as I start to imagine how I can tap dance around a direct question about whether I think the undead will eventually overtake mankind.

After a moment of tense silence and some fairly docile looks between a few of the group members, everyone shakes their heads. I sigh in relief as I slide myself across the floor and into my bed, partially out of exhaustion, and partially to avoid discussion. With my body running on fumes and rational, conscious thought becoming more difficult by the moment, I fall asleep before the lights are turned out.

10-16-04, SATURDAY

I wake up feeling awful, perhaps from missing my cathartic cry last night, but I can only concentrate on running my tongue against the bottom of my incisors to feel the solidifying layer of pond scum accumulating on my teeth. After a few seconds of attempting to force my rancid breath toward my nose, I open my eyes to see Anderson awake and staring out the window.

"Jesus, Anderson, do you ever sleep?"
"Fuck sleep. You sleep when you die."
"Not anymore."

He turns back and gives me a sly grin as I pull myself out of my makeshift bed. "I gotta piss, and I *really* need to brush my teeth." He points out one of the doors and keeps staring forward, out the window. "Okay..." I mumble as I make my way out the door. "Wait a second..." Anderson says as I exit. I turn back to see him looking at everyone else still asleep on the floor. He motions for me to come close and the two of us begin whispering.

"Why aren't we telling Rob about the girl?"
"I don't know... what if he cracks?"
"What do we do about the body?"
"Burn it?"

Anderson nods and gives me a thumb up. I turn left out the door and find the nearest bathroom. I awkwardly step back into the room, unsuccessfully trying to avoid cold spots on the floor. First I shit and piss, then take a good long time to brush my teeth. I walk back into the bed area to see that Melody is making use of the tea kettle. I yawn. "You our resident cook now?" I ask her. "I'm no Julia..." She doesn't finish. It seems it was all I needed. "Oh Jesus, I'm sorry..." Melody says as I sit down, and she wraps her arms around me. "It's okay..." I manage to get out. "Just hurry up with the tea." Sure enough, the tea kettle starts whistling and she pours the cups. I can tell Anderson feels awkward about the fact that I'm crying. I manage to stifle the moans, but after a few seconds, I feel too exposed, so I take my blanket and hunker down in the corner for ten minutes.

"So Grey, we gonna check out the high school today?" Anderson asks moments after I return to the group. I blow my nose and wipe my eyes in a tissue that Melody hands me. "Yeah, absolutely. After breakfast." One by one everyone wakes up, and after some talk about what to do, everyone gets themselves ready to go. Once on the bus, I hesitantly give Rob the walkie-talkie that used to belong to Julia. Along the way to the high school I take notice of the few undead drawing toward the wake of the bus. I point two fingers on my left hand and pretend to shoot at them. We make it to the high school less than a minute later, and the first thing I notice is the broken window where Julia, Melody and I exited only a few nights ago. The front doors, which were all locked, don't appear to have been broken or damaged. "Do we lock it down?" Rich asks Anderson and me as we approach the auditorium doors.

"You mean the auditorium?" Anderson asks.

"Yes."

"No. I don't think they can get up on the flowerbeds, so we'll just lock the doors. There's about forty dividers in the loft we can use to block the windows…"

We go inside the same place I originally entered the school the previous Saturday night, instantly encountering the nauseating smell of rotten flesh and feces. "I think for the first level we reinforce all the windows and pull down the shades." Anderson says. "We should park cars against the doors." Jake adds. I nod in agreement. "And the band rooms… too many windows. Gotta clear 'em out first…" As we walk along the hall, I notice Melody looking up at the lack of ceiling panels, leaving the pipes, wiring, and ductwork exposed.

"Was this place ever *not* under construction?" Melody asks.

"Looks like they left their tools again." Jake adds, ineffectually picking up a hammer.

"Lucky us." Anderson mumbles.

The high school reconstruction effort has been taking place at least since my first year in 1999. It was supposed to be finished by 2003 at the latest, but many of the school's hallways are still littered with scaffolding, drop cloths, ceiling tiles, piping, concrete bricks, cement, caulk, and power tools. We continue down the hallway and suddenly a few of the undead shuffle out from behind a corner, causing us all to leap back in fright. Once we've taken them in, I get the impression that everyone is relieved, as though there was something worse we could have encountered. Are we already becoming desensitized to the undead? Anderson takes the initiative to beat their heads into a pulp. After he's done exerting himself, he looks back to see us staring at the corpses.

"First thing's first, we need to clear this place out."

"How do we run it?" I ask.

"There's seven of us... you, Karen, Melody, Rich downstairs... the rest of us up."

"Uh... let's start in the auditorium. You guys get the loft... we'll check the shop and the dressing rooms."

"Done."

As soon as we head back to the auditorium, I begin to wish I had taken the loft. I didn't see and didn't ask what happened to Ava, and I'll want to know at some point. A few seconds after we enter the auditorium, I hear someone beating something with a crowbar, so I turn my radio on. "Everyone else, radios, and hit your flashlights." The shoulder lamps come on as we ascend the six stairs up to the stage. Melody looks over the auditorium as Karen and Rich walk through the open drapes. Once in the center of the stage, Rich knocks the bottom of his crowbar into the floor, producing a hollow thud.

The thud bounces off the walls with no response, so we walk through the dressing rooms and the shop, finding no Zombies, but a lot of scaffolding and scrap wood that will doubtlessly find use later. I try to keep in mind that there are three doors behind the auditorium; one leads directly in the back, one is centered between the two dressing rooms, and one is in the back of the shop. With nothing to be found, we turn off our flashlights, venture back into the hallway, and head back toward the band and chorus rooms.

Despite a seemingly real threat when we came down to find clothes and bottled water, the band rooms are also empty. There's a door into the back of the band room and another attached to the chorus room; the chorus room has windows facing the contained courtyard interior, and the band room has no windows, which means this area will be relatively easy to defend. When we emerge, Anderson and his group are waiting for us.

"How many?" I ask.

"Seven. You?"

"None."

"We'll have to clear the bodies in the next day or so."

"Already put them on the roof, but first thing's first. Check every classroom..."

"We don't need to do that."

"Why not?"

"They can't open doors."

"Wait, so how'd they get upstairs?" Melody asks.

"Fair point... alright, they *probably* won't open doors. And I don't think they'd stop to close them."

"Alright..." Anderson starts. "Check out any open doorway. Once you've checked a room, close the door behind you."

With no more instruction needed, Anderson's group heads upstairs as my cluster patrols the lower hallways. I make it halfway to the main lobby before I get radio chatter.

"We want to go about the same speed, so check in at every junction. Over."

"Copy."

"Jeff?" It's Karen.

"Yeah?"

"I don't know if I can... if I'll be able to hit 'em."

"...the Zombies? You haven't killed one yet?"

"Yeah... well, maybe outside the supermarket."

"Well, I hate to put you on the spot, but the first one we run into's yours."

"We don't have to make her do that..." Rich offers.

"She's gonna have to get used to it sooner later."

"You get used to it pretty fast." Melody says, presumably to comfort her.

"Alright... well... do you have any method of doin' it?"

I turn to face her, hold out my hand, and she hands over her crowbar. I illustrate without making contact, but she still winces.

"Side of the head, then top of the head. Takes about three to four blows and they stop coming as soon as they're down. Don't think of them as people... pretend it's whack-a-mole or something, anything. I just let myself get pissed."

"About what?"

"...do you have to ask?"

After checking five more classrooms and the special ed teacher's offices, we've made it to the main lobby.

"Anderson, we're at the lobby, over."

"*Gotcha, almost there. Over and out.*"

"Uh, it's gonna take awhile to get through the offices and the gym, you want to check the basement and the courtyard in the meantime? Over."

"*Sounds good. Keep in touch. Over and out.*"

I realize after I attach the radio to my belt that there are six undead wandering in the hallway that leads to the nurse's office and the gym. "Alright, Karen, you're on deck." We walk with her as she cautiously sidesteps along the wall, holding her crowbar out diagonally in front of her. I notice as we continue that the floors are covered with dried mud, and up by the nurse's office there is a crusty, reddish brown stain where John Squared lost his struggle. Desiccated bits of organ still cling to the floor, but there is no corpse to speak of. As we approach, I notice the smell of old feces and rotten meat; it's present throughout the school, but even stronger this close to the undead.

The first one Karen approaches is an overweight woman, probably a week old in terms of transformation. Fortunately, the rest are about fifty feet away. Rich steps forward to stay behind her, but I motion for him to stay back. Karen winds, squeezes her eyes shut, and bangs the crowbar into the side of her head, sending her to the floor before she plants another blow close to the top of her head. "Like that?" I watch the body writhe on the floor for a moment.

"She's still moving." I step forward and hold my hand out for the crowbar. I look at Karen for a second before I unleash three blows at the temple of her target, sending chunks of skull across the floor. "Like that." I turn to hand her the crowbar back, seeing the terrified expression on her face. It takes me a moment to notice the catatonic expressions fixed on the faces of Melody and Rich as they stare down the hall. Melody's hand comes up to point.

For some reason, I wasn't expecting this; it's John Squared, free from his trench coat with his entrails reduced to a few torn lumps of meat dangling through the hole in his stomach. His clothes are torn up and his body is covered with bite marks. I sigh as he staggers out of the group toward me. "I can't watch..." Melody says. I stare into his eyes, violating what Anderson must have told me a thousand times is a cardinal rule of killing someone. I see echoes of his terrified face, accompanied by the screams he bellowed as we failed to help him. I remember our last theological discussion. We could have spent years going back and forth.

I take off my backpack and rest it on the floor. Taking two quick steps forward, I blast the crowbar into the side of his head, his weakened legs bringing him down faster than I'd imagined. His one arm comes up, extending straight up to my face as he takes his last look. I tap the appendage out of the way and land three more blows. He won't be getting back up again. The burst of adrenaline I expected doesn't come, but I'm still not exhausted, so I finish off the rest of his friends one at a time. I walk back to the group, still catching my breath as Karen meekly accepts her crowbar. Keenly aware that everyone is staring at me, I take up my walkie-talkie.

"Anderson, what's your status? Over."
"*Nothing in the basement, heading to the courtyard. You? Over.*"
"Just found John Squared. Over."
"*Wow... you okay? Over.*"
"Fine. Over and out."

I pick up my backpack and start adjusting the strap. "Karen, you want check the nurse's station, see if there's anything we can use?" Her eyes linger on the woman before she looks up and meekly nods. With Melody standing next to me, I sip at the straw of my CamelBak as Rich and Karen go through the room. When they emerge we go to the main office, where I switch to my katana as Rich and I go to work dispatching another five. Out of the gym, the locker rooms, the showers, the pool, and the adjoining two classrooms, the only thing of interest is the heavenly light shining down from the gym ceiling, bringing back a rush of images I didn't need to remember. We head back out to the main hall and finally check the bathroom, which is also vacant. After I take care of my discharging needs, the rest of the group filters in one at a time, and I lift my radio.

"Anderson, we're back in the lobby, over."
"*Good... took care of some in the courtyard, we're in the science hallway by 218. What've you got? Over.*"
"Gym, nurse's office, main office, pool, locker rooms... just a couple more. Headed to the cafeteria next. Over and out."
"Anyone else tired already?" Melody asks, exiting the bathroom.
"Little bit."
"Absolutely..." Karen responds.
"We need a break, or are we good? We've got a lot to do..."
"Let's just get it done." Rich offers.

With no complaints, we make our way through the next swatch of the school, finding nothing from the cafeteria to the history halls with brief stops in the new wing and two of the stairwells. The technology hallway, containing a graphic arts lab, computer lab, metal shop, wood shop, and media lab, comes last. Each room is unsurprisingly empty. As we exit the media lab and head back toward the stairwell that connects to the breezeway, I again take up my walkie-talkie.

"Anderson, we're done, where are you?"

"...headed to the breezeway and we're done. What'd you see? Over."

"From the looks of it, we're all set. We should just seal off the new wing. The main entrances each have two sets of doors, so we just have to plug up that little airlock... uh... we'll have to check both sides of the school to see if the cars sealed up the side doors. The library, main office, and the pool are gonna be a bitch, but the back of the school is pretty closed off. We should seal off the courtyard from the outside so we can use it. What about you, over?"

"Well, no one's gettin' in the second floor. Basement is fine, we can't repair the windows, but we can seal up the classroom doors... we should close the gap between the gym and the cafeteria. We can park a few cars in the courtyard loading dock and slash the tires, maybe hang one of the auditorium curtains over the pool windows. Other than that, we should be pretty solid. Over."

"Check the greenhouse? Over?"

"Figured we'd all do that together. Over."

"Copy, headed up there now, over and out."

We take to the breezeway stairwell and link up with the rest of the group before venturing to the greenhouse. I notice as we get closer that the floor is littered with little chunks of broken glass and wood, and, like the hallway leading to the office, the tiling is covered with mud.

"You don't think there are any still in here?" Melody asks.

"We would've heard 'em by now." Anderson responds.

"Agreed." I offer. "But when we start renovating, no one ever does anything alone. We'll make a sweep every day when we enter the building and another just before we leave."

"Good plan short man."

"We're the same height."

Anderson chuckles ineffectually as we head up to the greenhouse. I poke my head in the doorway and immediately notice that the glass door to the greenhouse hasn't been shattered or even torn off the hinges. I wonder for a moment if I can even remember the sound of glass breaking as they ran through. The smell of decayed flesh that permeates the rest of the school is even stronger up here, and just as I'm about to vocally chalk it up to the number of undead that passed through, I notice that Steve is still attached to the table.

As I fully open the door he springs to life, attempting to thrash through the yards of gray tape binding his limbs. Anderson comes in behind me, followed by Melody. "Jesus, he's still up here?" She asks rhetorically. Anderson turns his head halfway toward her. "Where was he gonna go?" As he responds, Melody scoffs. Thoughts flood into my head as I look at Steve, and before I can think to control them, they pour out of my mouth. "Maybe Steve gave us away." As I finish speaking, I ask myself if I said that out loud. Melody instantly confirms that I have.

"Gave us away... how?"

"Eh..."

"Are you saying they're... telepathic, or something?" Jake asks.

"Eh..."

"That guy on TV said they can't..."

I slam my eyes shut in shame as I think about what I said for a moment, and then try to validate my ill-formed assertion.

"Well, what says he doesn't give off some... I don't know, beacon?"

"Yeah, but... *really?*" Rob asks, coming inside.

"They say we only use a certain percentage of our brain, so...?"

"You think they turn psychic when they come back?" Jake asks.

"Well... how would you know?"

"Maybe they release pheromones..."

"...to tell you the truth, it just slipped out. I didn't mean to say it."

"Alright, but... if he can tell the others where he is, isn't he leading them here now?" Melody asks.

There's a moment of silence before we simultaneously run at Steve. Anderson pulls out his Beretta and presses it against the whitish-gray skin of his skull, pinning him to the table. As he's about to pull the trigger, I reach across and push the safety on. "Don't." I say softly. "Why not?" He asks, clicking the safety off again. "This might sound stupid..." I start, putting the safety back on. "...but we know how long since he's eaten, so we can find out how long it takes them to starve to death. He can still help us." Jake snickers and looks at me. "So what is he now, Hugh the Borg?"

A big smile escapes from my face, since I had just assumed that Star Trek was lost on most people in my generation. "Not really, but good reference." I look up and notice we've formed a circle around Steve. Melody pokes her head between Anderson and I to speak. "We can't keep him inside." Anderson acquiesces, reluctantly holstering his pistol as I lead the group out to the greenhouse balcony.

If he really does have a direct, coherent telepathic link, there's not much we can do besides shoot him, and if the undead use this ability to trap humans, he'll share that we keep coming back to this spot. However, if it's more of an animal instinct, we can leave him out there and he'll either keep us safe, or he'll draw in new ones that will find the area uninhabited and wander off. I realize how idiotic this thought train is, but remind myself that the dead have returned to life and are attacking the living. Trapped in a world where the ridiculous has become the new order, I can't find any fault with tangential thinking.

"Toss him." I say firmly. Anderson doesn't hesitate before bringing Jake and Rich inside, using the knives on their Leatherman tools to cut the gray tape, seal him so that he's immobile, and bring him outside. Once we mount the greenhouse fence, Anderson drags him to the edge by nestling a crowbar in his armpit. "Put his feet over first."

Anderson says. Rich, Jake and I support his shoulders and his head as we push him off. Still moaning, his body strikes the grass with a wet crunch as his fractured tibia and fibula split through the meaty skin of his right leg. I can't tell if he's moaning any harder since the sock is still jammed in his mouth, but once he settles from the fall he starts to kick around.

Looking up and beyond the parking lot, I observe the back of the school, including both football fields and both tennis courts. The same number of cars are still present, and, shockingly, so are the undead. I look around the corners of the field and realize that there's no way for them to leave aside from the gate in the cemetery. High fences and bushes stretch from the driveways along the side of the school and connect in the back behind the football field, none of which could be easily traversed by the undead, meaning that we'll need to defend just one side of the school. I glance over at the gym and take notice of the pool building only moments before Rich derails my thought train.

"So, stage curtains to cover the windows…"

"As long as we don't go inside… I mean, I'd like to go for a swim as much as the next guy, but we can't risk making that much noise…" I say.

"We can empty the pool to keep the corpses…" Rob says. "Cover the smell with chlorine…"

"If a rescue party comes through we can drag them outside and burn them to attract attention. The difficult thing is locking it down."

"Why?" Melody asks.

"If we use the bathrooms, it might draw them in."

"But the girl's showers are inside and don't have any windows."

"I hadn't considered that…"

"So, the main doors…" Anderson starts. "First priority."

"We get the keys, plug the airlocks… pack them with desks and black out the windows… I'm more concerned with the office."

"All the same, we'll have to shut down the athletic structure… and we'll have to do it so we can still get to the showers and the pool." Rich offers.

"What about the classrooms?"

"We'll have to block off hallways too."

"How?" Anderson asks.

"Well," Jake jumps in. "A lot of them have retractable gates. I don't think even a hundred of them could get through... if they clog up the hallway, we can pick 'em off..."

"I didn't know that. Good. We can plug up the cafeteria-gym opening with cars or dumpsters or something."

As Anderson finishes, I notice that Jake has the hammer he picked up earlier stuffed in his pants.

"We stock the fridges, get some DVDs, books, computers, a garden... this is gonna be awesome." Rob says with a smile.

"Let's not get ahead of ourselves." I add. "First off, we need to take care of the basement... and we need a way in and out that's Zombie proof."

"How about a rope ladder in the staircase next to the auditorium?" Anderson adds.

"We've talked about it enough." Karen says flatly. "We should start doin' somethin'."

"All right, where do we start?" Melody asks.

"Block the exits." Anderson and I say in unison.

"Thirded." Rich adds. "Basement first and work our way up?"

"Alright? Alright, let's get to work."

Like many of the upstairs hallways, the basement floors are covered with mud, chunks of broken glass, and bits of splintered wood. As I walk through the clutter, I'm reminded again that the basement was essentially a dungeon used to house the juvenile delinquents. Rumors persisted that they needed teacher escorts to travel anywhere, even if they were just going for water. As Anderson suggested, the damage to the windows is irreparable; we wouldn't want to repair them even if we could, and boarding them would be an enormous waste of time. "Alright..." I start. "First thing's first, sweep up the glass... no reason to risk anyone getting cut... second, we move everything out of the classrooms we might need..."

"...still got some live ones..." Anderson interrupts. He opens the door and stalks toward the far left corner where he destroys a long-haired young man. I grab the door frame and jump as Rich slaps his hand on my shoulder. Before I can ask him why he did that, I follow his extended arm toward the shattered window frames; there's a Zombie in a band uniform pulling himself across piles of broken glass, unable to stand as he's more or less detached from his legs.

I expect at this point Rich recognizes our band uniforms and is afraid that we're going to find the corpse of someone we know, but since everyone had the chance to change out of their uniforms, I'm not particularly concerned. I climb up on the heating unit and brush the glass fragments out of the way as I step over the divided torso of our next victim. He continues to pull himself along, raking sharp slices of glass along the concrete with his fingernail-free hands. "Oh god..." Rich says, hooking his crowbar under its left arm to turn him over. It's Matt Hughes. "You've got to be kidding me..." I mutter as Rich pushes the crowbar into his chest to keep him pinned down. Thankfully the guts and chunks of flesh clinging to his exposed hipbone and ribcage don't smell too bad after a few days of drying.

"What is it?" Anderson asks.

"He was with us the first night..." I respond.

"...what?"

"He left... didn't tell anyone."

"Alright, so what?"

"He *left*... we didn't see him again... but he knew we were in here."

"Shit..."

"Poor bastard was probably trying to get back in..." Rich mumbles.

"Wow... so, kill him now?"

"Yeah."

Rich turns as Anderson savages his skull, putting him to rest. Rich, still wincing and unable to turn, speaks with his back to us. "So, are we agreed that no one else needs to know that happened?" Anderson and I turn to each other and nod, and despite not seeing us, Rich seems to get the message. "Okay... Rich... take Rob and Karen, go pick up some supplies at the woodshop. The rest of us are gonna sweep and clear the rooms." Nodding again, Rich hops down off the heating unit and gathers his group.

For the most part each room is filled with miscellaneous junk and boxes filled with papers, but Anderson insists we move everything out, even if we just end up using it to reinforce some other part of the building. In a half hour, the other group returns from their woodshop excursion and helps us remove the last remaining bits from the classrooms. Without further discussion, Anderson and I go inside the rooms to nail the doors into the frames from the inside, removing the handles as well while Rich and the rest of the group go about reinforcing them from the inside. Once they've been nailed in, we caulk all of the holes and hinges extensively, leaving the wire-embedded windows in each door exposed so we can still see inside if need be.

He and I exit via the giant gaping window holes, reenter through the auditorium doors where Melody is waiting, and go back down into the basement. I'm thinking about Julia the whole way. When we return, we discover that the door nooks have been jammed with two desks apiece and the doors have been nailed from the outside. Beneath and on top of the desks are boxes of paper, the density of which will hopefully help the structural integrity of the doors, but we nevertheless reinforce the doorways with more desks stretching to the parallel walls. Because of this, the width of the hall is totally obstructed. There is a door that leads into the basement from the front of the building, but it has been locked for ages and trips an alarm if opened. The only other way in now is the small entrance we came through the first night we spent in the high school.

We track our way outdoors via our entrance the first night and Anderson notes that the metal steps descending to the basement door give us a lethal forty foot drop. The area across the bottom is only twenty feet and the stairway itself is narrow, so we can block the top of the staircase with a dumpster so it can't be seen from the ground level. If it can't be seen or guessed as a method of getting inside, it could make an excellent emergency exit.

We go back through the noisy generator room and head back up to the ground level, exiting via the doors to the main lobby. Once outside, we examine the area where the undead had gotten in the night of their siege, standing on the grating by which I exited the school moments after John Squared was torn asunder. We jump off the far end onto a short set of concrete steps that leads down to a landing where an open chain-link fence gate is all that stood between the undead and the basement windows. Anderson pulls the gate shut and fixes it closed with a rock climbing karabiner, making a crack about something this simple confounding the undead, but my concern lies with any poor bastard who makes it to the basement with the intention of getting in. Like Matt.

The final door to the basement is adjacent to the gate. As expected, it's locked; this door leads directly into the obstructed hallway. I express my concern that we should better block the door from either the outside or the inside, and Anderson finally feels the time is right to call it a day. He gets no complaints, so we rally at the front entrance, board the bus, and head back to the community center.

I take my seat near the back of the bus and watch as my weary comrades board, taking particular note of Anderson's strained, flagrant stretching. Unsubtly, he leans over Karen's seat just enough to get her attention, then turns to face front, putting his hand on the seat back as he stares out the front windows. Rich boards last, and as he makes some adjustment to his seat, he looks up at Anderson, starts to stand, and kneels back to the base of his seat, but not without looking directly at me.

I debate whether I should just go up and let them know how awfully their plan of being discreet is unfolding. I don't know what they're talking about, but I know it has to do with me, and they're trying to make some sort of group decision, so I can only assume from there that it has to do with Julia. I catch myself trying to look out the window in an effort to disappear from the equation, knowing, of course, that it won't work.

The bus starts... and Anderson takes a seat. Now it looks like they're having some casual conversation. Maybe my mind is playing tricks on me. A quick glance around the bus on the way back reveals

Jake sleeping, Rob staring vacantly at the back of his seat, and Melody occasionally glancing over at me. A hundred feet or so before we turn into the community center, I turn my attention forward and see Karen approaching me.

"How are you doin'?"

"I don't mean to be rude... but that's kind of a stupid question..."

"I know... nursin' habit. At least I didn't ask how 'we' were feelin'."

"I'm grateful for that. So what about me were you saying up there?"

"Ah, uh... well, there's no point in bullshittin'... it's Julia."

For the first time since it happened, I get a flash of her putting on that blindfold. The last time I saw her. I shut my eyes, fully aware that Karen is standing in front of me, and watch the bandana go on over and over and over again. We should have closed our eyes *before* we put on the bandanas. I shouldn't have kissed her on the forehead after we kissed on the bus. I shouldn't have let it happen to her.

"You want to know what we're gonna do with the body."

"Yeah."

"Cremate it."

"Yeah... this place used to be a school, right?"

"Yeah."

"It probably has a kiln... we just... don't know what to..."

"Just take her clothes off and do it..."

"I know... but... we don't know what... it's gonna, uh..."

"...smell?"

"Yes... you think it'll...?"

"I don't know. I don't know... I don't know. Can we just..."

"You know, don't worry about it... we can deal with it."

When they burn her body, it's going to smell. How awful. They're going to undress her limp, lifeless corpse and try to manipulate her limbs so she fits inside a tiny dark closet that will cook her until she's reduced to ash. By the time we make it back to the community center

Karen has returned to her seat and I'm crying uncontrollably. I bury my head between my knees and no one bothers me, even after the bus has emptied out. I've been to a few funerals, so the pageantry of death in society is not lost on me. Bodies are treated with care, embalmed, made up, the funeral procession is allowed to pass through red lights before the body is finally put to rest. In between, doctors and morticians work with the body. They're the ones who know what death is really like. I'd never thought of it before, but a corpse is truly devoid of anything. Especially dignity. Julia's body, flaccid and frail, unconcerned with her naked form being exposed to Karen and Rich, is an image I never wanted.

I disembark to find Anderson waiting by the door with a pile of cigarettes at his feet. He lets me in without a word and doesn't follow. I make it halfway across the gym before stopping and turning back, and by the time I make it to the door, he's already started another cigarette.

"What's up?"
"I don't feel like talking to anybody."
"...okay...?"
"I just wanted you to know... I'm going to the roof for awhile. I'll come back down eventually."
"Okay."

It's tough to avoid attracting anyone's attention in this place, but I somehow manage to grab food from the kitchen, make it to the stairwell, and finally arrive on the roof without anyone noticing. Once there, I ravenously eat some canned fruit and vegetables, then dig into my backpack and start on a cigar. I try to lie down to smoke it, but I realize that's not going to work, so I finish it off so I can lie down and look at the stars, which seem brighter and more numerous than usual.

Feeling like I need to cry again, I start going through images of Julia in my mind. Prom. The first kiss. The poem. Inane conversations. Loving her. Hating her. Disappointing her. Watching her sit silently and wondering if she was thinking about cheating on me. Trying to detect the small moments preceding a fight so I could avoid it.

Feeling so irritated by her that I'm unable to speak. Trying and failing to mask my thoughts about her. Watching her try and fail to mask her thoughts about me. I spend an hour thinking these things through. What a waste of time, and now that she's gone, I have no choice but to internalize the blame for every argument, every silence, every curse, and every tear shed. One more way, I suppose, that her suffering is over.

Is my endless desire to make people happy a hollow charade I've constructed to avoid confronting my own misery? I've always been capable of experiencing happiness vicariously through other people, and I've spent so much time being miserable about menial things that other people are my best chance for happiness. Should I feel guilty that, after a year and a half of mostly petting, our relationship took a violent step forward? Did she do it because it felt like the right thing to do, or was she just doing it for me? If she were still alive, I would have kept this thought from her.

I feel guilty remembering the sensation of her warm, radiating skin brushing against mine, the orchestration of her heavy, nervous breaths, and the casual contact of our sex organs that had never found proper use. I feel aroused remembering the humid grasp of her mouth, the view of her soft curves and perfectly contoured body, and her glassy eyes washing over with contented sexual bliss. I am forever denied her certainty in sexual advances, just as I am forever denied the reshaping of her body with age.

Once again, the crying has stopped, and my body hurts. I remember when I used to enjoy crying as a quick cathartic release that would allow me to sleep or otherwise get along with my day. Now, it's like watching a movie that doesn't end, and I'm chained to the chair. I enjoyed the first and second act, but they keep pushing out one cathartic moment after another, and I feel cheated by it. I want to go inside and have a normal conversation, but even if one gets going, I'm going to feel like the other person is just agreeing with me or humoring my bullshit theories for fear that any sign of disapproval will result in me breaking down. Then they'll feel guilty. Is acquiescence in conversation with someone who's having a bad time just fear of experiencing guilt, or is it because they genuinely don't want me to be depressed?

I smell terrible. Thank god I never picked up smoking as a legitimate habit because I can smell the cigar fumes steaming off my lips and feel the greasy smoke lodged in my scalp which now smells like an ash tray, or somewhere between charcoal and burning hair. I run my fingers through my hair and smell my knuckles; no, my hair is a bit dirty and carries the scent of the cigar, but nowhere near what I'm smelling. Did I set something on fire?

I stand quickly and look down to where I flicked my cigar over the roof, finding Anderson standing outside the door parallel to the road that leads to the high school; he's easy to spot due to his haircut and the tiny white skeletons of spent cigarettes next to him in a pile, but even from up here I can smell the menthol. Maybe it's going away. I walk back toward where I was and it returns with a vengeance; the stench is so powerful that I reactively step away, pinch my eyes shut, and wave at the air.

It's like leather, pork, and steak being dropped on a fireplace heated by charcoal with a hint of stale perfume. It's Julia. Somehow excited, my eyes dart across the roof until I can find the source of the smell, and that's when I see a vent pouring husky black smoke into the cool night air. Blistering flesh, red-hot strands of hair curling into nothingness, tendons snapping in the heat, and a perspiring eyeball boiling. I gag so fast I don't have a chance to breathe in, and I'm stuck almost choking on my own vomit. The second heave comes after I manage to catch my breath, spilling the contents of my stomach on the roof. I grab my backpack and run as far away from the vent as I can.

When I can finally take a seat, I wash my mouth out with a bottle of water before drinking it all, lamenting the food I wasted at dinner. Despite having finished crying no more than half an hour ago, I'm back at it again. For some reason, I remember when I told her I motherfuckin' loved her. The smell drifts my way, and something from my throat makes my cheeks puff out before one last dry heave causes me to pass out.

I wake up while it's still dark and manage to peel myself off the roof long enough to make it down the steps. Everyone else is asleep, so I again slide myself back into my sheets and try to concentrate on something that won't make me put a gun to my head again.

10-17-04, SUNDAY

When I wake up it still seems dark outside, but I turn to the windows to see the shades pulled down. My eyes are quickly drawn to the only source of light generated from Anderson peeking around a shade. "Jesus, Anderson, when do you sleep?" He glances over at me. "You're the only one still asleep." I sit up quickly and look around to find us alone. "What time is it?" He scoffs and looks at his wrist. "1:50." In the midst of standing and clearing the crust out of the corner of my eye I look down at the .45 lodged in my police belt. "What?" Anderson asks, having noticed me standing feebly in the middle of the room with a fixed expression.

I kneel down and pull the pistol out, loosening the magazine; I haven't bothered to reload it since the hospital. I space out until Anderson repeats the question.

"Nothing... it's nothing."
"Uh..."
"I don't know... I just feel weird with guns now."

I wonder if he can tell that I was about a half second from killing myself just by looking at me with the gun. I don't even think I can look at the bullets again without getting queasy. I switch out the magazine and put the .45 back in the holster, stopping myself from chambering a round. After that I piss, take my pills, eat some breakfast, and get dressed. Once dressed, Anderson radios the others to let them know I 'm awake. In a few seconds, a response comes.

"Jeff, someone called for you on my cell phone..." It's Melody.
"What!? Who, when!?"
"Alan, like an hour ago..?"
"Get up here now."

I shouldn't have said that like such an asshole, but fortunately, for now, I'm impervious to backlash. Only a few minutes pass before she's back in the room to hand me her cell phone.

"So, he called, and you answered?"

"He left a voicemail... he sounded kinda nervous, like he wasn't sure it was the right number or something..."

"Has anyone else called you?"

"Yeah, I guess..."

"Who?"

"My mom, and a few numbers I didn't recognize..."

"What were the... is your mom okay?"

"I couldn't get a hold of her, but she said she was going to my aunt's in New Jersey."

"Did anyone else leave a message?"

"No, but my friends don't leave messages, 'cause they know I don't listen."

"Well... did Alan leave a number?"

She hands me a scrap of paper from a small notebook and I dial the number immediately. The phone only rings twice.

"Hello?"

"Alan, it's Jeff."

"Hey... are you alright"

"First off, how did you get this number?"

"Your mom called my mom, my mom called me..."

Our mothers have known each other as long as I have known him, about a decade and a half.

"Heard from my brother?"

"No."

"Have you tried calling him? Have you gone to his apartment?"

"Tried calling a few days ago, haven't gone to the apartment."

"You with Jack?"

"Of course."

"Anyone else with you?"

"Heather and Nancy, two girls from down the hall. Also Nick and his roommate Dan."

"The Nick I know?"

LIFE AFTER: THE ARISING | 339

"No, the other one."

"Alright, finally, how is everyone?"

"We're alright."

"Have you seen a lot of them?"

"A lot of..."

"The undead."

"Only a couple."

"How many people are still up there?"

"Not many..."

"And which floor are you guys on?"

"The fourth."

"Alright. If you haven't done it already, police up the building for people and supplies, then hold up on the upper levels. Go shopping if you can... anything canned and imperishable, and lots of water. Drain your accounts if you have to. Once that's done... Penn State doesn't have a gun shop, does it?"

"Don't think so."

"Well there must at least be a hardware store or something... pick yourself up some crowbars for hand-to-hand weapons. I don't know... get everyone together and make a list of stuff you'll need. Once you get back and get settled block off the stairs and entrances."

"Gotcha."

"And one final request... if you can..."

"Yeah?"

"Stop by Dave's apartment... and see if you can find him?"

"No guarantees... but we'll try."

"I appreciate it. Last thing... if someone gets scratched or bitten or anything... you have to kill them. You have a few hours depending on the severity of the injury, but there's no escaping it. A gun just makes it easier."

"Yeah, I've seen the movies... so, uh, are you guys all right?"

"Terrible."

"What? Why?"

"It's... Jules..."

"Oh Jesus... what..."

"Not now..." I choke, holding back. "Just... get your shopping done as soon as you can. If you have any problems, call me here."

"Who's there with you?"

"Anderson, and a bunch of people you don't know."

"Where are you?"

"The community center… and we're trying to reinforce the high school."

"Yo, uh… Jack wants to talk to you."

"Alright, put him on."

"Yo yo G, what's up?"

"Not much…"

"Kill anybody yet?"

"Plenty. Unfortunately, I'm not in a joking mood. Are you armed?"

"Yeah, I've got my knife, and those steel playing cards."

"I'd stick with the knife."

"Can do."

"Get guns too, I don't know how much money you guys have or if they have any gun shops up there, but stock up. Lever action rifles and pistols, okay? If there aren't any gun shops in town, and you remember how to get to the old cabin, you might consider going to the general store. Just stick with the group you're in, don't leave them unless you have to. You and Alan take care of yourselves. Contact me at this number only if it's urgent. Otherwise, we'll call you."

"Uh, yeah, dude, is uh, Drew with you?"

"No. I haven't seen him or heard from him… you?"

"No… I mean, I talked to him awhile ago… he said he was trying to find a bomb shelter…"

"I saw… did he?"

"Dunno."

"You heard from Nick or Kaito?"

"Nah."

"Well, all right. Look, Jack… I'll talk to you later."

"All right, later dude."

I toss the phone back to Melody. "Got your charger?" I ask. She pulls it out of her bag, plugs it into the wall, and plugs in her phone.

"All right, we all ready to get going?" I ask.

"Yep…" Anderson says, popping off his perch and heading straight for the door.

"Wait, should I bring the phone?"

"Don't bother."

"What if someone else tries to call?"

"We'll take care of it later... just turn the ringer off."

Anderson comes back in the room with Karen just behind him. She's holding a tall jar full of gray ash that she doesn't hesitate to hand off. It's heavier than I expected at about five pounds, and the jar has the words *Quattro Stagioni* raised in the glass. "Do we know what this means?" I ask. No answers. I manage to nod at Karen and she seems to appreciate the gesture. I place the jar next to my pillow, ignoring the images that instantly enter my head. After a quick and somewhat noisy stretch of putting on coats and backpacks and grabbing weapons, we head out to the bus and make our way back to the school, making the decision to bottle up the courtyard while on the way.

We go through the front doors and through the first available stairway, and once outside an undead individual in formalwear greets us. Anderson is about to shoot it, but I push his rifle down. "Let's give Rob a shot." As Rob lifts his rifle, Anderson starts giving him instruction. "Hold the butt tight to your shoulder. Aim for something small, like an eye socket. Hold your breath while you aim, and when you have a shot, exhale slowly, and squeeze the trigger... don't jerk it." Following these rules, Rob squeezes the trigger, sending a high powered round through the bridge of his nose and gray porridge out the back of his head.

Anderson and I congratulate Rob with a pat on the back and begin dragging the corpse by the legs out past the band room door toward the cars jammed into each other near the parking lot's exit. I stop to admire the wealth of cars as Anderson pulls the body through the maze of bumpers toward the grass. I take a moment to look up at the trees and the sky as I take notice of the birds still chirping. Anderson smacks his hands together a few times and freezes as he looks into one of the car windows.

"What is it?" I ask.

"Most of these still have the keys in the ignition."

"Really…"

"Are you thinking what I'm thinking?"

"Probably?"

"We block the courtyard with cars ass end out. Use SUVs, it'll be tough for them to get over. And we can move them if we have to."

"What about the ground clearance? Can't they climb under?" Rich asks.

"I don't know."

"Just park smaller cars in front." Melody says.

"Yeah, but what if they use them as a stepping stone?"

"We'll worry about that later." I say.

Rob, Rich, Melody, Karen and I start looking for cars while Anderson and Jake cover us. The first car I find with keys, gas, and a working battery is a massive black SUV. I start it up and press the sucker into reverse, barreling into the car behind me. I pop the car into four wheel drive and navigate it over the trunk of the sedan in front of me. I scream with laughter as I drive over the cars that are next to the new wing, pull into the narrow 'loading dock' area, and climb out the sun roof.

Melody pulls in next to me in a truck as well, Rob pulls up next to her in another SUV, and Karen and Rich pull cars beneath the metal roof segment I once used to climb up on the roof. Fortunately, neither of them requires instruction on getting their vehicles flush against the support beams. "Everybody hang onto the keys?" They all dangle them from their fingers. "Toss them on the roof, we'll get 'em later." They abide. "And while we're out here, let's get some more driving done." Jake gets into a car with me and Anderson gets into a car with Melody. Karen, Rich, and Rob go together. I take a crappy sedan from the tail end of the car line and back it into the rear lot. Rich and Melody pull up on either side of me and roll down their windows.

"What are we doing?" Melody asks.

"Blocking the exits. You and Rich drive your cars into the gap between the gym and cafeteria, then I'll take you to get more cars."

"Jeff, there's still some buses, just use them to block the cafeteria."

"Yeah, sure, start one up... block the back door to the new wing as well. Take someone with you."

"Radios on, everyone." Anderson says.

Jake, Karen, and Rob get in the car I've taken, Anderson gets in the trunk to cover, and Melody and Rich get in a car together and drive down to the buses. I drive my group to the entrance at the rear lot to find that it is also thoroughly plugged with cars. "Guys, try to find some working cars and drive to the main rear entrance. Anderson and I will cover." Anderson and I hop out of the car and walk toward a few of the scattered undead as our compatriots spread out. I look off to my left to see Rich backing a bus out of the space between the gym and the cafeteria in a diagonal, scraping the building as he straightens out.

Anderson beats down two of them as a few more in the distance let out some stomach churning moans. For a moment, I consider taking them out with my rifle, but Anderson preempts me and runs toward them with his crowbar pulled back behind his head. Between the two of us we take out another eight before I see three cars driving to the rear entrance. I decapitate another two while I watch another school bus drive toward the rear exit. A few moments after it disappears, my radio begins to crackle.

"Jeff, this is Rich. The bus barely fits in the opening, over."

"What do you mean barely?"

"...I mean I'm scraping the sides, over."

"Perfect. Pull it up as far as you can go."

"Jesus, Grey... say over when you're done talking." Anderson grunts as he lays into one of the undead.

"Sorry... anyway, Rich, let's tighten up the entrance and exit from the back. Any suggestions? Over."

"There's still about six buses left... we park those against the back of the cars. Nose to nose, they cover a lot of space. Over."

"Yeah, but there's still all that space..." Melody cuts in. *"Can't they crawl underneath? Oh, over."*

"Anderson, any ideas?"

"I'm busy." He says calmly as a downward swipe causes a mushy burst of pulp shoot past his shoulder.

"Okay, uh… slash the tires? Over?"

"*…that might do it. I don't need to remind you that we'd have no way of fixing that. Over.*"

"Obviously, but with all those cars blocking our path to the main road, what else are we gonna use the buses for? Over."

"*Excellent point. Over.*"

I turn to see Anderson finish off another one of the undead before turning back to me with his walkie-talkie in hand and a cigarette dangling from his mouth.

"After that, we seal off the opening to the cemetery. And we need to take care of the path down to the baseball field. Over."

"Shit, I totally forgot about that…" Anderson mutters.

"*How big is the opening? Over.*" Rich asks.

"Well, about as big as one of the buses, over."

"*Perfect, over.*"

"Knock one down," Anderson replies, stomping out his cigarette. "No room for error there. Over."

"Agreed. Karen, go with Rich to speed this up. Anderson and I will continue to cover. Over and out."

I attach the walkie-talkie to my belt and walk over to Anderson as he lights up another cigarette. As I get close, I notice several walkers heading toward us from across the parking lot. "Don't worry," He starts, preempting my question. "We're on break." He pats the trunk of a car and sits down, suggesting that I do the same. I join him as he motions a pack of cigarettes to me. I hold my hand out and shake my head. "Don't you get tired using that thing?" He asks, referring to my katana.

"Not really… if you know what you're doing, it isn't very taxing… bitch to clean, though."

"How do you sharpen it?"

"Same thing as cleaning it, more or less."

He nods. The length of the silence makes the implications of his next question obvious.

"So?"
"Yeah, I know."
"Well, talk."

I sigh.

"I don't know if I'll be the same again."
"Aren't you the one always telling me we never stop changing?"
"Yeah, yeah... there's something about you that never changes... that's how you stay you. What I mean is... well, you know."
"Yeah. I don't just mean Julia."
"Right. Sorry. You're right, I just..."
"I know, dude. You miss everything... even the fights. You'd give anything to be in a fight."
"Yeah. She saw right through me."

Anderson immediately chortles and I can't help but smile.

"Seriously... I always had her when I faced adversity."
"Grey, I'm gonna let you in on a little secret."
"Sure."
"You haven't faced any adversity."

I also chortle as he smiles back.

"Not until now, anyway. I mean... I don't need to remind you I got kicked out of my house after high school..."
"Or that your mom died while you were in second grade and your dad shacked up with his psycho mistress. Or that your brother was an addict. Or that your other brother is retarded. Or that, until recently, you faced a very real threat of being sent to Iraq..."

"Right."

"My college was paid for, my parents stayed together, and I'll be able to live with them when I... or, would have graduated if it wasn't for this."

"We're all in the same shit spot now."

I look at him as he stares off at the distant phone towers in Manayunk, then turn back to see one of the school buses driving toward the back entrance.

"I don't need to tell you that what I'm about to say isn't a good thing... but now you're down to my level."

"Or up."

"No... down. It's definitely down. Point is... you've been there for me. I was forced to deal with my own shit... I had no way around it. You didn't have to make it your problem. Now I get the chance to return the favor."

There is a reasonable silence as he takes a long draw from his cigarette and exhales. After a moment, I nod softly and take in a breath to speak.

"You know... I'm not really scared anymore. But I know it's not gonna stay this way."

"What do you mean?"

"Someone else is gonna die. I mean... it has to happen. Try as we might to stop it."

"You'll drive yourself nuts thinking like that."

"I know. But it's true. You watch horror movies and read novels, and you can always tell yourself that you'd have done something different... hidden somewhere else, chosen better weapons, planned a better escape route... I don't know if there's a perfect way to do this."

"You know what? Fuck that. People who think that way are full of shit. We review our actions after training exercises in the Guard and they tell us what we did wrong... but they know they can say it because they had time to analyze it. Time we didn't have. No one makes a... Zombie survival plan that'd work in practice. Even if you prepared, imagine you're at a mall, or a football game..."

"Or a marching band competition..."

"Right... all that shit you have at home isn't gonna do you any good there. You have to think on your feet. A good plan today is better than a perfect plan tomorrow."

"That yours?"

"George Patton."

"Nice."

Finding that line of conversation totally sewn up, I watch Anderson approach the end of his cigarette, holding my question for the moment he tosses the butt.

"Wanna kill some Zombies?"

"Boy howdy."

I leap off the back of the car, finding that the Zombies who were previously halfway across the lot have gained more ground than I expected. Anderson and I approach the scattered masses and tear into them with reckless abandon while the school buses continue to transit around the back lot. The most important part of our slaughter revolves around making sure Anderson is outside my engagement range since being off by even an inch could leave him bleeding to death. Occasionally Rich will radio to ask if we're okay, and occasionally we'll take a break to rest our arms and lungs, but we spend most of the next hour putting down walking corpses indiscriminately. I wonder whether this is therapeutic for me as it's the one activity during which I don't focus on Julia.

Rich pulls up next to us in the last bus and yanks the door open. "We'll need some help to knock her down." Anderson and I leap on board and Rich drives us along the back of the parking lot to the exit that leads to the lower football fields. Rich shimmies the bus as close to the entrance as he can get; there are fences to the left and right across the grass and a large gap in between for the road, but passage to the field by car has been limited due to some small metal pillars.

Rich gets out first to estimate how much space we'll need, then backs the bus up and lines it up parallel to the pillars. Once he's finished, he takes everything useful off of the bus and ushers everyone out.

"Rich, call it, how do we do this?" I ask.

"Okay, Jeff, you're gonna slash the tires. We're gonna stand on the other side, and once the tires are flat, we're gonna push it over."

"Sounds simple enough." Anderson says, shrugging.

"It's not going to fall over on me when I slash the tires, is it?"

"I don't think so."

I stare at him for a moment, but he doesn't respond.

"When you slashed the other tires, did they fall over?"

"We didn't slash them, we stabbed them."

"Wonderful. Well… let's just get it over with."

Everyone gathers on the other side of the bus when I yank out my katana. I line up my intended slice, then quickly execute it and spin out of the wake of the fall. The tire tears surprisingly easily, but the bus just dips down about a foot. Fairly certain it won't tip on its own, I run to the other end and slash those tires, causing the back half of the bus to drop down as well. Seeing, again, that it won't tip on its own, I join my compatriots on the other side.

"What kinda push are we gonna need here?" Karen asks.

"Hard as you can…" Anderson says, backing up.

"Put your hands high to raise the center of gravity…" Rich says. "One, two, three…"

Anderson drops his shoulder and rams the side of the bus while the rest of us push. It immediately starts to give, so we all back off and cover our ears as it explodes into the ground. "Wow." Jake says. Rich runs around to the other side and pokes his head around after a few seconds. "Let's see if we can't get it snug. Everyone, put your shoulders into it." We oblige, but it doesn't move an inch. "Well fuck," Anderson spits immediately. "Doesn't do us much good if there's space for them to get through." Rob pats his shoulder and points toward the exit from the back parking lot.

"What... oh, we just drive another car into it."

"That'd work if we hadn't just plugged up all the entrances with buses and cut the tires." Jake says immediately.

"Well... shit."

"Relax," Rob says, shakily reaching in his pocket. "My car is still parked back here."

Anderson and Rob disappear and a car returns a few minutes later. "Done." Anderson says as he exits the car. "What next?" Rich asks. "Inside." I say. The group walks up a slight incline toward the back doors, finding them already been blockaded with cars. While I'm thinking, Melody points to Steve as he uselessly thrashes against his bindings. Rich uses the medical kit from the bus we just destroyed to fashion him a blindfold.

"Uh... I guess the new wing entrances... dammit, we plugged those too." I rub my forehead in aggravation. "You didn't slash the tires on the one blocking the path between the gym and cafeteria, did you?" Rich shakes his head as we breathe a sigh of relief. After crawling under the bus and going through the basement, we head to the back entrance to start locking doors.

"Okay, Anderson, Melody, Jake and I are group one, Karen, Rich, and Rob are two. Rich, your group gets started on the front door, and we'll get started on this one. Radios on. Once you've finished with a set, go clockwise around the school."

"We don't have any keys..." Jake offers.

"The locking mechanisms are in the doors... but Grey and I are going hunting for a set of keys. Get to your entrances and get your hands on as many student desks as you can find." Anderson says.

"What about all the bodies," Karen asks. "They're rotten. You just want to throw them out back or somethin'?"

"Balls." I say instantly.

"Pool." Rob offers.

"Whatever." Anderson mutters, heading off to the main office.

"Works for me. Rich?"

"Move to close."

"Excellent. We'll get started on that while you guys get started on the front door. Let's keep firing to a minimum."

As the rest of the group runs off, I chase Anderson to the main office in search of a master key or a set for all the doors and gates. We find the set quickly and move on to the auditorium to find a curtain we can use to drag the corpses, and while we walk around on corpse detail, Jake goes into the pool control room and looks for the drain. When we finally get inside the pool is half-full and audibly draining. Once the shallow end has completely drained Anderson attaches the curtains to his waist via karabiners and drags the tarp into the pool the same way a bull would drag a plow.

Melody and I kick a few of the remaining corpses down as Anderson climbs the ladder and gets back out, telling Jake to stop draining the pool when there's about four feet of water left. While the pool continues draining Anderson takes one of the pool rods and pushes the corpses down the ramp into the deep end. Once that's finished, we vow to figure out how the chlorine system works and leave the pool. We next return to the back entrance to join the effort of collecting desks to fill the doorways with as many as we can fit. Once finished we fill the staircase that leads up to the greenhouse from the science hall, then lock the door that leads outside.

After surveying our work we head to the last major entrance, the one designed to allow public access to the gym, and block that as well, leaving only eight places to enter the school. Three entrances are attached to the auditorium; one to the front stage, one to the shop, and one to the dressing rooms. One door is at the foot of the steps to where the undead broke in, two of them are part of the library, another is alongside the entrance to the rear parking lot, and the last one is attached to a stairwell between the main entrance and the auditorium entrance. After some discussion, we decide that one door must be kept unlocked so we can get in and out without deciding which door it will be. Satisfied with the amount of work we've done for the day we go back to the community center, eat, and collapse into our beds by the time night has fallen.

"God, I'm *so* tired..." Melody states over someone in the group mumbling quietly.

"A lot of work, a shitty diet, mental fatigue..." Anderson offers. "In the guard they have us eating 4,000 calories a day to keep our energy up."

"Mental fatigue?"

"Yeah. We've had a lot of shit to think about..."

I'm not sure if he had something else to say, but we are both distracted by the source of the mumbling we'd both heard only seconds before: in what passes for a shabby religious relief, Rob is on his knees, lit dimly but dramatically by the moonlight from the windows as it strikes rectangular polygons across the floor. His hands are pressed together about an inch from his nose and his eyes are pinched shut as he continues murmuring to himself.

"...the sea gave up the dead which were in it, and death and hell delivered up the dead which were in them, and they were judged every man according to their works... and death and hell were cast into the lake of fire. This is the second death. And whosoever was not found written in the book of life was cast into the lake of fire..."

"Dude... are you *praying?*" Anderson asks.

"...reciting Revelations... then I was gonna pray."

Anderson audibly chuckles; as he does, my blood pressure rises due to my fear of confrontation, but the fear is instantly washed out by a wave of banality. Who cares if he's praying?

"Something funny?" Rob asks, challenge apparent in his voice.

"Yeah... you're not gonna get saved by a bed time story."

"But as for the cowardly, the faithless, the detestable, as for murderers, the sexually immoral, sorcerers, idolaters, and all liars, their portion will be in the lake that burns with fire and sulfur, which is the second death.' Revelations 21:8."

"'There's an invisible man in the sky who watches everything you do. And he has a list of 10 things he does not want you to do, otherwise you'll go to a place filled with fire and smoke and torture where you will live and suffer and burn and choke and scream and cry until the end of time. But he loves you, and he needs money!' George Carlin."

The thought that this is headed nowhere is overpowering, and it makes me just want to go to sleep.

"Any reason why you quote George Carlin?"

"Any reason why you quote a fairytale?"

"A fairytale that's a source of comfort, enlightenment, and morality for over a billion people?"

"And if everyone else in the world listened to the Backstreet Boys, would you?"

"Okay, anyone around here religious?"

"I'm Jewish, but I don't believe in God." Jake says.

"Christian." Melody responds.

"Atheist." Rich offers.

There is a long pause.

"Jeff, how about you?" Karen asks.

"It's too long to go into."

"We appear to have plenty of time."

Silence follows as everyone apparently waits for my response.

"Alright. I believe everything in the Universe is unified by subatomic matter that functions as an all-powerful, non-sentient being. I believe the soul is the only thing about a person that never changes. I believe that the term 'God' represents the perfection of humanity."

"Wait, what's that last part?" Jake asks.

"If you reach total enlightenment and gain total knowledge, you reach the balance of Superego and Id. At that point, the Ego disappears and you react on instinct. God, to me, is not some all-powerful deity saying who's right and who's wrong… it is a man or woman with ultimate knowledge."

"Not too many of them, huh?"

"I like to think of myself as a tolerant Atheist…" Rich offers. "And if I was forced to take up some kind of spiritual view, it'd probably be close to that."

"It's called Pantheism." Rob adds.

"Yeah…organized religion is for the birds… closes people's minds…"

"…not having religion makes life empty and takes away moral balance… Rich, I can tell you don't have any faith."

"When you've lived my life you can only afford to have faith in yourself. The lord doesn't provide, and when he closes a door he does not open a window. This is 48 years of experience."

"Seconded." Anderson adds forcefully.

"But you're alive… how many have died? Perhaps you were denied certain things in the past, but now you have your life. It's all part of God's plan."

"Sounds like a reappropriation of Samsāra." I add.

"Or it's all coincidence." Rich boasts.

"A we a… prope… what?" Melody asks.

"Samsāra. If our actions come from karma, Samsāra is the chain of cause and effect."

"It could be coincidence…" Rob starts. "But it could be part of an elaborate plan."

"I thought God gave us free will." Rich states.

"He did…"

"Well if everything is part of God's plan, then we never really make any choices, he makes them for us."

"The plan is a blueprint… everything is built, but it's up to us to decorate the rooms and live our lives in them."

"You know from experience?"

"No, I experience it through faith."

"Well, faith isn't something you *know*. It's a feeling. Besides, were you raised Catholic?"

"Yeah."

"Your parents were Catholic? There are thousands of religions out there, and you're gonna tell me you just *chose* the same one as your parents?"

"You were educated in public school, right?"

"Yeah..."

"Were your parents Atheists?"

"No. Episcopal."

"Then how did you end up like this?"

"Easy, I asked questions."

"And look where it got you."

"...I'd rather have free will as an indigent than get lied to about the salvation I'm supposed to get once I die... stupid Republican bullshit."

"Rich, name one group who does more for the homeless than the Catholic Church... second, I'm a Republican, and those things have *nothing* to do with each other."

"You know any non-Christian conservatives? Christians and Republicans go together like gin and tonic..."

"But not Democrats, right?"

"...all that political shit about evolution, global warming, gay marriage... where do you think the Republicans get it?"

"I also know plenty of Democrats, and they're all alike... they say everyone should be allowed to have their own opinion, but get pissed if anyone thinks differently... all talk and no action, and if they had their way and got rid of guns, where would we be now? Any party that can kill babies but can't agree to put down hardened criminals has a moral compass that could get them lost in a map store."

"We're not talking about abortion... all the same, you're barely old enough to vote."

"...what?"

"If you're gonna make political arguments, you gotta understand politics. You don't understand until you get older."

"I don't expect you to understand today's issues because you're too old to matter."

"How does being pro-life, pro-death penalty, pro-war, homophobic, xenophobic, misogynistic, and anti-gun control fall under the purview of *today's* issues?"

"I'm protecting my beliefs; I don't change them every time some group of pinko whiners says I oughta."

"Pinko! Pinko! You were, what, *four* when the Soviet Union fell? That's exactly my point, you're falling back on this archaic idea..."

"...what, I can't use a pejorative to refer to liberals? People still call the gays faggots, but they're not literally comparing them to a bundle of sticks..."

"Does that somehow make what you just said better?"

"...instead of going after the words I'm using, why don't you tell me how you justify Democrats killing babies?" Rob asks.

"I don't, but it's not my choice."

"What isn't?"

"Abortion. Being pro-choice means you support people's right to decide for themselves. And the choice between having them in a sterile environment with a licensed physician or in back alleys with coat hangers is no choice at all."

"But how do you justify ending a human life?"

"How do you justify it?"

"I don't."

"Well, you apparently support the death penalty... besides, you eat meat, right?"

"Yeah..." Rob mutters.

"How do you justify killing cattle?"

"We need meat to live, and we're higher on the food chain."

"But you have options... you could go vegetarian or vegan."

"I don't want to though."

"What if someone said you had to change your diet for the health and well being of cows across the country?"

"They're *cows*! They're bred for slaughter."

"So? Don't you think life is sacred? Besides, you're a man, you can't give birth."

"It takes two people."

"Yes, but it's in the woman's body. Besides, look at the effects of people who felt morally obligated *not* to have abortions. People throw babies in dumpsters or drying machines, beat 'em, starve 'em... if they never wanted kids, why bring an unloved, unwanted child into this world?"

"Because like everything else, they deserve a chance to live."

"Including cows, right? Besides, that's a false equivalency... in the early stages the collection of cells you're callin' a child is like a tumor..."

"How could you possibly compare..."

"It's a living growth and it may be unwanted. Tumors are living flesh too. If life is sacred, you should refuse medical attention. Don't viruses and diseases have a right to life too?"

"That's... no. Not even remotely. Look, it's a human being we're talking about. I'm sure you're glad your parents brought you into the world..."

"Doesn't matter either way."

"You know, Rich, we're not getting anywhere... I'm not changing your mind and you're not changing mine... we *were* discussing faith, something you don't understand. You may think anyone believing in something bigger than themselves is an idiot, but you're talking about most people on earth."

"What's your point?"

"You're the outsider here... we've got a Christian, a Catholic, a Jew, a Pantheist... you're the only one that believes in nothing..."

"That's the second time you've brought up that 'strength in numbers' shit... most people in the United States have an IQ below 100, does that somehow make them smarter than the rest?"

"My point is *you're* alienating everyone else. You have no right to discuss the soundness of religion, it's obviously not something you've studied, and I'll hear no more preaching from you on the subject since you can't comprehend how someone could have something as simple as faith."

The silence that follows makes me wonder how many people this has put to sleep. As I lay thinking, a quote rolls into my head and comes out my mouth.

"'A walk through a lunatic asylum shows that faith does not prove anything'."

"Who said that?" Rob asks impatiently.

"Nietzsche."

"Grey, you're a quote machine." Anderson says sleepily.

"Yeah. I'm a tired quote machine. Goodnight."

"Proof denies faith..." Rob adds. "...and without faith there is no religion. Look it up in a dictionary, they're conflicting terms."

"I think Nietzsche meant faith is a delusion."

"You don't have any faith either, so why should we listen to you about it?"

"Oh, shut *up*..." Melody adds. "He said he believes in something, so shut up."

"And you have to listen to her... she has tits." Anderson adds.

This elicits a strong laugh from the group, followed by a considerable silence.

"Jeff... didn't you say a few days ago you thought that the undead were the perfection of people?" Karen asks.

"Funny you should mention that..." I finally reply. "I don't think of them as God... they're the antithesis... unthinking drones wielding collective power, fulfilling an underdeveloped Id. Like Nietzsche's supermen..."

"There's that name again..." Melody interrupts. "Who is this guy?"

"19th century philosopher... he popularized the term 'God is dead', not because he believed there ever was a God, he felt religion was no longer a viable source of ethics... he believed the Enlightenment was a failure, and that life after was just coming to terms with it. I'm mincing his words by equating the two, but the supermen are the next step... beings strong enough to create a new morality. By comparison, we're apathetic, weak-willed... in his words, the last men. The last men."

The silence after I speak is deafening, I assume because I've put people to sleep.

"I've been thinkin' about reincarnation..." Karen starts. "When people die and come back, is it the same soul inhabitin' the same body, or does the soul leave the body at all? And if less people are being born, are there leftover souls... I mean, since they had that idea, the population shot up... maybe this is just a chance for the souls to catch up."

"Interesting..."

After that there is relative silence, except what I think is the sound of Rich and Karen whispering to each other, their mumbles interlacing to make a constant low drone on which I concentrate to go to sleep. I roll over and look at the jar of ashes next to my head. I'm tired, so the meaning doesn't totally register. Staring at the jar through my heavy eyelids while hearing Rich and Karen murmur, I pass out.

10-18-04, MONDAY

When I wake up, I go into autopilot. I eat breakfast, drink my tea, get dressed, and wait for everyone else to wake up. Though she keeps quiet about it, I can tell that Karen is as sore as I was a week ago, and in another few days, she'll be as sore as I am now. After the bathroom and breakfast preamble, which includes Anderson monitoring what we eat to be sure we have the proper caloric intake, the seven of us board the bus and head over to the high school. When we pull up in front, Anderson and I exit the bus to test the front doors, finding them to be quite secure. We then enter through the only unlocked door in the building and Anderson gets inspiration from seemingly nowhere.

"Let's use the big lockers from the band room to block the hall-way... lay them sideways, fill them with heavy shit, stack 'em, and reinforce behind it."

"And hang the rope ladder from the top of the railing... sounds good." I reply. "Rich, see if you can get your hands on a tape measure. Anyone know where to find a hand truck?"

"Sure do." Jake chimes.

"Superb. Anderson, caulk gun. Melody, Rob, Karen, you're pull-ing desks with me."

The group splits as specified. In twenty minutes, Anderson and Jake return with the lockers to find us having acquired the necessary desks. When Rich returns, he measures the hallway, then the giant lockers to find that they measure eight feet and the hallway is eight and a half. With Anderson's help, Jake trucks two lockers into the hall and Anderson generously caulks the floor before we lay down the first; as predicted, the locker on its side is three and a half feet off the floor.

Anderson leaves and returns toting cinder blocks with the hand truck, placing several inside the locker at the corners and the middle before applying more caulk to the top of the door and disappearing again. Once the next locker is in place the wall is eight feet long, four feet thick, and seven feet high. Once set in place, we all move the desks in to reinforce it. Anderson returns with a rolled up paper under one arm and the rope ladder under the other, promptly hanging the rope ladder from the railing above and setting it in place with several kara-biners.

"Where do you get those things?" I ask.

"Guard."

"…alright, what's next?"

Anderson unfurls the paper, revealing a basic layout of the school.

"Where the hell did you get that?"

"Main office… I saw them pull it out to talk about the renovations when they had me in there once. Now… library should be pretty simple…"

"Block the doors with bookcases?" Melody asks.

"We can move 'em when we need to drag corpses off the lawn."

"And why do that?" Melody asks.

"You don't want them stinking up the lawn …"

"Right, then… dammit, we can't cut off the library…" I say.

"Why not?"

"If we're here for awhile, there won't be much to do besides read."

"Shit, good point."

"But we're in luck…" Jake says pointing at the map. "Those gates I was talking about separate the library, the gym, and the pool from the rest of the building…"

"Why do we want to close it all off?" Melody asks.

"God forbid we don't put one of the bastards completely under." I reply. "And it gives us two chokepoints."

"Let's not take any chances though…" Rich starts. "There are a few outer doors by that end, so let's get those sealed off from the outside… we find as many sets of keys as we can so we can get in and out of the wings when we need to."

"But if we need to get in and out of the library…"

"Park cars in front of the doors… leave them in neutral. Keep the keys."

"Excellent point." Anderson says. "Grey?"

"Move to close."

We follow Rich's suggestions and spend the next hour shutting the gates. Anderson, Rich and I enlist Jake, Melody, Karen, and Rob to get black paint from the art rooms to coat the ground level windows before the three of us go outside. Once there, we drop the sections of grating above the basement windows such that they create a cage covering the shattered frames. Once the last one is in place, Anderson steps away, wipes the sweat of his brow, and lights up a cigarette. I step up next to him.

"Something the matter?"

"Winter. It's gonna be a bitch to do anything then. We've got no one to plow the streets, and what if we can't get the heat working?"

"Don't worry about that..." Rich says. "My dad worked in home heating... he did contract work for the school district."

"...how did we miss talking about that before?"

"I don't know... but I'm worried more about locking this place up and getting food."

"Yeah... maybe we can get the satellite working..."

"What if they freeze to death?" I ask, chuckling.

"You actually believe that?"

"Can't be sure..."

"Did you hear that?"

As he finishes speaking, Rich points out to the street. "Too late..." Anderson says, pulling the rifle off his back. As if the rifle were a cue, a dozen people wearing hospital gowns appear around the edge of the fence at the left side of the school two hundred feet in front of us, running at full speed. I'm not the best source of speed, time, and distance measurements, but I estimate we have about 20 seconds until they reach us.

Before anyone else can speak, Rich and I loose our rifles and start running for the doors. "No, no, no!" Anderson shouts, breaking off to the left. Instead of going inside, he climbs on top of a chain link fence that surrounds an outdoor electric meter. In a flash, he's scaled it and is climbing on top of the metal canopy intended to protect bus-bound students from the rain. Ignoring my instincts to run in, I chase him up and Rich follows me. By the time I've pulled myself on the canopy I can hear a trigger click followed by a bolt working without the explosion of a gunshot.

I lie down next to Anderson on the canopy and pull up my rifle. "Rich, don't shoot unless they get too close." Anderson says in the midst of pulling the trigger. I reach in my pocket for my glasses and put them on. As I'm sighting I watch a cloud of red mist spray out the back of another head as Anderson pulls the trigger again. I rest the rifle against the rim of the roof and sight one, pulling the trigger and blowing apart another head as if it were made of wet cardboard. I work my lever as Anderson takes down another. I shoot and miss, and then Anderson does the same. The remaining eight are just about on us.

"This is going to be close." Anderson says, shooting and getting another. I kill the sixth one with a shot that removes his head. Anderson shoots again, missing, and I do the same. After reloading, Anderson takes out the seventh and I miss again. "Dammit, you're right." The five remaining ones hit the driveway simultaneously, growling as they see how close they are to the meat. Rich leans over the rim and prepares to fire his shotgun. I lay down my rifle and pull up my .45. The trigger clicks.

I yank back on the slide and fire two quick shots that brain the next one, spraying chunks of skull and eyeballs on the ground with a sickening splat. Anderson kills the ninth one with the rifle and switches over to his hand gun. The remaining three stop beneath the canopy and try jumping to get us. When one reaches his maximum height, Rich pulls the trigger on his shotgun, blowing apart everything above his sternum. When the corpse hits the ground, blood sloshes out like a spilled water cooler. Anderson and I stare in awe for a few seconds.

With his wits about him, Anderson fires two through the top of a Zombie's skull, causing him to fall over in a bleeding heap. Rich pulls up his crowbar and swings it underhand for the final one, the curved edge lodging in her mouth with a sickening crunch. Her body falls over when he pops the crowbar out. "Well, that was fun. Let's get these cleaned up." Anderson says. We drag the corpses through the library, gym, and finally into the pool before we head back into the main hallways.

It doesn't take long to notice that many of the windows on the ground level have been painted black. Following Anderson's specific instruction, one window on either end of the classroom has only been partially painted so we can still see out if necessary. Using a similar caulk and locker stuffing tactic, we block off doors that lead into the auditorium from the interior of the school over the next hour. Anderson makes sure to cover the window he broke at the auditorium entrance a week ago with taut plastic before he nails a board over the opening. The task totally seals off the auditorium, but also leaves our supply of hefty lockers depleted. After that, we fill as much of the new wing as we can with desks and chain the doors shut, then we trigger the school alarm system. It works for all the main doors and the one that leads into the basement from the outside.

As part of the interior defense, Anderson and I seal off the girl's bathroom from the rest of the gym structure so it can only be accessed from one interior hallway. Before lowering the gates in the hallway between the gym and the pool, Anderson and I get a hold of as many gym mats as we can and push them against the side doors, further blocking off the exit to the rear parking lot entrance. "You know what that means?" Anderson asks as I look out into the mess of cars just outside the windows.

"Hmm?"
"All the doors are blocked."
"Alright then... next, someplace to sleep?"
"I was going to say 218."
"Hmm... no windows, close to the inside of the school, plenty of space... good pick."

Room 218 was constructed as a lecture hall featuring multiple levels comprised of ten wooden steps to allow every student an unobstructed view of the chalkboard from the long, flat desktop on each level. We decide that the best thing to do is to remove all the chairs and keep the table tops when Anderson points out that we can steal ourselves some cots from the military barricades that will fit the levels.

"All right... we bring in cots, stock up on food..." Karen starts.

"...and alcohol." Rich adds.

"...right. We search the school for supplies... then what?"

"Well," Anderson says. "The first level's solid, there's only the one way to get in, we've got the windows blacked out. Jeff?"

"Computers, televisions, VCRs, DVD players... all the technology we can muster. Priority one is safety. Priority two is food. Priority three is staving off insanity. If they do manage to find out we're in here, they'll stay until they rot into dust."

"We can take them out," Jake says. "No problem, we've got the guns, and once we get the alcohol we can make Molotovs. Fish in a barrel."

"Yeah, but how many fish?" Anderson asks. "They get wind of us, they'll just keep coming."

"How do you know that?"

"Mark my words... if we slip up and they start pouring in, we won't have a chance to fix that mistake. Now let's stay on task..."

"What else is there?" Melody asks.

As Anderson retrieves the map, I attempt to do a walkthrough of the first level in my mind. He returns having already studied it.

"First level's solid... we can still get out on the roof. The security alarms are on... I've got it. Lock the classroom doors."

"I can handle that." I offer. "Maybe with one other person..."

I look at the people around me and notice that Rob isn't present. "Where's Rob?" I reach in my trench coat pocket and pull out my radio. "Rob, can you hear me, where are you, over?" After a few seconds of static, his strained voice crackles through.

"I'm okay. I'm in the bathroom."

"Rob, you've gotta tell us when you're gonna do that. Over."

"Sorry, I'm just... not feeling so well."

"Well, we're upstairs in room 218 when you come out. Over."

"All right, I shouldn't be too long."

I put the radio down.

"Anyone else get the feeling there's something wrong with him?" Karen asks softly.

"Nah, he's just worn out." Jake adds.

"He *talked* to you?" I ask.

"Yeah... he's a good dude."

"He *does* look fatigued..." Karen adds. "But it's more than exhaustion..."

"Well he *did* just say he was sick..." Jake says.

"If he's ill, we have to take it seriously... but if it's somethin' else..."

"It's probably just a cold or a stomach virus..."

"Jake, are you protectin' him?"

"...protecting him from *what?*"

"I don't know..."

"He just needs some privacy, nothing wrong with that..."

"Relax." Anderson says softly. "It doesn't matter why he's in the bathroom. We *do* need to stick together, and he *does* need to tell us where he's going. Anyway, I was gonna say something... Grey."

I look at him inquisitively before I notice everyone looking at me. "You look beat. You should get some sleep." I nod. "Yeah... is that alright?" I get no objections, so I walk to the back and drape my trench coat over myself. I can hear conversation behind me about what they want to do next as I begin slipping in and out of consciousness. After either a few seconds or a few minutes, Anderson comes back.

"Grey, we're gonna make a food run. You want anything?"

"Yeah. Hard lemonade, tortilla chips and party mix."

"...anythin' sensible?" Karen asks.

"You guys know what to get. Tea, I guess… Earl Grey and English breakfast. Oh, and I put a bunch of meat in with the frozen food at the supermarket."

"…for what purpose?"

"Freeze it, so it'll last. Also, anything with an extremely long-term expiration date. And water."

I roll over as Anderson mutters something else. "Melody's gonna stay here with you." I hear someone call from across the room. I think I have enough muscular power to nod my head before I pass out.

I wake up in darkness, hearing someone breathing close by. Terror rings its hands around my spine as I consider how vulnerable I might be. I'm about thirty feet from the light switch with a lot of tables in the way, so if there's someone or something in here I'm going to have to fight in the dark. I quietly pop the clasp on my holster and reach my hand out, squinting as I pat along the floor. Instead, I hit something soft; it's a person. A woman lets out a sigh, and then draws in a deep breath and stretches. Hoping that the sound will miscue anyone or anything in the room, I pull the shoulder lamp off my backpack, click it on with my hand over the bulb, and then jerkily point it at different corners of the room, swiping past Melody on the step above me. They did tell me she was staying here. I turn off the light as she continues alternately stretching and exhaling hard through her nose.

"Did I wake you?"

"I don't know. Maybe." She responds. "What was that about?"

"You don't ever get paranoid, waking up and not being sure if there's someone in a room?"

"I… didn't really think about it until now. Thanks for fuckin' that up for me."

"Sorry."

"I'm kiddin' ya." She yawns. "You were talking in your sleep."

"Oh?"

"Yeah. A lot."

"What was I saying?"

"'You can't take it away', 'my last bullet', 'don't leave'... do you talk in your sleep a lot?"

"Don't know... I never slept next to anyone before this week..."

"What'd you dream about?"

"Don't remember... I usually dream about... something that happened..."

"Like what?"

"I had this friend at college who used to lie compulsively. He said he knew all these famous people... he told me he was friends with the guy who directed both Bourne movies. They were directed by different people. It was just embarrassing to hear him talk about it. One night he was drunk at a party and he admitted he makes shit up all the time. The next day I talked to my roommate about it and he assured me that it never happened. I dreamt it."

"Weird."

I sit back as tear rolls down my cheek. "What?" Melody asks, hearing a depressed sigh. I shake my head as I wipe it away.

"I didn't even have the chance to think about her this time."

"...sorry."

"Why are you sorry?"

"Sorry... I don't know what to say..."

"...I've always had a concept to describe depression. It's... lying naked in a reeking, squalid dumpster on a rainy night, starving, freezing, sick, soaked to the bone, completely exhausted, losing blood from an infected wound in your stomach and addicted with some drug you can't identify and didn't want. You know you won't live to see the morning, and no one will care when you're gone."

"...is that how you feel?"

"This is worse."

"...all the time?"

I sit up and squint, trying to make eye contact.

"You said you lost someone... do you find yourself thinking about how you wronged them?"

"Yes."

"I remember a rough patch we had about six months ago... she wanted space, I couldn't give it to her. That went on for almost two months... we barely spoke... I embarrassed myself regularly trying to find ways to talk to her... it's all I could think about. I couldn't remember the last time I kissed her and it was driving me crazy..."

"You had that night together at the mall."

"Yeah..."

"She wouldn't tell me what it was for..."

"That was her way."

"I guess you won't tell me either?"

I stare into the darkness as she interprets my lack of an answer.

"Well... can I ask you something?"

"Go ahead."

"Did you... are you still... you know... a..."

"Yes."

She looks down for a moment.

"It's... you guys shouldn't have waited."

"You don't think it was worth it?"

"It's worth waiting for... I'm saying you guys didn't need to. I should know, I've had plenty of experience..."

I nod solemnly.

"Mostly bad..." She continues.

"I figured."

"What makes you say that?"

"A few days ago... you... implied you've been hit before."

"Yeah... a few times. You learn to avoid it, though..."

"Why... put up with it?"

She says nothing.

"I'm sorry..."

"Don't be..." She starts. "If I think of a way to put it into words..."

"Did, uh... never mind."

"What?"

"I don't want to offend you."

"You won't."

"I don't know... did your parents ever...?"

"Oh-no, no..."

"Sorry."

"But I... I'd never... I didn't put up with it for long..."

"Did it happen to you friends?"

"Yeah."

"I don't know, they say... they say your parents set up the dynamic for your relationships."

"Yeah... one time a guy told me what his father used to do to him... he... cried, when he told me. The next day, he pretended it didn't happen. That happened all the time... you fight, shit happens, you apologize... and it happens again."

"I wonder how people can do that... I mean, it's not like I've never made the same mistake twice... but you've gotta take something away from it at some point."

"Some of these guys... they just... I don't know... it's like they *act* tough all time... well, around their friends anyway. I guess we all do that sometimes."

We both pause uncomfortably, but after a moment, I don't know why this particular silence is making me uncomfortable.

"Does Anderson hate me?"

"What? No one *hates* you..."

"But... someone doesn't like me?"

"What gave you that impression?"

"The tone of your voice."

"Honestly? Ava wasn't your biggest fan..."

"Obviously..."

"That's it. You're definitely not the person I thought you'd be."

"...what?"

"...that didn't come out right... I had this... perception of you that fit in with how I thought of popular girls. Like if I tried to strike up a conversation with you, you'd ignore me, insult me, or treat me like crap... in high school, that's about the worst thing that can happen."

"I wouldn't have done that..."

"Well, I know that now."

"...what makes you think that?"

"An attitude in this school district... I moved here in second grade and was immediately disliked. By middle school, I realized no one cared what I had to say."

"I think more people appreciate you than you think."

"Do you know something I don't?"

"I used to hear stuff about you..."

"Like what?"

"Well... it's like, you weren't quiet enough to be scary..."

"Wow..."

"...but, like... you'd talk to anyone. One of the girls in your grade told me what a good listener you were."

"No doubt... I was the guy no one wanted to date... and I was too afraid to ask, so I became a listener."

"...I like talking to you... and you *are* a good listener."

"When I'm not talking about evolution..."

"Well, whatever. Besides... I feel a lot better about being here now."

"I feel better about you being here too."

She stares at me blankly a second.

"That was a joke."

"You know, half the things you joke about are really true."

"Half the things *I* joke about?"

"No, like, everyone."

"It was seriously a joke. What time is it?"

"Uh, it's 9:45."

"We should see if they're back."

I stand up, throw on my trench coat, pick up my weapons, and head out to the hall. From there I go down the steps into the empty cafeteria, power walking toward a serving area separated from the rest of the room by a wall with massive windows. As I approach the back, I can hear someone moving hefty cans of food around.

I jump over the stainless steel counter and pass into the back of a decidedly average high school kitchenette; giant sinks, a walk in freezer in the far corner, and three large counters taking up most of the space in the room. The first one has an oven and racks with cooking tools, the center one has two more sinks, and the last one is just a flat surface. There's an office on the far right side, next to the freezer. For a moment, as I approach, I hear muffled talking. "If only we had MREs." When the sentence is finished, I know it must be Anderson. I walk in and confirm it immediately as he continues.

"One of my pals in guard said he heard this from a guy who came back from Iraq: peanut butter plus crackers plus coffee plus sugar plus creamer plus coco base powder... you crush it up and add some water, and it's like the best thing in the world."

"Hey fellas..."

"Yo Grey, check it out... three hundred cans of food, cereal, canned drinks, dehydrated milk... that trick you pulled with the meat in the freezers?"

"Yeah..."

"Good idea. We stocked our freezer with every meat product we could find and dropped it down to zero. But you know how you broke that gallon of milk?"

"...yeah?"

"Bad idea. The whole place stinks and it pulled 'em in."

"W-... uh, I... wait a second, half the shit in there's probably going bad..."

"I know. I just wanted to see if I could get a rise out of you."

I'm not amused.

"How long until the meat goes bad?"

"Depends on the meat." Rich replies. "Most of it will be good for-ever… it's just a question of quality. If you know anything about cooking you can tell which meat has gone bad just by smelling it cook."

"We also stocked up on anything that was in bags… well, except dog food." Anderson chimes in again.

"Nice. How about water?"

"Well, in addition to the hundreds of bottles of water we already have, we cleaned them out. Check this out…"

He walks me out through a partition in the left side of the room. I glance around, unsure of what to look for until Anderson taps my shoulder: he opens the first of three refrigerators against the wall to show that every inch of available shelf space is covered with bottled water. The next refrigerator is stocked similarly. "Got tap filters too." He boasts.

"How much dehydrated milk is there?" I ask, walking back toward the grocery bags that people are unloading. "Between the powdered and evaporated stuff, both of which just need water… I don't know, a hundred gallons worth? You got those calcium pills though… and those cereal bars have the equivalent of a bowlful of milk. It won't last forever, but we've got one hell of a head start. And once we hook up tap filters, we can just reuse the bottles." I open up a box of cereal bars and chow down on one, then another. "We have a kettle or some-thing?" I ask with a mouth full of cereal. No one understands, so I wave it off and find one myself. I boil some water and get my hands on a box of sugar packets, then rifle through the bags until I find some Earl Grey.

Once the ingredients come together, I start drinking my tea. "What is that? You've been the only one making it for like a week now, and it smells good." Jake says as he approaches. "It's Earl Grey. Captain Picard's choice. Try some." Five minutes later, I have three other peo-ple drinking it with me. Holding my paper cup, I drown out the conversation around me. It's nice not to have any obligations, and for a moment, I think that my predictions about controlling some aspect of a Zombie apocalypse were correct.

Before I can develop that thought to the point of being depressed, I interrupt the other conversation when a few words spill out of my mouth. "What's the story on the entrances?" The conversation abruptly stops; it's still comforting that I can say whatever I want and have people listen. I wonder when the buffer from Julia's death will disappear.

"What do you mean?" Anderson asks.

"How easy is it for us to get in, how well defended are they?"

"Well, since we know where to get in, it's not a problem. Any door but that one is solid."

"Did we lock the classroom doors?"

"Nah…"

"Give me the keys, I'll do it."

Rich tosses them to me.

"Mind if I come with?" Karen asks.

"Sure."

We walk silently out the cafeteria doors to the English hallway. I quickly locate the skeleton key and begin locking doors while Karen keeps an eye out in the halls. We only survive in silence for a few minutes.

"Have a good nap?"

"Good enough…"

"…I hate to sound like your mom, but you should probably eat more… you'd have a lot more energy."

"I'll keep it in mind." I lock a door and turn back into the hallway.

"So… how about those… Zombies?"

"…yeah?"

She scoffs uncomfortably.

"Well, I don't know... you said this was your birthright..."

"Yeah... yeah... well, my parents are safe, you guys are safe, don't know about my brother, and Jules is dead..." I lock another door. "...they've exceeded my expectations in terms of being terrifying, but they've also proved to be about as manageable as I expected. Does that answer your question, or do you want me to talk about Jules?"

"Just strikin' up conversation... do you feel like... we're in the driver's seat?"

"I'm... not sure what you mean?"

"Do we have this under control?"

"...as much as we can, I guess... I'm pretty set in believing the world is deterministic."

"So... you don't blame yourself for Jules?"

"I have... and I will... but... I don't know, it's just such a ridiculous thing... like, I know how World War I turned into World War II, and it's hard to imagine that, given the circumstances, it could have happened any other way... this is different. In the end... I don't know... wasn't my fault, wasn't hers."

"Well, I'm glad you're talkin' about it at least... better than sufferin' silently."

"Get to know my friends and they'll confirm that's not a possibility."

This scoff is more amused than uncomfortable.

"Well, give this another week or so and I won't have to ask those questions." She responds.

"That's interesting... I suppose if this blows over we're never gonna forget each other."

If. I wish John Squared were still here. And Jules. Even Ava. A few seconds of awkward silence follow as I lock a few more doors. I've probably locked at least two dozen, now we're on the second level. I stop at one of the doors that's been left open; the room inside has been torn asunder by the undead, leaving the barren teeth of cracked glass clinging to the broken window pane. This strikes me as being a good enough deflection from the last sentence, so hopefully engaging her on what to do with this room will encourage her to forget asking about our chances of this blowing over. "What's our chance of survival?" Karen asks. I should have spoken sooner.

"You mean the group?"
"Yeah."
"Uhm... I'll have a better answer in a week."
"What happens in a week?"

I decide to lock the door and deal with it later.

"If we don't start turning things around by then... I don't know, it'll get a lot harder. Whoever said that a few days ago is right, though... they spread from this area... so I we're in good shape."
"You think they can they cross the oceans?"
"I doubt it... I doubt *one* of them could make it cross country in one piece."

There are another few minutes of silence as I finish up locking the top level, except for the bathrooms, which I unlock. When we head down the stairs that are adjacent to our only entrance, Karen pipes up again.

"So, a couple more days until this is all set up?"
"Something like that."
"What do you suppose we do then?"
"Stock up on more food... once we have a place to come back to we can go out a lot farther. We'll go through each room one at a time and find ways to make it safer... start figuring out a way to plant food in the courtyard and the greenhouse. We can figure out the best ways to fight the undead... start exercise routines to stay flexible..."
"I hear that..."
"You can teach us what you know about healthcare, Anderson can teach us about the military, Rich can teach us about street survival... Melody can... do you know what she does?"

"Works for a hair salon."

"…keep us trim and stylish? I don't know. As long as the power holds out, I can teach people about movies, though that hardly seems relevant."

"And what do we do about… *them?*"

"Well, if the military doesn't do something about it…"

"…what?"

"We hunt 'em down… we gotta police up the town if we're gonna stay… draw 'em out, kill 'em, pile 'em up, burn 'em."

"I… what?"

"Or however we can do it… house to house…"

"Jeff, you're not serious are you?" I lock another door.

"…yeah."

"I… can… is that the way to do it?"

"Unless you have a better one."

I lock the last door and go into the cafeteria to find everyone just sitting around. In short order we head out the only exit and get into the bus. On the drive back, I have Anderson help me clean my rifle, and when we get back I have him help me clean my pistol as well. It's easy enough, so from now on I can probably do it by myself. Once in the sleeping quarters we put on the television again as we sort out making our canned dinners around a hotplate. As we bring the news up we find two shabbily dressed men with poor makeup, but I smile as I see Lon Miller finish his sentence.

"… this that or the other. We're simply not at a stage where we can debate that."

"Well, what about the present situation with insects, we understand you have been doing various laboratory tests with insects, specifically mosquitoes."

"Correct. It seems that mosquitoes can easily distinguish between the flesh of humans and the flesh of the specimens, and 100% of the time they reject the undead."

"So the infection cannot be spread in that fashion?"

"No. And again, I stress that nothing about our studies to this point suggests that there is a pathogen… that a pathogen is the agent at work."

"…following the question of insect spread, what is the relationship of carrion animals to the undead?"

"Very similar, and it's the same for scavengers, decomposers, and detritivores. No animal or plant we've seen has involved itself in the decomposition process, which means that the reanimated dead will putrefy very slowly, unless burned..."

"What about other animals, such as cats, dogs, and wildlife?"

"I'm sorry, uh..."

"Are they capable of being, well..."

"Affected? There have been very few reported cases of affected animals, but the syndrome seems to have a similar effect on them. Revived animals share the same traits as risen humans; stiff joints, moaning, and heavy salivation. They should be avoided at all costs."

"Now, as far as burning goes..."

"Absolutely the only way to get rid of possible contagion... burn them, otherwise the body will eventually rot, leaving the affected tissue where it lies. The blood and tissue, it has been found, make soil unusable for planting, but other than ingestion, there is no method of affectedness made possible by the mere presence of an affected corpse."

"Now, what is the procedure for burning one of the undead?"

"Take it out to the street and douse it in some kind of flammable liquid, they burn surprisingly easily. Stay away from the smoke, as the effects of inhalation are, as yet, unknown. Once it has burned into ash, leave it in a white plastic bag by the side of the road and it will be collected by waste management."

"So, there is no time for funeral arrangements?"

"Well, to paraphrase one of my predecessors, the dubious comforts of a funeral must be forgone in the interest of public safety."

"We're just now receiving breaking news, so we will switch over live to our national affiliate."

The program switches with a series of graphics and music, finally settling on a man in a studio with a picture of the earth next to him. I become aware of a sinking feeling in my chest.

"Good evening, this is Robert Jensen with a special bulletin. Breaking news out of Boulogne, France indicates that the crisis of the dead returning to life afflicting the United States in the past week has spread to Europe. Earlier today, panic was reported on the streets of Paris as dozens of infected... uh, affected rampaged through public squares. No footage has been released despite an earlier assertion as such, and it would appear that a state of emergency has been declared. The French military was reported setting up a

blockade around the affected region, but no further information has been released. It is believed that the cause of the outbreak stems from a group of American tourists. More on this story as it develops, including a press conference with the French Prime Minister within the hour."

Another outgassing of graphics and music returns us to our regularly scheduled program.

"Thank you, Robert. For those of you recently joining us, we've been discussing the as-yet unnamed affliction causing the bodies of the recently dead to return to life and subsequently attack the living with CDC epidemiologist Dr. Lon Miller. Staying with this topic, we have a map to show how the infection appears to be spreading. The, uh... red dots forming clouds on the map represent locations of known affected presence, while the surrounding purple cloud denotes areas where it is assumed the undead have spread. As you can see from this graphic, the crisis has overtaken much of the northeast. Reports are surfacing from all corners of Pennsylvania, New York, New Jersey, Connecticut, Rhode Island, Massachusetts, Vermont, Maryland, and Delaware. The states reporting infection in more than 75% of their geographic value are West Virginia and New Hampshire, and 50% of Ohio and Virginia. Canada's National Guard is holding the borders and they have no interior signs of infection. Now, the original site of infection has been narrowed down to the adjacent towns of Broomall and Newtown Square in Delaware County, Pennsylvania. The nearby rescue centers have been reporting inoperative for some time, others... appear to be doing the same in a similar order to when the nearest town first reports an infection. Dr. Miller, is there any cause for this?"

"Well, yes. My colleagues and I have speculated that the emotional stress from the dead encircling a building is often too much for the occupants to take... this can result in attempted escapes and in some cases suicide. The military has been instructed to abandon any site that has been severely compromised, and this appears to be happening at an astronomical rate."

"Now, it has been the position of state and local authorities all along that private residences should no longer be occupied..."

"I love how they keep revising their story." I say.

"...safe houses are proving to be easily compromised, what is the suggested tactic for those who live near the areas where the infection is spreading?"

"Again, we can't be certain that there's a pathogen at fault..."

"...right..."

"...we're in a position where we are forced to reconsider the methods by which something of this magnitude can spread. As far as attempted shelter and rescues, there is no unified opinion on what to do... some townships are evacuating and others are staying put, so referring entirely to local broadcasts and emergency management services is the only recourse."

"Now, Dr. Miller, have there been any updates on the hunting patterns of the undead?"

"Well, following the suggestions of outside experts, we've begun setting up a series of maze tests with captured specimens... the CDC is still in the early stages of collecting data, but from what we've ascertained the specimens are able to hunt a human with surprising accuracy in a variety of conditions. Though anecdotal in nature, preliminary reports make prevalent the ability of the undead to cut off escape routes when humans are present..."

"And they use no standard form of communication to coordinate these attacks?"

"None that we know of, though it is possible that they know they're surrounding a target based on hearing each other's moans... that and whatever means they use to nominally hunt the living."

"Any clues as to those mechanisms?"

"Isolated sensory testing revealed little or no hindrance to their hunting in the dark. We've performed other tests intending sensory deprivation or confusion such as scents, lights, sound and temperatures, but none offer a noticeable decline in detection abilities. In the limited testing we've performed with unaffected individuals the best results came from instructing the person to remain absolutely still."

"So, they hunt mainly by sound then?"

"Again, we tried playing sounds and using smells to simulate a human presence... their patterns changed in a way that would suggest a lack of motivation in getting to their target. We are beginning to think, as far fetched as this sounds, that they can hunt by changes in air density... vibration."

"That would explain why they are drawn to main roads."

"Indeed, the smells, sounds and vibrations serve as an attraction. With this in mind, we tried an inanimate vibration test, but it would appear that their hunting patterns are triggered by certain types of vibration... the one getting the heaviest response was that of your average bipedal human walking in a normal indoor environment. Outdoors, they are much more likely to be confused by other vibrations. This is leading civil services to believe that the best option is underground or soundproofed safe houses."

"Recapping the biggest story of the century... for those of you just tuning in, the dead are returning to life and attacking the living. The bites of the

undead have proven intractably fatal, and the bodies of those bitten will re-
turn to life. The crisis has engulfed almost the entire Northeast and is
spreading rapidly South and West. Please, leave your homes in favor of mil-
itary sanctioned rescue centers..."

As he's talking, I turn and look at the rest of the room; everyone
else is either asleep or lying down, so I turn off the television. I lay
back for a few minutes, staring at the ceiling and cursing the length of
my nap earlier in the day. I let a bit more time pass before I get up and
check my trench coat pockets to find some cigars and my new lighter.
I grab my rifle and head up to the roof.

Once up there, I light up a cigar and have a seat, dangling my legs
over the edge of the building. The street is dark enough that I can't see
any of the undead. As always, part of me expects to hear sirens and see
wild fires in the distance in addition to rampant screams and gunshots,
sort of an exaggerated version of the first night on the roof of the high
school. I suppose that storm has passed, but I can't imagine how things
are shaping up in downtown Philadelphia.

I fantasize that computers will go a long way in preserving our
cultural heritage, but I concede quickly that a loss in power will render
them nothing more than expensive doorstops. Nevertheless, it feels
paramount that I get my own computer back. All my poetry, all my
short stories and novels, various school projects, not to mention songs
and videos fill that hard drive.

I look down at my lit cigar and the words of Dave from the community college come back to me: *They can see a lit cigarette from a mile
away!* I pull the rifle off my back and point it at the street about 200
feet away. I let out a small sigh and check my rifle, and to my great
surprise, it isn't loaded, so I start pulling rounds off of my bandolier
and do so, repressing the associations the name Dave brings about in
my mind. Once I've finished reloading, I get up and walk around the
roof holding my rifle with both hands; a lazy scan of the rooftop yields
only a concrete structure with a metal door that I hadn't noticed before.

I pull the door open and look inside to find nothing except a window parallel to the door. It seems as though it had been built

somewhat recently and hasn't really served a purpose. Thinking nothing of it, I walk back out to the edge of the roof, throw my cigar over, and head back inside. I have a moment of feeling slightly criminal, which I suppose is more of a leftover impulse in my brain telling me that I am trespassing and might get caught. Having been used to feeling this way when climbing the high school roof, it's hardly surprising. On the other hand, though I knew that one of the downstairs doors was always inadvertently left unlocked, I was never brave enough to actually venture inside.

While walking down the hall, I suddenly hear what sounds like vomiting coming from one of the bathrooms. I approach cautiously and place my ear against the door only to hear gagging and dry-heaves followed by fluid splashing into a toilet bowl. "Hello?" I inquire, hearing scuffling. "Be out in a minute..." It sounds like Rob. "Rob, what's going on? Are you okay?" It sounds like he shatters something in the intervening seconds before he responds. "I'm okay, I just... need a minute." I decide I can't just let it go and walk in to see his feet sticking out of one of the closed stalls. I softly place my hand on the door and push it open to find Rob sitting on the floor, his eyes bleary and his mouth encrusted with vomit, a broken hypodermic needle beside him. "Jesus *Christ*, Rob..."

"No, it's... it's not what you think." He says, stuffing a small bag of white powder in his pocket. "Roll up your sleeve, let me see your arm." I say softly. He shakes his head. "Rob, roll up your *sleeve!*" Reluctantly, shakily, he rolls his sleeve up to reveal several tract marks up his forearm, one of which is bleeding slightly. "Oh for the love of god..." He turns over and starts picking up the broken pieces of the needle, a lighter, and a spoon, stuffing them all in his pocket. "It's not as bad as you think." He mutters to the toilet bowl.

"How much worse could it get? What is it, cocaine, heroin? You know what, I don't need to know, just give it to me." Rob shakes his head. "No, I... no... it's not that bad. I just need enough to keep me... normal, you know?" I let out a deep sigh and look at the floor before moving my eyes up the wall. "Karen!" I shout. *"Don't!* No one has to know!" I yank my arm away before he can grab it. Seeing a blank, lost expression on his face, I reach into his pocket, pull out the bag of white powder and flush it down the toilet. "NO!" He screams as he pushes me back. "KAREN!" I shout.

When he pushes me again, the rifle comes up and bangs into his elbow. I reflexively let go, the barrel slides down the stall before the stock hits the ground, and it lands behind my feet. My heels go back into the rifle which then catches both sides of the doorway and sends me flailing past the door to the cold tile. I roll over on my stomach and start to kick as I hear Rob clambering across the floor followed by the unmistakable sound of my rifle being picked up.

I freeze before slowly rolling over on my side. He's pointing the barrel right between my eyes. I put both my palms on the floor, push myself away slowly, and stand up. "Jeff, what is it?" I hear from outside the door; it's Karen. I slowly hold my arms out. "Rob, what do you think you're doing?" He grits his teeth and prods my forehead with the end of the barrel. I pinch my eyes shut as I get an image of him prodding and pulling the trigger simultaneously. I just loaded it. For a moment, I think I can feel my brain pushing itself against the back of my skull and trying to spread out to avoid getting hit.

"Do you have any idea what that cost me? *Do you!?*"
"Rob..."
"JEFF! We're coming in!" Karen shouts.
"Stay *out!*"

I try not let my anxiety escape, but I think I'm failing. I'm starting to shake and my throat cuts off my sentences before I can start them. I've had a gun pointed at me once before, but it was Anderson, and he was shooting at something else. This is someone I barely know and he's on drugs and pissed. I imagine the pop of the gun and the ringing in my ears, so loud it offsets my balance. I wonder if the lights would go out all at once, if I'd have the chance to feel pain, or if I'd go numb and maintain consciousness for a few minutes. The exit wound would probably be about the size of a tennis ball.

"I don't have any more left and it's YOUR FAULT!" Rob shouts.
"Rob, please... put the gun down. You don't want to shoot me..."

"You deserve it, you *motherfucker*!"

"Rob. Put the gun down, and we'll talk through this."

His still looks pissed, but tears are gathering in his eyes. I'm not sure if it's because of the drugs or because I'm getting to him, but after staring him down for a moment I start to feel like it's the latter. This isn't so bad. I can talk him down. Just use his name as much as possible, stay calm and reasonable, and he'll have no choice but to oblige. "Rob..." The trigger clicks. Both of us freeze. My blood runs cold. I didn't hear a shot. My ears aren't ringing. All at once, the sensation that I'm still alive rushes back through my body in the form of a rage that boils over in an instant.

Almost without realizing it, I grab the barrel and smash him in the face with the butt, producing a sputter of blood from his nose followed by a thick stream that resembles chocolate syrup. Rob falls back with a strained cry as his hands come up to cover his face. Somewhere in the back of my head, I thank Anderson for advising me to not chamber a round until I know I'm ready to shoot.

I spin the rifle around and push the barrel between his hands as he continues weeping on the floor, prodding his forehead with the muzzle. "DON'T YOU EVER, *EVER*, POINT A GUN AT ME!!!" I scream. He continues weeping. "TRIED TO *SHOOT* ME!?" I work the lever, chambering a round, and prod his face with it again. With that, Anderson comes into the bathroom behind me.

"Whoa, Grey, what are you doing?"

"Target practice..."

"Grey, ease down..."

"That sounds like me, right before he put the barrel against my head and *pulled the motherfucking* trigger!"

"Are you okay?"

"WHAT DO YOU THINK!?"

"Grey, I'm serious, just put it down."

I turn back and look at Anderson. He steps forward slowly, puts his hand around the barrel and the trigger guard, and snaps the rifle out of my hand in one motion. Karen rushes past us and goes to Rob with a medical kit. I continue staring at Anderson. "Are you okay?" He asks again. I can still feel the tears pouring down my face. "He tried to shoot me! TRIED TO FUCKING SHOOT ME!" I shout, attempting to dive at him, but Anderson holds me back.

"Ease down, Grey. We need him."
"We need him like we need a… albatross…"
"…what?"
"Take everything away from him. Don't let him have any guns, nothing."

He looks up at me as Karen tends to his face, and as soon as we make eye contact, he glances away. "Don't look at me, ever. Don't even get *near* me. *Look* at me when I'm talking to you!" He looks up at me again and sobs loudly, choking it back. I look him straight in the eye before speaking slowly and clearly. "If you touch me again, I will kill you."

Caught in the same daze that began with me breaking his nose with the rifle, I walk out of the bathroom, go to the bedroom and pick up a crowbar. "Jeff, what are you doing?" Melody asks me sleepily. "Blowing off steam." As I purposefully walk out of the room, Anderson follows me. "What are you doing?" He asks. "Blowing off steam… I'll be back in a few minutes." I slip on my leather gloves. Anderson starts following me as I walk out. "Just leave me alone, I'll be *back* in a few minutes…" I mutter as he continues to follow me. "Grey, we're not lettin' you go out by yourself." I stop and quickly turn back to him, talking fast.

"Look, is it safe to say I've had a pretty shitty week?"
"We all have."
"*You* didn't lose your girlfriend, *you* didn't have someone put a gun to your head… if you do me one favor for the rest of my life, you'll let me go… and I *will* be back in a few minutes."
"*What* are you *doing?*"
"I'm saving his life. Okay?"

"Okay."

I walk down the steps toward the gymnasium. I pat my right side and yank my .45 out of the holster. I pull out the magazine and remember that two of the rounds are spent, so I have five shots left. I kick the lever on the gymnasium door, blasting it open. Spotting a fire extinguisher, I turn back and whip the crowbar into it, causing the top to blast off and instantly fill the hallway with white powder. I emerge from the cloud covered in it, but I don't stop to shake it off. Instead, I run for the exit. With the door in sight, I take two quick hits off my inhaler.

The large parking lot is lit dimly by street lamps, casting my shadow twenty feet in every direction. The top of a shadow crosses the foot of a fresh Zombie wearing a business suit. I holster the .45, bring up the crowbar and swiftly lodge it in his skull, popping it out and slamming it into his rib cage to hear several satisfying snaps. While I pry the cold steel out of his chest cavity, I hear a feminine moan just behind me to the right. "Shut up!" I swing the crowbar like a baseball bat, creating a dent on the side of her skull and knocking her back. When she tries to get up I slam the crowbar into the back of her neck and she goes limp. I repeatedly crush it into her spine, moving up and down until I hear every vertebrae snap. Her head is still twitching, so I raise my boot and stomp on it; it cracks and splits as brain matter squirts out, but that doesn't stop me from stomping harder and harder. Another one, a male, gets close to me. I pull out my .45 and buffalo him.

Holstering the pistol, I lift up my crowbar again. I swing it like a golf club so that the point gets lodged under his jaw and comes out his mouth, then I wrench it sideways and his lower jaw gets torn off with a sickening pop. I swing again, this time breaking through his orbital socket and mashing his eye into white gelatin before beating his skull until I'm satisfied. "Bring it!" I charge the next one and whack him in the back of the head. When he's on the ground, I place his mouth over the curb and he absently attempts to bite it. I raise my leg and stamp on the back of his head as hard as I can, hearing his teeth snap off at the gum line. I beat his skull until thick, viscous drops of chunky blood are raining from his ear.

"COME ON!" I spit, keeping my voice low. When the next one gets close to me, a woman, I pistol whip her as well. She falls back, and when her head starts coming up I press the muzzle against it and pull the trigger, resulting in the vaporization of the back of her head. The pavement becomes painted with little pieces of skull, mushy brain, and sparse blood. Another woman comes closer and I kick her back from my kneeling position. I stand, walk over, and stomp on her neck until it has the consistency of a ripped bag of wet gravel. She attempts to bite my boot, but I take the crowbar and whack her head off.

I have to run to get to the next one, a man. I bring the crowbar over my head and hook the curved part through the top of his skull. His arms drop and his entire body starts convulsing violently. "HAH!" I shout at his vibrating corpse, popping the crowbar out and rushing at the next one, gouging it through his eye socket and pushing him to the ground. I don't stop pushing until the crowbar makes contact with the back of his skull, then I put my foot on his neck and pull it out with a wet sucking sound. I turn to the next one and give him a jumping front kick to the jaw, causing his teeth to dribble out of his mouth as he falls back. I then quickly displace him with a shot to the forehead.

Then I see another female running at me. She looks relatively light, so I step back and brace myself, letting my butt hit the ground when she's five feet away and sticking out my foot. As expected, she runs directly into my foot and a combination of a swift kick and her momentum send her flying over my head. I scramble to my feet and blow her brains out when she tries to stand up. "Pussies! All of you!" I choke out as the next two approach. They're relatively close together, so I holster my pistol, step forward and launch my crowbar at them sideways, hitting both in the neck and knocking them down. In that same motion, I pull out my katana and undo their necks while they're on the ground.

Breathing deeply, I pull off my gloves and drop them as I look around for more targets. Not seeing any, I step forward and stare into the dead eyes of the last two I killed. I lift my foot to stomp on their skulls, and suddenly, I find myself incapable of doing it. I grab my face and rub my hands around hard as I start shaking. I bang my head softly into the blacktop, listening to the moans of more undead in the distance. I fight to keep images of Julia out of my head, but I only end up compounding them with images of my mom crying herself to sleep every night in her hotel room. I next get the image of my brother being forced into a wall, screaming and crying in protest as they sink their teeth into his arms and he's forced to submit as another one tears him apart at the stomach.

I close my eyes and pound my fists into the ground. When I open them I can't see through the tears, but I can still hear them moaning in the distance. "Stop…" I mutter as visions of ex-girlfriends succumbing enter my head. I start putting together images of my aunts and uncles feebly trying to fight back against the undead and failing miserably, only to rise again a few hours later. The moans are getting closer. "Just stop…" I think about my brother's painful desperation, the hopelessness as he looks up at his assailant and prays that something, anything will save him. His pulse races as they pull away his flesh, filling his last moments with intense, unbearable agony before he peaceably blacks out, but not before the realization that in a few hours, he'd be one of them. "I don't…" I cry harder, out loud now.

Every person I love has been conditioned to believe that this scenario is something out of a horror movie and perhaps acted as incredulously as they said they never would in the safety of movie theatres. They may have even believed that they were doing a fine job surviving at some point, and believed that they had begun to accept the situation as reality. I pinch my eyes shut again, hard, and open them; I'm still here.

As the moments turn from desperate to grim, as these common, everyday people become surrounded, as all hope should disappear, the fantasy comes back. They look on with disbelief, dubiously hoping that it's all been a prank and their attackers would suddenly start laughing to signify that the joke was over. They may even try reason in their last seconds, but the fantasy ends the moment those teeth sink into an extremity and the pain makes proof of a reality that was impossible to accept.

I pinch my eyes shut again. "I want to wake up." I whisper. I open my eyes, unable to see anything other than the watery lights superimposed over the darkness. I close my eyes.

10-19-04, TUESDAY

I wake up inside on a shoddily arranged pile of blankets with un-real levels of tightness and soreness eclipsing my entire body. I wipe the drool from my lip and pull out the magazine from my .45; it's empty, so last night was definitely not a dream. Was I brought inside, or did I come in on my own? Did I fire any more shots? The sudden realization that I have a headache takes precedence, however, so I find the medical kit and take more ibuprofen than I probably should. After I do, I look over to see Rob on the ground. Sleeping. Vulnerable. Tied up. His nose covered in bandages. I jump when I see Karen looking at me.

"Jesus, Karen..."
"Are you okay?"
"Yeah... just a headache."
"I mean... you're not gonna..."
"Well... I wouldn't leave us alone together..."
"What happened?"
"I heard him throwing up in the bathroom... he's on drugs..."
"Do you know what it was?"
"White powder... I flushed it down the toilet. He didn't take kindly to that."
"Maybe an intervention might've been the way to handle that?"
"Was there gonna be a *good* way to handle it?"
"No, but he coulda killed you... now we have to..."
"Rehab him ourselves."
"It's hard enough to do in a clinic with doctors and time..."
"Can we do it?"
"Do we have a choice?"
"So we'll do the best we can..."
"I know, I know, we don't have a choice."
"Look at the bright side... if we had done an intervention, he'd resent everyone... not just me."

She fakes a smile as she shakes her head softly.

"So what do we do?"

"What do you figure?"

"Twelve steps, but we've gotta isolate him when he goes into withdrawal."

"Great."

"I can't say from experience, but cold turkey ain't easy. As you say, look at the bright side... there's no chance he'll relapse."

I wrap my hands around to the back of my head and uselessly scratch, tousling my hair. I then move them up and down my face and rub my eyes. Karen continues looking at me.

"You alright?"

"Yeah, just... never mind."

"...I'm not gonna let it go."

"Just thinking about... last week."

"What specifically?"

"I was in college... still feels like I can just go back. I'm having trouble remembering anything before that. That happen to you?"

"Mmm... not really. You had, what, two more years of college?"

"Yeah, hopefully... why?"

"It's interestin'..."

"What is?"

"You may not end up bein' what you wanted to be... but you're doin' what you're best at."

"Well, that's the part that gets me... I might never find out what I was supposed to be best at. You have any unfulfilled dreams?"

"...I don't know."

"Paris, skydiving... anything? You seem pretty independent..."

"Nothin' I can think of. I'm guessin' you're codependent."

"I was."

I shake my head and look up to see Anderson standing over me.

"How much work is left at school?" I ask.

"Plug up the side entrances and the front with cars, see what else we can tighten..."

"What then?"

"Cots and mattresses. And we're gonna have to make some more food runs."

"All right. How about you, me, and someone else go for cots and stuff, and everyone else works on the cars?"

"Uh... Karen's gotta stay with Rob, someone's gotta stay with her... is one person doin' the cars?"

"...okay, we bring Rob on the bus, Karen stays with him, one person guards the bus, the other two on car detail. Good?"

Following an explanation to the rest of the group, breakfast, bathroom trips, and some poor attempts to stretch, Rich takes us to the school. Once there, Anderson and I take a particularly large truck to run our errands and instruct everyone to leave their walkie-talkies on. "I'm glad no one ganked my car." I say as we drive past the bus parking lot. "Yeah, that would have been a bummer." Anderson confirms absently while looking out the window. I consider addressing the uselessness of our exchange, but I opt not to as we drive silently through a series of back roads to get out to West Chester Pike.

Once we make it to the check point we both hop out of the truck, and before we can make it more than a few feet, Anderson hands me a surgical mask to cover the smell. Anderson takes the initiative to hop over the weakness in the middle as I stop to survey the slaughter in the mid-day sun before looking off into the distance. The road breaks off as an on-ramp and an off-ramp in many places, but it also continues straight down a hill on a slight angle before curving back up about half a mile away and disappearing behind dense foliage and Mercy Community Hospital.

Anderson gets my attention with a nod as he brings back his second cot. "Most of these are soaked... we aren't gonna get more than ten or twelve." I don't respond as I fix my eyes on what I think is a moving object. "That's gonna suck if more people come lookin' for help." He continues as I begin to pat my pockets until I find my glasses.

I turn to see Anderson adjusting a pair of Y suspenders over his shoulders when he finally stops to look at me. "You gonna help?"

"Look at that." I say, pointing into the distance at the thick lines of undead walking along the road toward us. "Think they see us from there?" He asks. "I have no idea. How far from the school are we?" Anderson steps away to think for a moment.

"Two miles. They walk, what, two miles an hour?"

"Looks about right."

"That puts them on top of us in fifteen minutes."

"And at the school in an hour."

"Provided they don't detour."

"Well, with all these cars they're bound to be slowed down, and they'll have to negotiate the check point, which won't be easy..."

"We could be in a world of shit in a few hours."

I jump over the barricade, run into the nearest tent and start looking for metal and nylon cots. I take two at a time and make three trips; with that and Anderson's cluster, we have all the clean ones, so we start the drive back to the school. Along the way he and I stop at a Wawa, filling eight trash bags with food and drinks before indulging in some Anderson-approved lunch, consisting of aged turkey sandwiches, granola bars, 5 Hour Energy, and whichever electrolyte-filled beverages we can get our hands on. We both discharge our breakfast before moving on to the mattress store around the corner.

We easily break in and take two queens and four singles before the truck becomes too full to carry any more, at which point Anderson makes use of his karabiners to latch the mattresses together at their handles before fixing them to the truck with bungee cords. Once we drive back the school, I can see clearly that cars have been crashed into the front doors. Rich stands at the edge of the driveway to greet us. "Looks like you guys did a bang up job..." I say, getting out of the truck.

"Yeah, Jake got a little overbearing..."

"He alright?"

"Thanks to the seatbelt and the airbags."

"Good to know."

"We also tightened up the auditorium security."

"Terrific. We got more food, now the task is getting it inside."

"And I got these..."

I look back to Anderson, who holds up a pair of grenades.

"Are those hand grenades?"

"M-18s, yellow smoke."

"Did you find any real grenades?" Rich asks.

"You'd have a better chance of finding Excalibur... first wave didn't get any frags, they thought it was protestors or sick people... but these'll do. I only have a couple though, so I'll only use them when we're totally fucked."

"...which situation would that be?" I ask with a snicker.

"If we have to run away from a fight."

"...we've run away from plenty of fights..."

"No we haven't. We've avoided them, or taken them down when we could. If we're in a fight we can't win, when we're *totally* fucked, I'll pop smoke, and you'll know."

Rich shrugs, hops in the truck, and I drive it fifty feet to the only way inside from the outside. With the help of Melody and Jake, the five of us move the mattresses, cots, and food inside. Melody points out that the queens won't fit in the room we've chosen as we're bringing them inside.

"Eventually we get our own rooms..." I start. "Once we get settled."

"How do we pick who gets what?" She asks.

"We'll figure it out."

"Doesn't matter." Anderson offers brusquely. "Is there more food and shit on the football field?" Anderson asks.

"Yeah, probably some." Jake says.

"You don't actually, like, *want* to go down there?" Melody asks.

"I do. How about you, Jeff?"

"Not really. No. Not at all, in fact."

"Rich?"

"Any food is good food."

"You're outvoted. Rich, want to come with?"

"No, I'll go." I say.

"But you…"

"It'll give us a chance to talk. Melody, Jake, Rich, sort the shit out. Put the mattresses and cots in 218 for now. Is Karen alright?"

"She's got Rob sedated for now, she's fine. I'll check on her." Rich says.

"Are we moving in tonight?" Jake asks.

"No, I forgot to mention, there's a wave headed this way, so we're going to stay at the community center until they pass through." I say.

"But isn't this place secured, and that place isn't?"

"I don't want to test the defenses until we have to."

"Yeah, I second that." Anderson adds.

I pull my rifle from around my shoulder and check to see that it's fully loaded. Anderson and I walk to the exit from the rear. I guess it could be construed as an inconvenience that we can't drive from the front to the back of the school, but we haven't a choice since many of the cars don't have keys, gas, or live batteries anymore. Once over the cars, Anderson and I pass Steve as walk across the back lot. "Is he ever gonna starve?" Anderson asks flatly. For some reason, this reminds me of something I tried to ask him earlier.

"By the way… before we got to the mall, I asked you if you guys were ordered to evacuate, and you said you couldn't tell me…"

"Yeah… I was still on orders."

"…to do what?"

"What I told you… escape and evade, that shit. If we were gonna link up with my unit, it was better if you guys didn't know certain things."

"Like what?"

"No harm in telling you now… our orders were to set up the check point and assess the situation. It didn't take long to figure out we had some kind of infection, or whatever, so we called it in, and that's when they authorized deadly force."

"Is that, like, a common thing?"

"No... not when there's civilians. Basically, we evacuated anyone who cooperated. Anyone who doesn't either gets arrested or shot, depending on what's going on. If there was any discrepancy, we were supposed to shoot first."

"Jesus..."

"The highest priority was containment. You know that shit about breaking eggs to make an omelet..."

"Of course..."

"You didn't get my message?"

"No, still don't have my phone."

"Well, if you did, you would've cooperated... we would've gotten you out..."

"Did you have to shoot any real people?"

"No, thank god. We had to turn some people away, but it never got ugly. It's a good thing you didn't show up, though."

"Why's that?"

"We had the evacuees loaded up on a deuce-and-a-half. I don't think they made it out."

"There wasn't a truck at the reservoir, though..."

"I heard it take off once I got away... at that point everyone at the checkpoint was either dead or dying."

We arrive at the gate that leads to the football field, and despite all the rain, there is still some blood on the bars and puddles that seem to have stained the ground below. Only a few corpses remain lodged between the iron bars, but they've been chewed up enough that you couldn't even make out their sex. Anderson stares in awe.

"They just put in that gate?"

"Yeah."

"Jesus, did *they* do this?"

"Remember all those..."

"I wasn't here..."

"Right. Sorry. Hundreds of people tried to get out here. You'd think they'd be able to slow down, calm down, or at least rush through fast enough to keep moving. They just packed in here like sardines."

"Hard to believe."

"It was disgusting."

After a moment, I glance over to see him staring up at the sky.

"What?"

"Looks like rain."

"One of the last things I talked to my mom about before coming home was that it was gonna rain a lot this week. We'll probably see some tonight."

"Interesting."

"What?"

"That something happened in our lives before this."

I immediately flush the surge of Julia out of my system by staring out across the football field and quietly reminiscing about the night it started. The sun settles into the clouds to my left, casting the blotchy artificial turf and the few remaining partially consumed bodies strewn across the middle of the field in a reddish-orange glow. Anderson and I walk along the track toward the concession building, the front of which has large windows covered by shutters. The rest of it is so full of track and field equipment that one would have to crawl between tightly compressed foam pads to get through it. Strangely, the metal shutters that cover the windows have been shut. I could have sworn they were open when we escaped the football field the previous week.

Anderson walks over but I stop him as he's about to open the door. "Wait... put your ear against it before we go barging in." I press my ear against one of the metal shutters, listening for a few seconds and hearing nothing. "Alright, open it." I say. He pulls the door open to reveal a dead person on the ground with a large gaping hole in his head. The lights inside are on. The concession area is narrow only because most of the building is devoted to the back room, which would be accessible were the doorway leading there not filled with a pole vaulting landing pad. "Cooler." Anderson says.

The cooler is open; there are several empty water bottles, various soft drinks, several half-eaten pretzels, and a bunch of candy bar wrappers. "Think someone was in here?" Anderson asks. I shrug, opening a second cooler behind the first one to find that it is also full of drinks, so I move them into one and start putting the soft pretzels in the other.

"Shit dude... how are we gonna get the meat group?" I ask.

"What?"

"The meat group, how do we get it in our diets in, like, a month? A year? And what about dairy?"

"We'll have to hunt. As far as dairy goes, I have no idea. Not much we can do about it."

"We have to get it into our diets somehow..."

"MREs... we'll need to hit up the check points and get as many of those as we can, or see if we can find some deuce-and-a-halfs cartin' 'em."

Once I have all the food together, I pick up the cooler. "All right..." I start, stopping the moment I hear a noise that resembles a person running their fingers against nylon. Anderson and I freeze and turn toward the doorway filled with the thick pad covered with blue nylon. It doesn't quite take up the height of the doorframe, leaving a pitch-black 12 inch gap at the top. I put down the cooler and lift my rifle. "Anyone there?" I ask. After a few seconds of silence, Anderson and I hold our breath to hear a third person breathing.

"Grey?" I hear from the next room, somewhat muffled. Someone back there knows who I am? "Who is it? Come out of there!" Anderson says. A pair of hands pop out of the gap, then pull back inside. Finally, two legs stick out, followed by a body that slides through and gracefully lands on the floor. Standing before me is a man of thin build with somewhat gangly limbs and ear length wavy brown hair. He has a goatee and stubble all around his face, he is wearing a tan corduroy jacket, and he is holding a three foot metal pipe. He is Colin Mursak.

"Mursak!? What are you doing here!?" I shoulder my rifle and hug him.

"Jesus... I've been in here for... I don't even know how fucking long."

"Since Bandrome?"

"Yeah... I mean... no... I tried to use the bathroom..."

"Jesus, you've been living off of soda and pretzels for a week?"

"What day is it?"

"Tuesday." Anderson says.

"...has it only been that long?"

"Jesus it's good to see you again." I say.

"You have guns? Wait, what are you doing here?"

"We're fortifying the school."

"Oh thank god... anyone else with you?"

"A bunch of people you don't know."

"What about Julia?"

My eyes sink toward the floor. Mursak reads me.

"Oh Jesus... I... I'm sorry."

"No, it's okay..." I say, fighting back some tears. I rub my face.

"How did...?"

"An accident..." Anderson starts. "We were in a hospital..."

"We shot her full of morphine... then we shot her." I finish flatly.

"Oh Jesus, I... I don't know what to say..."

"...let's get back to the school."

Anderson pulls out his Beretta and hands it to Mursak as I head through the door. "Might as well defend yourself with something better than that thing." Mursak holds onto the pole as Anderson and I cart the coolers. "...so ...can we go back to my house?" Mursak asks after only a few seconds of silence.

"I wouldn't advise it, it's spread too far."

"How far?"

"New York, states surrounding PA, parts of France."

"Jesus, you're kidding."

"No, so we're not going back to any of our houses."

"But... what about Elena?"

Elena is Mursak's four-year-old sister. Anderson and I keep silent for a moment.

"...can't risk it." I finally say.

"Grey... I understand where you're coming from, but I'm not... I can't leave Ellie alone... I *can't* leave her."

"Mursak, there's a good chance..."

"I know. I know. But, Grey, if Jules were still at home, you know you'd go back for her."

"Yeah..." I respond.

"I don't need to tell you ... I couldn't risk going back before, but... I mean... I don't want to put you guys at risk. I really don't. Even if... I'm too late... you know... I have to know for sure. I'll go alone if I have to."

Anderson bites his lip hard and stares at him.

"Alright."

"How did you survive it?" I say in an obvious change of subject.

"Oh... jumped off the side of the bleachers. I saw what happened at the front gate, so I ran for the tennis court. I could see... if I ran to the parking lot I was pretty sure I'd get run over. The back door of the hut was open, I remembered all that track and field shit in there, so I climbed on top of the landing pad and pulled the door shut. I just sat on top of it and... covered my ears. You guys were in the high school?"

"I was... Anderson was on duty."

"God... the screaming. At first it was just... all over the place. I could tune it out... then, as I got used to it, I could pick out the individual screams. They got louder, faster, closer together when they'd... get someone. In between you could hear the... it was like... static. Then they'd get someone, and it just cut through... didn't matter if you covered your ears. You could *feel* it. Finally... it got quiet enough, around four I think. I crawled down to look out windows... I took a few bottles of water and climbed back in. God, the stuff you hear people scream..."

For a moment he can't continue.

"A couple hours later it was quiet... it's so dark in there, I don't know when the sun came up. I tried to get out, but I couldn't run for long with my leg..."

"Your leg's *still* bad from the track thing?" Anderson asks.

"Yeah. I needed some way of... I-I... kept thinking of Ellie..."

"How long did it take you to realize they were Zombies?" I ask.

"Not long. My first thought was 'Where's Grey when you need him?'"

"Hah. Well, it's a shame you didn't just walk to the high school."

"Yeah, what did you do?"

Anderson and I spend the rest of the walk bringing him up to speed. When we finally arrive at the front of the school, Rich, Jake, and Melody are already waiting in the bus. Rich jumps out immediately.

"Holy shit, who's this?"

"Richard McKnight, Colin Mursak." I say. They shake hands.

"Good to meet you." Rich says.

"Yeah, you too." Mursak responds.

Jake and Melody walk out of the bus next, so we continue the introductions.

"So how did you guys make out?" I ask Rich.

"We unscrewed a lot of the chairs in 218 like we talked about. We left the first few rows in so we can watch movies and stuff."

"Fantastic. Well, we ought to get back... the wave is coming."

We all get back on the bus to find Rob still passed out. We make our introductions with Mursak and head back to the school, where Karen quickly isolates Rob in the classroom next to the one we've made our home. We get everyone situated while Karen does a basic physical on Mursak and loads him up with a bunch of pills to combat his malnutrition. I consider taking a nap, but as soon as Karen finishes with Mursak, he silently joins Anderson and me. I know exactly what he wants, but for some reason I can't put my finger on, I skirt the issue.

"What time is it?"
"6:10." Anderson replies.
"Mursak, you want to try it tonight?"

I can instantly interpret his blank face as an answer.

"Alright... tonight."
"Wait, what are you guys doing?" Melody asks.
"We're gonna see if we can get Mursak's little sister." Anderson responds.
"How far?" Karen asks.
"Couple miles."
"How are you gettin' there?"
"...we'll have to take a golf cart." I say.
"And who's goin'?"
"Anderson's the army guy, Grey knows Zombies, and I need to get my sister. So, the three of us." Mursak responds.
"Well... be careful."

Rich removes his shotgun and bandolier, handing it off to Mursak, who stares back blankly. "Good luck." Mursak nods and takes it. The three of us run outside and take my car from the bus yard to the high school, taking an empty gas can at Anderson's insistence. Once inside, we make our way to the hall just outside the band room where there are two golf carts waiting. Anderson does a systems check while Mursak and I watch. "This one's got more fuel in it. I say we siphon the other one and take at least an extra few gallons with us."

After we siphon the other cart, we end up with half a container of extra fuel and start up our ride. As I get used to the controls, Anderson runs into the band room and comes out with a large umbrella, 'incase it rains'. I drive the cart up to the main entrance via the auditorium, and then Anderson and Mursak clear a space in the desks at the auditorium entrance. Once the cart is through, they place the desks back as best they can, then we're on our way. While I drive the cart up to West Chester Pike, Anderson takes my car back to the bus yard. Unsurprisingly, he makes it to the bus depot a lot faster than I do. He's finishing off a cigarette by the time I pull up.

"How's she runnin'?"

"Got her up to twenty-five." I say.

"I would have figured fifteen, max... we've chased it down before." Mursak adds.

"I guess no one ever floored it."

Anderson takes the rifle off his shoulder and plants himself in the back as I speed toward the main road. Once alongside the Pike, I turn left and head west toward where the traffic ends. It takes another seven minutes to get to Bryn Mawr Avenue, which will thankfully take us almost all the way to Mursak's house. I see a Zombie walking across the street almost immediately upon turning on Bryn Mawr. I fight the urge to hit it, because that would mean almost certain death to Mursak and me, so I lightly turn the wheel, steering to the other side of the road.

I don't feel like I'm going particularly fast when my foot is pressed against the pedal, even with the wind ripping past me. The road we're driving is almost entirely lined with trees and grass, but every once in a while a suburban house or a posh elementary school will poke through the hilly terrain, and every few minutes or so I have to avoid a Zombie milling around. Twice along the way I have to steer my way around car crashes, and many more times I have to steer around abandoned vehicles. In several places, the road is barely big enough to fit the cart.

"What kind of gas mileage does this thing get?" Mursak asks.

"Probably worse than your average car." I respond.

"I thought shit like this got better mileage." Anderson says.

"Uh, maybe. I guess it depends on the carburetor."

"Do any of us know what one of those does?"

"No."

"No." Mursak says.

"Just wanted to make sure."

"Grey, do you have your DVDs?"

"...in the golf cart?"

"No, idiot, at the community center."

"Yeah... took a whole bunch more at the mall... got Zombie movies for reference."

"Hah. That's priceless."

"Actually, they were."

My expression drops from a half smile to a flat grimace as Julia crosses into my mind again, and this time something strange happens. Up until this point when riding through barren streets and seeing a world almost literally at a stand-still I would get a great swell within, taking in the ominous grandeur of abandoned highways and empty sidewalks. Now, the road seems cold and frightening, mirroring the way I felt before leaving my house. Just being in a tidy suburban neighborhood brings with it a certain level of unspoken comfort. Security. Even togetherness. I used to enjoy writing in the wee hours of the morning, having always felt as though a kind of psychic energy that engenders creativity is produced when sleeping people are nearby, and I have to imagine that this unspoken comfort made that possible. I'll never know that again.

I catch myself daydreaming moments before passing through a traffic light, and just as we do, a car goes speeding through the intersection perpendicular to us. "Jesus!" Mursak shouts. We all turn to see where it went, but it's already gone. "Probably for the best." I say, turning my attention to my surroundings as we continue past a hospital. A few seconds later, we approach a majestic bank with a car pancaked into the side; the intersection before it is littered with broken glass and twisted metal, so we evade a possible flat tire by driving on the sidewalk.

This particular road, Lancaster Avenue, is the main extension of what is referred to locally as the Main Line, after the old Pennsylvania railroad. The Main Line extends roughly from Philadelphia out to Amish country, but Bryn Mawr, anchored by Bryn Mawr College, is arguably the heart of the stretch. The surrounding area is notoriously wealthy; Gladwyne, in particular, has a median family income nearly twice that of Beverly Hills. Although a non-native could mistake the stretch for a particularly well-to-do section of Philadelphia, it is safely nestled in the middle of suburbia.

Despite my expectations, the Main Line is drenched in silence; no fires, no gunshots, no screaming people, just the sound of the wind and the uneasy whirr of the golf cart motor that likely attracts every walking corpse in earshot. "We should stop at the sporting goods store on the way back." Mursak says. "That sounds like a horrible idea." Anderson responds flatly, looking back at us. As I look suspiciously at the buildings, I notice that Mursak and Anderson are doing the same thing. Cars are conspicuously absent and the abundance of stores facing out at us appear to have elegantly closed as though today were a holiday. As I gaze upon the road ahead, I feel as though the earth could suddenly rise up, blot out the sun, and crush us.

"Why is it so quiet?" Mursak asks.

"It's the Main Line... it's far enough from Broomall, so they had plenty of warning and plenty of money to get out of here in a hurry." I reply.

"What's money got to do with it?"

"I don't know... they've all got cars, can afford guns, head to the city and take a plane out of here... they've got an awful lot more options for fight or flight than poor people."

I make a left past a supermarket and continue over a tree-covered bridge that extends over the R5 Septa line; the bridge curves up and slopes down heavily enough that I again feel the weight of a possible ambush crushing me to the ground, but I am once again greeted with silence. We make a right on Montgomery Avenue, adjacent to the rail line, and continue along the tree draped street until we can make an angular left that juts off diagonally toward Mursak's house. Anderson and Mursak chuckle as I turn toward Mursak's street.

"What is it?" I ask.

"I guess old habits die hard... you went out of your way to go the right direction on a one-way." Mursak affirms.

"Well... shit, I guess I did."

I slam on the breaks as we pull into the driveway of Mursak's house, miscued by a sheet of plastic billowing out of a window frame. The rest of the house, three stories tall with an exterior crafted in stone, looks to be in good condition.

"That's probably a bad thing." Mursak says.

"What?" I ask.

"That." He gestures toward the window. "They finished construction a while ago. That plastic wrap wasn't there when I left."

Frozen by the statement, we all stare blankly at the house as the engine continues running. As I'm about to switch it off, Anderson reaches forward and grabs my hand.

"Probably best to stay mobile."

"Why?" I ask.

"Incase they followed us... I don't want to be stuck in there."

"So, who stays?"

"I do. I'm fine being alone, you guys just get whoever's in there the fuck out."

"Wait, shit, can we fit his mom and dad on this thing?"

"We're gonna find out, but hurry it up... remember that wave we saw coming from the east?"

"Shit..."

"Maintain radio contact."

I jump off the cart as Anderson takes the driver's seat, backs out of the driveway, and speeds off toward the main road. The silence, apart from the crinkling plastic sheet, is maddening. I quickly turn on my radio as Mursak and I walk up the driveway, feeling an intense, dizzying pressure build in my mind as I nervously wrap my fingers around the handle of my katana. I've been up this driveway so many times to pick him up so we could play computer games. Now, we're on a rescue mission.

I look over at Mursak, and, as much as could be suspected, he looks like he's dreading going inside. I wish I could know what's going through his head. Are his parents alive? Is his sister? Are they going to insist we stay, or come along with us and incorporate into the group? Is Mursak going to be able to leave without her, knowing that his parents are trying to keep her safe? Are they even here? Are we going to make it out alive?

Mursak knocks gently on the door. Silence. "That's bad..." Nala, his enormous guard dog, is obviously not here. I try to look through the windows, and for no apparent reason I remember what his basement looks like. The idea of going down there carries with it shades of *The Blair Witch Project.* Mursak pulls a key out of his pocket and slowly opens the door.

I enter behind him, touching my index finger to my lips when he shuts the door. The steps to the second floor ascend immediately to our left, next to a narrow path that leads into the kitchen. The pale white walls are cast in an almost equally pale blue light from outside. The soft sound of something making contact with wood can be heard down the hall. I pull up my pistol, then take the lead and sidestep quietly toward the kitchen. As we get closer, it becomes audibly clearer that someone is going through the cabinets. I turn my radio down, fearing a sudden outburst.

I poke my head around a corner to see the kitchen, the center of which has an island tabletop covered with canned food. I continue easing myself in until I see Mrs. Mursak entering the cabinets next to the sink. "Mom?" Mursak says softly. She turns quickly. "Colin? Oh god, where have you been?" Her words are equally soft, but totally lack emphasis. Shouldn't she be relieved to see him? As he walks past me, I notice the bandage tied around her left forearm with a small brown stain in the middle. Her eyes are cold, bleary, and bloodshot like she'd been crying. As he gets closer to her, I get overwhelmed by an impulse of tact and step out of the room, making sure I'm able to listen from the hall.

"Mom, are you okay?"
"Where have you been?"
"I was at the high school."
"Colin... you've already graduated, why did you go back?"
"Mom... are you okay?"
"I'm just... so tired..."
"Mom, where's Ellie? Where's dad?

I still feel like an intruder. Usually Mrs. Mursak is personable and smiles a lot when Mursak has company over, but this quiet anxiety is disconcerting.

"Your father's sick..."
"Were you bitten? Was Ellie?"
"She's upstairs. Colin... just, help me..."
"Mom, I... help... help you with what?"
"Valium."
"...in the cupboard?"
"I don't know, Colin..."

A board creaks upstairs, and an instant later I hear Mursak rush through a door in the kitchen that leads to the second floor. Taking his cue, I go the opposite direction and run up the main stairwell. We meet at the second floor landing, and his face makes my blood run cold. I hesitate before I follow his glance down the hall to find his father staggering along the carpet, headed towards what I know to be Elena's room. Aside from his pale skin and sickly frame, he doesn't look much different despite the fact that a massive lump of muscle has been taken out of his left calf.

Mursak pauses. "Dad." Mr. Mursak doesn't stop. "Dad..." Mursak lifts his steel pipe back behind his head to the left. "Last chance." His arms come up as he draws closer to us. As Mursak steps forward, I clench my teeth and pinch my eyes shut; the pipe hits Mr. Mursak's skull like a clam being cracked on a rock. After a moment, I turn back to see Mr. Mursak take one last awkward step over to the railing before he flips over, followed immediately by the tumbling crack of his body slamming into the hardwood floor below. Mursak lifts the rug on the floor, wipes the blood off of the steel pipe, and runs into Elena's room.

"Ellie!?"

"Hi Cowin!"

"Come here, we're leaving."

"Mommy and daddy are sick..."

"I know, Ellie, we're leaving them for a while."

"Where are we going?"

"Away. We're gonna stay with some other people for awhile..."

"Okay."

Mursak reemerges with Elena in his arms. "Hi Jeff!" She says, and I smile at her. "Hi Elena. Ready to go?" She nods. "Grey, get my pipe?" Mursak says, starting to take her to the steps, pressing her head into his shoulder. I nod, holster my pistol and pick up his steel pipe. I reenter the hall at the crux of both stairways, seeing him look down the steps that lead to his father's corpse, then the steps that lead to his sickly mother. "I'll take Ellie outside, *you* deal with *her*..." I say. Mursak turns back, hands me Elena, takes back his pipe, and looks at me for a long, sullen moment. "Do I have to...?" He asks. I shake my head. "It's up to you." He nods, turns, and walks down the steps.

I switch Elena over to my other side, holding her head tight against my chest so she doesn't have to see her father as I run down the main stairwell. Holding her with one arm, I exit the front door and pull up my walkie-talkie. "Anderson, do you copy? We need evac, over." The static rings for a few seconds.

"I couldn't breathe when you did that..." Elena says.

"Oh, I'm sorry hun, I won't do it again."

"Why did you do that?"

"Ah... the hall downstairs smells like someone went to the bath-room... I... I-I didn't want you to have to... Anderson, we need you *now*, come back!"

Elena giggles at my comment. A sudden clatter from the kitchen turns me back in a reflex action, but I turn away just as quickly, biting my lower lip as I pick up the walkie-talkie again.

"Anderson, back here, like now!"

"What was that sound?"

"I... you know, I don't know hun... but I thought I saw one of those little pink elephants in your kitchen..." That was physically pain-ful to say.

"No you didn't!"

"Sure did! I'd take you back, but we're trying to leave now... An-derson, this is kind of important!"

I hear the door open behind me and only catch a brief glimpse of Mursak's face before it breaks into a welcome smile. I pass her off im-mediately.

"He said there was a pink elephant in the kitchen!"

"Pink elephant? You should know never to listen to Grey... it was a Wonder-Lu-Lunky!"

"No it wasn't!"

I shake my head as I hold up the walkie-talkie again, but Anderson thankfully cuts me off.

"Copy. Rolling to you. We've got company. Bunch of hungry sons of bitches. Over."

"Anderson, watch your language. We've got Elena."

"Copy that, sorry. Be there in a second. Over and out."

Mursak runs along the driveway, and as I follow him, I fight the urge to ask what just happened. When we get to the street Anderson rolls up in the golf cart and moves to the passenger seat so I can take over behind the wheel, and once Mursak and Elena get in the trunk I start heading back the way we came.

I glance down at the console to search for the headlights, finding a cumbersome switch to the left of the wheel. As soon as I get the light on a Zombie steps out from the left side of the street, crossing out from behind a tree. Able to see nothing but him in front of me, I feel like I'm on a theme park ride. As I swerve away, Anderson perks up, steadies himself as I turn, and fires a shot that blows a soggy lettuce-like substance from the back of his head. I think I can hear Elena crying and Mursak trying to calm her down. "Anderson, can you save that for when we need it?" I ask, loosening the strap securing my .45.

"Testing my moving accuracy..." I nod and turn left, looking back to see a runner chasing after us. Anderson gets ready to shoot. "Dude, he can't catch up. We're going twenty-five." I look forward to see one running down the street toward us, his shoulder length hair swaggering with his uneven steps. Instinctually I pull up my .45 and point it at the center of his head. Before I swerve, I steady the pistol with both hands and pull the trigger; I forgot to reload it. "Reload!" I shout, dropping the gun in Anderson's lap.

I pull the cart onto Lancaster Avenue just in time for Anderson to slap in what I believe is the last full magazine in my belt. When I glance off to my left I get a chance to see what Anderson was referring to on the radio; thick clusters of the undead stretch back as far to the east as I can see through the patchy darkness, but thankfully only a few of them have made it up this far. "God what I wouldn't give for a Molotov about now..." Anderson says, pointing the rifle behind us as I cut across the street toward the sidewalk. "OH GOD, HELP ME!" A voice shouts from the left; I can only imagine we all turn in unison to see a woman running out of the public library, blood freely flowing from a small wound in her neck. Anderson pops open the umbrella and lays it on its side in the back so Mursak and Elena aren't able to see behind us.

I look over for a moment to see Anderson grimace, pulling the silencer out of a holster on his belt as the woman continues screaming behind us. I think about saying something, but I face the road and veer to the right to avoid a bench next to the sidewalk. When I look back, Anderson again has the rifle hugged up tight to his shoulder. "Dude, knock it off!" I shout.

"Shut up, just hold it steady!" I glance quickly between him and the rear in just enough time to see him fire off a shot that rips through the top of the woman's skull. If I didn't put so much attention into safely making a left turn, I might have thanked Anderson for the last act of mercy that woman would ever know. "Oh fucking hell…" I mutter the moment we straighten; the undead are scattered through the road, shambling off to the west as though they've all escaped from a mental hospital to the east. "Pipe… pipe!" Anderson shouts, shouldering his rifle. "It's gonna be *close*…"

Weaving away from one means steering into another as I try to negotiate the street, knowing that two more blocks will see us to a stretch of road without another major intersection until West Chester Pike; in the midst of just such a maneuver, Anderson winds up, swipes over my head, and clocks one of the undead who was close enough to touch me. "Favor my side, dammit, I don't want keep swinging over you!" I obligingly swerve to the left and Anderson merely pokes at one getting too close.

It's dark enough now that I'm having trouble seeing anything not directly in the headlights, and the stark realism of the bodies shuffling into these pathetic beams of light is not lost on me. I get the feeling like I'm on a theme park ride again, though now I feel as though I'm going considerably slower, and the danger is imminent. A ragged corpse growls at me as I'm forced to veer right; the golf cart shutters violently as I clip one at the knee, but Anderson swipes again and stops him from barreling over the two-foot hood. I glance behind me again quickly, seeing a corpse bathed in red light desperately trying to claw at the umbrella separating Elena from a lifetime of nightmares. At this speed, he barely misses what could have been a prime opportunity to seize our backseat passengers. "EYES FRONT!" Anderson shouts.

Without looking, I swerve left, luckily missing another potential accident. Five hundred feet in front of us the undead are packed together tightly enough that we won't be able to make it through. I hear clothing tear next to me.

"Anderson, what…"
"Shut up, I'm dealing with it!"
"Make it fast…"
"SHUT *UP!*"

Anderson's lighter ignites just to my right. I glance over just in time to see him standing up in the passenger's seat, holding our other can of gas with a swatch of my flannel shirt poking out the top. Before I can say another word, the swatch is lit and Anderson lobs it in front of us. The plastic gas container smacks into the road, the cap pops off, and a tiny flame explodes out in a fat stream to the left, carrying with it a report that could doubtlessly be heard for a mile in every direction. Just as quickly as that happens, the undead instinctively recoil in all directions, revealing a path in the middle of the flames. Shelving my inherent fear of fire and death by explosion, I speed through the middle fast enough that nothing on the golf cart catches fire.

I turn to look back, watching the undead feebly dive in all directions unable to extinguish themselves. As I turn back to face a relatively empty road, I become aware of the fact that my jaw is hanging open. Suddenly, Anderson's infectiously stuttering laughter boils up from my right as he slaps my shoulder hard. "Did you see that!? Did you see *that!?* Holy shit, I can't believe that fucking *worked!*" I manage a heavy sigh through a wave of nervous laughter as the light from the fire disappears behind us. Mursak pokes his head up from the back seat. "What the hell just happened?" I think for a moment as I concentrate on the empty road in front of us, but I can only shake my head. Anderson laughs again, elbowing his seat cushion to exhaust some of the adrenaline currently causing his body to shake.

The rest of the ride is thankfully much smoother, remaining uneventful despite a higher volume of the undead. By the time we pull the cart outside of the community center the rain has begun and it's pitch black outside. After the initial joy of everyone seeing cute little Elena, Karen grills Mursak for a medical history which he essentially provides. Once we've finally settled down, we turn on the news.

"... will insure that Delaware County residents still have power."
"SHIT! I can't believe we just missed that." Mursak says.
"...the President today met with congress in a meeting closed to media, a meeting that is speculated to precede the introduction of national martial law. It is widely believed that such a motion would pass unanimously and could be announced as early as this evening. In local news, a barricade set up around Philadelphia with the intention of sealing the inner city has met with catastrophic results. It seems that in the midst of the battle, several fragmentation grenades were dropped when the undead were within reach of the barricade... this not only injured the soldiers, but also created an opening in the wall... we, uh... again, we apologize for moving quickly through these stories, but there is a lot to report... and now, speaking on the reverse flow of the undead, we go to our epidemiology expert, John Toland..."

The camera reveals a distinctly uncomfortable man standing in front of a blue screen featuring a close up of the northeastern states. It closes in on the Broomall area as he speaks. *"Thank you David. As you can see, we've outlined the start location of the crisis with this red dot. The red dot, when expanding, represents the flow of the undead..."* The dot grows outward with serrated lines, illuminating the name of a town as it passes through. *"As you can see, they move outward in an expanding circle. Instead of weakening as they spread out, they've only grown stronger, reinforcing their ranks at an astronomical rate..."* Several dots appear and transform into growing rings like dozens of rocks being tossed in a pond.

"What we're seeing here is those leaving Broomall after the outbreak, transitioning to an undead state in their home towns. If you'll notice, the undead en masse appear to only expand outward, avoiding covering the same ground twice. When two circles meet in an area, the undead seem to gravitate to the forefront of the expansion, the places they had not crossed before." When two circles intersect, the intersection line dissipates facing outward and makes the individual circles into one large amorphous blob. *"Now, one of the many curiosities was what would happen when they hit something they could not pass, such as a mountain, or an ocean. Since the*

undead seem to gravitate toward roadways, mountains don't seem to impede their progress. However..."

The picture closes in on New Jersey's shoreline. *"As you can see here, this group is approaching the shoreline. Once struck, the cluster reflects back, a pattern we liken to ripples in a pond. The information we've been given has suggested that this reflection occurred approximately 35 hours ago, meaning that a large wave of the undead will be crossing back through the Broomall area at some point tonight..."* The first part of the group hits the shore and immediately reflects back, headed west again, but the effect suddenly freezes. It looks like it wasn't supposed to happen, evidenced by the look of surprise on the newscaster's face.

"While many of the undead remain in larger cities, a large cluster of them are headed west again, and have been for a few days now. Now, recent reports have come in that the border to Canada has been compromised and part of the wave is headed north, but also large groups that have hit several of the great lakes are pushing back south again. As you can see from this map... uh, perhaps not this map in particular, but the infection has spread as far west as Michigan, uh, the southern half, and as far south as North Carolina. Back to you, David."

The camera stays on John, even as David speaks again. *"As far as the infection in France is concerned, there appear to be no signs of slowing, but..."* John, the man currently on camera, puts his hand to his ear and squints. He looks to the cameraman and mouths the words *did you hear that.* All the while David is silent, even as a bumbling thump echoes from the studio. The cameras start switching back and forth between three angles rapidly. John runs to the left, then back through the frame toward the right as the undead spill over the desk and catch David off guard. He falls backward, screams, and a thin plume of blood squirts upward. The image goes black and is followed by the station logo overlain with sounds of attack before the sound cuts out as well, leaving us speechless.

"Where's that station?" Anderson finally asks.

"Just off City Line Avenue." I respond flatly.

"So... they said they'll be back... *tonight?*" Melody asks.

"Yeah." Anderson responds. "Grey, with me locking doors. Jake, Melody, move everything out to the bus except the blankets. Karen, you stay up here and try to get Elena to sleep. Don't forget your walkie-talkies."

Anderson pulls the blinds down and turns out the lights as Karen turns the lantern on and sets it in the middle of the floor. I stop Jake as he goes for my backpack. "Give me a second…" I unzip it, needlessly looking inside to see if there's anything I need. I should have enough ammo and food to last through the night, but I do rifle through my back pocket and stuff my inhaler into my jeans pocket. I seal the pack and let Jake continue as Mursak stands and follows us to the door. "Take Rob's weapons." Anderson says. Mursak picks them up and follows us downstairs. "All right," Anderson says as we run down the steps. "Grey, you take the gym. Mursak, take the front. I've got the auditorium." We come out at the bottom and prepare to run, and then Mursak stops us. "Wait, how do we lock the doors without any keys?" Anderson responds, walking backward. "They've got latches. Get moving."

The first level of the school is almost entirely black save for the orange glow emanating from the infrequently spaced exit signs. Melody and Jake are behind me with everyone's survival bags and a duffel with the rest of our food, leaving only blankets and weapons behind. Once through the gym doors to the parking lot they go directly to the bus while I start flipping the latches on all of the doors. Once I'm done, I hold one open and wait for them to return from the bus. "Move it." I say. They come back in and Melody follows me as I run to another set of doors along the side.

"What are you doing?"

"…giving you a hand?"

"Don't. Go upstairs and make sure your gun's loaded."

"…okay."

An exit sign provides just enough illumination for me to make out her ass as she runs down the hall. I shake my head and turn back to the door just as a bloody corpse slams into the glass, howls, and starts clawing. My scream comes out as a brief, terrified crescendo of primal fear.

One eye is nothing but a quivering oyster of dark yellow tissue; he's missing the other, along with most of his orbital sockets. His jaw hangs below his face like it was broken in a fight, and his skin is colored like forest green vinyl crackling with veins drawn from rotten romaine hearts. The fact that he can still move in this state of decomposition greatly contributes to what may be the most horrifying image I take away from this crisis. As I ponder how oblivious I was to how altered the human body could appear, my thoughts are overridden by the idea that the only way for me to stop him from getting in is by opening the door and flipping the latch. Not happening.

He smashes his fists against the glass and seemingly tries the handle, but he can't get through. I notice a putrid smell in the hallway, a smell that freezes me as the hairs shoot up on the back of my neck. I turn quickly to face the pitch black hallway and resist the urge to start looking for a light switch, reaching back for my katana handle, but I must have dropped it with the stuff to go out to the bus. "Oh... corpse in the locker room." I say softly, catching my breath. The smell probably attracted that one, and it would probably attract more. I slide myself away from the door and watch the perverted aberration devised of elemental fear try desperately to fight his way inside. Once I think I'm far enough away I stand and run, snatching the walkie-talkie off my waist.

"Anderson, Mursak... there's one at the door; they know we're in here."

"*Copy that. Heading upstairs. Over.*" Anderson responds.

"*Headed up.*" Mursak adds.

I march up the steps again, wait for Mursak and Anderson at the top, and close the door. We return to the main bedroom to find everyone there with one exception. "Where's Rob?" I ask. "He's in the other room... tied down." Karen says. Jake walks over to the window and peeks out into the street. "I'd limit the amount of times you do that." Anderson says. "Alright, jeez..." Jake moves away from the window and lies down on his sheets. I rub my face hard and drop my head to the floor, fighting back the idea that the Zombie I encountered downstairs has the superhuman ability to dull my senses with incapacitating fear, and some deeply rooted defense mechanism gets me to chuckle when I nonsensically imagine that his mutant name would be Corpse-O. Other than my short, uncomfortable laugh, the only sound in the room is that of the softly intensifying rain.

"What do we do if they attack?" Melody whispers.

"Run for the bus." Rich whispers back.

"What if they've blocked the exits?" Karen asks. Everyone is now whispering.

"We'll just have to find another way around."

"Or shoot our way through." Jake adds.

"We're *not* wasting ammo." Anderson responds.

"Well what do we do with the junkie?" Mursak asks.

"Someone can help him out." Melody says.

A tear rolls down my face, and for the first time in about a week, it's not because of Julia. As the conversation engulfs the room, the lantern starts to dim. The light begins to visibly fade, quieting everyone down until no one speaks. Anderson gets up and tries to prime it, but it only lets little flashes of light escape. Finally, it just goes out, drenching the room in darkness. A scream rips through the wall of the adjacent room, but no one moves. Melody begins silently cursing through tears as I start to get up, but Karen places her hand on my shoulder and goes out the door. She comes back in thirty seconds dragging Rob, who continually whimpers like a frightened dog.

"What the *fuck* is going on!?" Anderson asks.

"Withdrawal." Karen responds.

"Tape his *fucking* mouth shut!" I spit.

"If he throws up he could choke to death!"

"Let him choke, just get him to *shut up!*"

A glass pane shatters below us, causing the room to audibly tense. Another window follows. Five or six shatters later, and everyone is up gathering supplies, just like the last night we spent in the high school. "Who has flashlights?" Anderson asks. There are only hushed curses. "I have one, does anyone else?" He continues. I pat the pockets of my trench coat until I find mine. "I do, anyone else?" I ask, only to be met with silence.

"Come on, everyone, the gym, let's go, let's *go*." Anderson says. As we spill out into the hall, more glass can be heard breaking closer than the previous shatters. "This way..." I say, leading the group in a different direction from the sound of the break. I turn off my flashlight in hope that I won't attract attention. Trotting in front, I lead everyone down the staircase closest to the gym, and then take them the opposite direction toward the doors that face the main road.

"The bus is *that* way!" Rich whispers forcefully, prompting me to adopt the same tone and volume.

"It's coming from the gym, we have to find another way!"

"They're gonna get us turned around in here..."

"They're gonna do that no matter what, but if we get outside, we have open space to run... now *move!*"

I can't remember the last time a simple hallway looked so ominous; without the flashlight, I have to guide myself by the sinister orange sparkles of vestigial locker latches reflecting the dim exit lights. The remaining darkness feels as though it could swallow me whole, and the absolute silence behind me allows me to imagine that everyone else is thinking the same thing. Stepping sideways and remaining on the balls of my feet, I slide myself up to the nearest door at the front.

I hold my hand out behind me and peek through the glass, leaping back and stifling a dry heave as I see about a hundred undead outside the window, rhythmically staggering toward us across the grass. I turn around and start walking back toward the group with a shake in my step, trying to stay calm. "Not that way." I say, choking back my fear. I take them back toward the gym; the hall is adjacent to the kitchen, which is ahead of us on the right. One of the giant windows that looks into the kitchen shatters and six walking corpses fall limply over the frame, and I know that this instant marks the end of a silent escape. I freeze and hold my arms out, stopping the group. "Through here!" Anderson mutters from the back.

Anderson clearly remembers the Friday nights we spent here in middle school, particularly the evening when we examined a shortcut from one classroom to another that leads into the hall adjoining the gym. He rips the door open and hits the light to reveal a Zombie in shambles facing away from us. How did he get in here? Mursak shoots him in the temple before he can face us. I expect Anderson to chastise him for using the bullet, but he knows as well as I that shooting our way out might be the only option. I jog toward the passageway in the far right corner of the room, finding several figures approaching from the darkness. "Shit! Go back!" I shout.

Screams accompany my desperate push to force the group into the previous room, likely because everyone else tries to push their way to the front the same way I do. The result is that I lose traction, watching clothes shake violently in front of me as I get the nightmare feeling like my feet are trapped in wet sand. "No, no... NO!" I shout, clawing for leverage. "GET DOWN!" I hear Rich scream, followed by the explosion of a shotgun. We all spill out into the hallway to find that the dead from the kitchen have spread out to our left. The hall to our right is empty, but it also leads to the front doors, which represent certain death.

Anderson charges the group to our left swinging his crowbar; I look past his shoulder to see the kitchen teeming with undead crawling all over each other, almost fighting to get through. Two people run off to the left while Anderson fights the undead, another two go to the right. I don't see any single person's specific trajectory because I run off to the right as well. The people in front of me, Jake and Melody, go straight for the front doors. "No! NO! THIS WAY!" I shout, going back up the stairwell. A fist smashes through the glass of the front door, prompting Melody to scream and jump back. "COME ON!" I scream, running up the steps with their footsteps distant behind me.

I get to the top and look both ways, turning back as Jake arrives at the landing. "Where's Melody?" I ask. He looks at me stoically with his mouth hanging open, but after a moment, we both react to a high pitched scream downstairs followed by two quick gunshots. "MEL-ODY!" I take a step into the stairwell and turn on my flashlight as I hear steps ascending. It's a runner. Jake shoots at him three times, the pistol report briefly illuminating the stairwell; one shot hits him in the forehead and downs him, but the following snap shots reveal a quickly advancing group of walkers behind him. When the light disappears I can still see dots of reflected light on the wet, wriggling backs of the corpses crawling up the stairs.

I run into the hallway toward our former room, seeing a figure ahead. I hold up my gun only to discover that it's Mursak with Ander-son's flashlight. "Where are the others?" I shout. "WHERE'S ELLIE!?" He turns his flashlight along with his body to see twelve corpses approaching silently from the rear. This really is it. We're done. As if to confirm my thoughts, Mursak lets out a short, high-pitched yelp and leaps toward us. "RUN!" He shouts. I bolt toward the stairwell as Jake runs toward Mursak; I reach back to pull him but miss, so he runs directly into Mursak and both of them fall over twenty feet behind me.

For some reason I freeze in place as the undead from the stairwell enter the hall and separate me from them, but the last thing I see before they block my view is Mursak and Jake slowly gaining their footing; one of them claws at the flashlight, sending out a flare of light obscured by the dancing shadows of shambling legs. I lift my rifle, but I can't shoot without hitting either Jake or Mursak. Before I can make any other decisions, four more spill out of the stairwell and start toward me.

I turn and run down the rest of the hallway, turn right, then run some more. "FIGHT!" I hear in the distance behind me, followed by several gunshots and short screams, mirrored by more of the same beneath me. I run down the next hallway safe in my assumption that there is another staircase down. The moans are getting louder and closer together as the building shakes from the staggering footsteps of the undead.

I only make it a few more feet before I find an exit sign above a stairwell. As asthma begins tearing at my lungs, my feet rip into the steps with accelerating ease until I reach the first floor and spill out the doors at the bottom; there appear to be a pack of them fighting over something to my right and I immediately know that someone in the group has to be at the bottom of the pile. I take a step over, thinking I can help, but quickly decide against it and turn around only to wind up in someone's putrid, disgusting arms. Before I can process this, my fist crosses his face and knocks him to the ground, but there are more behind him.

I pull my rifle off my shoulder and run at the cluster, butt-ending the first in the stomach and whacking the one to the left of him across the face with the stock. If I fire a shot, I'll draw too much attention. Without taking a step, I smash the butt into an undead face, and then take another step forward and cross-check one of them in the nose with the length of my rifle. I then swing my rifle by the barrel and take out two of their legs, but it goes flying out of my hands and clatters across the hall. "*Fuck!*" I think for a moment that I can get it back, but I apparently failed to realize just how many pairs of legs occupy this hallway. Now it's only clear enough to get back up the steps, so I return to the stairwell while entertaining the notion that my exit options are dwindling.

Once I get back upstairs, the moans are overwhelming. I look the direction I came from to see the undead spanning the length and width of the hallway. As lightning flashes outside I find them closing in from the other side as well. Upon seeing me, one in front quickens his gait just enough to make me shiver. The smell is starting to get to me. It's more real now than it's ever been.

I almost take a moment to slap myself for stalling, but I instead opt to enter the nearest classroom, slamming the door shut behind me and immediately pushing the teacher's desk against it. As my body takes me to the window, I again realize that I've gone into autopilot, and the development that sees my leg firing out to shatter a window is a surprise even after it happens. I shove my feet through the open pane and take hold of the frame. As I ease out, the frame falls toward me about a foot and my body starts to brace for impact, but it seems that my weight merely forced open the window mechanism. It's pouring outside.

I look below to where I plan on dropping, but there are about fifty beneath me trying to climb through the windows, testing the limits of their stiff limbs as they frantically claw at the glass. As I avoid wondering how long I can hold on before my arms give out, I glance at the window of the next classroom window. Struggling to hold on with one arm, I yank my pistol free and smash the glass. After I've cleared the frame of visible fragments, I shimmy across and grab it. Pulling myself inside requires every ounce of strength in my body, a fact that makes cutting my upper chest on the glass shards irrelevant.

I spill out on the floor keeping the pistol pointed away from my body, and when I can finally lift my head, I'm relieved to find that the room is empty. Once I manage to relax, I can hear them breaking into the room I came from via the clattering desks and chairs. I stare at the door and bite down hard on my lower lip, praying that they all ran in after me as I watch the shadows moving down the hall via the frosted glass in the door. Realizing this might be my last opportunity, I take a moment to catch my breath while slowly advancing toward this room's only official exit, and when I finally have my face up against the door glass I can see dozens of them fighting to get in the room from which I just escaped, so I quietly open the door. Once I'm sure they don't see me, I run down the hall.

I try to run around to the steps next to the classroom in which we slept, but the stairwell is still blocked, leaving me only one more place to go. I bolt up the steps to the rooftop, explode through the door, and jog over to the edge facing the road we use to get to and from the high school. There don't seem to be as many as before outside, likely because most of them are already in. I roughly run my hands up my face and through my hair before running across the roof of the gym toward where the bus should be. When I find only empty blacktop I expect myself to be mad, but I'm more relieved that someone actually made it out. It doesn't seem like too far of a jump to get down, but I would be hitting concrete.

I run back to the steps only to be given a swift, painful reminder that I'm asthmatic, so I brace myself against the door for a moment in a vain attempt to catch my breath as I take my inhaler from my belt. It's empty. I remember that I've had this one for years without even entertaining the notion of an asthma attack. In high school, on my bus rides home from school, I used to spray it repeatedly in my mouth and breathe out hard to make it look like I was smoking. If I had the opportunity now, I'd strangle my younger self.

Realizing that my lungs are at about three-quarters capacity, I pull the door open, shut it behind me and take three steps before I take out my flashlight to reveal four Zombies in the stairway. Knowing it's my only way out I yank out my pistol and gun down the four of them with seven shots, and as I pull the trigger the last time I realize that I've just spent my last round. I bolt down the steps to the open door and another one steps in the way; I lift my gun in a vestigial display as another two come behind him. I start backing up, checking the magazine pouches in my police belt, and it's immediately apparent that both of my spare clips are empty, so I run back up the steps. After making sure that it was repeated to the group that magazines don't have an infinite supply of ammo, I was stupid enough to not reload any magazine I've loaded since we first went into the gun store.

I lost my rifle, my katana is on the bus, and I have no extra ammo. What was I thinking? I slam the door shut behind me and run to look over the edges of the roof, but there isn't a good place to jump off. I eye the flag pole, thinking for a moment that I can jump out, grab it, and slide down. I take a few steps back and prepare to charge, but then something bangs on the door. I scramble the opposite direction, thinking I can hide behind the door when it opens and try to trick them into emptying out before I slip behind them, but then I see that little concrete room. I run inside and pull the door shut, sitting across from it and staring forward.

I listen to the sounds of the undead trying to get on the roof, and to the sound of the rain pinging against the ceiling like the report of distant gunshots. A rumble of thunder is followed by an explosion as the stairway door bursts open. I only have a few minutes. No death-defying escape plans, no way to write myself out of this. I've got nowhere to run and the only people that can help me are gone or dead. I could jump off the roof, either dying on impact or crippling myself so that they can have their way with me. I can hear them scuffling across the roof in different directions, trying to hunt down the meat. I remain totally still inside the shack, only blinking and breathing. It must be hard for them to hunt in the rain with all the vibration. I entertain the stupid notion that I can slip past them, but I remember that they have sharp eyes, sharp enough to see a lit cigarette a mile away.

I wipe my hand down my face and neck, and then begin rubbing it hard into my upper chest as my heart accelerates. Calm down. Lower your heart rate. Think of something. I look down to see blood on my hand from where I cut my chest climbing through the window. Even if I'm quiet, they'll be able to sniff me out. I had often wondered how I would deal with knowing that I would be dead soon. It was one of the many thoughts I'd entertain when I knew most other people's brains would be switching to autopilot. When I imagined it, I didn't think I would avoid the subject so much. I pretty much figured I would just cry like a ninny, but here I sit, changing the subject, letting my thoughts wander. I try to think about Julia, but the thoughts aren't coming naturally.

The moaning gets louder as they draw closer. I look at my feet, up my legs, into my lap. Still a virgin, no more Jeff Greys to enter the world. Before that thought processes, I look at the bulge on the side of my jeans; I managed to forget that I pulled my inhaler out of my backpack and stuffed it in my pocket. Taking it as a sign that I've done something right today, I pull it out and a bullet falls out of the mouthpiece. I have another round for my Colt.

Staying as quiet as possible, I remove the magazine from my pistol, pop the bullet in, slide the magazine back in, and chamber the round. This is the bullet I almost used to kill myself. *Put the gun in your mouth,* a totally calm and rational voice says inside my head. The voice is so calm and so rational that I actually place it in my mouth and bite down on the barrel. The cold metal makes my teeth shake like when I watch someone chew tinfoil. I let out a small laugh, but I think about what I'm doing, what it means, and how sick laughing at it is.

I start weeping. That it didn't take long. This is my fault. It was because of me that we stayed in a giant, completely undefended building based on the assumption that we shouldn't test the defense at the high school this soon. Somehow, I thought we'd just wait it out, failing to address the possibility that the wave of undead would crest and engulf us. I screwed myself and my friends with my stupid, lifelong insistence upon saving the best things for later; hot tea on a cold night, sleep for the moments before I collapse from exhaustion, sex for when I would truly appreciate it, and a fortified citadel for the final stage of completion.

Tears pouring down my face, I contemplate what it means to be alive, and how that's the one thing I've taken for granted. I'm about to deny myself continuing existence, which brings about more tears and harder sobbing. A sick thought comes to mind and I start singing the only song that feels appropriate, and I wonder if suicide really is painless. I squeeze the trigger a little bit and start crying even harder. I can imagine what this bullet is going to do to the inside of my head. There's no dropping a pen this time, this is it.

I distract myself by singing the second line. Nothing can describe this like the act itself, and it makes me cry still harder. I can hear the click and pop inside my head, then imagine everything in my brain disappearing in an instant. My life, my memories, the person that I am will be gone in an instant thanks to a few ounces of lead. I don't even feel like I'm just killing myself, I feel like I'm erasing my existence from the past as well.

Here comes the chorus. I think about my brother. My father. My mother. What would she do if she saw me like this? I imagine someone else giving her the news. I imagine her inconsolable, lying on a bed, and crying hard enough to welcome a disease that her body would contract due to her refusal to stave off death. I understand how Julia felt, but I have no morphine to make it easier. I have my finger wrapped around a trigger, and it doesn't get much harder than that.

Second verse. Julia drifts into my mind as a progression from the previous thought. I wonder how she would react to seeing this, and before that thought can register enough to make me start bawling, another pushes it out: *If you die, you're with Julia again.* I wait for her voice, but she doesn't say a word. Maybe she agrees. Maybe I'll end up with her again. A scratch at the door returns me to reality. They know what's in here, but not whether it's alive or dead. I'm in limbo, like Schrödinger's cat. Like them.

I look down and reconsider my earlier thought that there is no dignity in death, and wonder if it's possible to die in any less dignified manner. They're going tear into my stomach, into the intestines I've taken for granted all my life. They'll mutilate my genitals. My other parts seem expendable. If the lights don't go out all at once, how much pain will I feel when they rip into my abdomen, grab a handful, tear it free, and start chewing? The scratching turns into pounding. I am a coward. I squeeze a bit harder and I can feel the hammer start to pull back. Final chorus.

My muscles tense with anticipation. I hum the next few lines and start getting calm. My body prepares for the evacuation of my brain, or at least enough of it to matter. I can already feel the burn of the flames on my lips, hear the ringing of the gun, and feel the release of energy in the five foot radius of where it goes off. The pounding crescendos and the door flies open. There's a Zombie standing there.

The barrel comes out of my mouth, allowing saliva to pour off of my lower lip. I don't want to end my life on a trigger pull. That can't be the last thing I do.

I stand up and blow the top of his head off, causing him to fall back into his compatriots as I reach across my body and catch the hot discarded casing with my left hand. I stuff the casing in my pocket and punch the next one in the nose before his hands can come up. I then connect with an uppercut to his jaw and knock him back. "I've got nothing to lose. Come on!" I punch the next one in the mouth until most of his teeth come dribbling out, then grab his head and snap his neck, and though he doesn't die, he does hit the ground. There are two at once now, and this is where I fall backward, and they're coming down on top of me. They've clearly won.

The glass shatters behind me and two arms pull me out, so they're taking me from behind as well. "Pussies." I mutter. My last words. "Pull pull *pull!*" Anderson shouts, freeing my legs from the edge of the window frame. We both fall back into the rain soaked roof as one of them quickly approaches from the right. I can't get the words out to alert Anderson to his presence, but it doesn't matter as the business end of

Mursak's metal pipe smacks into her forehead hard enough to send her sailing over the edge. "You came back..." Anderson looks down at me, still dragging me across the roof.

"Shut up, we're gettin' out of here."
"How!?"
"Jump off the roof... and pray we don't break anything."
"I'm going first." Mursak adds.
"But the bus left!" I protest, standing up on my own.
"Grey... trust me."

We run to the edge of the roof by the gym entrance and this time the bus is parked flush along the side of the building. "This is impossible." I say, rubbing my face. "Just like Zombies are impossible?" Anderson asks. "Or me having this?" I turn to see him presenting my rifle. I smile, stuff my pistol back in my holster, and sling the rifle over my shoulder. I turn back to see the undead shuffling after us. "Down!" Anderson shouts. Like an idiot, I duck. Anderson points down to the section of roof fifteen feet beneath us.

The three of us grab the edge and lower ourselves, and between the lengths of our bodies and outstretched arms we eliminate about half the distance down. Having repeatedly scaled the roof at the high school and made jumps like this, we all bend our knees when we make contact and no one breaks anything. The next challenge before us is jumping across the six foot gap between the bus and the roof. Fortunately we're jumping down about two feet, but the roof of the bus is wet. I can't believe I almost killed myself a minute ago.

Without warning, Mursak jumps and lands on the roof, sliding about a foot in the rain as lightning strikes in the distance. The white emergency hatch on the roof flops open. "Did you get him?" A voice asks. "Yeah!" Mursak yells back. I take a few strides and jump, also sliding as I brace myself with my hands. I look down below to see the undead trying to get into the bus. I won't say a word to Anderson. "Come on!" Mursak and I shout together. Anderson looks back at the dead at the border of the roof as they approach the moment where they'll pitch forward and fall on top of him; Anderson's not as good of a jumper as Mursak, so he runs back against the giant windows of the gym, takes five massive strides, and jumps. When he's in mid air four Zombies fall down and smack into the roof where he was standing. Both of his feet land on the edge of the bus, so Mursak and I reach out and pull him toward the hatch. "Drive!" I shout.

The bus jerks forward and the three of us slide back. I take hold of the ceiling escape hatch closest to the rear as Mursak and Anderson grab the one closer to the front. As Rich turns onto the street to take us back to the high school, we swing toward the left side of the bus. A glance over the edge reveals Zombies in the street, a fact that greatly incentivizes staying on the roof. I watch the stragglers wiggle through the front door of the community center to join the raucous chorus of moans and percussive staggering feet already inside. What little light there is illuminates each floor, highlighting the movement of the un-dead as they shuffle through the corridors like dispassionate parents at a high school art show.

The bus shakes hard as we presumably hit a Zombie in the street, causing my hatch door to rip open, flop against the roof, and send me backward far enough that my legs dangle over the edge. I clamber to regain a solid hold as the bus swerves. Finally, Rich speeds into the school parking lot, making a sharp right into the front lot. The force of the turn sends Mursak flying off the edge, his pipe hitting the black-top with an ear-shattering clang. "Keep driving!" Anderson yells inside. Anderson and I release our grip and let ourselves get thrown off along with our friend.

I hit the grass unbelievably hard, letting out a low groan as I force myself up. "Everyone alright?" Anderson asks through the rain. I cough hard and nod as Anderson helps Mursak to his feet. Thank god I didn't land on my rifle. There are a few walking corpses absently milling around the front, but Mursak and Anderson dispatch them with their melee weapons as Rich parks the bus against the doorway, leaving just enough space for us to get through. As we run between the bus and the wall, the far door opens up to let us inside, and for a moment the people scrambling to get their gear together is more con-fusing than a flock of birds trying to peck my eyes out. Melody hugs me the moment I get through the door. As I stifle a latent sniffle, I look down to see a pile of equipment on the floor. "All right, this is every-thin' from the bus." Karen says.

"He's got my guns." I look up to see Rob looking down at Mursak's guns, his mouth hanging open and his lower lip glistening with drool. When he sees me looking, he turns his head, and Karen quickly shuffles him away. I grab my pillow, crowbar, katana, and my survival pack, and then climb up the rope ladder. "Lock the doors." I say to Rich as I go up. From the top level, I look down. "When you're done pull up the ladder. Just for tonight." I look back to see Mursak behind me, then I pause and look over the edge again. Jake, Elena, Karen, Rob, Rich, and Melody all survived.

My limbs suddenly wobble and I fall back against the wall, barely able to keep myself from falling down the steps. With my hands shaking, I reach into my pocket and grab my inhaler, quickly taking a hit. I feel like crying, but I hold myself back with the proviso that I can do all the crying I want when I get in bed tonight. As Mursak clambers over the railing, I fantasize over the beautiful proposition of lying on a mattress with a pillow and sheets. Once Mursak helps me to my feet I manage to muster the strength to get myself into the hall unassisted.

"When'd you decide to come back?" I ask, stroking my free hand through my soaked hair.

"You want the long version, or the short one?"

"Long."

"Rich was the first one out with Ellie, I followed Karen upstairs, and when she got Rob and went down, I ran into Jake..."

"You were surrounded..."

"Shot our way through and got back downstairs. I found Anderson... he was just walking through a hallway lined with bodies covered in blood... and he asked where you were. He told us to get outside... Karen and Rob were already on the bus, then Melody came running around the side of the school, and finally Anderson came out the gym, saying he couldn't find you. We drove around to the other entrance... Rich wanted to wait, but Anderson wouldn't have it, so we came in... he was like a *machine*. We heard the gunshots on the roof. There were dozens of them, so we lured them away, then ran around the other side and went up..."

"Got it... thanks. I mean, really... thanks... I thought I was dead."

"Yeah, well... you'd do the same for us."

"I hope so... god, I hope so."

The tears start up again as I free my Colt from the holster. I yank back on the action, confirming that I am totally out of ammo. Once inside 218, I grab one of the queen sized beds and carry it up to the top of the platforms where I find that it actually fits despite the width. I cover it with sheets and put blankets at the foot of the bed, and my survival gear goes up against the wall parallel to the end of my bed along with Julia's ashes. I put my arm against the wall and notice the faded phone number written in marker on the back of my hand. I rifle through the drawers in the desk at the front of the room until I find a permanent marker and carefully write it on the wall next to the phone. My thought train then leaps unexpectedly toward the weapons. "Rich, what did we do with the ammo?" I ask.

"It's in this closet here." There is a trapezoidal bulge behind the teacher's desk with a door facing us. Rich opens it to reveal little more than a light bulb on the ceiling and shelving around the walls, and a large space has been cleared on the shelf with a label marked *Ammo* and several more beneath it that tabulate where each type of bullet is kept. After refilling my rifle and bandolier, I take twenty-one ACP rounds to fill my Colt magazines.

As I stare into the bullets, I can't help but think that all of our supplies are easily exhaustible, and if things get any worse, all industrial production will shut down. Stores carrying weapons and ammo will be raided or bought out, leaving us with only melee weapons. I turn around to see the rest of the group arriving to set up their beds, so I take a seat on top of the front desk and draw their attention with an exaggerated wave.

"Um... first... I don't know how we just did what we did... but, if you can remember *how* you did it..." They all snicker. "As tired as most of us are, we're gonna have to keep watch. Let's try to keep the movement and talking at a minimum... let's let 'em think this place is abandoned..."

"Understood... that's fundamental." Anderson says. "From now on, we're just gonna call that a yellow alert. That means you don't reload, you don't flip a light switch, you don't even go to the bathroom without me, Jeff or Rich saying so. You stay away from the windows. You walk softly and quietly on the balls of your feet... what?"

"Which part is the ball?" Melody asks.

"Where your toes meet the rest of your foot. Anyway, phones off, radios on minimum volume... we'll come up with a way so you can remember the specifics, but it boils down to being as quiet as possible."

"Jeff, are we puttin' up signs lettin' people know we're in here?" Karen asks.

"We'll talk about how we'll handle that later."

"The short answer is yes." Anderson states.

"...we need to think about it first..."

"Sure, the best possible way... we're gonna get that roof rotation thing goin' again, just make sure they can't see you from the street."

There is a moment of silence.

"...we need to talk about the signs..."

"What about them?"

"I'm... not sure we *should*... not for awhile, anyway..."

"Why not?"

"Well... should we really be advertising?"

"*Why* not?"

"We-I... well... it's hard enough trying to... I mean it took us this long to... you know, trust each other."

"What are you *talking* about?"

"I don't know, *this*... we bring more people in here, we're gonna have to explain this shit to them, get them to follow along, get them to listen to you, me, and Rich...what if they're not into it? We just throw them out? We give ourselves away, and who knows what they could do?"

"*What* are they gonna do?"

"Come on, I can't be the only one that feels this way, anyone… anyone…?"

Their silent gazes are locked on me.

"So… we're not gonna let anyone know we're in here… and if someone gets in and doesn't stick with the plan… we, what… execute 'em?"

"No, that's *not* what I'm saying…"

"Could you trap someone outside? Could you deny anyone the means to get in?" Karen asks.

"Look, just hear me out. I'm saying too many people is a risk…"

"Well…" Anderson starts. "…we're not talking about bringing a hundred people in here…"

"But that's my point! Where do we draw the line? If we leave the signs down, we're not inviting that kind of trouble…"

"Jeff, that's almost puttin' people in harm's way…" Rich adds.

"I didn't *say* we should turn people away, I just don't know if it's a good idea to broadcast. That's what the safe houses did, and we know how that turned out… this isn't a military stockade… we don't have k-rails and fences and sand bags, some of these doors are just reinforced with *desks*…"

"Look, we can keep arguing about this, but they're coming, and we have to keep quiet…" Anderson states. "We pair off… two in the front corners and two in the back."

"What about the sides?" Rich asks.

"Cars have it cut off pretty well…" I add.

"Alright, so Rich and Jake together, Jeff and Melody, me and Mursak. Karen stays here with Rob and Elena…"

"I don't want my sister near that addict…" Mursak blurts out.

Rob looks at the ground dejected, but stays silent.

"Fine, then Elena goes with us, but for Christ's sake, keep her quiet."

"What do I do about Rob's screamin'?" Karen asks.

"Can we spare some morphine?" I ask.

"We… can I talk to you for a second?"

As I nod, Karen walks over to me and takes the two of us to the corner as Anderson starts talking about god knows what.

"You *do* know that morphine is where heroin comes from, right?"

"I didn't."

"If they can't get a fix…"

"Are you saying it's not a good idea?"

"We can't keep doin' it."

"Well, we have two choices, and I leave it up to you… give him morphine and have him detox for longer, or don't and have him give us away."

"That's not much of a choice."

"Just for tonight…" Anderson says, sticking his head between us as Rich talks to everyone else. "It's *very* important they pass us by. Melody and Jeff on the southeast corner, Jake and Rich take the back; Me, Mursak and Elena are in the southwest end. Every once in awhile I'll head downstairs… I've been trained in recon."

Everybody somewhat noisily starts picking up their weapons and filing for the door, but Anderson stops them with a loud shush.

"Shut. Up. Remember what I said? Alert condition yellow. *Think* quietly."

"Melody, whisper if you see something." I say.

"No problem…"

"Karen… you're gonna be okay with him?"

"Don't worry about it."

"You know I will."

"Then don't worry too much."

Before I turn back, I see her go to our supply bag for the medical equipment. Once in the hall, I watch Anderson walk off with Mursak in tow as Elena lies asleep on his shoulder. Jake and Rich silently march down a hallway toward the back of the school as Melody and I walk to the end of the hall, entering the last classroom on the left and quietly closing the door behind us. Once there, I scoff at our visibility; the library cuts off most of the view on the left side so we can only see to where the street meets the parking lot entrance. Good enough, I suppose.

I go directly for the far left corner of the room and ease myself onto the counter beneath the windows, warming my aching muscles on the sparse wheezes of lukewarm air leaking out of the vents of the heating unit. I lean against the wall and despite the uninviting discomfort of lead-painted cinder blocks, I can relax my back. I reach into my pocket and pull out my bullets, carefully resting them in my lap before taking out an empty magazine and filling it.

"Jeff... you see anything?" She must not have been looking at me because she clearly didn't notice that I wasn't paying attention. I peer out the window, struggling to see as the wind whips through the skeleton branches of the tree at the edge of the property, obscuring the wet, black shine of the street. "No." The room is totally silent, save for the quiet clicks of me pushing bullets into a magazine. "I can't see anything." She says softly. More silence.

"Are you scared?"
"I'm tired..."
"Me too."
"Are *you* scared?"
"Not like I used to be."
"Getting used to it already."
"You are?"
"I used to write about it... one of my professors at college had us read a book that said people like gangster movies because they vicariously enjoy the gangster's power, money, drugs, women... in the end, the gangster gets caught or dies... by then we've separated ourselves, so we can enjoy crime getting punished. Zombies did that for me... you develop some survival plan and assure yourself you can make it...

and then... I don't know. I guess there's a point where you stop planning ahead... assume you get rescued."

"You're only human..."

"Only human..."

After gently sliding the last magazine into my .45 and slipping it back in the holster, I pull my legs up close to me and wrap my trench coat around them. I can't wait to get in bed. I can't wait for this to be over. I finally look back at the window to see nothing stirring in the street. What I wouldn't give to be holding Julia right now. "I almost killed myself tonight." I say suddenly. I don't have to look back to see her staring at me.

"And that's not something I want repeated. I just... if... what happened to Julia... was earlier today, I would've done it. If we hadn't been together, I would've done it. If it were just the two of us... I don't even know. I can't explain why I'm still here..."

"I think maybe, you're trying to make it mean something."

"...the fact that I'm still here?"

"Yeah."

"Are you saying it doesn't?"

"Well, no... I... yeah, I'm saying it doesn't."

"It doesn't mean anything... huh."

"I'm not saying you don't matter..."

"No, I get it. You're right."

Another long moment passes.

"You think... things'll ever be the way they used to be?"

"No. Might get better, eventually... but if it gets any more out of hand first... I mean, can you imagine going back to school after something like this? We'll adapt, but... think about it a thousand years from now. Maybe they'll have an explanation... it doesn't change anything about it for us. If we make it through, we'll be the last generation who had to adapt. Just like we're the last generation to remember life before the internet."

"If things don't get better, we might be the last ones to use it."

"Hadn't thought of that."

"What was the last song you heard on the radio?"

"Don't listen to it. What about you?"

"Destiny's Child, *Lose My Breath*."

"Don't think I know that one."

She hums the tune.

"Oh, okay."

"I'm wondering if it's the last new song I'll ever hear."

Finally, I think I can see some of the undead coming up the street. It's hard to tell with the darkness and rain, but after a few seconds it's clear the horde from down the street have realized there was nothing left to eat in the community center. Seeing the undead in a different light seems to be the recurring theme of the past few weeks. Perception of them changes, depending on whether you're hunting them or running from them. From this vantage, in a building I know to be well fortified and quiet, they don't look very imposing. In fact, they're quite boring. I wish they would speed up so I can at least know whether we'll have to fight them off or if we can get some sleep tonight.

It takes several minutes for the group from the street to finally get to the school, but once they get close to the door they pass out of my sight range. "Maybe we should go to another room?" Melody asks, getting up. I suppress her movement with a slight hand motion. "We wouldn't be able to see them beneath the canopy anyway." I reach forward and wrap my fingers around the latch for the window. I take almost a full minute to pull it down, and then slowly push the window out. Melody speaks so softly I can barely hear her. "What are you doing?" I simply hold my finger to my lips. I close my eyes and nod my head back toward the wall as I listen to the rain. I hear nothing else. It takes only a few more seconds until I can hear a gentle pounding on the front door. From the sound alone, I can guess that they aren't trying particularly hard.

After another minute of listless thumping, part of the group disperses toward the street. Part of me wonders if Anderson is downstairs at the moment. Given the situation, it would probably be better if he were not. I hear some more pounding somewhere further down the building, but I can't pinpoint where. When that ceases, I spend a full minute gently pulling the window closed again. My eyes travel up the side of the exterior library wall until they begin focusing across the street to where the undead are staging an assault on the exterior of a house. "They must think there's someone in there." I say softly. I then pull up my walkie-talkie.

"Rich, status report? Do you see any back there?"
"None back here, over."
"Anderson? Status? Over."
"You see them trying to get in the front? Over."
"Yeah…"
"Didn't look like they were trying very hard. Over."
"No, thank god. But they look like they're going for the house. Over."
"Copy, we'll keep an eye on it. Over and out."

A large portion of the horde from the community center breaks off and heads toward the house, banging on the walls and crowding the front door. "Think there's someone in there?" Melody asks. As if that were the trigger, someone in jeans and a sweater comes wriggling out the side window on the first floor. It's a girl, about my age, and she's running past them toward the street with her arms waving around. She's coming toward the school. "What do we do?" Melody asks. My response is silence as I watch her run across the grass, sucking every dead person in the area toward her.

"Jeff? What do we do?" I continue watching. If we let her in the undead will know there's someone in here. They won't stop looking for her until they rot into dust. At the same time, she's alone and terrified. The radio crackles. *"Going for her…"* Anderson says, out of breath. *"Rich, get the bus, over."* Melody jumps up and rushes over to my end of the counter.

Anderson appears on the grass shouting and waving his arms. "OVER HERE! IN HERE!" She runs past him as he continues to stand on the grass waving his arms. I then hear the sound of the bus starting up, followed by a sharp beeping sound as it backs up, then the roar of the engine as it starts driving toward the street. "Is he insane!?" I spit through my teeth. He starts beeping the horn and flashing the lights, which must be visible from a country mile. Anderson starts running toward the street as Rich stops the bus by the sidewalk, and then runs toward the emergency exit at the rear as the undead start crowding the bus. As he pulls away down the street, every walking corpse funnels after him.

"What's he doing!?" Melody asks loudly, prompting me to yank the window shut and silence her. "They can *hear* us!" She puts her hand over her mouth, then whispers. "What's he doing?" About six of them head toward the side door the woman just went through while the rest follow Rich. *"Jeff, it's Sak... he's leading them away... Anderson's betting on them thinking she got on the bus. She's inside now."* Anderson's voice then crackles over the radio from the bus.

"That's big roger on that... they've definitely taken the bait..."

"Anderson, what are you *doing*!? Seriously! There's a couple *thousand* out there!"

"We just saved her life..."

"At what cost!? What if they only take the bait for a few seconds? What if a bunch of them trail off and head for the door she came in?"

"Rich and I both think it's worth the risk, so..."

"But Christ, you could have *said* something!"

"Well, it's done now. She's inside, and we're gonna circle. We'll make sure we've lost them before we come back. Over and out."

"No, you don't just... god *dammit!*"

"Do you think we should have let her in?" Melody asks.

"I don't know."

"...you've got to have an opinion."

"What do you think?"

"We did the right thing..."

"Yeah, but now that's another mouth to feed, another person to secure bedding for, another person to eat up ammunition..."

"Jesus, Jeff, I know *you* wouldn't want to be left out there..."

"I know, I know..."

"...were you seriously gonna let her die out there?" She raises her voice and stands up.

"*Shh*! Remember what they said on TV, about safe houses? God forbid she's been bitten, then we have to deal with that too... if we keep adding people..."

"Could you *act* like a human being for thirty seconds and try to think about what it's like to be alone out there?" Tears well up in her eyes.

"Look who you're asking. Of course I've thought about it..."

"Yeah, because you wrote a fuckin' *story* about it..."

"*Hey, you* followed *me* and look where it got you. Maybe you want to consider that I might have a point?"

"I just wanna see you look in that girl's face and tell her why we shouldn't let her in... 'I'm sorry, it's bad for us that you're here...'"

"You can stop right there. Maybe it is bad for us that she's here."

She stares at me.

"You want an explanation? Because it's not difficult... people assume that humans are generally good, we just need to be shown the error of our ways once in awhile... well, we're not. The world sucks because we're inherently predators..."

"What the..."

"Look out the window... and tell me the predator isn't the only human thing left in them."

"Look," She drops her volume but maintains a sharp tone. "I'll just make this simple... you're an asshole... and a hypocrite... you want me to sit here and listen to your shit and agree because you think you know what you're talking about? Who *cares* what we're supposed to be? At some point, you make a *choice* to screw someone over or take the easy way out... you're right, I followed you in here... when we saw those people running out front, and I wanted to yell and scream, but you wouldn't let me? You were right... if we made enough noise, maybe they'd come after us instead... there were, what, nine of us? And how many people died out there? How many people spread it? Maybe if they came in here *we* would've been screwed, but this town would've had a chance..."

"What about the buses, going to the other towns..."

"There's nothing we could do about that... and maybe I wasn't thinking like that before, but I just wanted to help those people... *you* pretend you're doing the best thing... but if we're all predators, if *I'm* a predator... then so are you. And so was Julia."

She picks up her rifle and walks out before I can respond. I can't remember if she had a good point or not as I stopped caring as soon as Anderson turned off his radio. What a bitch. She wasn't so hot on bringing Steve upstairs that first night, where was her humanity then? She just brought up Julia because she knew I wouldn't be able to say anything after that. So what if Julia and I were predators too? We're all slaves to our own biology, I just happen to know how we're chained.

I'm sure this fight will continue to be annoying for several days and probably end up being an undercurrent to every plan we make going forward. If Anderson's ill conceived notion pays off and they clear out, we'll have days, weeks, maybe even months to sort it out. I'm probably not going to change anyone's mind about this, but maybe I can at least get them to understand my thinking.

Perhaps I'm getting ahead of myself. Things haven't totally gone to shit yet. The military could be mobilizing this very instant, trying to contain the infection. Maybe there's a cure and we can return to life as usual in a few months. I doubt it though. It may be thinking a bit too apocalyptically, but it's largely possible that this group could end up being one of the last pockets of civilization. Being one of the three leaders, I'll have to make some big decisions, and tonight wasn't a good start. But we're here in our veritable safe haven, the place we've been working on for the past week and the place we've wanted since the outbreak began in earnest. It wasn't overly difficult to make it a stronghold, which means it won't be overly hard to penetrate.

Regardless, it's our place to stop. There won't be any running around, aside from getting food and more supplies. There won't be any daily action, aside from talking, watching movies, and reading books. I certainly won't try to go far from here since it's my home now and I want to defend it. But how long will that last? Even if we can hold this place down, what can we do besides wait to die? The circumstances outside our control, like looters, disease, insanity, cabin fever, and the undead are crushing us to the ground.

It seems clear that we can't just wait here. After a while, maybe even a couple years, we'll have to work to get society back on its feet. I may even have to work toward a future by impregnating one of the women in my group, but how does one go about raising a child in this world? Some places on this planet were bad enough before, but now this had to happen, and I'm still on the fence as to whether or not this is a good thing.

This curse of consciousness continues to act on me as I sit on the counter for hours and watch night give way to dawn. I doubt Melody will return, but the radio chatter from the rest of the group confirms that everyone inside is safe. I wonder if everyone else is falling asleep at their post when I notice my eyes forcing themselves shut. In a last ditch effort to sustain consciousness I reach in my pocket and start playing with the casing of the bullet that must be my Schrödinger's cat, representing an existential state of quantum superposition. Before I pass out entirely, I think about the fact that I was supposed to have potential and how meaningless this idea is in the current paradigm. It's not as though anything I had written is going to make an impact now. I smile as I think that times like these make me long for the indifference provided by a space between life and death.

ACKNOWLEDGEMENTS

As a first-time published author, this novel would not have been possible without the generous participation of Neil Ross, who trudged through early drafts providing concise, brilliant criticism and guided my path through rights issues, editing, and publication. Neil, if my gratitude ever appears to die out, you can be sure that it will rise again.

John Henderson, veteran of the Pennsylvania National Guard, helped with the ideas that formulated this novel and provided me with invaluable technical, logistical, and emotional support throughout the writing process. Thank you for your help, service, and friendship.

Ryan Korsak endured the pains nagging about making a book cover for months, and his final product absolutely validate that nagging. You are a disturbingly brilliant artist, and I look forward to harassing you for another cover in the future.

Thomas J. Chandler has given me endless technical support throughout my travails in understanding everything there is to know about computer hardware and software. Tom, thank you for always being patient.

Joseph Harrold engaged me in a long talk about the ins and outs of home heating and the differences between oil, gasoline, and diesel fuel, and his contribution will ensure the survival of anyone searching for a means to get around in a post-apocalyptic landscape.

John Johnston, who is not presented such as he is, but had too good of a name, and nickname, to pass up as a character.

The teaching staff at Marple Newtown and Temple University; were it not for you, I would not be able to write or think for myself.

Lon Miller wrote the piece of Zombie fiction that influenced my writing the most of any one author, and his *Alomal-137 Epidemiology Case Study* will forever stand as the most influential document on the undead ever created.

Neil Fawcett (*Homepage of the Dead*), Julie Leeds (*Tom Zombie Festival*), Curtez Riggs (*Zombie Pop*), and Miguel Gomez (*Viva Video*) have all provided me with great publicity opportunities and believed in my work without even reading a word of it, and I wouldn't be able to sell it outside my family and friends without them.

Cecil Adams, whose site *The Straight Dope* is more intellectually fulfilling and illuminating than anything else I can find on the internet.

Tom Miller provided me with specific geographical information that will bear fruit in the novels I hope to follow. Even if they do not, he has my thanks.

Thomas Lamb gave me his blessing in making reference to a far off vacation destination I plan on visiting if I manage to find success.

Anne M. Boothe, the Executive Director of the PhillCo Economic Growth Council, Inc. gave me concise, literate information about subjects I could not study personally, and she too has my thanks.

Timothy P. Hofer, Eve A. Kerr, and Rodney A. Hayward wrote an article on effective clinical practice that, again, gave me something I could not have otherwise validated and whose research will hopefully appear in further novels.

The book text is Crimson font (Sebastian Kosch), the header and information is Share font (Ralph du Carrois), the title and chapters are Dirty Ego font (Misprinted Type), and they were all found thanks to FontSquirrel.com.

ABOUT THE AUTHOR

Bryan is a graduate of Temple University and lives near Philadelphia, where he writes novels, articles, short stories, and screenplays.

Made in the USA
Columbia, SC
10 April 2018